EVERY KISS YOU STEAL

A Redeeming Love Novel (Book 7)

J.E. PARKER

Edited by SARA MILLER

Beta Read by CHRISTINA YOUNGREN

Cover Design by LETITIA HASSER

Publication Date: 10/22/2019

Dedication

Ziggy Bear

You were more than just a dog.
You were my companion and my anchor.
You were the glue that helped hold me together.

Losing you has shattered my heart,
but I know that one day we'll meet again.
Until then, I'll hold every precious memory tight.

Thank you for loving me, Zigs.
You were the best furbaby I could've ever asked for.
I love you, sweet boy.
Forever.

Playlist

"Rescue Me" —Daughtry
"Ocean" —Lady Antebellum
"Mercy" —Brett Young
"I Know She Ain't Ready" — Luke Combs
"What Happens In A Small Town" —B. Gilbert
"Make You Feel My Love" —Adele
"Someone You Loved" —Conor Maynard
"Kiss Me" —Ed Sheeran
"Beautiful Soul"—Jesse McCartney
"You Say" —Lauren Daigle
"Wanted" —Hunter Hayes
"Be My Baby" —The Ronettes
"At Last" —Etta James

Part One

BEFORE LOVE CAME SORROW

"Life had broken her but she was still there persisting in the shards of her broken pieces."

— Atticus

Chapter One

ASHLEY

I can't breathe...

Covered in a fine sheen of sweat, I stared out the front windshield of the luxury four-door sedan where I sat, my starved lungs struggling to pull in enough air to satisfy my pounding heart.

The low hum of the car's engine filled the quiet space, giving me something to concentrate on besides the well-dressed man seated next to me, his intense gaze fixed on the illuminated screen of his phone.

Mere inches separated his arm from mine, causing fear and disgust to slither through my veins. Fear for the pain he could inflict; disgust for the vile and twisted things he'd done in the past.

Things which he'd done to *me*.

Hands tucked firmly between my knees, I fought to block out the horrid memories that flashed through my head, one after the other, like a movie reel on repeat. With the smell of his expensive cologne still clinging to my damp skin, doing so was impossible.

None of this is your fault, I told myself.

It was a truth my heart refused to believe.

I jumped, almost coming off the seat when he dropped his phone to the console and turned, now focusing his rapt attention on me. "Look at me," he demanded, his voice deceptively soft.

I shut my eyes, refusing.

It was a mistake.

His hand clamped down on my thigh, the pressure creating a throbbing ache. I bit the inside of my cheek, refusing to cry out. If I did, he would tighten his hold, causing even more agony.

It's what he always did.

Without fail.

"When I tell you to do something," he said through gritted teeth, "you will do it. Do you understand me?"

Though I didn't want to obey *him*, one of the many villains that starred in the unending nightmare that was my life, doing so was inevitable. If I didn't listen, the night would end with the back of his hand colliding with my already bruised face.

That couldn't happen.

Not when my body was still reeling from all the pain he'd caused just hours before.

With no other choice, I twisted in the leather seat, facing him head-on. Our eyes met, and my throat tightened.

"Good girl," he whispered, tracing a knuckle down my jawline. "You did well tonight. Worth every penny I paid."

His words were a dagger to my chest.

Razor-sharp, they cut me deep.

Blinking back tears, I reached behind me, fumbling for the handle. "Can I go now?" I asked, my voice small and shaky, revealing the shame and terror that pulsed through me like a second heartbeat.

Both of which he reveled in.

"Manners, darling." His dark, cold-blooded eyes dropped to my lips. "I'm your number one client, which I believe entitles me to a kiss before you leave."

I froze.

"I c-can't," I stammered. "It's against the rules. If Dominic finds out—"

"I am more than familiar with the rules," he interrupted, his palm sliding up my bare thigh. "But they've been broken before." Grabbing my arm, he lifted it, exposing the ink on my inner wrist. "This"—he nodded at my tattoo—"is proof of that. Is it not?"

Fire roared to life in my belly.

Jerking free of his hold, I covered my wrist with my hand, hiding every piece of beauty that it represented from his view. He chuckled in return, and my fingers twitched with the need to slap his cruel face.

It was an action I didn't dare take.

I was angry, but the crippling fear possessing me still overrode the rage that nipped at my spine, demanding to be let free.

One day I'll be brave, I told myself.

Then, I'll fight back.

"Now"—he leaned closer—"about that kiss."

I curled my shoulders, turning in on myself. "It can't happen," I started. "Dominic will—"

He gave me no chance to react before sliding his hands into my hair. Dark locks clutched tight in his fist, he wrenched my head back, sending jolts of pain careening through my scalp.

I cried out, but my voice was silenced when his mouth slammed down on mine, possessing it completely.

Searing panic engulfed me.

Adrenaline spiking, I pounded my clenched hands against his broad chest and screamed into his hungry mouth, hoping he'd let me go before it was too late.

He never got the chance.

Behind me, the window suddenly shattered, sending shards of glass flying into the car. Before I could comprehend what was happening, the door popped open, and I was being yanked from the vehicle by my neck.

My back and elbows hit the concrete sidewalk, ripping flesh from bone. "You motherfucker!" A voice which I feared more than any other, screamed from above me, sending my pulse into overdrive. "What *the fuck* do you think you're doin'?"

"Careful, Dominic," the man warned. "Remember who you're speaking to."

Scared out of my mind, I studied Dominic, the man who I'd once believed to be my savior, yet who had turned out to be anything but.

Face contorted with fury, his muscular body was drawn taut, his calloused hands fisted at his sides.

He looked murderous, something which didn't bode well for me, or the man who sat in the car, an ugly sneer etched on his even uglier face.

Furiously wiping my palm across my lips, I prayed he hadn't witnessed the kiss.

Deep down, I knew that he had.

His rage was evidence of that.

And now he'll make me pay...

Forearms resting against the car's frame, he leaned forward, ducking his head inside. "Remember who I'm talkin' to?" he repeated, a mixture of disbelief and hatred plastered on his face. "What, you think I'll bow down to you just because you're the goddamn DA, Ellington?"

He chuckled, but there was no humor behind it. "Look around you, *pendejo*. This isn't your fancy downtown office. I run these fuckin' streets, and you just crossed a major line. You know the rules, and yet you pull this bullshit with *my* girl? You got a death wish, man? 'Cause others have died for a lot less."

I almost vomited upon hearing Dominic say the man's name. Though I'd learned it the first night he'd hand-delivered me to the pay-by-the-hour motel room the man had rented, I'd always refused to use it.

Acknowledging who he was only made the time I was forced to spend with him that much more gut-wrenching.

Jeffrey Ellington.

Toluca County District Attorney.

Happily married.

Father of three.

Unaffected by the threatening words being spewed in his direction, the man slid his eyes to me, his pervy gaze skimming over every inch of my bare flesh. Unlike everyone else, he showed no fear of Dominic, a man who'd taken more lives than I could fathom.

Whether it was because of the arrogance he wore like a second skin or just plain stupidity, I had no clue.

"I understand your infatuation with her," he said, casually leaning back in his seat. "I've tried all your girls out, but she's worth more than all of them combined." My stomach rolled, the urge to puke returning with a vengeance. "If you ever decide to thin your stock, I'd be willing to make a deal."

It was the *wrong* thing for him to say.

In one swift move, Dominic pulled a shiny black revolver free of his jeans and pointed it inside the car. "That's not happenin'," he said, his mental instability making its presence known. "No one will ever get my *Tesoro*, especially a white-bread *hijo de puta* like you." The gun made a clicking sound as he cocked the hammer, ready to fire. "If I were you, *Jeffrey*, I'd kick rocks while you still can."

Angry as I'd ever seen him, the man pulled a brown, cash-filled envelope from his suit jacket and tossed it out of the car. It landed on the sidewalk at my feet, crisp hundred-dollar bills visible from the open flap. "The next time you point a gun at me, D-boy," he snarled, addressing Dominic by his street name, "there will be consequences. *Lasting* ones."

Dominic stepped back, lowering the gun just as the man shifted his sleek, black Mercedes into drive and took off. The door was still open, the busted window raining bits of broken glass in its wake.

I should've been relieved to see the car fade into the distance, but that wasn't what I felt. Instead, it was heart-stopping anxiety. Well aware of the trouble bearing down on me like a runaway freight train, my fear grew tenfold.

And for good reason too.

Dominic had hurt me before.

Many times.

But this time would be bad.

Like, *really* bad.

Eyes wide with fear, I pushed to my elbows as he turned, his hard face now devoid of all emotion. Finger resting on the gun's hair-trigger, he stepped over me, straddling my hips with his feet.

"You've betrayed me, *Tesoro*." My lungs froze. "And you know what the consequence for that is."

"I told him not to kiss me!" I cried. "I swear I did! But he didn't listen and—"

I screamed when his heavy fist met my left cheek, splitting the skin wide open. I turned to the side, blood streaming down my jaw and pulled my knees into my belly, covering my face with my arms. The move was one of protection, but it did little to protect me from the blows raining down.

Clutching a chunk of my hair with his free hand, he yanked me up off the ground, wrenching a yelp from my throat. "You goddamn *whore!*" he screamed, spittle flying from his mouth, his nose nearly touching mine. "How could you do this to me?"

Terrified beyond belief, I didn't reply.

It was yet another mistake.

My heart slammed against my ribcage when he snarled and dropped me back to the concrete. "Dom," I whispered, my voice barely audible. "Please... p-lease don't hurt m-me."

My staccato plea fell on deaf ears as a handful of people gathered in the various yards lining the nearly abandoned street, all of them watching the scene before them unfold. I held my breath, waiting to see if one of them would step in and stop the suffering I knew was coming, but like always, no one did.

To some, Dominic was their pimp.

To others, he was their loan shark.

To most, he was their dealer.

But to everyone, he was *el diablo*... the devil.

"You fucked up," he said, pointing the gun at me. "And now you'll pay."

I screamed as he pulled the trigger.

Then, everything went black.

Chapter Two

ASHLEY

I came to on my back.

Vision blurry, I blinked up at the hazy ceiling, burning pain radiating throughout my right shoulder. Mind completely blank, I worked to remember how I'd ended up on the ground, the top of my dress warm and sticky.

Confused, I started to sit up.

"Ash, don't move," a soft voice, one which brought immediate comfort, said from beside me. "I just got the bleeding stopped."

In an instant, everything came rushing back.

The unwanted kiss.

The broken rule.

The sound of the gunshot.

Panicked, I jerked my head to the right, locking eyes with one of my only two friends. "Jade..." My mouth was dry, my tongue heavy, making it hard to speak. "Dominic, he..."

"I already know," she whispered, pressing hard on the wad of fabric she held against my shoulder. "He made sure to tell me what you'd done the minute he carried you inside earlier. It was his sick way of warning me not to break any of his stupid rules, I think."

I rushed to explain. "I didn't want it. I swear I didn't. I told him no, but he didn't care and—"

"I have no doubt," she interrupted, a sweet smile on her freckle-covered face. "Ellington is a psychopath. Everyone knows that. It's why he pays so much money to spend time with girls like us. He knows he can do whatever, whenever, and no one will—"

She snapped her mouth shut when the bedroom door suddenly burst open and bounced off the graffiti-covered wall behind it, sending broken pieces of busted plaster flying through the air.

"*Dios mío!*" Carmen, friend number two, screamed as she rushed our way, the threadbare fur coat she always wore swirling around her ankles. Words rushed, she was panicked, her cinnamon-colored eyes filled with fear and confusion as she looked from my blanched face to the blood-soaked cloth Jade held. "What the hell happened?"

"Dominic shot her," Jade answered matter-of-factly. "Well, he grazed her. You know he wouldn't actually shoot her. I mean, he would, but if he did, she wouldn't wake up." Visibly cringing, she paused. "I should probably shut up now."

Bronzed cheeks tinged red with anger, Carmen crossed her track-mark covered arms over her chest. I wasn't sure when she'd last shot up, but it wasn't recently. Her sweat-soaked skin and dilated eyes were proof of the withdrawal beginning to set in.

Seeing her like that...

It made my heart hurt. Badly.

"That *cabrón!*" she shouted, her ruby-red lips trembling. "I ought to smash his *huevos* with a sledgehammer!"

My heavy-lidded eyes flared as Jade sucked in a breath. "Carmen, for heaven's sake," she fussed quietly. "Don't say that. If he hears you—"

"The no-good shit-stain won't hear me," Carmen snapped before stomping to the front window that overlooked the street below. Staring out the dirt-streaked glass, she sneered, her jaw ticking. "One of his lackeys jacked up a dope delivery, so he's outside handling him." She glanced over her shoulder, meeting my gaze. "Guess you won't be the only one getting a bullet tonight."

I flinched, and her face fell.

"Sorry, *Chiquita*. That was a rotten thing to say." Stomping back across the room, she dropped to her bony knees beside me and gently cupped my face. "Who did he send you to tonight?" she asked, tracing her shaking finger over each lavender-colored bruise that bloomed against my porcelain skin. "Which *pendejo* did this?"

"Ellington," Jade spat, answering for me. "That psycho is the entire reason Dominic flew into crazy mode and almost killed her."

Carmen's jaw ticked. "Explain."

Jade opened her mouth to speak, but I beat her to the punch. "He kissed me," I mumbled, the pain in my shoulder growing. "The man broke the rules and kissed me. Dominic saw him and—"

"To hell with Dominic!" Incensed, Carmen dropped her hands. "I am sick and tired of him and his rules! I've met a lot of *idiotas* in my life, but he is the stupidest *puta madre* I have ever met! He claims you as his own, acts like he's obsessed, but then sells your body to other men repeatedly, yet later almost kills you over a kiss?"

Hearing my sins laid bare was too much for my heart to handle, and for the second time that night, I broke. "It's my fault," I cried. "Everything... all of this... it's *all* my fault."

Jade's brows rose nearly to her hairline. "How?"

At her question, I thought back to the day Dominic found me outside the Toluca City bus station, alone and scared to death. Thanks to being kicked out of my shitty childhood home—*thanks for that, Mom*—I was homeless, half-starved, and desperate for a place to sleep.

I'd been the perfect prey.

When Dom, who was a seasoned predator, approached me, I never stood a chance.

I hiccuped, my stomach churning with disgust as I recalled the effortless way I'd believed the many lies that had fallen from his cunning lips, beautifully disguised as everything my heart had always craved, but never experienced.

Acceptance.

Love.

Safety.

I'd been so stupid.

So. Damn. S*tupid!*

"Answer her," Carmen demanded, freeing me from the fog of misery possessing my mind. "*How* is any of this your fault?

"Because I believed him..."

It was the only explanation they needed.

Jade nibbled on her bottom lip, her pain mirroring my own. "I believed him too," she whispered, confessing a truth I already knew. "We all did, in some way or another."

A heavy silence filled the air.

Then, "You know what? This shit is ending *tonight. El diablo* has stolen enough from us already." Carmen's eyes locked on my tattoo, anguish flashing in her irises. "You especially, *Chiquita.*"

Painful memories stirred at her words.

Wrist burning, I held it to my chest.

Don't think about it...

Not now.

"And I will *not* stand here and let him steal another precious thing." Carmen took one of my hands in hers, followed by one of Jade's and held them tight. "There isn't a thing in this twisted world that I wouldn't do for either of you. You know that, don't you?"

"I do," I whispered, truthfully.

Jade nodded, silently agreeing.

"Good." She sighed in relief and then pulled in a deep breath. Chin wobbling, she glanced up at the ceiling. I had no idea what was going on, but something wasn't right.

I felt it deep in my gut.

Righting her head, she looked from me to Jade. "I need both of you to make me a promise. One that you have to keep, no matter what."

My brow furrowed. "What kind of promise?"

A lone tear rolled down her cheek. "I need you to promise me that once you're free of Dominic, that you'll go back to school and get your diploma. Maybe even go to college."

Free of Dominic?

That would never happen.

He'd kill us all first, me especially.

It was an oath he'd made clear from day one.

Point blank, there was no escape.

"It may not seem like it now," she continued, "but at sixteen, you two still have your entire lives ahead of you."

Right then, that feeling in my gut, the one that screamed '*this isn't right*' intensified. Carmen looked resigned to the crap deal we'd all been handed, the fight she normally possessed noticeably missing in action.

I didn't like it.

Not one single bit.

"So do you," I replied, wanting to see her eyes glowing with the fire to survive once more.

Shaking her head, she released our hands, a second tear falling. "I'm thirty-four years old, *Chiquita*. I may have once been Miss Colombia with the world at my feet, but that girl is *long* gone. The only thing that remains of her is a street whore with a penchant for shooting poison into her veins." Standing, she tapped her chest twice. "Trust me, there's nothing left in here but a couple dozen broken dreams and enough self-hatred to take down a million-man army. Not a bit of which is worth saving."

Her words weren't true.

At all.

Like Jade, Carmen was worth more than words could ever say. Drug-addicted prostitute or not, she was one of the most loving souls I'd ever met. Protective and loyal to a fault, she was everything beautiful in a world filled with a lot of ugly.

"Carmen—" I started.

"Save it, *Chiquita*," she interrupted. "Now, back to what I was saying." She paused and ran her fingers through her long, tawny hair. "Once you're both clear of this shit-hole and everything that comes with it, I want the two of you to get your *culos* back in school and make some friends." A genuine smile, one filled with warmth, brightened her face. "Maybe even fall in love with a boy your own age."

Fall in love with a boy my own age?

Not likely.

If by some miracle I ever escaped Dominic, I'd never go within twenty feet of anything that possessed a penis again. All men did was cause pain. Besides, how could someone ever love me? Whether it was my choice or not, I was nothing but a whore. As painful as it was to admit, girls like me weren't meant to be loved by boys worth loving back.

Period.

"I can't do any of that without you." Jade's panicked voice broke through the silence that had fallen over us like a velvet curtain, cracking my heart. I hated when she was scared, which was most of the time. "Without either of you."

"You *will* do it, little one," Carmen replied as she crossed the room, each of her steps quicker than the last. "Because *I* want you to." Stopping next to a busted dresser, she opened the top drawer and pulled out a wad of hundred-dollar bills, all of them Dominic's. "*Idiota* just leaves money lying around," she mumbled. "Thinks no one has the *cojones* to steal from him. *Hijo de perra* is wrong."

Eyeing the nearly closed door, she headed back our way. "Take this," she said, slapping the money into Jade's hand. "Once the coast is clear, I want you to take Ashley and run to the shelter over on Sycamore Street as fast as you can. Take the back alleys and use the shadows as cover. And no matter what happens, you do not slow down, you do not stop, and you do not look back. Got it?"

"The battered women's shelter?"

"Yes, the battered women's shelter, " she replied, answering Jade's question. *"You'll* be safe there. They'll give you food, clothes, and help you find somewhere permanent to stay. The people who work there are good. Don't be afraid to trust them. I wouldn't send you there if I had any doubts about them—"

The sound of someone climbing the rickety wood stairs down the hall reached our ears.

Jade and I froze.

Carmen though? She didn't.

Finding her fight once more, she whipped open her coat and pulled a rusty switchblade from the top of her thigh high. "Remember what I said," she said, flicking it open. "You do not look back. Not for any reason. And if for some reason push comes to shove, you fight." My panic skyrocketed as she slipped out of her worn red heels, exposing her stocking covered feet. "You *always* fight."

Turning, she crept forward.

Next to the door, she crouched low and glanced back at us, an emotion I couldn't decipher flashing in her eyes. "I should've saved you *chicas* a long time ago." Hand in the air, she blew Jade and I both a kiss. "I love you both"—she covered her heart with her free hand —"with every broken piece of me. *Never* forget that."

I jerked upright, ignoring the searing pain that stole my breath. "Carmen!" I cried out, louder than I intended. "Don't do this!"

My words didn't dissuade her.

Her decision was made.

"It's the only way, *Chiquita*."

"No, it's not! Just listen—"

My voice disappeared, dissipating like vapor as the door burst open a second time, and Dominic's large frame stepped into the room, an insidious aura surrounding him. Eyes narrowed, he glared at Jade. "What the fuck are you doing up here? I told you—"

A battle cry ripped through the air as Carmen leapt up and lunged forward, taking Dominic by surprise. Hands gripping the knife tight, she swung it with all her might, sinking it deep into his side. Blood instantly wept from the wound, staining his fitted white t-shirt crimson.

Eyes blazing with fire, he threw a single punch, one which met Carmen's jaw with a bone-jarring crunch. Momentarily dazed, she stumbled back, losing hold of the knife. "You crazy fuckin' bitch!"

Murderous intent bled into his eyes as he ripped the blade free of his flesh and stared at it, his chest rising and falling in rapid succession. Enraged, he jerked his head up and took a single step toward Carmen.

Chin raised, she showed no fear. Arms extended, she wiggled her fingers, beckoning him to move closer. "Come on, *papi*," she urged, shifting her one-hundred-pound weight between her feet. "You want to rip my throat out? Then come on and do it!"

Dominic didn't need to be told twice.

Wearing a twisted smile, he hurtled forward, eating up the space between them. In the space of a heartbeat, he had one of his hands wrapped in her hair, while the other held her own blade against her lithe throat.

Jade jumped up. "Carmen!"

Knowing she was about to charge—and likely get killed—I climbed to my knees, then to my feet, ignoring the way my head spun, and grabbed her arm, holding her in place.

"Dominic, don't!" I screamed, praying that his infatuation with me would somehow sway him.

I should've known better.

"She's gotta die, *Tesoro*!"

Carmen glared up at him, her smiling face still absent of fear. "You first, *pendejo*."

In one quick move, she grasped the revolver tucked in the front of his waistband and ripped it free. Leaping back, she raised it high, pointing the barrel at his chest.

"I will *not* let you hurt my girls!" she screamed, victory dancing in her eyes. "Not another damn time!" Losing the remaining grip she had on her emotions, she blinked, one fresh tear after another cascading down her face. "For almost two years, I have watched you cause them pain, Ashley especially, and I am fucking done! Do you hear me? I am *done*! I may be a worthless whore, but I'm about to send *el diablo* back to where he belongs." She widened her stance, steadying her aim. "See you in hell, Dominic."

She pulled the trigger, and I braced for the bang that would swiftly follow.

But it never came.

Instead, a clicking sound did.

Confused, Carmen looked at the gun, her eyes wide. Fully expecting it to fire, she pulled the trigger once more.

A second click followed.

"You stupid fuckin' cunt." Dominic chuckled, his face devoid of amusement. "The chamber is empty. The last round is buried in the sidewalk out front." His rage-filled eyes cut to me, but I said nothing as Jade clutched my trembling hand, lacing our fingers together.

Ripping off his shirt, he held it against his muscular side, staunching the flow of blood. Attention focused back on Carmen, along with the useless gun she still held, he sneered.

Bloodied switchblade clutched in his free hand, he twisted his neck, cracking it. "That mistake you just made, bitch? It'll be your last."

Dropping the shirt, he moved quickly.

Unprepared, Carmen never stood a chance.

Using the blade she'd stuck in him minutes before, he stabbed her in the side, then in the belly.

Repeatedly.

Instinct took over, and without thinking, I rushed forward and slammed my small body into his large one, not caring if he killed me too. The hit was hard, my aim perfect, but he didn't budge.

Losing my balance, I stumbled and screamed. Loud. "Dominic, stop!" I clawed his arms and wrists from where I kneeled, too dizzy from the impact to find my footing again. "I mean it, *stop!*"

He didn't stop.

Hit after hit, he continued to plunge the knife into Carmen's flesh until her legs finally gave way. Pale-faced, she dropped to her knees, her heart slowing with each beat.

Arms opened wide, I caught her as she fell, her fur coat soaked through with blood. Chin resting on my injured shoulder, I held her against me, hugging her broken body tight. "I f-failed," she whispered, her voice losing strength. "Failed my *ch-chicas*..."

"You didn't fail," I replied, wanting to ease her mind in what I knew were her last moments. "But Carmen, you have to hang on." My mind whirled, my chaotic brain trying to figure out a way to get her help.

She absolutely could *not* die.

Without her, Jade and I wouldn't make it.

"Carmen, p-please," I cried as I squeezed her tight, my voice breaking. "Don't leave m-me. You can't ever leave u-us."

When she wheezed, her chest rattling against me, but said nothing in response, I knew there was no saving her.

Turning my head, I buried my face in her caramel-colored hair and kissed her for what I knew would be the last time. "I love y-you, Car. With every broken piece of m-me."

Her reply came in the form of a raspy exhale.

It was her final one.

I bellowed, my heart cracking into millions of irreparable pieces as her body went limp in my arms.

Ten feet away, Jade bent at the waist and screamed, the pain she felt pouring out of her in waves. Over and over she yelled, her agony tearing me to pieces as sob after sob racked my own body, causing my petite frame to jerk uncontrollably.

She's gone.

El Diablo killed her, and now she's gone.

Forever.

Consumed with grief, the world around me fell away.

Blinded by pain, I missed the moment Dominic hobbled to the other side of the room, a sick expression on his face and kneeled down, pulling a second gun out from beneath the mattress where he violated my body each and every night.

But I sure as hell took notice when he started to hobble toward Jade, his blood-soaked hand holding the loaded weapon tight.

"You stealin' from me, sweetcheeks?" Eyes widening, her cries fell silent, yet no answer came, which further enraged the homicidal psycho headed her way. "Fuckin' answer me when I speak to you!"

Terrified, she dropped the roll of cash Carmen had given her minutes before. My broken heart sank as it floated to the hardwood, fluttering in different directions.

Dominic's jaw ticked. "No need to speak. I've got my goddamn answer."

Collapsing against the wall behind her, Jade held up her hands, palms out, her frantic eyes bouncing between the monster looming over her and me. "Ashley," she cried, her voice so laced with fear it was nearly unrecognizable. "Please..."

Having no other choice, I gently laid Carmen's lifeless body down and stumbled to my feet. Determined not to let her be harmed, I rushed to her, moving my battered body as fast as I could.

By the time I reached her, Dominic had already raised his hand, the gun he held aimed at her chest, ready to fire.

Wedging myself between her and the gun, I shielded her body with my own, protecting her as best as I could.

Just like before, I didn't care if I died.

What I did care about was making sure that Jade kept breathing.

I'd already lost Carmen.

I refused to lose her too.

"Get out of the way, *Tesoro*."

Shaking my head, I stood tall, refusing to back down. I may have been terrified of Dominic, but I would not back down, the consequences for my defiance be damned. "I won't let you hurt her!"

Jade clutched my dress and buried her face between my shoulder blades.

The sight of Carmen's corpse, combined with her terror-fueled tears streaming down my back caused every protective instinct I possessed to rise, flaring to life. "You are *not* taking her from me!"

El diablo's dark eyes hardened. "Watch me."

Unimaginable pain ricocheted through my head when he brought the butt of the gun down on my left temple in a brutal strike. Blinding light flashed before my eyes, and I stumbled, losing my balance. Unable to right myself, my hip slammed onto the hardwood. I yelled out in pain, failing to bite back the sound.

Jade's muted voice screamed my name.

Dominic's deep timbre followed.

I looked up, finding them both.

My mind was foggy, my vision wavering, but I could still read the scene playing out before me, my heart pounding in time with each of Jade's screams for help.

Knowing I needed to save her, I attempted to regain my bearings as Dominic stepped closer to her.

No, no, no!

Rolling to my belly, I tried to push to my hands, but I slipped, falling on my face. My nose cracked against the floor, but I paid the blood pouring down my lips and chin no mind. The only thing that mattered was reaching her.

Come on, I told myself. *Get up!*

My body failed me as I worked to stand once more. The ground felt as though it were moving, making getting to my feet impossible. I raised my head, my hazy vision focusing on the girl who'd helped hold me together ever since the day *el diablo* stole the only good thing that ever came from me, truly shattering my entire world. Eyes locked with hers, I extended my arm, my fingers reaching for her. "Jade…"

Shoulders shaking, her face fell.

Acceptance flashed in her eyes as she pulled in a deep breath and lifted her trembling hand, blowing me one final kiss, just as Carmen had done. "I love you, Ash," she said, her voice cracking. "With every broken piece of me."

I wanted to tell her that I loved her too, but the words didn't come quick enough. "I—"

Pop!

I felt my soul shrivel up and die as I watched her body jerk from the force of the bullet Dominic fired into her. Stumbling to the left, her eyes slid closed, blood seeping from her wound as she swayed, and then collapsed, falling to her side on the filthy trap house floor.

There, she took her final breath.

Chapter Three

ASHLEY

Three Months Later

*J*ust keep breathing.

Heart and soul in shambles, I stared out the car's windshield, eyes locked on the emptiness before me, the scene eerily reminiscent of the one from months before.

The only difference between now and then was that instead of being parked next to the curb under the dark night sky, in front of a known trap house, Ellington's Mercedes idled in the middle of a hotel parking lot, the afternoon sun beating down on its black paint from above.

Ninety-four days had passed since that fateful night, the same in which the man I hated like no other murdered the only two good people in my life, stealing them away from me forever.

Without Carmen and Jade, my life had eroded, becoming nothing more than an unending hell.

I couldn't eat, could hardly sleep, and God knows my every waking moment was filled with the agonizing pain of losing them.

Even after I managed to cry myself to sleep, which seemed to take forever, the torment never stopped. Over and over, I watched my girls die in my nightmares, and though I fought to stop their deaths each time, I always failed.

Just as I had the night they were killed.

It's all my fault.

"What are you thinking so hard about?"

The grief suffocating me briefly abated, allowing unchecked anger to take its place at the sound of Ellington's cruel voice. Back teeth clenched, I glared over at the sadistic bastard, the sleek Armani suit he wore the picture of both wealth and arrogance.

Like Dominic, I hated him.

With the passion of a thousand blazing suns.

"Nothing, *Jeffrey*," I replied, no longer worried about facing who he was or the consequences for speaking his name. "I'm not thinking about anything at all."

His eyes narrowed. "You know better."

I *did* know better.

I just didn't care anymore.

The night Carmen and Jade died something other than my heart broke. Sometimes I wondered if it was my sanity; I wouldn't have been surprised if it was.

At seventeen, I'd been through more than most would ever experience and lost more than I could ever admit. Even before my girls' deaths, a huge piece of my soul had been ripped from me.

One which I'd never get back.

Pissed off at my smart mouth, Ellington clamped a hand down on my left arm and dug his fingertips into my bruised flesh, ripping me from the painful memories beginning to echo through my head. "Ever since Dominic disposed of those other two whores, you've developed quite the attitude, my little pet."

The sick name caused my skin to prickle, the need to teach him a lesson, one which he'd never forget, becoming nearly overwhelming.

"At our next meeting, I'll need to do something about it"—he smiled, ignoring the rage bleeding from my pores—"before it's too late."

His words made me smile because although he didn't know it yet, there would be no future meetings between him and me.

Not ever again.

He had used me to satisfy his sick and twisted desires for the last time. Satan would serve ice water to every burning resident of hell before he violently took pleasure from my unwilling body again.

I was done.

Completely and utterly *done*.

Right hand on the door handle, I conjured the long-forgotten bravery that was buried deep in my belly, mentally preparing myself for what I was about to do.

With escape being my only focus, I hadn't gotten the chance to pay Dominic back for the horrible things he'd done, but one day, I would get my pound of flesh and force him to pay for every ounce of pain he'd inflicted. Even if it killed me to do so, I would finish the job that Carmen started when she plunged her blade into him, a blade which, unbeknownst to *el diablo*, I now possessed.

As for Ellington, his day of reckoning had come.

Closing my eyes, I gripped the door handle tight as Carmen's voice echoed through my head.

This is push meeting shove, Chiquita.

It's time to fight.

I nodded, determination setting in. "It's time," I whispered, hoping that wherever she was, she heard me.

"Who are you talking to?"

Eyes popping open, I jerked free of Ellington's hold and slipped my left hand between the seat where I sat and the center console. A malicious smile tipped my lips when I touched the familiar switchblade.

Stealing it from Dominic had been easy.

While he was busy getting stitched up by the gambling-addicted doctor he kept on call for emergencies a mere hour after murdering Carmen and Jade, I'd snuck away and hidden it in the tank of the upstairs toilet.

He never even noticed it was missing.

The idiot.

Gripping the knife tight, I looked at Ellington, my rage reaching a boiling point. "Don't you *ever* call them whores again."

His eyes flared. "Excuse me?"

Calmness spread through me. "Their names were Carmen and Jade," I answered, tightening my hold. "And they were beautiful!"

Giving myself no time to second-guess my actions, I lifted the blade high into the air and then drove it into Ellington's thigh, slicing through his slacks and puncturing his flesh. He howled in pain and knocked my hand away, but it was too late. The knife was sunk deep, the rusted tip touching bone.

"You little bitch!"

It was wrong, but seeing him wither in pain momentarily calmed the maelstrom of emotions swirling inside me. Grasping onto the relief working its way through my veins, I clutched the blade once more and twisted it—hard—snapping the handle clear off.

Blood pouring from the wound, Ellington screamed once more, and I knew I had to move quickly. In no time at all, his pain-filled bellows would draw the attention of others.

If that happened, I was done for.

"Listen to me, you sick bastard," I said, inching closer to the door. "From this moment forward, I want you to forget that I ever existed. If you don't"—I forced a smile—"well, as you once told Dominic, there will be consequences. *Lasting* ones."

His eyes filled with unspoken questions.

Ones which I was all too happy to answer.

"Let me be clear," I snarled. "If you so much as utter my name to the police about this little incident, then I will be forced to make a few confessions of my own. And those confessions? They will destroy you."

It was the absolute truth.

Ellington knew it too.

Not giving him time to react to my words, I snatched his phone—the same one he used to record all the twisted things he'd done to me—

off the console where it laid. "This," I said, holding it just out of his reach. "Is my insurance policy."

His face contorted, his expression morphing from pain to rage, and though I felt brave as could be, fear suddenly stirred in my chest.

Knowing that I needed to go—like, right then—I popped open the car door and jumped out. My stiletto-covered feet hit the scorching Georgia asphalt, and like a bat fresh out of hell, I took off.

Letting my adrenaline drive me, I raced across the parking lot and then up an alley that hugged the side of the hotel. Long and narrow, it led to the back of the new fire station, which sat at the intersection of Sycamore and Pine Street.

Sycamore was my destination.

At the end of the alley, I tossed the broken knife handle into an open storm drain, made a sharp right, and then bolted across the fire station lawn, followed by its small parking lot. My eyes bulged, and a yelp fell from my lips when I almost careened headfirst into a dark-haired fireman headed toward a black truck, a duffle bag thrown over his shoulder.

Thankfully, he moved fast, quickly stepping out of my way. "What the hell, kid?" he yelled as I passed him. "You alright?"

Ignoring his question, I kept moving.

Arms pumping wildly, I willed my tired legs to move faster. My lungs were screaming, my feet aching, but I didn't slow down. If anything, I ran harder, pushing my beaten body to its limits.

Reaching the intersection I needed, I sprinted across the busy two-lane road and down the opposite sidewalk. A hundred yards later, I came to a stop in front of a closed, wrought-iron gate, the metal sign attached to it acting as a beacon.

Toluca Battered Women's Shelter, it read.

It was the third time in as many days that I'd stood outside that gate, reading that same sign, but it was the first time I intended to pass through it. I only hoped that Carmen had been right about the people who worked inside.

If they turned me away, I was dead.

I wasn't worried about Ellington because although he was a predator, he wasn't stupid. After stealing his phone and now in possession of the evidence it held, he knew I had the power to sink him into oblivion if he so much as uttered my name to the cops.

But Dominic? He'd kill me.

His obsession with me be damned.

"Please," I whispered, wrapping my shaking fingers around my wrist. Teeth gnawing on my trembling bottom lip, I rubbed my thumb over my tattoo in slow, comforting strokes. "Please let them help me."

When no one came, doubt crept in.

Growing more panicked with each passing second, I wanted nothing more than to turn around and run in the opposite direction. Going there had been a mistake. Even if the people were good, Dominic would never let me go. It didn't matter how hard I ran or how much distance I placed between us.

He'd never give up searching.

I took a step back, ready to take off

Just as I turned, about to dart across the road, the front door of the shelter swung open, and a woman, followed by a man, walked out.

I froze, my feet glued to the sidewalk.

The man was big like Dominic, with inky black hair, tanned skin, and intimidating features.

But it wasn't him that drew my attention.

It was the woman.

I'd never seen her before, but there was something familiar about her fierce expression, something which reminded me of Carmen.

Overcome with grief at the realization, I stumbled back.

Her icy blue eyes flared in response, and she moved faster, her golden-blonde hair blowing in the wind. "Honey," she said, her thick Southern accent comforting. "Please don't run. I just want to talk."

Reaching the gate, she silently wrapped her hands around two of the wrought-iron bars and looked me over, taking in every inch of my disheveled state.

I could only imagine what she thought.

The curve-hugging dress I wore was two sizes too small, showcasing my abnormally thin frame, and my worn stilettos were sky high.

Face caked with garish makeup, my dark hair was pulled on top of my head, the locks messy thanks to Ellington's wandering hands.

I looked every bit the harlot I was.

Disgusted over who I'd become, I crossed my arms, the shame overwhelming.

Unable to stand the silence any longer, I jerked my face up, fully prepared for the woman to sneer in my direction, and then demand I leave.

Thank God that's not what happened.

Warmth spread through my frigid soul when instead, her hope-filled eyes locked with mine and Carmen's words, the ones she'd spoken moments before she died ricocheted through my head.

The people who work there are good, she'd said.

You can trust them.

With no other choice but to return to the streets, I held my tattooed-wrist against my thrumming heart and made a decision that would change my life forever.

And that decision? It was to trust the beautiful woman standing before me, her soul calling to my own like a siren's song.

Turns out, it was the best decision I ever made. Because that woman, her name was Shelby Mason.

And she was my salvation.

Chapter Four

ASHLEY

Three Weeks Later

I felt sick.

Overwhelmed with dread, I sat in the middle of the shelter's main office, my stomach twisted in a million knots. Scared of what was to come, I stole a peek at Maddie Davis, the shelter's manager, who was seated across from me and next to Shelby.

Though a gentle smile played on her full lips, I couldn't look at her without feeling as though I was a half-second away from breaking down. With her sparkling green eyes, freckle-covered face, and sweet disposition, she was a walking, talking, reminder of Jade.

It killed me.

"You okay?" Her soft voice chipped away at my heart, intensifying the ache flourishing in my chest.

Without speaking a word, I forced a tentative smile and nodded before sliding my trembling hands under my thighs, hiding them from view.

"You sure, sugar?" Shelby asked, her tone filled with concern.

Neither woman looked convinced that I was alright.

Every Kiss You Steal

And rightfully so.

Anyone with eyes could see that I wasn't being truthful, and though I loathed lying, I still insisted on acting as if I were coping just fine. It was a stupid thing to do considering I was teetering on the edge of a breakdown, dangerously close to losing what remained of my mind.

That's *if* I hadn't lost it already.

Which, let's face it, was a distinct possibility.

The rolling chair Maddie sat in squeaked as she leaned forward, placing her elbows on the large oak desk separating us. "If not, all you have to do is tell me, and I'll do whatever I can to help you." She nodded toward a silent Shelby. "We both will."

My throat burned as another lie danced on the tip of my untruthful tongue before slipping free. "I'm sure."

"Okay," she replied, her voice filled with skepticism. "But if you ever find that changes, then find me, Shelby, or one of the other ladies. It doesn't matter what the problem is, we'll do everything we can to help you."

Of that, I had zero doubt.

The women who worked at the shelter had already gone above and beyond to help me. From donating clothes, both new and old, to rousing me from the dark dreams that tormented me each night, they'd done everything they could to make me feel safe and cared for.

For that, I'd be forever grateful.

Lump in my throat, I nodded once more, not saying a word. Consumed with too many emotions to count, I couldn't have replied if my life had depended on it.

Still smiling, she picked up a blue pen and leaned back, lifting a sheet of paper from the desk. "Alright," she said, tucking a strand of chestnut-colored hair behind her ear. "The reason Shelby and I asked you to come in here is because we need to talk to you about long-term placement."

I froze, my lungs seizing.

Placement?

What did *that* mean?

29

"Don't panic, beautiful girl," Shelby said, reading the terror flitting across my face. "She just means that we need to figure out the safest place for you to live after you leave here."

Leave?

I had nowhere else to go.

Well, nowhere other than the morgue which is where I'd end up if Dominic found me.

Anxiety ensued, sending both my heart and mind into a frenzy. "Are you...?" My throat felt as though it were closing. Swear to the heavens above, I couldn't breathe. Could. Not. Breathe! "K-kicking me out?"

Eyes bulging, Shelby jumped up. "Girl, it'll be a cold day in hell." I blinked, my throat continuing to tighten. "Sugar, you have a place here as long as you need it. Don't care if I've gotta make you a pallet in the hall, so damn be it." Her unflinching eyes drilled into mine. "You're not going *anywhere* until you're ready to. You hear me?"

A smidge of relief unfurled in me.

Chewing on her bottom lip, Maddie stood and rounded the desk, taking a seat in the chair next to me.

My attention went to her pregnant belly.

Pressure built inside me.

"You just turned seventeen," she whispered, stating something I already knew. "As a minor, I legally have to take certain steps to ensure your safety."

The relief I felt seconds before vanished.

"What steps?" I asked, bouncing my legs nervously.

"Well," she replied, her hands resting on her stomach. "For one, by law, I'm required to call Children's Protective Services and inform them that you're here. They'll want to talk to you and—"

I stood so abruptly my chair skittered backward and slammed into the wall. "I am *not* letting CPS send me back to Kentucky," I snapped, my tone harsher than I intended.

"Is that where you ran away from?" Maddie asked.

"I didn't run away from anywhere," I replied, confessing one of my awful truths. "I was kicked out and forced onto the streets."

"By who?"

I didn't hesitate. "By my mother."

Mother.

Yeah, right.

The woman who birthed me had been anything but. A dog would have cared for me better than she had. At least they had maternal instincts, something Wanda Ward severely lacked.

Eyes full of sympathy, Maddie looked from me to Shelby, then back to me again. "Your mother kicked you out?"

"Yes."

Frustrated by the tears welling in my eyes, I turned, giving both women my back. They'd seen me cry enough since my arrival. They didn't need to see me break down again.

Wanting to comfort me, Maddie touched my arm. I flinched; the feel of her skin on mine was nearly intolerable. "Tell us about her," she whispered, jerking her hand back. "I know it's probably a hard subject to broach, but the more we know, the better we know how to help."

I gnawed on my bottom lip, surprised that she didn't know more about my ugly past since I'd spilled everything to Shelby the moment I'd shown up at the gate, terrified and out of options.

Most everything, anyway.

I'd left out the most hideous parts of my past for numerous reasons, the most prominent being both shame and fear.

Shame because my sins were vast, the scars marring my soul deep; fear because of the horrendous—not to mention *illegal*—things I'd both witnessed and been forced to partake in since I was a child.

I was the definition of a walking liability.

To more people than just one.

"My mom is *not* a good person," I said, putting the truth mildly.

"Did she hurt you?" The sadness I'd seen in Maddie's eyes moments before bled into her voice, making the sympathy she had for me clear.

"N-no," I replied, my voice cracking, much to my dismay. "She did something w-worse."

"Ashley, sweetheart, it's okay. If you aren't ready to tell Shelby and me every—"

Unable to stop myself from divulging the vile confession, I turned to face them once more and wrapped my arms around my belly, holding myself tight. "She let her boyfriend, more than one, harm me." The tears filling my eyes began to fall, each sliding down my cheeks faster than the last. "And she didn't even care what sick stuff they did or how badly they hurt me. Not as long as she was kept knee-deep in pills and whatever cheap liquor with which she chose to wash them down."

Shelby inched closer until her chest almost touched mine. Having her in my space, her warm body so near mine should've made me uncomfortable, but it didn't.

To my surprise, I wanted her close.

"What did they do, sugar?" She reached out and wrapped an arm around me, resting her palm on my back. "How did they hurt you?"

My insides twisted as memories, ones which I'd tried to block out, flared to life.

The smell of their rancid breath.

The feel of their grimy hands covering my mouth.

The sound of my muffled screams.

Every gut-wrenching detail came rushing back, making me want to vomit up what little I'd eaten that day.

"I've got you, Ashley," Shelby whispered, her fingers rubbing slow circles on my back. "Trust me."

Call me crazy, but I *did* trust her.

Immensely so.

Feeling her strength bleed into me, I sucked in a calming breath and forced the words to come. "They touched m-me."

The room fell silent.

Heaviness filled the space.

Then, "You are *not* going back there," Shelby practically hollered, her eyes filled with fire. "I will be damned!"

"No," Maddie agreed, clearly upset. "She's not going back there. Not ever." Wiping her tear-streaked cheeks with the back of her hands, she looked over at Shelby. "I'm not sure how CPS will want to handle this since she'll be a legal adult in less than a year, but if it comes down to it, she can live with Hendrix and me until then. He won't mind and getting licensed as—"

"Oh, back off, Cupcake," Shelby interrupted, causing Maddie to snap her mouth shut. "I found her"—she dropped her hand from my back and placed it on her cocked hip—"and that means I get to keep her."

My head began to spin.

Keep me?

I was so confused.

"It's plain and simple," Shelby continued, explaining herself further. "If she's going to live with anybody, it'll be Lucca and me." Looking my way, she smiled, her pretty eyes crinkling at the corners. "My little man would love having you around. Then he'd have someone else to harass besides me."

The vice squeezing my chest eased at the mention of Shelby's toddler son. The first time I met him, he'd wiggled his way into my broken heart.

Just like his mama had.

"So, what now?" Shelby asked Maddie, shifting her weight between her cowgirl-booted feet. "Do I need to go down to Children's Services and fill out some paperwork or what?"

Maddie's eyes widened. "You're serious, aren't you?"

Shelby looked confused. "Why the hell wouldn't I be? She needs somewhere safe to live, and I can give her that." Her eyes met mine. "You'd rather stay with me than go back to Kentucky, right?"

There was no hesitation on my part. "Yes."

"See," Shelby said, shrugging. "Far as my Southern behind is concerned, it's a done deal. I may be so poor I can barely afford to pay attention half the time, but my house is clean, the pantry has food in it, and my sofa is mighty comfortable. Even if it is older than dirt. Besides, my lil ol' duplex is better than some random foster home. And before you jump my rear end, let me just say—I know some foster families are great, but some, well, they just ain't." Turning, she lifted her phone from the desk and clutched the cracked screen tight. "So work whatever magic you have to, Mad, 'cause this needs to be taken care of. Pronto."

The air in the room shifted, becoming lighter.

"Lord, Blondie." Wide-eyed, Maddie shook her head. "What's next? Are you going to adopt her too?"

Shelby blinked. "Will they let me?"

A smile tipped my lips.

It felt strange on my face.

When was the last time I smiled?

"You're something else you know that?" Maddie asked, eyes twinkling.

Cocking a hip, Shelby sassily flicked her hair over her shoulder. "If by something you mean fabulous, then why yes, yes I am."

That earned a chuckle from me.

Tossing a wink in my direction, she hooked her thumb and pointed toward the door. "Alright, y'all, if we're done here, I need to go help Hope and Clara. Last I saw, they were stripping beds, and Hope's tiny self looked ready to fall over." Scrunching her nose up, she shook her head. "The girl just ain't made for manual labor."

Maddie waved a dismissive hand in the air. "It's fine, go. I've got calls to make anyway since you're determined to steal Ashley from me."

Shelby's eyes narrowed. "I found her—"

"—So you get to keep her," Maddie finished for her. "Yes, I know, crazy, I heard you the first time."

Shelby rolled her eyes. "I'll show you crazy."

"Please don't." Maddie turned and rounded the desk. "I am not prepared to deal with it. Especially not after finding out Grandmama was passing out moonshine at church yesterday. Seriously, y'all, my limit for handling crazy has been reached for the week."

I snickered at the mention of Grandmama.

Maddie's grandmother, she was a colorful force of nature. Utterly inappropriate on the best of days and completely scandalous at her worst, she was one of my favorite people, even if I didn't know her too well.

"Hey, ladies..."

My spine snapped straight when Carissa and Heidi, two sisters who worked at the shelter, walked into the room. Both were close to my age, with only a couple of years separating us. Carissa, who was the oldest, shot me a sweet smile, while Heidi, who was deaf, waved in my direction.

I liked both girls, but there was something about Heidi that made me breathe a little easier when she was near. I couldn't explain it, because even though she didn't talk much, she brought me comfort.

Carissa nibbled on her bottom lip, her eyes bouncing between Maddie, Shelby, and me. "Did we come at a bad time? Because if so, we can head back out—"

"It's fine, C," Maddie interrupted, her smile growing. "We were just talking about where Ashley will live once she transitions out of emergency care." Her gaze cut to Shelby. "And Blondie over here is adamant about keeping her all to herself; therefore, she's insisting we find a way for Ashley to live with her and Lucca."

Carissa blinked, the shyness she wore like a coat of armor disappearing. "That's not really fair, is it? I mean, shouldn't we get to vote or something? What if I want her to live with Heidi and me?"

Shelby's eyes narrowed. "For the second time today, I will be damned—"

"Okay," Maddie said, cutting in once more. Hands up, palms out, she waved her arms around. "I'll need to work closely with CPS on this, and they'll have the final say which will include all sorts of stipulations and rules I'm sure, but it's up to Ashley whether she wants me to pursue this."

She looked at me.

"Honey, I know this is a hard decision, and it isn't one you have to make on the spot, but it's your choice whether you want to stay with one of us. If not, we understand. But if you do, then all of us will open our homes to you. Clara and Hope included."

I shifted my weight between my feet, an unfamiliar emotion stirring inside me.

I was being given a choice: a first for me.

And I was unsure of how to react.

"Your voice matters, Ashley," Carissa said, her tone gentle as could be. "It may not have in the past, but it does now."

"She's right," Shelby added. "From now on, it will *always* matter."

Heidi nodded her agreement, her blue eyes awash with moisture.

"As I said," Maddie started once more. "You don't have to—"

"I want to stay with Shelby and Lucca," I blurted out, cutting her off and surprising myself. "If that's okay with her." Feeling a bit nervous and a lot foolish, I ducked my head and stared at the floor. Mere minutes had passed since Shelby stated that she wanted me to live with her, but that didn't stop my anxiety from planting seeds of doubt in my head.

What if she'd changed her mind?

Or what if she hadn't really meant it?

"Thank you, sweet baby Jesus." I jerked my head up, my wide-eyed gaze landing on Shelby when she spoke. "I am so glad you picked me, sugar," she said, "because I am not above begging."

Her eyes twinkled; my heart beat faster.

Closing the small space between us, she extended her arms. "Can I hug you?"

Again, I didn't hesitate. "Yes."

Her warm arms embraced me, and I leaned into her, resting my cheek against her chest.

"Thank you for picking Lucca and me," she whispered, swaying me from side to side. 'You won't regret it. Promise."

Her words, as nice as they were, made no sense to me. I had no idea why she was thanking me. Shouldn't it have been the other way around?

Leaning back, she ran her hands through my hair, pushing the errant locks from my face. "And just for the record, I swear on everything holy that I will not let anyone hurt you again. Not today, not tomorrow, and not ten years from now. Got it?"

It was a vow I prayed she'd be able to keep.

"I've got it."

Dropping her arms, she took a step back. "Well," she said. "Since this is all settled, I guess I should go find Clara and Hope. Lord knows Itty Bitty has probably keeled over by now."

Carissa scrunched her nose. "Let's hope not because I don't think Evan would handle that too well," she said, referring to Evan Morgan, the shelter's head of security, and the man who acted as Hope's shadow.

I didn't know what the deal between them was, but he was always up her butt. Normally, such a thing would've made me uncomfortable, but it was obvious that Evan's behavior was okay, maybe even welcomed as far as Hope was concerned.

I didn't understand it. At all.

Then again, I was no expert on relationships. My experience with men consisted of unwanted touches, constant abuse, and sadistic behavior.

Who was I to judge what was normal?

Or even healthy?

Shelby's eyes widened, grabbing my attention. "That's no joke."

Smiling big, Maddie tapped Shelby on the arm and pointed toward the door. "Get your tush out of here and go help the girls before Hope works herself to death, and Evan has a coronary in response."

Shelby glanced back at me. "You want to come?"

I rocked back on my heels, crossing my arms. "Is it okay if I go outside instead? I know I'm not supposed to but—"

"It's fine. The gate is closed, so you'll be safe. Just don't stay too long. It's hotter than blue blazes out there." Having given me her answer, she turned her attention to Maddie. "I'm taking C and Heidi Bug with me. You call Children's Services and then try to take a nap. You look exhausted."

Hand on her belly, Maddie nodded, her eyes heavier than before. "I swear this little one is sucking the energy right out of me. I can't even pee without—"

I'd heard enough.

Heart aching, I headed for the door before Maddie could finish whatever she was about to say. "Be back soon."

No one said a word as I hoofed it out of the room, but I felt their eyes on me until I reached the very end of the hall and turned the corner, disappearing from their sight.

Shoving through the exit, I burst into the afternoon sunlight, the meltdown I felt brewing earlier barely restrained.

Racing around the side of the building, I hid behind a large dumpster, taking myself out of view of the security cameras.

Chest tightening, I let my legs give way and slid to the gravel-covered ground beneath me in a heap of weary bones and battered flesh. Knees pulled in, I wrapped my arms around my shins, holding myself tight.

There, I allowed myself to break.

Chapter Five

ASHLEY

I woke up screaming.

Back pressed against the cot where I slept, I kicked away the thin white sheet blanketing my sweat-slicked skin and jerked upright, heart in my throat.

The nightmare that had invaded my dreams, stealing the breath right out of my lungs still lingered, making it impossible to fight off the demons that lived inside me, their cruel taunts destroying me bit by bit.

Like the day before when I'd recalled the horrid things I'd been through at the hands of my mother's lovers to both Maddie and Shelby, every heartbreaking detail of that fateful night—the one which came two months before Carmen and Jade's deaths—rushed forward.

The memories…

They hurt.

So damn bad.

Hands pressed against my ears, I rocked back and forth, agony gripping me as the reminders of my past bombarded me, forcing me to relive a hell I'd never truly escape.

The smell of fresh blood.

The sound of my screams.

The echoes of her cries.

Stomach churning, vomit climbed the length of my esophagus. Knowing I was about to be sick, I clamped my hand over my trembling lips, jumped off the rickety cot, and headed for the bathroom.

Halfway there, I almost ran smack dab into Shelby, but by some miracle, she managed to jump out of the way just in time, avoiding a collision. "Ashley!" she hollered, her cowgirl boots clicking against the hallway floor as she chased after me, matching me stride for stride. "Wait!"

Wait?

That wasn't possible.

Demons were nipping at my heels; I ran faster, my heart splintering. Bursting through the bathroom door at top speed, I dropped down in front of the toilet, my knees slamming onto the tiled floor, and emptied the contents of my belly into the porcelain bowl.

Shelby rushed in behind me.

Pulling my hair back from my face with one hand, she used the other to rub circles on my back. "It's okay, sugar," she whispered. "Everything is alright."

I liked Shelby, but she was wrong.

Nothing would ever be alright again.

Not without them.

Done getting sick, I plopped back onto my butt just as the first sob hit, jerking my entire body. "He took her from me," I cried, holding my tattoo against my chest. "He took *all* of them from me!"

Unable to stand the pain, I leaned forward and curled my hands before slamming my fists down on my thighs over and over.

Breaking apart at the seams, I then screamed, putting my grief out there for any and everyone to hear.

Kneeling behind me, Shelby wrapped her arms around me tight, and pulled me back, taking all of my weight when I collapsed against her. "Who, sugar?" she asked, her erratic pulse bleeding into my back. "Who did he take?"

I dropped my head back onto her shoulder. "Everyone," I whispered, my insides twisting. "He took everyone I ever loved." More sobs, more tears. "Now they're gone, and I'll never get them back."

It was a truth I didn't want to face.

Because without Carmen and Jade, and without *her*, I knew the torment embedded in both my heart and soul would last until the moment I took my final breath.

———

Dressed in a soft pink tank top and light grey pajama shorts that had once belonged to Hope, I sat atop a picnic table next to the shelter, my eyes closed and head tilted back, letting the blazing Georgia sun dry my tear-streaked face.

How long I'd been sitting there, my body still trembling from what happened an hour before, I hadn't a clue.

Not that it mattered.

Finding comfort in the quiet that surrounded me, I could have stayed in that same spot, my skin baking in the mid-morning light, all day.

Everyone seemed content to let me do it too. Other than Heidi popping her head out the side door every few minutes to check on me, I'd mainly been left alone.

For that, I was thankful.

Nearing a complete mental breakdown, I wasn't in the correct state of mind to answer any of the concern-filled questions headed my way from the ladies once I stepped back inside.

Questions about the nightmare.

Questions about who *they* were.

Questions I couldn't answer.

Being forced to relive Carmen and Jade's murders each time I closed my eyes was bad enough, but being asked to explain the harrowing events that came months before would be my demise.

"Ashley!"

Ripped from the chaos that was my life, I snapped my head

forward, a chill racing down my spine at the sound of a familiar, albeit panicked, voice.

Hand shielding my eyes from the blinding sun, I looked toward the front gate, searching for the woman it belonged to.

My eyes found her immediately.

Upon seeing her, surprise and a lot of fear flooded my veins, triggering my panic once again. "D-Darcy?" I stuttered, hopping off the table. "How"—I paused—"how did you find m-me?"

If she found me…

Hands wrapped around the wrought iron bars that kept the shelter safe from the crime-ridden streets of Toluca, she glanced over her shoulder, then back to me.

"Ashley, help me!" she screamed, tears streaming down her bruise-covered face. "Please, he's coming! If he catches me—"

Her words faded, becoming muted.

I didn't need to ask her who *he* was.

I already knew.

Dominic.

He was coming.

Oh God…

"Please, Ashley…" Her entire body jerked as she sobbed, continually looking over her shoulder. "I don't wanna die."

Before I could think about what I was doing, my feet began to move. As risky as helping her was, I couldn't let him kill her too.

Granted, she had been nothing short of awful to me ever since we'd met, but I didn't blame her for that.

I blamed *el diablo*.

From the beginning, he'd pitted every girl in his stables against one another, relishing in the additional pain it caused each of us to be at one another's throats.

It only made matters worse when he claimed me as his own, putting me on a pedestal no other girl could reach, making me the envy of all the others, except for Carmen and Jade.

The entire thing was sick and twisted.

Just like the man who'd orchestrated it all.

At the gate, I paused, a semblance of sanity swirling in my head. "I need to get one of the ladies," I said, taking a small step back. "Evan too. He can protect you if Dominic—"

"No!" she screamed, cutting me off. "You can't go back inside. It'll take too long, and I need your help now. Ashley, *please*. If he catches me before I get inside, he'll kill me." Her knees bent, close to giving way. "Just like he killed Carmen and Jade."

Her words were my undoing.

Determined not to let her be hurt, I let my unstable emotions drive me, and without hesitating, I lunged to my right and slammed my hand down on the hidden silver button that powered the gate.

It was a mistake.

Heart nearly exploding, I squeezed through the small opening the retreating gate created the moment there was enough room for my body to fit, and extended my shaking hand, offering it to her.

She didn't take it.

Right then, I should've known something was off. But I didn't. "Darcy, let's go," I said, my words rushed. "We have to hurry before he gets here and kills us both."

Lower lip trembling, she suddenly stepped back, an emotion akin to regret swirling in her dilated eyes. "I'm sorry," she whispered, moving back further. "So sorry."

Before I could process what she was saying, a large body, one that I knew all too well, appeared from behind the brick pillar that held one end of the gate in place.

"Missed you, *Tesoro*," Dominic said, his dark eyes lit with fury. "Time to go home, baby."

A scream tore from my throat as he suddenly sprang forward, a twisted smile locked on his devilish face.

Fight or flight kicking in, I fell back, my butt hitting the ground and struck out, doing my best to keep him from getting his murderous hands on me.

He grunted as the bottom of my foot connected with his right knee, but the move didn't help.

It only served to piss him off further.

"You stupid little bitch!" he hollered, leaning down and fisting a handful of my shirt. Jerking my upper body off the ground, he glared at me, the evil that lurked inside him shining bright. "You're going to pay for that, along with all the other goddamn problems you've caused me!"

Hand raised, he slammed his knuckles into my cheek, backhanding me.

The hit was hard.

The pain brutal.

Dropping me back to the ground, he clutched my shirt and began to drag me across the traffic-less street, following Darcy to an idling SUV parked next to the curb.

"Let me go!" I yelled, struggling against his hold, the bravery I feigned driven by fear and stoked by instinct. "I am *not* leaving with you!"

He moved faster.

My adrenaline surged.

"Help me!" I screamed, fighting against him with everything I had as the concrete bit into my bared flesh, ripping my skin. "Someone help me!"

"You stupid fuckin' cunt," Dominic growled, moving faster. "You'll be goddamn lucky if I let you live past sunset." Clenching my shirt tighter, he glared down at me. "Keep it up, and I'll gut your troublemakin' ass and toss you in the same swamp as your two favorite whores."

Anger blinded me.

Until that moment, I hadn't known what happened to Carmen and Jade's bodies. The only thing I did know was that one of Dominic's fixers, a dirty cop with a thirst for things only a drug dealing pimp could provide, had disposed of them. But knowing that he'd ordered them thrown into the swamp...

I couldn't handle that.

Fueled by rage, the thought of getting loose and running straight to the police ricocheted through my head, but I squashed the idea right away.

Though I wanted nothing more than to see Dominic behind bars for the rest of his natural-born life, getting help from the law would be impossible.

Especially not with Ellington as the DA.

Between him and the half dozen dirty cops *el diablo* had in his pocket, the charges would never stick. That's *if* they even arrested him to begin with.

Which I doubted they would.

Not to mention, with my luck, if I reported the crimes I'd seen, I would likely end up tortured and killed for turning snitch. Or I'd be locked up on false charges and silenced with the threat of spending my life in prison. A place the powers that be would guarantee was hell for me.

Corrupted beyond redemption, there was no length the scumbags of Toluca County wouldn't go to in order to steal my voice, along with anyone else who found the courage to speak up against them.

Keeping quiet was my only option.

For now.

Clinging onto every bit of fight that I possessed, I dug my heels into the ground, hoping it would slow Dominic down, at least until someone realized what was going on and came to my rescue.

If he got me into his car, it was over.

But hard as I fought, we didn't slow.

Not the least bit.

It didn't matter though.

Help was on the way.

And that help? She. Looked. *Pissed.*

Terror stabbed me right in the heart when I caught sight of Shelby running full-bore toward me, her arms pumping wildly as she came closer, the crazed expression on her face nothing short of manic.

With only a few feet separating her from us, she lifted her arms in front of her before slamming her body into Dominic's back, ripping his hand from my shirt.

Taken by surprise, the hit knocked him to the ground, all the air leaving his lungs in an audible swoosh as Shelby flipped forward, tumbling a good five feet.

I jerked up, the sound of my pounding pulse filling my ears, blocking out the surrounding world. Gaze locked on the scene before me, I watched in horror as Dominic jumped to his feet, hands fisted at his sides.

Shelby scrambled backward, Dominic stalking her every move, then stood. Panting for breath, she glanced at me, her eyes pleading with me to listen to whatever words she was about to say. "Ashley, run!"

I didn't run.

Instead, I remained paralyzed with fear, glued to the spot as *el diablo* turned his head, shooting me a glare over his shoulder. "Bitch, you better not—"

His words turned into a pain-filled grunt when Shelby took advantage of his momentary distraction and slammed the pointy toe of her cowgirl boot into his crotch, nailing him where it counted.

Like a rock, he dropped.

A mixture of shock and awe washed through me when his formidable frame hit the sidewalk with a crack, his mocha-colored complexion losing all color.

Not missing a beat, Shelby lunged for him and in one quick move, ripped the ever-present pistol he kept tucked into the front of his waistband free.

Just like Carmen had the night she died.

My terror-filled eyes flared as she and Jade's faces flashed before me.

This can't be happening.

Not again.

"Shelby, don't!" I screamed, watching as Dominic fell forward, his chest nearly hitting the ground. "He'll kill you!"

Even as I shouted the words, I didn't believe them.

Not because Dominic wouldn't do as I said—he certainly would—but because Shelby dying wasn't an option I was willing to entertain. I'd already lost the most important people in my life at the hands of the monster laying ten feet away, his hand cupping his—hopefully busted —junk.

I wouldn't let him hurt her.

History would *not* repeat itself.

Of that, I was damn sure.

Climbing to my feet, I took a shaky step forward, prepared to do whatever I had to in order to keep Shelby safe.

Even if it meant sacrificing myself.

She had a beautiful little boy, one who I cared about more than was logical given the circumstances, and I wouldn't let her be ripped from him. He needed his mama, just as she needed him.

But no one needed me.

Not anymore.

Indispensable, I was completely worthless.

I'd only made it two steps when Evan suddenly blew past me, almost knocking me over.

Jaw locked tight, he came to a sliding stop next to Dominic. "You motherfucker!" Lifting his arm, he slammed his elbow down on *el diablo's* back. A cracking sound followed, and right or wrong, I couldn't help but smile. "I should kill your worthless ass!"

Pulling a pair of zip-tie looking handcuffs from his back pocket, Evan then yanked Dominic's hands behind his back and secured them in place, making escape impossible.

Knee pressed into the back of one of my many tormentors, he looked over at me, his enraged gaze searching my body for any signs of damage.

Seeing none, he focused back on the monster beneath him, one who hadn't said a word since Shelby drove his nuts high into his stomach a minute before.

It was surprising.

As combative as he was, I expected Dominic to curse, to fight, to do anything other than lie there on the sidewalk and take being restrained like the criminal he was without complaint.

But I shouldn't have.

I may not have understood it at the time, but men like Dominic never went toe-to-toe with another man.

Especially not one like Evan.

Abusers in every sense of the word, they lorded their power over weaker people, making a career of harming the most vulnerable of us.

Evan wasn't either of those things.

Dominic had no power over him.

"Ashley!" I jumped, my heart lurching into my throat when Carissa appeared beside me, her expression alarmed. "I need to get you back inside," she said, gently wrapping her hand around my wrist. "Where it's safe."

Torn between the desire to flee and the need to stay and make sure Dominic didn't hurt anyone else, my head and heart were conflicted.

I didn't move.

Didn't speak.

I'm not sure I even breathed.

Carissa's head jerked to the right as the sound of approaching foot-steps reached my ears. I had no idea who they belonged to, but one look at her suddenly pinched lips, and I knew I wouldn't be happy with whoever was headed our way.

I was right.

"Miss Ashley."

Chills raced down my spine at the sound of the deep voice. Ripping my arm free of Carissa's, I spun around, coming face to face with one of the scariest looking men I'd ever laid eyes on.

In an instant, fear flooded my veins.

"Chris," Carissa said, speaking to one of Evan's security team members. "We need to get her inside. If we don't, Evan will—"

He held up his hand, halting whatever she was about to say. "Miss Ashley," he repeated, his infuriated eyes never deviating from my terri-fied ones. "Like Miss Carissa said, we need to get you inside." His gaze raked over me, just as Evan's had, assessing my thin body for any injuries. "Can you walk? Or do you need me to carry you?"

Overwhelmed, my head started to spin, and my mind began to shut down. I couldn't have answered him if my life had depended on it. The darkness that came for me each time the world around me became too much to handle was beginning to circle, its suffocating arms outstretched.

Fingers tingling, my breathing became labored. Growing weaker with each second that ticked by, I swayed, my legs turning to mush.

Chris reached out and wrapped a muscular arm around me, stopping the nasty fall I was about to take dead in its tracks.

My skin burned at the feel of his touch, and though I knew he wouldn't hurt me, my fear intensified, slingshotting me headfirst into the black hole that awaited me.

Feeling myself float away, I dropped my head back, my face tilted toward the cloudless Georgia sky.

"Ashley!" Carissa's panicked voice echoed around me, but she sounded so far away. Wrapping a hand around my jaw, she squeezed it tight. "Oh my God, Ash, breathe!"

Ash.

No one ever called me that.

No one except Jade.

The realization was too much.

I simply couldn't cope.

And just like that, it was lights out.

———

My hands wouldn't stop shaking.

Momentarily free of the panic that had stolen my grip on reality twice in the previous three hours, I watched as Dominic was not-so-gently placed in the back of a police cruiser, his busted face a testament to the beating he'd been handed by the plain-clothes police officer arresting him.

A man whose name I didn't know.

Swallowing around the lump clogging my throat, I rested my forehead against one of the shelter's front windows. "Who is he?"

Shelby, who was busy cleaning the backs of my scraped thighs with peroxide soaked wipes, blew out a frustrated breath. "His name is Anthony," she whispered. "Anthony Moretti."

There was something about her tone... "Do you know him?"

Still facing the window, I didn't see her nod. "You could say that. He's my..." She paused. "Well, I guess he's my—"

"He's her boyfriend," Clara, who stood next to me, her fiery red hair pulled into a messy bun atop her head, interjected. Nose scrunched, her eyes twinkled with mischief. "You see, Shelby here doesn't like to admit it since she has commitment issues and all"—she smiled—"but Detective Moretti is her man all the same." Leaning to the side, she peered behind me, finding Shelby. "Right, Blondie?"

Shelby growled. "Right."

My lower lip trembled as the man, Detective Moretti, placed hand-cuffs around a crying Darcy's wrists and led her to a second cruiser. I wanted to be angry with her for the stunt she'd just pulled, but doing so was nearly impossible.

She was terrified of Dominic, and being terrified of him meant that he could bend her to his will, making her do things she normally wouldn't. Fear, as horrible as it was, had the power to make you do all sorts of things.

It was a truth I knew all too well.

Adrenaline waning, I wrapped my arms around my torso, digging my fingers into my sides. "Is he good?"

Shelby's hand stilled, the cool cloth she held resting against my tender flesh. "Yeah, sugar, he is," she answered, her voice barely a whisper. "I know it may not seem like it, considering he slammed D-boy's face into the sidewalk earlier, but he got combative when Tony showed up to arrest him."

She was right.

Dominic did deserve it.

That and a lot more.

One day...

"I know you have zero reason to trust me," she continued, standing. "But, I swear that Tony is nothing like them."

Them.

The single word pinged around my head, reminding me of the confessions she'd made the day I'd shown up at the gate, on the run for my life. *I know what it feels like to be threatened by someone with a soul blacker than coal*, she'd said. *And I know how terrifying it can be to take that first step towards escaping.*

Like me, a man who promised to love and protect her forever had hurt Shelby.

Clara too.

It's why I *did* trust them.

They understood.

Exhausted, I gnawed on my bottom lip, lingering fear, and anxiety pulsing through me. "Will he be angry if I come and stay with you?"

Though I knew Anthony didn't live with Shelby, I wasn't sure how he'd react to her letting a homeless teen prostitute move in with her and Lucca.

That's *if* CPS even approved it.

Which, who knew if they would or not.

Shelby's eye twitched. "Shit no!" she hollered in a thick accent. "He won't say a single word against it." After dropping the blood and dirt-streaked wipes into the trash, she placed her fisted hands onto her hips. "But even if he did, I'd tell him where he could shove his two cents. And trust me, it's a part of his body where the Southern sun doesn't dare shine."

Clara laughed, and if I hadn't been so scared, I might have too.

Placing a single finger on my jaw, Shelby turned my face to meet hers. "Now," she said, her stormy blue eyes filled with a myriad of emotions. "We need to talk."

My stomach dropped to my feet. I didn't want to talk or face the music for the reckless way I'd acted earlier. At that moment, the only thing I wanted to do was sink into the floor and disappear.

For good.

"It was wrong of me to open the gate," I said, tears welling. "I realize that. But I thought Darcy needed help, and I couldn't let him hurt her. I know I'm stupid but—"

Shaking her head, she palmed my cheeks. "You are *not* stupid." Her words surprised me. "Impulsive? Yes. But stupid? Never."

I blinked, unsure of what to say.

"She's right, you know," Clara added. "What you did was something we all would've done. No questions asked."

Fire danced in Shelby's eyes. "Exactly! That's why I didn't think twice before coming after you, the consequences of not waiting for back-up be damned."

"W-why?" The stuttered word rolled off the tip of my tongue before I could stop it. "You know Dominic could have hurt you. And I'm not worth you being hurt over. Not when—"

"You are worth more than you'll ever know, Ashley Ward," she interrupted, squaring her shoulders. "And you *never* forget that. As for why I did it... I swore that I wouldn't allow anyone to hurt you again." She paused and pulled in a deep breath. "And, sugar, I always keep my word."

Head bowed, I didn't try to stop the sob that broke free, its mighty force nearly ripping me in half. Legs shaky, I fell into Shelby, twining my arms around her warmth like vines.

She held me in return, her strength pouring into my very soul. "Please," I cried, my cheeks resting against her chest. "Don't ever let go."

If she did, I feared I'd shatter.

Yet *again*.

Arms tightening around me, she buried her face in my hair. "I'll never let go," she replied, her tone steady. "On my life, I promise I won't."

It was a promise she kept.

And one she never came close to breaking.

———

"What's your name?"

I snapped my head up at the sound of the masculine voice, one I'd never heard before.

A twinge of fear flared in my belly when my eyes locked with a pair of steel-grey ones that belonged to Detective Moretti.

Sucking in a small breath, I leaned back against the plastic chair, where I sat next to Heidi, who held my hand firmly in hers. "Ashley," I whispered, not wanting to anger him. "Ashley Ward."

He jerked his chin down once. "Ashley, my name is Anthony Moretti. I'm a homicide detective at Toluca Police Department." Unclipping the shiny badge affixed to the front of his pressed slacks, he held it up for me to read. "If you have a minute, I'd like to talk to you about Dominic West."

I hunched my shoulders.

Then sunk in the chair.

Reading my anxiety-riddled expression, he clipped his badge back in place and slowly moved my way. When only three feet separated me from him, he squatted, bringing us eye to eye.

Though I knew he wouldn't hurt me, having *him*, a man I didn't know so close almost sent me into a tailspin.

Leaning against Heidi, I ducked my head, pushing a stray lock of hair behind my ear. "I don't have anything to say about Dominic."

Liar! The voice in my head screamed.

Tell him about Carmen.

Tell him about Jade.

Tell him about Ad—

Mind in free-fall, I ripped my hand free of Heidi's and fisted them, refusing to listen to the words repeating on a loop in my head.

As much as I wanted to disclose every horrific crime I'd witnessed Dominic commit, doing so wasn't an option. For one, as much as it hurt to admit, I doubted anyone would care, especially that he'd killed Carmen and Jade.

Despite being the most beautiful people I'd ever encountered, to some, they were nothing more than worthless whores, the dregs of society. Being murdered by their pimp, a man as vicious as he was vile, was just par for the course.

Two, deep in my heart, I knew Carmen wouldn't want me to divulge what happened that night. Instead, she would've wanted me to move on, to finish school, to fall in love, and to live a happy life—the very thing Dominic stole from her and Jade both.

And right or wrong, I wanted to make her proud.

Unable to hide the tsunami-like emotions whirling inside me, I let the tears that had been blurring my vision fall.

Heidi, Lord bless her, hugged me in response, holding me close. Ever since Shelby and Clara left the room twenty minutes before, she'd been by my side, the silence that had stretched between us nothing less than comfortable.

"I understand you don't want to talk about Dominic," Moretti continued, his forearms resting on his thighs. "And I'm sure you have plenty of reasons for wishing to remain silent."

If he only knew.

"But I need you to understand something."

Convinced his words were the start of a well-delivered threat, my heart flew into a tizzy, thumping away at warp speed. He may not have been a fan of Dominic—that became clear the second he slammed his face into the sidewalk—but what if he was on Ellington's payroll?

"I won't t-talk," I stammered. "Not—"

"He's not going to hurt you, Ashley," he said, interrupting the slew of panic-stricken words about to roll off my tongue, rapid-fire. "Not ever again."

Heidi froze. "How?" she asked, surprising me. It was one of the few times I'd heard her speak, and I'd be lying if I said I didn't love the sound of her voice.

It was different but beautiful.

Just like her.

"How can you be sure?" she added, her narrowed blue eyes full of suspicion.

"I can be sure," Detective Moretti replied, "because, after today, Dominic West won't ever walk the streets of Toluca County again."

It was my turn to freeze. "What?"

His eyes softened. "This is strike number three for him."

I didn't understand.

Like, at all.

"I don't... I mean, I don't get it."

He nodded and stood, crossing his arms over his chest. "D-boy," he snarled, "already has two violent out-of-county felony convictions, something I was just notified of. And now, after his latest stunt, he'll be charged with a handful more. Attempted kidnapping, possession of a firearm by a felon, drug trafficking, not to mention assault and battery on a female. None of which he has a prayer of beating in court since the entire event was caught on the shelter's security cameras."

My hillbilly genes were coming through strong because I still didn't comprehend exactly what he was saying. Not even close. "What does that mean?" My voice was high-pitched, my words rushed, making it obvious that I was working myself into hysterics.

"It means he's going away. For a long time."

Going away? "To prison?"

Detective Moretti nodded. "To prison."

"How long is a long time?"

"My best guess? Twenty years."

My world stopped turning.

My lungs quit working.

And my heart? I swear it stopped beating.

"Twenty years?" I wheezed in disbelief.

He smiled. "Twenty years."

I didn't bother to wipe away the tears that spilled down my cheeks. "He's going away," I croaked, the relief clogging my throat nearly choking the life out of me. "And I'm finally free."

Heidi hiccuped, tears of her own falling.

"Yes, you're free," he whispered, sliding his hands into his pockets. "And from this day forward, you always will be."

His words were the truth.

Because that day, I got a second chance.

As for *el diablo*? Just like Anthony said, he later got twenty to life.

Part Two

FROM DARKNESS CAME HOPE

"He stepped down, trying not to look at her, as if she were the sun, yet he saw her, even without looking."

— Leo Tolstoy, *Anna Karenina*

Chapter Six

CHASE

Seven Months Later

*I*t was a Saturday, at half past six.

Both mentally and physically exhausted, I sat in the middle of the sofa, my bare back pressed against the supple leather cushion behind me.

"Chase," Bianca, the annoying-as-hell brunette straddling my lap, purred, her soft hands massaging my shoulders. "Why don't we go to your bedroom?"

Shifting her weight, she rolled her hips, trying her damnedest to seduce me into giving her the exact thing she'd been fighting like hell to get the past two years. "There's something I want to show you."

She wouldn't be showing me shit.

When I didn't speak or make a move to get up, she upped her game. Raking her tongue over her bottom lip, she pinched the hem of her tank top and began to lift it over her head, exposing her flawless skin to me, one slow inch at a time.

The move was meant to be seductive, but it didn't entice me to touch her.

The only thing it did was irritate me.

More than ready to put an end to whatever game she was playing, I gently wrapped my hand around one of her wrists, halting her from revealing the top half of her tits. "You need to stop."

A well-rehearsed pout formed on her gloss-coated lips, annoying me further. "Why?" she asked, grinding her crotch down onto my non-existent erection. "I know you want me."

I almost laughed.

The chick was crazy.

I didn't want her.

Not at all.

But that truth, one I'd made perfectly clear plenty of times in the past, hadn't seeped in yet.

"No," I said, making myself clear yet again. "I don't. How many times do we need to go over this?" Sounding like a complete dick wasn't my intention, but it couldn't be helped. I was beyond tired of her clingy shit. "I'm not interested, Bianca. Never will be, so do us both a favor and give it a rest."

Surprise crossed her face at my words, but it morphed into straight-up pissiness when I lifted her off my lap and deposited her scantily clad ass onto the cushion beside me, crushing the magazine she'd been looking at earlier.

Leaning forward, I rested my elbows on my thighs and nodded toward the door. "It's past time for you to go." I stood, grabbing my shirt from the back of the sofa and slipped it on, hiding my tanned skin from her view.

"So, that's it?" Bitch mode activated, she jumped up, crossed her arms over her chest, and glared at me, her bony hip cocked to the side. "We're not even going to make out?"

I blinked.

She couldn't be serious.

One look at her face, and I knew that she was, in fact, serious.

"Oh, for fuck's *sake*," I hissed, crossing my arms over my chest. "Did you not just hear what I said?" When she didn't reply, I took a deep breath and continued. "Bianca, listen to me. I. Am. *Not*. Interested. So why in the hell would we make out?"

Her mouth gaped. "You have got to be kidding me!" she screeched, fisting her small hands. "I swear, Chase, if I didn't know better, I'd think you were..."

"You'd think I was what?" Chin raised, I urged her to keep talking. "Go ahead, finish what you were about to say."

A malicious smile curved her lips. "I'd think you were gay." Eyes shining bright, she flicked her long hair back over her shoulder. "You're not, are you?' Cause if not"—she reached out and ran a manicured nail down the center of my chest—"then why don't you prove it?"

Fuck this.

Reaching my limit, I took a step back. "Trust me, Bianca, I'm not gay. Not that it's any of your business," I said matter-of-factly. "I just have no interest in sticking my dick in a hole that's already been plowed more than a county mile's worth of cornfields."

My words were harsh.

But they were the truth.

Most people would've found it hard to believe, but at eighteen, I understood that sex was about more than just getting off.

My older brother, Ty, the man who'd raised me after rescuing me from our abusive father, started pounding that fact in my head the moment I hit puberty.

Women are more than a place for you to bust a nut, he'd said, over and over. *You treat their bodies with respect, or you stay away from them altogether.*

I'd listened.

"You bastard!" Bianca screamed, her cheeks tinged red. "How dare you!"

I shrugged. "Just calling it like I see it."

Mad as hell, she snatched a glass of water off the end table and slung it at my head. I moved to the side, dodging it just in time and turned, watching as the spiraling glass hit the wall behind me, shattering.

I whistled, the quarterback in me impressed with the throw. "Well, hell, Bianca," I said, wide-eyed. "Maybe you should try out for the football team. With an arm like that, Coach may bench my ass in favor of you."

She shrieked again, this time louder, but said nothing as she stomped toward the apartment door, her heel-covered feet slamming against the hardwood with each step.

I chuckled, her antics reminding me of a pissed-off toddler. "And people wonder why I stay away from chicks," I mumbled to myself.

The front door burst open just as she reached it, and my brother, of all damn people, stepped inside, his blue eyes filled with alarm and confusion.

"What the fuck is going on?" he asked, looking from me to Bianca, then back to me again. "I heard someone yelling all the way down in the parking lot. Sounded like a cat was being tortured to death."

Bianca's eyes narrowed. "You're *such* an asshole, Ty," she snapped before shooting one last sneer in my direction. "Guess it runs in the family."

Without another word, she stormed past Ty and disappeared into the hall, leaving nothing but ringing ears and the smell of expensive perfume in her wake.

Shaking his head, my brother shut the door. "Tell me you're wrapping up with her."

I froze, my shoulders tensing.

"Pack of condoms in the bathroom hasn't been touched, Chase, so don't bullshit me," he continued, his tone accusatory. "Unless you're buying your own, then I don't know what the—"

"There isn't shit to wrap up," I interrupted, the urge to shove my fist into his face growing with each word he spoke. "I know better than to stick my dick in crazy."

Arms crossed, he stared at me with an inscrutable expression. "You mean to tell me as much time as that girl spends over here, that you're not fucking her?"

I was offended. "What did I just say?" I may have been a lot of things, closed-off, angry, and selfish just to name a few, but I wasn't a liar. "If I say something, I damn well mean—"

"Calm your hot-tempered ass down," he said, interrupting. "I was just asking a question."

"No, you were insinuating," I fired back, my temple pulsing with a heartbeat of its own. "And I don't like that shit."

Eye twitching, he moved closer. "If you two aren't screwing around, then why is she always over here?"

I slid my hands into the pockets of my sweats. "Just because I'm not giving her my dick, doesn't mean she isn't trying to get it." Again, it was the truth. "And just so we're clear, I never invite her over. She always tags along with one of the guys. Tonight, it was Grant. When he dipped to go see Emma, she stayed."

Much to my annoyance.

Ty nodded, understanding finally making its way into his thick skull. "Good, because a girl like that"—he paused, shaking his head once more—"she's not what you need. Not when your entire future is on the line."

Having already heard this lecture more than once, I moved back to the couch and plopped down, stretching out my sore legs.

"Don't worry, big brother, I know," I replied, lacing my fingers together behind my head. "My football scholarship is gone if I mess up again."

And by mess up, I meant that I couldn't beat anyone else's ass like I'd done a year before when a rival player tried to manhandle one of our cheerleaders after a game.

I had no tolerance for that bullshit.

Already pissed from losing, I'd seen red when he tossed her over his shoulder despite her pleas to be left alone. Without thinking, I'd reacted and beat the prick until he lost consciousness, a move which resulted in me being thrust into court-mandated anger management classes.

Despite knowing I took the beating too far—*prick deserved it*—and having to deal with the fallout and nearly losing my full-ride to Charleston Southern, I didn't regret my actions.

Not the least bit.

The girl, Ellie, had needed help.

I'd given her that.

"As long as you understand what's at stake, then I'll back off," Ty said. "But Chase, I'm telling you, if you slip—"

His words dissipated when someone pounded on the door three times in rapid succession.

Boom!

Boom!

Boom!

I dropped my head back. "Please tell me that isn't Bianca again."

The sound of Ty's footsteps filled the apartment as he moved back toward the door. "It's not, Bianca," he said, wrapping his hand around the knob. "It's someone crazier. If I were you, I'd suggest you grab your cup out of your gym bag and put it on fast-like. Christ only knows what's about to happen."

Had he lost his damned mind?

"What in the Sam Hill are you talking—"

"I heard that, you dadgummedmed blond-headed troublemaker!" Doris Davis, or Grandmama as most called her, shouted through the door. "Now open the door before I pull out my flyswatter!"

"What did you do?" Ty turned, his eyes meeting mine. "The only reason the Crazy Old Biddy would show up here is if she's ready to throw one of us a beating."

"I didn't do shit," I replied, standing. "What did you do?"

He shook his head. "Nothing."

"Lord have mercy," Grandmama mumbled from the other side of the door. "Listen here, you two. I ain't got time for this. I'm busier than a one-legged cat in a sandbox, and if you two dummies make me late for where I gotta be next, then I'm gonna take out my swatter and pop you both right on your scrumptious behinds."

I cringed at the thought.

Not because I was scared of a flyswatter, but because I knew Grandmama would pinch my ass a time or two before whacking me.

Besides being the town busybody, she was a self-proclaimed Granny Cougar.

No man was safe around her.

"Ty, let her in before she shoots the door open. Christ knows she's probably already digging her gun out of that massive bag she totes around everywhere."

Did I mention that she owned a gun?

Because she did.

And she'd used it before too.

More than once.

As the saying around town went...

One did *not* fuck with Grandmama.

Blowing out a breath, Ty pulled open the door and stepped to the side, letting the oldest hell-raiser I'd ever met into our apartment.

Wearing a floppy purple sun hat, turquoise framed eyeglasses, a floral dress that looked more like curtains than clothing, and fuchsia-colored lipstick, she looked every bit the nut she was.

Eyes narrowed, she pointed a hot pink-tipped finger at me. "You," she said, lips pursed. "You're the one I need to speak to."

Ty chuckled. "Good luck, bro."

If he'd been within reach, I would've punched him.

Hands up, I took a step back. "Don't know what this is about, Grandmama," I said, truthfully. "But whatever it is, I can assure you I didn't do it."

She rolled her eyes, putting her dramatic side on full display. "Lordy, boy, I already know that," she replied while looking at me as if I were the crazy one in this exchange. "That's why I'm here.' Cause there *is* something I need you to do for me, and it's a whole lot important too."

I blinked.

Not missing a beat, she dropped the oversized purse dangling from her curled shoulder to the ground and bent at the waist, digging through its contents.

I looked at Ty, who shrugged.

After a moment, Grandmama stood. "Ah-ha!" she said. "Finally found it." Holding on tight to what looked like a small photo, she sucked in a breath. "I'm getting too old to be bending over like that." Hand pressed to her chest, she exhaled. "Feel like I'm gonna pass out."

A mischievous smile crossed her face as she glanced back at Ty. "If I faint, you best be giving me CPR, Troublemaker. And make sure you take one of them selfies while you do it too, so I can show all my ladies down at the bingo hall. Dadgum hussies will be green as toads with envy."

Chuckling, I pointed to the picture, paper, whatever it was, that she held. "What's that?"

"This," she said, beaming from ear-to-ear, "is my newest grandbaby."

Confused, I arched a brow.

It was no secret that Grandmama claimed half the county as her own, blood relation be damned, but I hadn't heard who the latest adoptee was. Not that I paid much attention to what was happening around town to begin with.

Sporting a thoughtful expression, she stared down at the picture. "She'll be starting with you down at Toluca High tomorrow," she said. "Hasn't been in a regular school for a spell, but she's been taking some of them internet class thingamabobs on the 'puter. Thought she was gonna graduate that way, but she done went and told her mama that she wants to spend her last semester going to class in person."

Online classes?

Why had she been taking those?

It was a question I didn't get the chance to ask because Grandmama kept talking, her focus still on the photo. "My grandbaby is smart as a whip, but it's still gonna be a big ol' adjustment. Can't help but worry that it'll be hard on her. Therefore, I'm asking you for a favor."

"What kind of favor?"

She didn't hesitate before answering. "The kind where you keep an eye on her for me."

Wanting no part of it, I gritted my back teeth together. "If she's in high school, why does she need me to babysit her?" It was a shit thing to say, but like the dickhead I can be, I said it anyway. "Isn't she old enough to look after herself?"

Fire danced in Grandmama's eyes. "'Cause, ya big dummy, she's been going through a rough patch here lately, and she doesn't need no more horsepuckey added on top of it. Poor girl has had to deal with enough."

Her reply made me feel like an ass. "What kind of rough patch?"

Grandmama opened her mouth to reply, but Ty beat her to the punch. "It's none of your damn business, Chase," he said, his voice stern and colored with disappointment. "Just keep an eye on her. That's all anybody is asking."

Somebody was in a pissy mood.

That much was obvious.

Jaw ticking, he moved over toward Grandmama, keeping his ass clear of the Crazy Old Biddy's traveling hands. "Ashley, right?" he asked her, glancing down at the picture over her hunched shoulder. "I've seen her with Shelby a few times, but I've never spoken to her."

"Yep, that's her," she replied, pointing at the photo. "Shelby took her in as a foster kid some months back, but after her no-good, white trash mama back in Kentucky signed over her parental rights, she and Anthony adopted her the minute they got hitched. The whole thing, including Ashley's name change, was finalized a week ago."

Adopted?

Who the hell adopted a high school kid?

"Had to grease the right gears to get it done so fast, but we made it happen," she continued, pride flitting across her face. "Ain't she one of the prettiest things you've ever laid eyes on?"

Ty's face softened, something that didn't happen often. Well, except when it came to Heidi Johnson, the chick he secretly pined away for. "That she is."

My curiosity was piqued. "Hold up," I said, extending my hand. "Let me see the picture."

Crossing his arms, my big brother glared at me, his eyes burning holes in my head. "You hear us mention how pretty she is, and now all of a sudden you want to see her? Convenient."

Normally, I wouldn't have blamed him for being suspicious of my curiosity.

But right then, I did.

Because he was wrong.

I didn't give two shits if the girl was the next Miss America, because I wasn't interested in chicks. I had enough on my plate already.

Mainly keeping myself out of trouble.

Still, hearing that she was going through a rough patch, as Grandmama called it, didn't sit well with me. Maybe it was because I'd been through my fair share of bullshit, but I didn't like knowing she was having a hard time.

I only hoped she wasn't like Bianca.

Because if she was...

Hell, I didn't even want to think about it.

"You gonna look out for her?" Grandmama asked, holding the photo against her chest. "Make sure nobody messes with her or gets her all upset?"

Without thinking twice, I dipped my chin once in affirmation. "Yeah, I'll keep an eye on her."

"And you are gonna keep your dadgummed hands to yourself? I know how teenage boys are.' Specially popular ones like you. Last thing my grandbaby needs is some jock with wandering hands to twist her up more than she already is."

"I'm not going to touch her," I replied, annoyed as hell.

"You better not," she replied, handing me the picture. "I mean it. No flirty looks, stolen kisses, or hanky panky. Keep it platonic. Else I'll jerk you bald-headed."

I didn't doubt that for one minute.

Taking the picture from her hand, I pulled in a breath, my fingers shaking the slightest bit. It was stupid as hell considering the circumstances, but for some unknown reason, I felt unsettled, entirely on edge.

It was ridiculous.

Turning in place, I gave Grandmama and Ty my back. Then, with my stomach in knots, I flipped the picture over.

And just like that, my heart stopped.

No joke, it *stopped*.

Chest tightening, I stared down at the most beautiful girl I'd ever seen, wanting to memorize her every feature.

Almond-shaped, coffee-colored eyes.

Small, upturned nose.

Full, bow-shaped lips.

Scarred left cheek.

Long, chocolate-brown hair.

"Christ," I mumbled to myself, rubbing my sweaty palm across my jaw. "I am completely fucked."

No truer words had ever been spoken.

Because at that moment, it didn't matter that the girl staring back at me was a stranger.

The only thing that *did* matter was that something deep inside me recognized her, and with only one look, I knew damned well that nothing would ever be the same again.

In the end, I was right.

Chapter Seven

ASHLEY

I *have a family.*

The realization stirred in my chest as I sat in the middle row of my family's SUV, my gaze flitting between the other four occupants, their loud voices, and warm laughter filling the space.

Seeing them, their smiling faces bright in the morning light, soothed my scarred soul, and knowing that they'd chosen to keep *me*, the girl with more demons than one could fathom, did funny things to my tattered heart.

Despite the horrific memories that still plagued me, and the excruciating feeling of loss that I'd never be rid of, having them by my side made the pain a whole lot more bearable.

"You ready for this?" Anthony, or the Dadinator, as I called him at times, asked from the driver's seat. "Because it's not too late to back out. If you've changed your mind, I'll go in the school and—"

"She's ready," Shelby, also known as the Mominator, interrupted. Flipping open her visor, she stared back at me from the mirror. "Aren't you, sugar?"

I nodded. "I'm ready."

It was a lie.

I wasn't ready, not at all, but the time had come for me to reclaim everything that had been stolen from me.

With Dominic no longer a threat, and Ellington out of the picture—hopefully for good if he had a lick of sense—my life had changed, and with it, I needed to change too.

Even if doing so scared me.

Like, a whole lot.

Besides, I had a promise to keep.

Carmen's words, the ones she'd spoken moments before her death, echoed through my mind, lighting a fire in my belly and renewing my determination to forge ahead, despite the anxiety that gripped me, threatening to send me into a tailspin at any moment.

I need you to promise me that once you're free of Dominic, that you'll go back to school and get your diploma, she'd said. *Maybe even go to college.*

Terrified of what was to come that night, I hadn't given her my word that I'd do as she asked, but I intended to do it all the same.

I owed her that, plus a lot more.

"Issy, ready!" Lucca, the best little brother I could've asked for, squealed next to me, his arms raised high in the air. "My issy ready to go, go, go!"

A lump formed in my throat each time he called me Issy, his version of sissy.

He was perfect.

Just like she would've—

Thumb caressing my tattoo, I fought back the memories that threatened to rise, bringing with them nothing but pain and sorrow. Needing to distract myself from the internal battle I never ceased fighting, I reached over and ran my shaking fingers through his curly black hair.

"Are you going to behave at daycare today?" It was a miracle my voice didn't break. "Or are you going to drive your poor teachers batty?"

"Batty!" he shrieked, nodding. "U-ka drive teach batty!"

Smiling, Anthony groaned from the front seat, his shoulders shaking the slightest bit as he chuckled. "Of course, he will."

"Well, duh," Shelby responded, shifting in her seat. "He's not my son for nothing."

"The lady speaks the truth," Felix, who sat in the third row behind Lucca and me, said. A once homeless Vietnam vet, he'd been taken in by Shelby—just like me—and now lived in the apartment above our garage.

Lucca and I called him Uncle Felix.

And to me, that's exactly what he was.

"Zip it, Fe-fe," Shelby said, turning in her seat. Eyes twinkling, she smiled. "I was only kidding, anyhow. We all know that he gets his troublemaking skills from Hendrix, not me," she said, referring to her older brother and Maddie's husband. "Ain't that right, little man?"

Bouncing in his car seat, Lucca clapped. "Un-ka Henny did it!"

That earned a laugh from me.

Poor Hendrix.

He caught the blame for everything.

"Alright, *Principessa*," Anthony said, his voice steady and gentle. "We're here."

Anxiety climbing, I looked at the building to my right as the car came to a stop. Stomach flipping, I took in its brick exterior, along with the various people, most of them around my age, that littered the sidewalk and breezeway beside it.

Just breathe…

Hand hovering over the door handle, I pulled my bottom lip between my teeth and bit down, cringing at the pain that zinged through me. "Guess I better go then."

My dad, the man who'd chosen to love me when he had no obligation to, stared at me, his eyes filled with reluctance. Over the past few months, he and I had gotten close—miraculously so—and I knew he wasn't ready to let me go.

That truth both warmed my heart and made it that much harder to take that first step.

But I had to do this.

If not for me, then I needed to do it for Carmen and Jade.

They wouldn't have wanted me hiding out in my room, buried

behind my laptop, taking one online class after another. Both would've wanted me to get out and live my life.

It was because of them that I found the strength to unbuckle my seatbelt and pop open the door.

I was just about to hop out when Anthony said, "I put some cash and a travel-size bottle of Mace in your purse. Attached a small Taser to your keychain too. If you need either, use them. No hesitation."

Frozen, I blinked. "I'll get in trouble."

The look that came over his face was nothing short of comical. "It's a good thing your dad is a cop then, yeah?"

I smiled. "It is."

Turning back around in her seat, Shelby handed me my backpack. "I made sure everyone's number was programmed into your phone. If you need any of us for any reason, you call us, sugar. Understand?"

I nodded.

"And," she continued. "If this all becomes too much to handle, you walk right out and hightail it across the street to the fire station. Hendrix and Pop will both be on duty all day."

My smile grew at the mention of Pop.

He was Shelby's father and my grandfather, but I had a hard time referring to him as such because the man didn't look a day over forty.

So I called him Pop like everyone else.

He didn't mind either.

The only thing he cared about was making sure his family was safe and happy, something we always were despite the different challenges we all faced.

"I'm going to be fine." I didn't know who I was trying to convince more—myself or my family. "No worries, guys."

A high-pitched bell suddenly rang.

Eyes wide, I sucked in a breath. "Okay, y'all, I'm going." Not giving my brain time to comprehend what my feet were doing, I jumped out of the SUV, slipped on my backpack, and looked back at my family one last time. After blowing a kiss at Lucca, who pretended to catch it mid-air, I waved good-bye to all three adults. "I'll see you guys when I get home."

Knowing that I needed to move before I chickened out, I shut the car door, not giving anyone the chance to reply.

Nervous as could be, I turned, facing the school.

Pulling my folded up schedule out of my back pocket, I gripped it tight, my hand shaking the slightest bit, and glanced at the building's front door. "I survived two years with Dominic," I whispered to myself, feeling my throat tighten. "Surviving high school should be easy."

At least that was my hope.

Determined and more than ready to get the first day over with, I headed inside, my strumming heart beating in time with my hurried pace.

Little did I know, I was mere hours away from my entire world being upended, and my life changed.

Forever.

Chapter Eight

ASHLEY

*M*y day was spiraling.

After not being able to get my locker open the half dozen times I'd tried, getting lost more than once, and being the center of the Toluca High gossip mill since the moment I stepped foot on campus, I was reaching the end of my rope.

I thought this would be easy.

I thought I'd be able to handle it.

But standing at the front of the crowded cafeteria, lunch tray in hand, I realized that I had been severely mistaken.

As per usual.

Not knowing where to sit, I ignored the numerous sets of eyes glued to my face, along with the hushed whispers that surrounded me, and headed to an empty table that sat along the far wall.

Once there, I sat down and sent up a silent prayer that everyone would then turn their attention back to whatever it had been on prior to me entering the room.

I should have known better.

"Uh, excuse me?"

Fork in hand, I snapped my head up at the sound of the bitchy voice. When I saw the pretty girl standing next to me, her expensive purse dangling from her forearm, I knew that whatever was about to happen, wouldn't end well for me.

Raking her harsh glare over me, she sneered. "What do you think you're doing, new girl?" she asked, one perfectly manicured hand on her hip. "You can't sit here. This is our table," she continued, amused. "And you are *not* one of us."

A giggle sounded from behind her.

That was when I noticed the three girls at her back, each of them wearing matching looks of disgust on their pretty faces.

Great.

Just great.

"I d-didn't..." She arched a brow, her ruby-red lips twisting into a vicious smile when I stuttered, the words I needed to speak refusing to come. "I didn't know."

"Well, you do now," she said, her tone growing more hateful with each word. "So if I were you, I'd get up and leave before we decide to—"

I'd heard enough.

Gripping my tray tight, I stood, the bravery I'd possessed earlier in the morning nowhere to be found, and rounded the table. Exit in sight, I headed straight for it, no hesitation.

Too bad I didn't make it that far.

After only two steps, my left foot caught on something, and I stumbled. Unable to right myself, I lurched forward, my lunch tumbling from my hands.

The world around me slowed as it hit the vinyl floor, its contents splattering in different directions.

A squeal slipped past my lips as I started to follow it down, my descent into a new hell quickly approaching. Eyes closed, I braced myself for impact.

Only, it never came.

Instead, a strong hand found my arm, stopping my fall in its tracks.

Heart pounding, I gasped when the owner of said hand pulled me up, helping me find my footing.

Steady once more, I looked up, finding the person who'd saved me from cracking my head wide open.

When his electric blue eyes, the prettiest I'd ever seen, met mine for the first time, I nearly forgot how to breathe.

Not even kidding.

Taking in his above average height, muscular frame, short, blond hair, and angular jaw, I may have squirmed a little.

Though I wasn't interested in boys, not in the least, even I could appreciate how cute he was.

And Lord, he was cute.

If I had been a normal girl—

"You alright?" he asked, his deep voice silky smooth and just as beautiful as the rest of him.

"Oh good God, of course, she's alright," the girl from before snarled, ugliness bleeding into her tone. "She didn't even hit the floor."

Embarrassment swamped me.

Chin wobbling, I jerked my arm free from his hold, my skin burning from the small amount of contact.

The guy whose name I didn't know, looked confused at the move.

Getting over it, he glared at the girl, whose name I also didn't know. "What the hell is the matter with you, Bianca?"

Bianca.

The name fit her well.

It sounded just as bitchy as she seemed.

"She was sitting at *our* table, Chase!"

"So, what," he fired back, his eyes narrowed. "You think that gives you the right to talk to her like a dog, and then trip her when she tries to leave?"

Realization struck.

The witch had tripped me.

On purpose.

Anger seeped in.

At that moment, I so wished I'd possessed the lady-balls to turn around and smack the meanness right out of her, something Carmen would've done without hesitation.

Shelby too.

Unfortunately, I wasn't ballsy or brave like them.

Where they didn't take crap from anyone, I might as well have been a doormat.

Well, except for that time I stabbed Ellington.

Don't think about that now!

Not wanting anyone to witness the meltdown I knew was impending, I stepped away from Chase—*I love his name*—and toward the back door.

The small move drew his attention.

Eyes back on me, he licked his lower lip, making my belly flip. "Let me go grab you another tray," he said, holding out his big hand. "Then, you can come sit at my table."

"What!" Bianca, screeched, clearly upset.

Ignoring her, Chase moved closer, erasing the step back I'd taken moments before. "Come on, Ashley," he continued, urging me to slip my hand into his. "You've gotta eat, beautiful."

My lips parted, shock gripping me.

I wasn't surprised that he knew my name since I'd been the focus of the Toluca High grapevine all morning, but what did surprise me, nearly to death, was being called beautiful.

I wasn't beautiful.

My skin was scarred, my soul stained with filth. There was nothing, and I mean *nothing*, beautiful about me.

"You don't even know me," I whispered, my hackles rising.

His brow furrowed. "I realize that," he replied, dropping his hand. "But that's something I plan on changing."

Heaven help me, the boy was obviously nuts, and given my history with crazy males, I needed to put as much space as possible between us.

Even if a tiny part of me didn't want to.

Shaking my head, I slipped my thumbs under my backpack straps and clutched them tightly. "Don't waste your time," I said, preparing to bolt. "Trust me, I'm not worth it."

Losing the fight to keep my tears at bay, I turned and took off, bursting through the exit.

Once outside, I ran for cover.

Chapter Nine

CHASE

*M*y chest hurt.

Quite fucking literally.

Holding a lunch tray in each of my hands, I pushed through the same exit Ashley had disappeared through minutes earlier, searching for her.

Where she'd gone, I didn't have a clue.

But I was damned sure going to find out.

Going on a hunch, I followed the sidewalk that led to the football field, a route I'd taken many times before.

Madder than I'd been in a long time, my hands shook. Hard as I tried, I couldn't get the look on Ashley's face as Bianca spewed her venom all over her out of my head.

She'd looked broken.

Completely defeated.

I couldn't stand it.

Whether or not I knew her yet, seeing tears fill her gorgeous eyes was worse than a well-aimed foot to the balls.

It made my insides hurt, which was a first for me.

Don't get me wrong, I wasn't an emotionless dick, but I'd never reacted to someone else's suffering on a visceral level the way I had hers.

The only time I'd ever come close to channeling another's pain like that was when my old man, the drunk bastard that he was, used to beat my brother to a bloody pulp whenever he felt like it.

But despite the similarities between that situation and this one, they were still different.

With the torment I'd witnessed Ty endure, regret was the emotion that took center stage in both my head and chest. How could it not when the lone reason he took those beatings to begin with was to keep me safe? Screwed up as it was, as long as our father's rage was focused on him, it was never on me.

But with Ashley and the shit I'd just watched go down, all I felt was anger.

A helluva lot of it.

I'd never hit a woman in my life, and I'd throw down with any man that did, but if Bianca had been a dude, she would've been leaving school in a lot worse shape than she'd arrived.

No joke.

Like the moment I first saw her picture, the magnetic pull I felt toward Ashley didn't make a damned bit of sense, and after spending over half the previous night trying to rationalize why I'd reacted so strongly to nothing more than a wallet-sized photo, the only thing I could deduce from the situation was that something inside me wanted to protect her, just as my big brother had always protected me.

Or at least *tried* to protect me.

But it didn't matter.

My feelings were my own.

And that was the end of it.

Nearing the ticket booth that preceded the stadium, the sound of Ashley's soft whimpers reached my ears. I picked up my pace once I figured out exactly where the sound was coming from.

Behind the booth, next to the woods.

Barely holding it together, I rounded the corner of the small building. Once I spotted her, looking just as beautifully broken as before, I came to an abrupt stop.

Back resting against the side of the building, she sat cross-legged, her purple backpack on her lap. Hugging it tight, her face was puffy and streaked with tears, her petite frame trembling.

She was falling apart.

And I hated it.

A hollow ache made its presence known in my chest, and I squeezed the Styrofoam trays tight, ignoring the way they creaked under my unrelenting grip. I wanted nothing more than to drop them to the ground and go to her, then scoop her up in my arms and hold her tight until every last tear she cried stopped.

But knowing I couldn't do that—not without freaking her the hell out—I cleared my throat and said, "Ashley, please don't cry." Startled by the sound of my voice, she snapped her head up, her terrified eyes locking with my anger-filled ones. "It tears me up to see you like that."

Unable to keep my distance, I moved closer, the need to make her feel better choking the hell outta me.

My steps faltered when her back straightened, and she slipped her hand into the small purse next to her. Without taking her eyes off me, she pulled out a simple key chain, which a small Taser dangled from.

Oh shit...

Extending my arms, I lifted the trays and took a single step back. "I'm not going to hurt you," I said, hoping she'd believe me. "I was just bringing you something to eat because I don't like the thought of you not having lunch." I forced a shaky smile. "So don't tase my ass, please."

Silence.

"I wasn't going to tase your butt," she replied, wiping away her tears with the backs of her hands. "But, I was planning on jamming it in your..." She waved the weapon, one which I was pretty sure was illegal, in the air, searching for the right words. "Ya know, your privates."

Surprised laughter erupted from my throat. "You're feisty," I said, the smile I wore no longer forced. "I like it." Keeping a reasonable distance from her, I sat down to her left, placing the trays on the concrete stretching between us. "I wasn't sure what you'd prefer," I told her, "so I got a bit of everything."

"Why are you doing this?" Her suspicion-filled eyes slid from me to the food, then back to me again. "I don't get it."

For a moment, I considered telling her that Grandmama had asked me to keep an eye on her, but that wasn't the reason.

It may have been why I originally agreed to watch out for her, but the second I glimpsed her wounded brown eyes in that damned photo, everything changed. But not wanting to tell her that—I wasn't completely stupid—I went with, "You look like you could use a friend."

It was a crap answer, and one she'd likely call bullshit on, but it was the truth all the same.

Plus I could use a friend too.

Yeah, I hung out with my teammates occasionally, but I wasn't close to any of them. Not really. The only reason most of them wanted anything to do with me in the first place was because of who I was.

Chase Jacobs, All-American star quarterback.

Besides, letting people in wasn't something I did, not when I'd seen first-hand the destruction and pain others could cause.

Thanks for that lesson, Dad.

"I don't need any new friends," she whispered, her voice lined with a whole lotta hurt. "Especially not those of the male variety."

Her words stung.

A helluva lot.

But that same sting disappeared when I recalled Grandmama's words from the night before. Though the Crazy Old Biddy hadn't elaborated on what Ashley had been through, her reaction to my presence gave me a clue of what it could be.

Dollars to donuts, she'd been burned.

Most likely by someone possessing a dick.

Angry didn't begin to describe how I felt.

Clearing my throat, I bent my legs and leaned forward, resting my forearms on my knees. "Did some asshole hurt you?" She stilled at my question. "Because if he did, I'd be more than happy to cave his face in."

My words were irrational yet true.

I was supposed to be keeping my head down and staying out of trouble, but if some jackass had hurt *her*, the most beautiful girl I'd ever seen, I'd have no problem throwing him a beating he'd never forget.

Fuck the consequences.

"You seem awfully angry." Still clutching the Taser, she nibbled on her bottom lip, making me want to do the same. *What the hell is this girl doing to me?* "Is that normal for you?"

I chuckled. "Admittedly so."

My half-joking answer made her more anxious, which wasn't my intent.

I'd only wanted to see her smile.

Did I mention that I was an idiot?

Because obviously, I was.

Climbing to her knees, she swung her backpack behind her, slipping it on. "Thanks for bringing me food. It was really nice of you," she said, her entire body quaking. "But, I should go."

She climbed to her feet, her movements quick, but before she had the chance to walk away, I jumped up, blocking her escape, and reached for her. "Ashley, wait—"

My words died on my lips when, in a move I'd seen performed by a younger Ty many times, she flinched and then lifted her slender arms, shielding her face.

She thinks I'm going to hit her.

The realization was like a sledgehammer to the gut. Swift and hard-hitting, it nearly made me crumble. Barely able to breathe, I grew even more pissed.

And that was saying something.

Blood boiling, I shoved my hands in my pockets and stumbled back. "I'm not going to hit you," I said, fighting to keep the fury currently working its way through my system out of my voice. "I will *never* hit you."

Trembling with fear, she wrapped her arms around her belly, seemingly holding herself together. Tear after tear spilled from her eyes, shredding my heart. "Yeah," she said, her soft cries turning to sobs. "That's what he said too."

I'd known—I'd damned well known—that a guy had done something to her, but hearing her confirm it made my hands twitch with the need to punch something.

Hard.

Without another word, she darted past me.

Consumed with rage, I stepped around the corner of the ticket booth and watched her run full-bore back toward the school. Frozen in place, I simply stared as she moved further and further away, despite every cell in my body screaming at me to give chase.

Mind reeling with mental images I didn't want to see, ones which involved her being hurt by some faceless douchebag, I turned, ready to slam my fist into the fucking wall.

But I stopped, my eyes narrowing, when I caught sight of something laying on the ground next to where Ashley had been sitting.

It was her purse.

Walking over, I picked it up.

I didn't know a damned thing about a woman's purse, but hers was small, the fabric it was made of soft. Her perfume, which was as sweet as sugar, lingered on the cotton-like material, making my chest burn.

Without thinking about what I was doing, I lifted it to my nose and inhaled, pulling her scent deep into my lungs.

"Fuck me," I muttered. "Seems I've got no choice but to go after her." I paused, mulling over what I would say once I caught up to her. "Let's just hope my dumbass can avoid scaring her this time."

Blowing out a frustrated breath, I turned.

Then, I went on the hunt.

Chapter Ten

ASHLEY

ust keep moving...

Still crying, I burst through the front door of the Toluca Police Department and came to a sliding stop in the middle of the empty lobby.

At the sound of my not-so-graceful entrance, the older desk sergeant, whose name I couldn't remember, snapped his head up, his wide eyes finding me from where he sat. "Miss Moretti," he said, face paling. "Are you okay?"

I shook my head because, no, I wasn't okay.

Not by a long shot.

Wrapping my arms around my middle, I shifted my weight between my feet, practically bouncing from one leg to the other, all the while looking around the desolate lobby, my panicked eyes searching for one of the half-dozen crooked cops I'd met thanks to Dominic.

If I encountered any of them...

Well, I didn't know what I'd do.

Thankfully, it was a problem I hadn't been forced to deal with. Not yet.

I wasn't sure if it was because they worked at a different precinct or what, but I prayed I wouldn't see any of them, plus a certain district attorney, ever again. Not only would coming face-to-face with them send me spiraling once more, I was terrified I wouldn't be able to hide my reaction from Anthony.

God knows if he, a strait-laced detective, ever discovered the multitude of favors they'd all done for *el diablo* before his arrest and subsequent prison sentence, he'd flip. Even more so when he learned more than one had harmed me in the vilest of ways.

With my luck, he'd kill them.

That's if Shelby didn't do it first.

Which she likely would.

But even if I wanted to see every dirty cop, along with Ellington brought to justice, I couldn't allow my parents to be involved.

Not when, for the first time in my life, I had a mother and father, both of whom loved me and my little brother with everything they had. Losing either of them to the penal system wasn't a risk I was willing to take.

I'd suffer in silence for eternity if it meant keeping my family intact. After all, the secrets I already harbored were vast, the memories that haunted me unending. If anyone could keep their lips sealed, it was me.

Across the lobby, the desk sergeant stood and opened his mouth to speak, but I cut in, not giving him a chance to utter a single word. "Is Anthony—" I clamped my lips shut and pulled in a breath. "I mean, is my dad here?"

He nodded. "Let me buzz him—"

Refusing to waste another second, I was moving before he could finish his sentence.

Pushing through the door that connected the lobby to the back half of the building, I hoofed it down the hall that led to his corner office. When I was ten steps away from his door, he stepped into the hall, a stack of papers clenched in his left hand.

I stopped in my tracks when he looked up, his grey eyes locking on me. "Ashley..."

My chin trembled, the tears that hadn't stopped falling since I left school continuing to slide down my cheeks, making my distress obvious. "I tried," I cried, my shoulders trembling. "I swear I did, but—"

I snapped my mouth shut when he moved toward me, his long legs eating up the space between us. Reaching me, he twined his strong arms around my back and pulled me into him. Nose pressed to the crown of my head, he held me tight, pouring both his strength and warmth into my heart and soul.

I nearly collapsed in relief.

Because there, at that moment, tucked in his arms, I felt safe, something that I'd never experienced until he and Shelby came along.

"It's okay, *Principessa*," he whispered, his New York accent thick with emotion. It was such a stark contrast to Shelby's Southern accent, along with my Appalachian one, that I couldn't help but laugh at times. "From this day on, we'll take this slow, sweetheart. One step at a time, yeah?"

I leaned further into him, letting his body take my weight, and fisted the front of his shirt in my shaking hands. "You're not disappointed?"

It was such a loaded question considering I already knew the answer. Still, it was one I couldn't help but ask. I needed to hear him say the words. As a girl who'd spent her entire life having conditions placed on what others pretended was love, I needed that reassurance.

He knew it too.

Unwinding his arms, he slipped a finger under my chin and tilted my head back, forcing my eyes to meet his. "Ashley Jo Moretti, you listen to every damned word I'm about to say." His words were harsh, but his tone wasn't. "I may be disappointed in some of the decisions you make in the future, but *never* in you."

Sliding his thumbs across my cheeks, he wiped away my tears.

"You promise?" I asked, my insides calming.

"I swear it."

"Good, because—"

I jumped in place when the door at the end of the hall, the one I'd come through minutes before, burst open and slammed into the wall.

I didn't have time to spin around and see who had made such a ruckus before the familiar sound of cowgirl boots clicking against the floor echoed through the building, bouncing off each of the walls.

A smile tipped my lips as I turned, coming face to face with my mother, followed by Felix, who was carrying a cat in his arms.

My eyes bulged.

Why in the world did he have a cat?

In a police station no less?

"I only have two questions," she hollered, pulling my attention from the content looking feline. "One, whose rear-end am I kicking, and two, how hard am I kicking it?"

"Sunshine," Anthony said to her. "Calm down."

"Calm down my ass," she fired back as Anthony raised his hands in surrender. He knew that once Shelby got like this, it was just best to let her run out of steam and not interject.

Coming to a stop right in front of me, she palmed my cheeks, raking her gaze over me from head to toe, no doubt searching for any injuries.

"Hendrix called the shelter in a panic and said he saw you running down the sidewalk, all upset." Her eye twitched. "So he jumped in the truck and followed you until you got here. Now"—she exhaled, her nostrils flaring—"I want you to tell me who upset you so I can shove my size nine boot up their soon-to-be-sore-as-all-get-out behind."

She quirked an expectant brow, and the words tumbled out of me, one after the other before I could stop them. "Uh, well, to start, a bitchy girl named Bianca tripped me at lunch." I paused, knowing Anthony would likely have a stroke over what came next. "But, I didn't actually fall because a boy caught me."

"A *boy*?" he growled. "What boy?"

I bit the inside of my cheek. "Chase."

"Chase who? I need a last name."

I raised my hands, palms toward the ceiling. "I don't know his last name," I replied, answering him. "All I know is that he kept me from face-planting in the middle of the cafeteria, and then after I ran out of the building like an idiot, he brought me a new lunch tray, because, according to him, he didn't want me to go without lunch."

I paused, regret washed over me.

I'd been so rude to him.

Even if I wasn't comfortable around people I didn't know—anger-prone men in particular—there was no reason for me to behave the way I had. For heaven's sake, he'd brought me lunch, and I'd run away from him like he was Freddy frickin' Kruger.

Despite my issues, that wasn't okay.

And to make matters worse, he probably thought I was completely nuts now, especially after I flinched, proving that I was terrified of his mere presence.

Lovely.

"Crap," I whispered, fiddling with the straps of my backpack. "I can't even remember if I told him thank you before I took off." I hoped I had. "Now I feel bad."

Shelby's eyes narrowed. "Why'd you run off?"

I fidgeted in place. "He scared me."

Anthony sucked in a breath, and I felt rather than saw his mood shift. He wasn't angry per se, but he was on edge. "How, *Principessa?*" he asked, his voice tight. "How did he scare you?"

I blinked, fighting to stop the tears that still fell. I was so sick of crying all the time. "Because when I told him I didn't want any new friends, particularly male ones, he asked if a guy had hurt me in the past." Until then, I hadn't realized how transparent I was. I didn't like it. Not one iota. "I didn't answer him, but he still offered to beat up said guy anyway."

Shelby smirked.

But Anthony?

He still wasn't happy.

It made me smile.

His overprotectiveness was such a dumb thing for me to be joyful about, but it made me feel like a normal teenage girl, particularly one who hadn't lived through hell and survived the devil himself.

"Is that all he did?"

I shook my head. "He seemed so mad that I asked him if being angry was a normal thing for him." Why had I asked such a question? It was *none* of my business. "When he said yes, I freaked."

"Ashley, honey, listen to me," Shelby said. "It's not okay for people to be angry all the time, but just because someone is upset, it doesn't mean they are going to hurt you. Now, don't get me wrong, I'd much rather you be cautious than reckless with that sort of thing, but—"

"It's all in my head, I know," I replied, cutting her off. "Trust me, I'm tired of being scared day in and day out. It's exhausting to think everyone is out to harm me, but no matter how hard I try, I can't silence the voice that compares everyone I meet now to the people from my past."

It was an issue that I was working on with my therapist. She'd assured me that my distrust of others would get better with time, but I wasn't so sure. It was such a negative thing to think about, but I some-times wondered if I was too broken to fix.

Deep down, I knew I probably was.

"That's just the PTSD talking, sweet pea," Shelby said. "I know it's easier said than done, but don't listen to the harsh words your mind speaks. Else you'll keep swimming in blackness instead of climbing out of it."

She was right.

I knew that.

Exhaling, I nodded. "I'll try. Promise."

She kissed my forehead before pulling me in for a hug. Holding me tight, she ran her fingers through my hair. The light caress was both calming and comforting. "One day at a time, baby," she whispered, rocking me side-to-side. "We're just gonna take it one day at a time."

"That's what I told her," Anthony replied. "Not that anybody ever listens to me."

I smiled at his teasing tone.

Shelby, though, she scoffed. "Well, if you weren't wrong all the danged time, then maybe I'd listen more."

"Sunshine," he shot back. "Don't start."

Stepping back, Shelby glared up at the stubborn man who'd chosen to be my father, not out of duty, but out of desire. Hand on her hip, she arched a brow in a direct challenge. "And what if I do?"

Anthony chuckled. "You know what'll happen."

Unable to stop myself, I gagged. "Oh gross," I said, side-stepping them both. "I don't want to hear that." Hands over my ears, I glanced from one to the other. "I'm already traumatized enough. Do you want me to need more therapy?"

Shelby tossed her head back and laughed.

Hard.

Anthony, though...

Redness bloomed on his olive-toned cheeks, making his embarrassment—something I rarely saw from him—known. "Christ, *Principessa*, I didn't mean it like that. I was just—"

"I know," I said, interrupting him. Smiling from ear-to-ear, I shrugged. "I just enjoy giving you crap every once in a while. Gotta keep you on your toes somehow."

His eyes narrowed. "You're just like your mother."

If possible, my smile grew even wider. "Good."

Shelby leaned to the side and bumped my shoulder with hers. "Smart answer." She winked. "Now, are you ready to head home? Because I say we blow this joint and go pick up a pizza or two."

I tilted my head to the side. "Don't you have to work?"

She shook her head. "I already told Maddie I wouldn't be back. Her and Hope have it covered." Looking over at Anthony, she placed a hand on his broad chest. "What about you, Stud Muffin? Think you can take the rest of the day off and spend some time with your girls?"

He didn't hesitate. "Wild horses couldn't stop me."

At his answer, the weight of the day began to lift from my shoulders. Blowing out a pent-up breath, I shot him and Shelby both a smile before moving toward Felix, who, up to that point, had been leaning against the far wall, his attention focused on the cat in his arms.

"Uncle Fe-fe," I said, standing in front of him. "Who's your friend?"

One side of his mouth tipped heavenward. "This here is my little buddy," he replied proudly, running his aged fingers through the long-haired tabby's fur. The perfect mixture of black, grey, and beige, he was beautiful. I hadn't even petted him yet, but I loved him already. "Found him behind the shelter this morning. Don't know if someone dumped him or if he got lost somehow, but I'm fairly sure he's blind. Poor fella kept walking into the fence."

That made my heart hurt a little.

"Are you keeping him?"

His eyes found Shelby, then Anthony. "I'd like to, but only if your mama and papa—"

"You're keeping him," Shelby interjected. "He needs a home, and what better place than with you?"

Felix's eyes twinkled, filling with unshed tears.

Nodding, he swallowed and hugged the cat close. "Thank you, Shelby. I promise I'll clean up after him."

I swear my heart swelled, nearly to the point of bursting.

Like me, Felix had issues, and I could already tell the cat, sweet as he seemed, would bring him immeasurable comfort, which made me happy as could be.

"What are you going to name him?" I asked, readjusting my backpack.

Felix took a breath, his fingers tracing invisible lines down the kitty's back. "The moment I saw him, he made my old heart feel a whole lot better," he whispered. "So I'm going to name him Angel, 'cause to me, that's what he is."

"*Shit*," Shelby hissed. "Now, I'm gonna cry."

I was right there with her.

"Carbs," she continued, shaking out her hands. "I need carbs to deal with this kind of emotion." Huffing out a breath, she pointed toward the hallway door. "Let's move, people. I need pizza and bread-sticks. Like, right the hell now."

I laughed, tears of joy rolling down my cheeks. "Can we pick up Lucca first?"

"Well, duh," she replied. "If we don't, he may burn the house down once he gets home and realizes we had pizza without him."

That was true.

I loved my little brother with every broken piece of me, but he was a nut. Then again, all it took was one look at our mother to see where he got it from.

Apparently, crazy is genetic.

The sound of Anthony shutting his office door grabbed my attention, pulling me from my thoughts. Keys in hand, he nodded toward the end of the hall. "Alright you three, let's head out."

Together, we all started to move.

Walking next to Shelby, I bumped into her shoulder with mine, just like she'd done to me minutes before. "Since Felix has a cat now, can Lucca and I have a dog?"

Her eyes bulged. "What kind of dog?"

"I want a husky. Preferably a white one with blue eyes."

"Yeah?" Anthony asked from behind us. "And what would you name it?"

My answer was immediate. "If it was a boy, Ziggy Bear."

"I like Ziggy Bear," Shelby replied, sniffling.

"Me too," Anthony agreed. "But where am I supposed to find a white Husky?"

Shelby shrugged. "I'm sure you'll figure it out."

She was right.

Anthony would figure it out.

And when that day came, it would be one of the best of my life.

Chapter Eleven

CHASE

839 Magnolia Street.

Holding Ashley's purse in my hand, I stood next to my parked Jeep, staring up at the blue two-story house across the street. With a white wraparound porch, perfectly manicured lawn, and bright blooming flowers planted everywhere, it was nice. But its beauty didn't compare to the girl who lived inside.

A girl who, after spending less than five minutes in her presence, hadn't left my mind.

Because of that reason alone, I'd hunted Grandmama down the moment the final bell rang. After finding her perched in a salon chair at a beauty parlor down the street from the school, I'd persuaded her to give me Ashley's address, something that sure as shit wasn't easy.

Not only did I have to take off my shirt and flex for her and the rest of the old birds occupying the remaining chairs, but she'd also forced me into agreeing to clean her gutters the following weekend.

Being gawked at by a bunch of crazy old women wasn't something I enjoyed, nor was home maintenance, but I would've done a whole lot more to find out where Ashley lived.

Sure, I could have checked her purse for the info, but I wasn't going to invade her privacy. Doing so would've been a douche move, and though I was a lot of things, that wasn't one.

And yeah, I could've waited until the following day and found her at school, but I wasn't in the business of denying myself the things I wanted. And let's be real here... I wanted to see Ashley Moretti again.

More than I wanted to take my next breath.

After she'd bolted during lunch, I'd searched everywhere for her, but she'd vanished, completely disappeared. I didn't know if it was because she'd dipped and left school early or what, but I was about to come out of my skin.

Between my inexplicable desire to have her near and the driving need to make sure she was okay, I was a second away from losing my mind. All afternoon I'd mulled over the way she'd reacted to me, and hard as I tried, I couldn't get the sight of her shielding her face when I came too close out of my head.

Seeing her do that...

It had broken something inside me.

No woman deserved to be abused. That was a gospel fact, but knowing that she'd been hurt at the hands of another only made me more determined to keep her safe.

From that moment on.

Frustrated as hell and unable to stand being so close, yet so far away from her a second longer, I started across the quiet neighborhood street. When a blaring horn sounded to my left, I immediately jumped back, removing myself from the path of an approaching—albeit slow as hell—Cadillac.

My eyes narrowed when the car came to a rolling stop in front of me, and I got a good look at the old woman seated behind the wheel.

Placing my arms on the open passenger window, I popped my head in the vehicle. "Grandmama, what the hell? You following me now?"

Rolling her eyes, she waved a dismissive hand my way. "I only follow men who are old enough to take me out dancing and drinking. You ain't but eighteen, which means I can admire your drool-worthy tush, but I ain't wasting gas on chasing you around town. Dadgum stuff ain't cheap. Anyway"—she waved her hand once more—"I see you found the place alright."

"I did, but what are you doing here?"

She quirked a brow and pointed to the yellow house behind me, the one I'd parked directly in front of. "That's my house."

Well, shit...

I didn't know that.

Then again, why would I?

"Are you sure?" I asked, glancing at the immaculate house over my shoulder. "'Cause I would've bet you'd have a couple of dick-shaped water fountains out front."

Eyes narrowed, she pointed a wrinkled finger my way. "One, I don't like that type of language. It's called a tallywacker, ya big dummy. Two, you ain't looked in the backyard yet now have you?" She cackled, and I couldn't decide whether she was screwing with me or not.

Knowing Grandmama...

"Well," she said, between bouts of laughter. "Guess I better skedaddle since the chicken I've got marinating ain't gonna fry itself, and I've got company coming." Dipping her head, she glared at me over the top of her glasses. "Make sure you get my grandbaby's purse back to her. And no funny business. You so much as make a single move, and I'll shoot your balls slap off and turn em' into Christmas tree ornaments. You understand me?"

For Christ's sake, she was batshit crazy.

Jaw ticking, I fisted my hands, my temper sparking. "If you're worried about me taking advantage of Ashley, you don't need to be," I replied. "I'd rather play chicken in rush-hour traffic."

"Thatta boy," she said, smiling. "You may not have the sense God gave a goose, but at least you ain't completely dumb."

"That's one helluva compliment if I ever heard it." Shaking my head, I took a step back and stood tall. Tapping my knuckles against the roof of the car, I tossed Grandmama a wink. "See you later, Crazy Old Biddy."

"See you Saturday, Hoodlum." She looked back out the windshield.

"You best be remembering what I said. I know you've got a tendency to get more confused than a fart in a fan factory, but I mean it—keep your danged hands to yourself. Else I'll be the proud new owner of your balls. Got it?"

I cringed. "I got it."

With a final nod, she stomped on the gas and spun into her driveway, then slammed on the brakes inches away from her garage door, nearly crashing through the damn thing. She climbed out and hobbled up the sidewalk, her giant purse swamping her aged frame.

When she saw me watching her every move, she placed her hands on her rounded hips and glared. "What?" she asked, her eighty-year-old sass on full display. "I was just checking to make sure the dad-blasted brakes worked!"

Sure she was.

Ignoring her special brand of crazy, I turned, my eyes once again locking on Ashley's house. "Alright, shithead," I mumbled to myself, heart in my throat. "Whatever you do, don't fuck this up."

Then, without hesitating, I crossed the street.

Chapter Twelve

CHASE

*A*nthony Moretti looked ready to kill me.

Blocking the partially opened door with his body, he glared at me, his hard eyes boring into mine. "You're Chase," he said, sounding more like he was speaking to himself than me. "The one who saved my girl from falling in the cafeteria earlier today."

I nodded. "Yeah, I—"

"You're Chase *Jacobs*," he said, cutting me off mid-sentence. "Clyde Jacobs' youngest son."

Pressure built in my chest at the sound of my father's snarled name.

It was bad enough the bastard had nearly killed my brother as a kid and made my life hell as a result, but to be judged because he was half of the shitty parent duo that created me?

Yeah, that wasn't right.

Not at all.

Biting back the fury that swelled in my throat, I crossed my arms, tucking Ashley's purse against my chest. "Son or not," I said, my tone failing to hide the anger raging inside me. "I am *nothing* like him."

As a cop, it was obvious that Anthony was familiar with my police officer father, who just happened to be one of the biggest scumbags to ever exist, both in and out of uniform.

A monster in every sense of the word, I hated him.

It may sound cold of me, but after the torment he'd put Ty and me through, I wouldn't have shed a single tear if he was run over by a semi and turned into a skid mark on the highway.

Not only did I have no respect for a man who'd spent a decade constantly beating one son half to death while forcing the other to watch, I had no love for him either.

The shit he did...

He deserved to die for it.

Slowly. Painfully. Surely.

Leaning a shoulder against the doorframe, Moretti lifted his chin in the air. "What do you want, Chase?"

The answer to his question was a simple one.

I wanted his daughter.

But to keep my teeth where they belonged, I didn't tell him that. If I had, he surely would have punched me.

Not that I would've blamed him.

"I stopped by to see Ashley," I said, holding her purse up for him to see. "She left this at school, and I intend to make sure she gets it back."

He reached for the purse. "I'll—"

"I'd like to give it to her personally, sir," I interrupted, jerking it back. "If you don't mind."

One look at his face, and I could tell that he sure as shit did mind. Sucked for him though, because I wasn't leaving without speaking to Ashley first. Even if it was only for a second.

I had to make sure she was okay.

"Look, kid," he started. "I'm not trying to be a dick, but—"

Whatever tirade he was about to go on was cut short when the door was pulled open fully, and a barefoot Ashley appeared beside him, her long hair pulled on top of her head in a messy bun.

Damn, she's beautiful...

Most beautiful girl I've ever seen.

Holding a toddler-sized kid on her hip, she stared at me, her heart-stopping eyes wide. "Chase," she said, her voice soft. "Why are you...I mean, what are you doing here?"

Bewitched, my mind blanked.

When I didn't answer right away, her lips tipped, a ghost of a smile appearing. "You feeling okay?"

Pulling myself together—the shit was hard, okay?—I found my voice. "I'm fine," I choked out, the sounds raw and guttural. Tapping my chest with my fist, I cleared my throat. "Just been a long day."

Ashley nodded as Moretti narrowed his eyes, obviously seeing straight through my bullshit.

"Can I, uh..." Hooking my thumb, I pointed to the space behind me. "Can I talk to you for a minute."

Eyes filling with anxiety, she chewed on her bottom lip, shifting her weight from one foot to the next. "Alone?"

Forcing myself to stand still, I shrugged a lone shoulder. "If you want. If not, I don't mind an audience."

Something I couldn't read flashed in her eyes at my answer.

After a few seconds of silence, she turned to her dad. "Is it okay if we talk on the porch for a bit? It won't be long, promise." Cheeks reddening, she paused. Leaning closer to him, she turned slightly, hiding her beautiful face from my view. "I told the Mominator that I'd try," she whispered. "This is me doing that."

Moretti looked from her to me.

Judging by the look on his face, I was convinced he was about to tell me to fuck off.

But that's not what happened.

Instead, he jerked his chin down once in a half-hearted nod and took the kid from her, a little boy who was shooting a puzzled look in my direction. "I'll be just inside," he said, his eyes on hers. "If you need me, I'm here, *Principessa*."

Ashley's face relaxed. "Thank you."

Moretti pressed a gentle kiss to her forehead before stepping back into the house. Hand on the doorknob, he looked over his shoulder, his gaze meeting mine. "Keep your goddamned hands to yourself, yeah?" Before I could answer, he kept talking. "Lay one finger on my daughter, and I'll deliver you to my wife on a silver platter."

I'd pass on that.

I didn't know Shelby all that well. In fact, I'd only talked to her a handful of times. But from what I'd heard around town, she was not one to be trifled with, especially when it came to her family.

She was Grandmama 2.0. If you hurt or threatened someone she loved, she'd just shoot you.

No questions asked.

"Yeah, Detective," I replied, watching as Ashley's small shoulders shook from silent laughter. If she hadn't been so damned pretty, I might've been offended. Here I was being threatened, and she was laughing. Part of me secretly loved it. "I've got it."

Ashley stepped onto the porch.

"Five minutes," Moretti barked, before softly shutting the door.

Shaking my head, I looked down at Ashley.

Hand covering her mouth, she was staring up at me, her eyes twinkling with amusement.

I couldn't help but smile. "Thought that was funny, did you?"

Dropping her hand, she shrugged. "It kinda was."

Chuckling, I lifted her purse in the air. Distracted by everything going on, she hadn't noticed it yet. "You left this behind the ticket booth at lunch. Thought you may want it back."

Face falling, her anxiety returned, making its presence known on her features. "You didn't have to bring it all the way out here. You could've given it to me tomorrow," she whispered, gently taking it from me. "But thank you."

Hands now empty, I slid them into my pockets. "I know I didn't have to, but it was something I wanted to do."

Head tilted to the side, she fidgeted in place. "Why?"

"Because I like you." The words slipped out before I could stop them. Not that I would have to begin with. As much as I didn't want to scare her, I didn't believe in holding back either.

"You don't even know me."

I'd heard that before.

Still didn't change how I felt.

Knowing that she'd likely need breathing room soon, I moved across the porch, giving her space. On the other side, I leaned back against the banister and crossed my arms over my chest. "Beautiful girl, listen. I'm going to be real blunt here, which in turn is probably going to make me sound crazy, but I'm not one to beat around the bush."

Pinching the hem of her shirt, she eyed me cautiously.

"What you said is right. I don't know you. Not yet," I stated truthfully. "But I know *pieces* of you."

Her brow furrowed. "What pieces?"

"The broken ones."

She jerked back as if I'd slapped her. Eyes filling with tears, she looked away. "You don't know anything about me, much less my broken pieces."

She was wrong.

And I was about to prove it.

"I know you've been hurt," I said, truthfully. "And I know it was a man that did it." Just speaking the words made my chest tighten. "A man I'd like to snap like a goddamn twig."

She swallowed, tears now cascading down her cheeks. "I'm sorry," she whispered. "But I can't do this."

Turning, she grasped the door handle.

Knowing that any chance I had with her would be ruined if she stepped foot back in the house, I dropped my arms and stood tall, my heart beating double-time. "My old man was abusive," I confessed quickly, the acidic tasting words burning my throat as they tumbled free.

Ashley froze, her hand unmoving.

Hoping I could make her understand, I continued. "For over a decade, he hurt my brother. Repeatedly."

Emotions stirring, I felt like puking.

I didn't talk about this with anybody, yet here I was, spilling my guts to a girl I'd only known mere hours. Either I was losing it, or my mind was finally catching onto what my heart already knew.

Ashley was special.

Real damned special.

"To this day, I don't know how Ty survived," I continued, wanting her to understand. Exhaling, I dropped my head forward and stared at the white-washed porch boards beneath my feet. "I know you've been hurt, Ashley because when I look in your eyes, I see the same brand of pain that gleams in his."

Silence filled the space between us.

Then, "Did he abuse you too?"

Looking back up, I shook my head, the guilt gnawing away at me. "No. He tried a few times, but Ty always intervened and took the beating for me."

She flinched, the heartbreak she felt for my big brother, the man I owed my life to, written all over her face. "I'm sorry."

"Don't be. It's life, as shitty as that is sometimes."

Turning to face me once more, she crossed the porch, surprising the hell out of me. Stopping next to me, she glanced up. Our eyes locked. "It shouldn't be."

"No," I agreed, shaking my head. "It shouldn't."

Arms crossed, she hugged herself tight. "The guy," she whispered, body trembling. "The one who hurt me... his name is Dominic." I remained silent, wanting her to keep talking. "And he's the devil."

Rage built inside me, making my head feel as though it would explode. "Where is he?"

"Georgia State Prison."

I bit my tongue, refusing to speak. Afraid that the words would come out wrong, it was best if I just stayed quiet. At least for the time being.

After a few moments of silence, she spoke once more. "Aren't you going to ask?"

I blinked. "Ask what?"

"What he did to me."

I shook my head. "No, I'm not. I figure if you want me to know, you'll tell me."

Part of me hoped she would tell me, while the other part prayed she wouldn't. The bastard was in prison, which meant he'd done more than slap her around a few times. If I found out he'd hurt her in other ways...

I wouldn't handle that well.

"I'll never tell," she whispered, wiping her cheeks with the backs of her hands. "Not just because I can't, but because talking about it makes it real, and right now, I just want to pretend none of it ever happened."

I could've sworn I felt my heart fracture.

It hurt.

A helluva lot.

"Then don't talk about it," I replied, wanting to wash away her pain. "We can chat about something else instead."

"Like w-what?" Her voice cracked, making the urge to pull her into my arms increase tenfold.

I forced a smile. "Like where we're going to sit at lunch tomorrow."

"We?"

"Yes, *we*." I leaned back against the banister again, my hands gripping the rail. "So tell me—you want to eat behind the ticket booth where it'll be nice and quiet, or do you want to stay inside and grab a table? Personally, my vote is for a table. For one, my ass hurts if I sit on concrete for too long, and for two, it's supposed to rain tomorrow. I don't know about you, but I'd rather not spend the afternoon walking around looking like a drowned rat."

My stomach flipped when she laughed, the sound soft and sweet. "How about the library?" she asked, smiling shyly. "It's inside, and they have tables plus books. Can't really go wrong there."

The air between us grew lighter, erasing the painful fog that had blanketed us seconds before.

Lifting my chin in the air, I inched closer to her, the invisible rope connecting us shortening. "You like to read?"

"I do," she answered, tucking a stray lock of hair behind her ear. "What about you?"

I snorted. "Do the Sunday comics count?"

She nodded. "Words are words."

I'm glad she thought so because I wasn't sure I'd ever finished a book in my life. CliffsNotes were my best friend when it came to the stuff I was required to read for school.

Maybe I should change that...

"You think you could help me pick out a book tomorrow? I just realized I haven't read much in the way of actual books. Should probably fix that."

It was the right thing to say.

Eyes shining bright, she rocked back on her feet. "That I can do. I know exactly what to pick—"

Freezing in place, she snapped her mouth shut when the front door opened, and Moretti appeared, his stern gaze taking in the scene before him. "*Principessa*, it's time to come inside. Your mama just called and said she'd be back with the ice cream in five minutes."

Pursing her lips, Ashley nodded. "Yeah, okay."

Turning her attention back to me, she smiled. "Can you meet me outside the cafeteria tomorrow? I really don't want to go through the line alone if I don't have to." Self-doubt slid over her features. "I mean, only if you—"

"I'll be there," I interrupted. "Promise."

"Okay." Purse in hand, she crossed the porch. Reaching the door, she stepped inside next to Moretti and turned, facing me one last time. "I'll see you tomorrow, Chase Jacobs."

I grinned. "Tomorrow, Ashley Moretti."

Without giving either of us a chance to say another word, a pissed-off looking Moretti wrapped his arm around Ashley's waist and pulled her out of the way before shutting the door.

Loneliness instantly crept in, stealing the warmth that had possessed me every second that she was close. I hated being separated from her, but what could I do?

Nothing that's what.
So, left with no other choice, I went home.

Chapter Thirteen

ASHLEY

"*H*arry Potter?"

Fighting to keep my laughter at bay, I clamped my hand over my mouth as Chase stared at me from across the library table, his pretty blues locked on me.

For the past two weeks, we'd occupied the same spot during lunch, hidden away from most everyone. Nosy teachers, gossiping pupils, and bitchy drama queens—hello, Bianca—included.

I secretly loved it.

There was just something about being there with him that was...

Magical.

Even though I was still the same broken girl as before, when I was with Chase, my demons didn't scream quite as loud. I may not have understood it, but just like when I was with my family, having him by my side made life hurt a whole lot less.

And by my side is where he stayed.

At least while we were in school.

When the final bell rang each afternoon, we both went our separate ways. Not because we didn't want to spend more time together, but because I wasn't ready.

Since escaping Dominic, I'd grown by leaps and bounds, but as my reaction to Chase the first day proved, there was still a part of me—a pretty big one—that was terrified and untrusting of most people.

Chase was still one of those people.

Don't get me wrong, I liked him. A whole lot. I just didn't trust my own judgment, which made trusting him nearly impossible.

It was a crap situation, one which I hoped would only improve with each day that ticked by. However, until my brain found a way to work past the issues that plagued my heart, we were taking our newfound friendship one baby step at a time.

"Seriously, Ashley," Chase said, pulling me from my thoughts. "Harry fucking Potter?"

Looking at me as if I were crazy, he picked up the book I'd checked out for him moments before and dropped his gaze to the cover, his full lips pursed. Turning it to the side, he shook his head the slightest bit and ran a finger over the spine. "How many pages is this? Two-fifty?"

My shoulders shook, the battle not to crack up at his expense nearly futile. "Closer to three-fifty."

"Oh, what the hell," he mumbled. "This isn't a book. It's a phone directory."

And just like that, the laughter stirring in my chest broke free.

"I'm *serious*," he hissed, holding the book up. "Damned thing could be used as a deadly weapon it's so thick. Hit somebody upside the head with it, and you'd knock them slap out." He smiled from ear-to-ear. "On that note, maybe I should buy the Crazy Old Biddy a copy for Christmas. Then she could give her prized flyswatter a rest."

Running my fingers through my hair, I pushed the errant locks back. "Just wait until you see the seventh book in that series. Ya know, since you already agreed to read them all." I paused for dramatic effect and cupped my hands to my mouth. Then, I whispered, "It's over seven-hundred pages."

Dropping the book to the table, he ripped his faded ball cap off and tossed it onto the chair beside him. "There is no way. Absolutely *no* damned way."

He looked close to panicking.

It only made me laugh harder.

Happier and more carefree than I had been in a while, I reached across the table and gently wrapped my fingers around his wrist, giving it a slight squeeze. "Don't freak out on me," I said. "If you want, we can read it together."

His eyes dropped to where our flesh touched. It was a first, and to my surprise, my skin didn't burn, not like it did when I touched most others.

"Yeah?" He swallowed. "And how will we do that?"

Suddenly feeling a tad bit overwhelmed, I jerked my hand back, my cheeks burning hot. "Well," I said, feeling beads of sweat form along my brow. "Pop bought me the entire series a couple months back, so I can call you every night, and we can take turns reading over the phone if you want."

I felt like an idiot.

Take turns reading?

We weren't ten for heaven's sake!

Not that I would know what normal ten-year-olds did. At that age, my innocence had already been stolen, and my childhood—if I ever truly had one to begin with—was over.

Don't think about it...

Just don't.

One corner of Chase's mouth tipped, pulling me from the darkness swirling in my head. "You're going to call me every night?"

Skin on fire, I was burning up. "If you want me to?" The words came out as a question, not a statement, adding to the embarrassment I already felt.

Leaning forward, he ran a finger down the back of my hand. I froze in place, watching as he traced invisible lines over my wrist and around each of my knuckles. Ears filled with the sound of my pounding pulse, I barely heard the words he spoke next.

Thankfully, I did.

"Why don't I just come over after I'm done with team workouts?" he asked, causing me to suck in a breath. "Football may be over for the season, but I'm still required to—"

"Sup, Jacobs," a voice, one which I'd never heard before, interrupted. "Who's the pretty girl?"

Pretty girl...

I didn't like the sound of that.

There was nothing overly salacious about it, but it reminded me of something one of my former clients would have called me.

At the thought, panic seized me, snaking its way through my veins. Letting the terror that climbed the length of my spine drive me, I slipped my hand into my purse, which lay on the table next to me. Fingers finding my key chain, I gripped the Taser my dad had given me tight.

I was just about to pull it out when Chase's hand landed on my free one. Eyes instantly finding his, I sucked in a much-needed breath. "Chase..." Close to bursting into tears, my voice was barely audible, the faint sound muffled. "I—"

"I have you, Sweetness."

Sweetness...

It was the first time he'd ever called me that, and despite the alarm working its way through my system, I *really* liked how the simple endearment sounded rolling off his tongue.

"Nothing to worry about," he continued. 'Trust me, beautiful."

"What the fuck man?" the guy asked, his tone dripping with annoyance. "You suddenly forget how to talk to anybody but hot chicks with perfect-sized tits?"

Chase held my gaze as he removed his hand from mine, stood to his full height, and then rounded the table. Stopping next to my chair, he turned, wedging himself between the guy and me, blocking my body from his view.

Crossing his muscular arms, he then widened his stance. With his broad shoulders and athletic frame, he reminded me of a wall, and for a moment—the briefest of seconds—I felt safe.

It was... unexpected.

"I didn't forget anything," Chase said, his voice deeper than I'd ever heard it. "But obviously you forgot your fucking manners, Ryder, so do me a favor and go find them."

My eyes nearly popped out of my head.

The guy, Ryder, chuckled, but there was no humor behind it. "Never seen you get territorial over fresh meat before," he replied. "She must be something special."

Fresh meat...

Two words.

That was all it took for me to snap.

Jumping up, I grabbed my backpack off the table, followed by my purse, and stumbled back, knocking over my chair in the process.

Chase spun around at the commotion. When his rage-filled eyes locked with my terrified ones, his jaw ticked. "Ashley," he said, clenching a single fist. "Sweetness—"

I didn't stick around to hear more.

After quickly sliding my backpack on, I slung my purse over my shoulder and headed for the exit. Upon reaching it, a distinct thump sound echoed through the room.

A pain-filled grunt followed, and even though I had a good idea of what had just happened, I didn't stick around to confirm my suspicions.

Instead, I bolted.

———

Chase caught up to me in the parking lot.

"Ashley, wait!" he hollered, his approaching footsteps growing louder as he drew closer.

Knowing that I didn't have a prayer of outrunning him, I slowed, then stopped.

Seconds later, he was standing in front of me, his chest rising and falling in time with each of his labored breaths. "Why'd you run?"

My lower lip trembled. "You don't understand..."

"Then explain it to me."

"That guy," I said, pointing back toward the school. "What he said"—tears began to cascade down my cheeks—"it took me back to a place I never wanted to be again." Unable to stop, I kept talking, letting every ounce of fear and anger clogging my throat free. "I am not a piece of meat to be shared, and I am *not* something for anyone to get territorial over."

Not. Ever. Again.

"Despite what anyone else may think, I am not an object to be possessed," I said, uncaring that the words I spoke likely made no sense to him. "Almost a year ago, I swore that from that day forward, the only person I'd ever belong to again"—lifting my hand, I pointed at my chest—"is myself."

It was a promise I refused to break.

In full meltdown mode, I expected Chase to balk at my behavior, maybe even roll his eyes, before walking away and writing me off completely. After all, I sounded like a crazy person.

But that's not what he did.

Instead, he smiled, surprising me.

Eyes crinkling at the corners, he crossed his arms over his chest, a move he did often. "Want to know something, Sweetness?"

There was that name again.

Even as upset as I was, it still made my belly feel all wonky. If I hadn't known better, I could've sworn it was butterflies dancing, the same ones people in love often spoke of.

But that couldn't have been what it was.

Broken girls like me didn't have butterflies.

Did we?

Nodding, I fidgeted in place. "Tell me."

Closing the space that existed between us, he slipped a finger under my chin, tilting my head back. Heart climbing into my throat, my lips parted. "I'm so fucking proud of you."

My mind blanked. "What?" I squeaked, half-convinced I hadn't heard him correctly. "What do you mean you're proud of me?"

"You think I didn't see you reach for that Taser?" He quirked a brow. "You've been through some horrible shit, Ashley Moretti, and even though I don't know all the details, I know you've been hurt. Badly." Reminders of things I didn't want to think of, his words stung. "Yet, you haven't allowed it to break you."

He was wrong.

So wrong.

Couldn't he see how fractured I was?

"Chase—"

"What you just said to me," he interrupted. "I felt that." Wrapping his fingers around my wrist, he lifted my hand and placed it on his chest. "In here."

Oh God...

"And for the record," he continued, his eyes never leaving mine. "I don't want to possess you."

Raking my tongue across my suddenly dry lower lip, I fisted the front of his shirt, holding it tight. "Then what do you want?"

"Right now," he said, dropping his gaze to my lips. "All I want is to kiss you."

In one quick whoosh, all the air left my lungs, leaving me fighting to suck in one breath after another. "Chase, I'm not—"

"—ready," he finished for me, saving me the pain that completing that statement would bring. "That's okay. I'll wait." Cupping my face, he caressed my cheeks with his thumbs. "For however long you need me to."

After brushing a stray lock of hair from my face, he dropped his hands. I immediately missed the feel of his skin on mine. "What are you doing to me?" I asked, completely breathless.

Rubbing his palm across his clean-shaven jaw, he smiled. "I could ask you the same thing."

I blinked, replaying the last few minutes in my head. "Did you punch that guy?"

His eyes hardened before mine. "Ryder?"

I nodded.

"No, I didn't punch him."

My brows furrowed. "Then what was that sound? I swear I heard—"

"I hit him with the goddamned book," he said, interrupting me once more. "Fucker had it coming."

"Why?"

"Because *nobody* talks to you like that," he said, his anger evident. "Ashley, you may not belong to me, but I will never stand by and watch somebody talk to you like a dog. You're too good of a person to be treated like shit."

His words were like a one-two punch to the face. They rocked me. "You really hit him with the book?"

"I did. Damned thing knocked him slap out. Just like I told you it would."

Countless emotions whirled inside me, making it hard to decipher one feeling from the next. Still, the most prominent of them came through loud and clear. "Chase, I..." Eyes sliding closed, I clenched my jaw tight. "Oh, screw it."

Without giving myself time to think about what I was doing, I opened my eyes and placed my hands on his shoulders, cupping the muscles that laid beneath. Standing on my tiptoes, I leaned forward and pressed my soft chest to his solid one.

Then, I touched my lips to his.

Our connection was gentle and sweet, but it was defining. Call me crazy all you want, but with just one stolen kiss, Chase's beautiful soul breathed life back into my suffocating one, and though I knew the feeling wouldn't last, for a moment, I felt whole.

Twining his strong arms around my back, he pulled me close, warming my small body with his big one. Chest heaving, he dusted his lips over mine, drinking my essence in tiny sips. "Ashley," he whispered, his mouth still ghosting over mine. "Baby, I need you to—"

I froze, my body as still as petrified wood when the roar of a car's engine sounded from behind me, followed by the sound of squealing tires seconds later.

"Son of a *bitch*," he cursed, his fingers digging into my back. "Talk about the worst damned timing." I had no idea what he was talking about, nor did I know who had come to a sliding stop behind us.

Curious, I glanced over my shoulder.

Who I saw jumping out of the SUV that idled less than fifteen feet away nearly made my heart stop. "Oh God," I whimpered. "He's going to kill us both."

Well, he wouldn't kill me.

Chase though? Uh...

Extracting myself from Chase's hold, I spun around, shielding his body with mine as my father—who looked nothing less than irate, I might add—approached us both. "*Principessa*," he said, his hard eyes locked on Chase. "Get in the car."

"Wait," I said, stomach sinking. "It's not—"

"Two weeks," Anthony barked. "That's all it took for you to convince her to skip class and do something she has no business doing."

If I thought Chase's words from before rocked me, then the ones my father spoke bit into my skin, each syllable lashing me like a whip.

Anger, raw and all-consuming, stole my breath as I gazed up at the man who I'd come to love with my whole heart. "He didn't convince me to do anything!" I hollered, tears filling my eyes. "I did it all on my own."

A whole lot hurt, I stumbled to the side, cold seeping into my bones. "I know I've made some bad decisions in the past," I said, looking him in the face. "But I'm not entirely stupid. And this"—I pointed from Chase to me—"was what *I* wanted."

Heartbroken, I made my way to the waiting SUV and climbed in the back, slamming the door shut behind me.

Outside the car, I could hear Anthony and Chase arguing, but I had no idea what either of them was saying.

Red-faced, Anthony turned and headed back to the vehicle, leaving a pissed-off looking Chase behind.

He looked so angry, and part of me was afraid to face him, even though I knew I had no reason to be scared.

He won't hurt me...

He's not el diablo.

"Issy..." Turning my head, I looked over at Lucca, who was sitting in his car seat, his big brown eyes full of confusion. "Issy sad?" he asked, causing the remaining hold I had on my emotions to break. "You sad?"

"I'm okay," I whispered as sob after sob jerked my body. "Promise I'm o-okay."

It was a lie.

I wasn't okay.

My little brother knew it too.

Wanting to make me feel better, he lifted his hand to his mouth. "Here, Issy," he said. "Catch!" The kiss he blew me was the second sweetest I'd ever had.

Pretending to catch it mid-air, I pressed it to my lips.

"Better?"

I nodded, tears still falling. "I'm better."

The smile that crossed his face warmed me the slightest bit. "You okay," he said, smiling. "My Issy always okay."

He was right.

Despite the hurt that boiled in my gut, and the demons that stirred in my chest, I knew that as long as I had him, I would always be okay.

And that was the truth.

Chapter Fourteen

ASHLEY

I was lying on my side, my knees pulled into my belly when Shelby stormed into my room, a livid expression plastered on her beautiful face.

Coming to a standstill next to my bed, she crossed her tanned arms and dug her slender fingers into her biceps. "I'm going to ask you a couple of questions, sugar, and I expect nothing less than the God-honest truth to spill from those pretty lips of yours."

Head pounding, I sat up. "I've never lied to you," I replied. "And I don't plan on starting now."

My words were only halfway truthful.

Though I'd never outright fibbed to her before, I had a mile-long laundry list of secrets I'd kept to myself. It was awful, and maybe so was I, but even though I wanted to spill every dark truth to her and Anthony both, doing so right then was impossible.

One day I would confess my sins.

But today wasn't that day.

"Alright," she said, jerking me from the crippling guilt that encapsulated me like a velvet cloak. "Question number one—did Chase Jacobs ask you to leave school with him?"

"No," I replied immediately. "I left the library and walked out on my own accord."

Brow arched, she cocked her hip to the side. "We'll get to why you walked out in just a minute, but first, I need to ask you a second question." She paused, her blue eyes growing stormy before mine. "Once you were outside, did Chase do anything inappropriate?"

It took a minute for the meaning of her words to sink in. But when they did, the hairs on the back of my neck stood on end. "No," I squeaked, my throat tightening. "He never even—"

"You sure, sugar?" she asked, interrupting me. "Cause if he did anything, anything at all, then you just let me—"

"He didn't do *a single thing*!" I snapped, slinging a heaping dose of attitude her way.

It was a first, considering most of the time I was quieter than a church mouse. But hearing her ask me such a question, even when I knew her intentions were coming from a place of good, pissed me right off.

"No disrespect intended, Shelby, but regardless of what you or anyone else thinks, Chase would *never* behave the way you're inferring."

My chest heaved, the anger brewing inside me increasing like a category-5 hurricane about to make landfall. "I know you have no reason to trust me, but he is *nothing* like Dominic."

My words surprised me.

For a terrified girl who claimed not to trust a certain boy, I sure was defending him a whole lot.

Unsettled by Shelby's questions, along with my reaction to them, I climbed off my bed and crossed the room. Standing next to the window, I looked across the street to Grandmama's house, spotting the Crazy Old Biddy right away.

Sitting on the front porch like she didn't have a care in the world, she held a glass of sweet tea in one hand and a magazine in the other.

At the sight, my heart clenched.

Why couldn't I be strong like her?

Sure she was crazy, but from what I'd been told, Grandmama had endured her fair share of pain, yet she didn't walk around a twisted up and crying mess.

Unlike me.

Why did I have to be so weak?

Shelby's footsteps padded across the carpet behind me as she moved in my direction. "Ashley Jo Moretti," she said, her voice more stern than I'd ever heard it. "Did you just get pissy with me?"

Leaning my forehead against the cool glass, I ignored the tears that slid down my cheeks. "Chase is a good guy," I whispered, all my fight vanishing. "And I'd appreciate it if you and the Dadinator didn't act like he is a teenage Jeffrey Dahmer."

"Turn around."

My chin wobbled as I followed the order she'd given and slowly spun, coming face to face with her.

Though irrational, part of me expected her to slap me right across the face. After all, it's what my birth vessel, Wanda, would've done.

But this was Shelby.

She'd never strike me.

Yell at me? Absolutely.

But hit me? Nope.

Still, I held my breath, fully expecting her to morph into a monster I didn't recognize, just as most others had done before her.

Thankfully, I was able to release that same breath a heartbeat later when she smiled and then said, "I am so danged proud of you, sugar."

My face fell. "Uh, why?"

Cupping my shoulders, she gave them a slight squeeze. "'Cause that's the first time I've ever seen you stand up for someone. And even if that someone is a boy—one whom I don't approve of, I might add—I'm still proud of you all the same."

Her words didn't make me feel any better.

Sure, I was glad that she was proud of me for finally growing something that resembled a backbone—*yeah right*—but I didn't like hearing that she didn't approve of Chase. "Why don't you like Chase?"

"I didn't say that I don't like him," she replied, dropping her hands. "I said I don't approve of him. There is a big ol' difference."

That made no sense to me.

At all.

"I realize I'm not the sharpest tool in the shed at times, but I don't get it. If you like him, then why don't you approve of him?"

She shrugged. "Because he's not good enough for you. It's as simple as that." I opened my mouth to reply, but she kept talking, not giving me the chance. "And before you get your panties in a twist, let me just say this—it doesn't matter how good a man is, he will never be good enough for *you*. Not in my eyes, and certainly not in your father's."

Her response warmed my heart, but at the same time, I felt like I'd been gut-punched.

"That's not true," I quickly retorted. "If anything, Chase is—"

I snapped my mouth closed when Anthony suddenly appeared in my doorway, a solemn expression on his handsome face. It was a far cry from the seething anger that had possessed his every feature an hour before. "You got a minute?"

Eyes narrowed, I thinned my lips, annoyed as could be. I may love the man more than words could ever say, but I was so upset with him.

Not because he'd reacted so harshly to seeing Chase and me kiss, but because he'd wrongly assumed that I'd been easily talked into doing something I shouldn't.

Given my past, I understood his rush to judgment, but that didn't dull the sting his words had created. And right or wrong, deep down, I couldn't help but wonder if my entire family thought I was stupid for ending up with Dominic in the first place.

They never acted like they did, but after today...

Well, I wasn't sure what to think.

"Ashley." Shelby softly tapped my arm, pulling me from the mess of tangled thoughts consuming me. "Sugar, answer your father."

I swallowed, unsure of what he was about to say. "Yes," I replied, teetering on the edge of a breakdown. "I've got a minute."

Crossing the room like Shelby had done minutes before, he came to a stop in front of me and slid his hands into his pockets. "I was wrong," he said, unexpectedly, knocking me off-kilter. "The way I reacted earlier was out of line, and the things I said weren't okay."

Shelby's eyes narrowed. "Did you really just admit that you were wrong? 'Cause if so, then I need to run downstairs and alert the media since this is breaking news and all."

A ghost of a smile played on Anthony's lips.

Ignoring Shelby, he continued. "Seeing Chase kiss you"—he paused—"it broke my heart."

Once again, I didn't understand.

I swear confusion was an ongoing theme for me.

"Why did it break your heart?"

He glanced at Shelby before meeting my gaze once more. "Because, *Principessa*, I just got you. And I'm not ready to lose you to another man, much less a hot-headed teenage boy."

His words...

They stirred something inside me, and if I hadn't known better, I could've sworn that one of my many broken pieces snapped back into place.

"You're not going to lose me. I mean, it's not like I'm getting married. I only kissed him once—"

"*You* kissed *him*?" Shelby interrupted, wide-eyed.

I bit my lower lip and nodded.

"Well, hells bells," she said, borrowing one of Grandmama's favorite phrases. "Didn't see that one coming."

Smacking Anthony's arm, she glared in his direction. "Why didn't you tell me that she kissed him instead of the other way around, Stud Muffin? If I had known that, I wouldn't have come up and interrogated our poor girl. Men, I swear..."

I erupted into laughter.

Anthony, though, he scowled. "I still don't like it. Don't like him either."

It was Shelby's turn to crack up. "Of course, you don't." Hands on her hips, she pursed her gloss-coated lips. "So, I guess now isn't a good time to tell you that he's downstairs playing with Lucca, huh?"

Mischief twinkling in her eyes, she added, "And by *him*, I mean Chase."

Heart slamming against my rib cage, I froze.

Chase was downstairs?

With my little brother?

Hearing that made me all sorts of happy.

"What?" Anthony snapped, his face swinging in Shelby's direction. "What the hell do you mean he's downstairs?"

Shelby's smile grew. "He knocked on the door a few minutes ago and said he was upset about what happened earlier. I threatened to castrate him on the spot, but he flat-out refused to leave until I let him visit with Ashley. Said he wanted to see for himself that she was alright, and since you were busy pouting in your office over God only knows what, I figured it was as good as time as any to let him in. Ya know, especially since I didn't know if I needed to kill him yet or not."

Oh for heaven's sake!

"Nobody is killing Chase." I looked from one parent to the next, projecting as much fierceness as I could muster, which admittedly wasn't much. "He's a good guy, and I kind of..."

I fidgeted in place, scared half to death to say what I needed to.

Buck up, Chiquita, a familiar voice in my head said. *Say the words.*

Comfort mixed with the feeling of soul-shattering loss swept through me. *Miss you, Carmen. Jade too,* I mentally replied, fighting to hold it together. *More than you possibly know.*

Taking a deep breath, I channeled my inner sass, or what little of it I possessed. Then, I did as Carmen's ghostly voice demanded and said the words I needed to. "Listen, y'all, I like Chase, and even though neither of you do, I'd really appreciate it if you didn't murder him in the living room."

My father scowled. "Not making any goddamned promises."

"Well," I said, flicking my hair back over my shoulder. "That's the best I can ask for."

Jaw ticking, he shook his head before nodding toward the door.

"Go check on your *friend*. Christ knows, your brother may have him duct-taped to the wall by now."

I didn't need to be told twice.

After kissing both my parents on the cheek, I took off. Darting out of my room, I ran down the hall and bounded down the wooden stairs. Reaching the bottom, I turned and bolted into the living room.

There, I found Chase, seated in the middle of the sofa with Lucca snuggled into his side, his strong arm holding my little brother close. A movie played on the flatscreen—Shrek, I think—but I paid whatever they were watching no mind.

My eyes were focused on them.

Looking back, I think it was right then, at that very moment, that I lost a huge piece of my heart to Chase Jacobs.

It was the first of many...

And one I'd never get back.

Chapter Fifteen

ASHLEY

Six Weeks Later

*I*t was a typical Saturday afternoon, and every store in the Toluca City Mall, the place where Heidi, Carissa, and I found ourselves bouncing from one store to the next, was packed.

And I mean *packed*.

I swear I couldn't move a foot in any one direction without bumping into someone. For me, a person who literally couldn't stand to be touched most of the time, it wasn't an ideal situation.

But I was coping.

Well, best as I could.

Truthfully, I was so busy keeping my body wedged between Carissa and Heidi's frames that I hardly noticed when a stray arm or hand came too close for comfort. It was a blessing because let's face it, the last thing I wanted to do was nosedive headfirst into a panic-driven meltdown in the middle of the mall.

A mall where, apparently, everyone in the tri-county area was busy shopping.

"For goodness sake," Heidi grumbled, dodging a group of girls that looked to be around middle school age. Busy giggling and staring at a trio of boys by the food court, they were standing stock-still, smack dab in the middle of our path.

Swooping and swerving, we navigated past them.

"Too bad your football star boyfriend isn't here," Carissa said, stepping the slightest bit in front of me to shield my body from a man who was walking a tad too close, his gaze locked on a brightly colored storefront window to the left. "He could just plow through everybody for us."

My brows rose. "I don't have a boyfriend."

Carissa looked at me, her blue eyes twinkling. "You sure about that, Ashley Jo?"

Was I sure? No, not really.

As silly as it sounded, I didn't have the slightest clue what Chase and I were. We hadn't exactly labeled our relationship, nor had we be an official date. Other than a single kiss, one which I'd stolen, and a half dozen hugs, he hadn't touched me either.

It was both disappointing and relieving.

Disappointing because he'd made no move to take things to the next level with me. It made little sense because him acting like a true gentleman in that regard should have been a good thing. But with my bottom of the barrel self-esteem, I spent half my time second-guessing whether he genuinely had those types of feelings toward me or not.

It was ridiculous.

Especially considering that the dark part of my psyche—the place where I fought to keep my demons locked away—felt nothing more than relief over the fact that he *hadn't* tried to touch me like that.

A simple kiss on the lips had been one thing, even if said kiss had turned my world upside down, but I wasn't ready for a whole lot more. Now, don't get me wrong, I'd gladly accept his mouth on mine once more, but as for full-blown sex?

That was a big fat nope.

Trust me, I'd fantasized about what it would feel like to have Chase touch me intimately—more than once—but when my mind went there, my skin would begin to burn as panic roiled to life in my belly.

It happened each time, without fail.

And I hated it.

Despite knowing that my reaction was normal given my past, I still feared that he would leave me, writing me off forever, if I didn't find a way to conquer the demons that came out to play whenever I imagined baring my body to him for the first time.

In my heart I didn't believe he'd walk away over such a thing, but the problem was, my brain had a hard time believing anything my heart said; especially since it had led me astray the day I made the damning choice to put my trust in Dominic after a handful of well-delivered, albeit phony, promises.

Because of him, every touch that my body had endured since I arrived in Georgia had been taken without permission. And because of my mother and her horrific choice in men, I'd learned what it felt like to have my innocence forcibly stolen from me when I was nothing more than a child.

Both truths made me absolutely sick.

"Earth to Ashley." Heidi's unique voice pulled me out of the heart-wrenching fog encapsulating me. "Did you hear me?"

Brows furrowed, I looked directly at her and shook my head. "No," I said. "What did you say?"

Being moderately deaf meant Heidi had a hard time understanding what was being said in loud settings where her hearing aids struggled to filter out background noise.

Ya know, like the crowded mall.

Because of that, Carissa and I both made sure to look at her when we spoke, giving her the chance to read our lips, a skill she thankfully possessed since, unlike C, I didn't know sign language.

It was a problem I was working to correct.

After Heidi and I started spending so much time together, she'd quickly become the closest thing I had to a best friend. Because of that, I figured learning ASL was something I should do.

So that's what I was working on.

One sign at a time.

Smacking my arm, she grabbed my attention once more. "Do you need to borrow my hearing aids?" Before I could aim a sassy remark her way, she smirked and then pointed to the other end of the mall. "Just look over there, Dimples."

Dimples...

I loved it when she called me that.

More than curious as to what she wanted me to see, I followed the trajectory of her finger. When I saw who she was pointing at, I almost came out of my skin.

Chase...

"He's here," I whispered, heart pounding as I drank in every inch of him, starting at the top of his blond head and ending at the tips of his sneaker covered toes. Dressed in a pair of loose, grey sweats that hung low—not to mention, just right—on his lean hips, along with a fitted white t-shirt that hugged his chiseled chest and strong shoulders, he looked enticingly beautiful and beyond tempting.

Coming from me, that was saying something.

"Careful, Ashley Jo," Carissa teased. "You're starting to drool." Dabbing her finger against the corner of her mouth, she added, "Right about here."

Wide-eyed, I shook my head, my unwavering focus traveling right back to Chase. "I don't even care," I replied, mouth suddenly drier than the Sahara. "I mean, *look* at him."

Laughing, Heidi jumped in front of me and turned. Walking backward—seriously, the girl was nuts—she dropped her eyes to my lips. "Did you tell him we'd be here?"

I shook my head. "No."

"Huh," she replied with a half-hearted shrug. "Wonder how he found out then?"

Brow arched, Carissa shot her little sister a look that screamed, *are you kidding me?*

"What?" Heidi asked, reading said look easily. "You know something we don't?"

"Oh come on, y'all," C said, rolling her eyes. "You both know *exactly* how he found out."

"We do?" I asked, clearly confused.

Carissa nodded. "Yes, you do."

"Uh," I said, the wheels in my head spinning a million miles per hour. "Could someone fill me in then because, as per usual, I have no idea what's going on." As soon as the last word left my lips, a lightbulb went off, stopping my brain from frying itself like an egg in a cast-iron skillet. "The Crazy Old Biddy told him."

It wasn't a question.

It was a statement.

Other than my parents, Grandmama was the only person who knew where I'd be, and with the way she rode Chase to watch out for me—something I'd only recently learned—I knew without a doubt that she'd likely called him the minute I jumped into the back of Carissa's car.

Not that our trip had been a secret or anything.

If I'd thought it could've been pulled off without causing the Dadinator to stroke out, I would've made arrangements for Chase to ride with us from the get-go. But, needless to say, after witnessing first-hand his reaction to our kiss, I'd thought better of it.

Despite him extending an olive branch of sorts over the past couple of weeks, neither he—nor the Mominator for that matter—approved of Chase and I becoming... well, whatever it was that we were becoming.

While Shelby stood by her opinion that he wasn't good enough for me, with Anthony, it was different. I couldn't put my finger on what it was exactly, but deep down, I knew there was something more driving his dislike of Chase.

That much was clear.

At least to me.

"Are you going to talk to him?" Heidi asked, still walking backward. "Or are you just planning on gawking at him all day? I know he's cute and all, but heaven's girl, if you don't go chat him up, some other hussy will."

My right eye twitched.

I didn't like the sound of that at all.

"I'm going to talk to him," I said, feeling my blood pressure rise. "You two wanna come?"

Readjusting the bags she held, Carissa shook her head. "No, we'll give you guys some privacy." Lifting one hand, she pointed to the crowded food court. "We'll be in there somewhere. Probably near the pretzel stand. Come find us whenever you're ready." Tossing a sweet smile my way, she added, "And bring the jock with you. I kinda like him."

I kinda liked him too.

Well, there was no kinda too it.

Because my feelings for Chase were *big*.

After waving at both girls, I quickly turned right, breaking away from them. Giving each person that I passed a wide-berth, I high-tailed it to the opposite end of the mall where I'd seen the most handsome boy I'd ever laid eyes on standing just moments before.

When only twenty feet separated me from said spot, my skin prickled with awareness, just like it did each time he was close.

At my approach, he looked up.

When our eyes locked through the sea of bodies stretching between us, I swear to the heaven's above that my heart skipped a beat—or two.

Unable to control the excitement crackling in my chest, along with the need to be closer to him, I moved faster, nearly doubling my pace.

He smiled as I gained ground, giving me a glimpse of his white and perfectly straight teeth. "Sweetness," he said, his deep timbre sending shivers racing down my spine. "It's about time you found—"

Wanting to feel his warmth against me, I slammed my body into his and wrapped my arms around his back the very second he was within touching distance. He grunted and stumbled backward, the force of impact momentarily knocking him off balance.

"Christ, beautiful," he said, chuckling. "You hit harder than most defensive ends."

I had no idea what a defensive end was, but I'd tackle him a million times if it meant that I got to spend more time together as we were right then—with my arms wrapped around him, and him holding me tight in return.

Sliding one strong hand into my silky hair, he gently tugged on my chocolate-colored locks, silently urging me to tilt my head back.

It was a request which I obliged.

His lips immediately found my cheek, and my eyes slid closed on their own accord in response. "Chase," I whispered as he leaned down, gently touching his forehead to mine. "What are you doing?"

Removing his hand from my hair, he lightly trailed his fingers down my spine, ghosting them over my heated flesh before resting his palm on my lower back. "I'm about to do something I should've already done," he whispered, dipping his face closer to mine. "After all, turn-about is fair play."

I had no idea what he was talking about.

I didn't really care either.

Not as long as he continued to touch me, each sensual move softer and more heart-stopping than the last. It was such a stark contrast to the way I normally felt, but right then, I didn't care to analyze my shift in feelings.

I just wanted Chase to come closer.

Much to my surprise.

Feeling the world beneath my feet tilt, I leaned further into him, giving him most of my weight. He willingly took it, tightening the arm wrapped around my back even more.

Swallowing, I gazed up at him with heavy-lidded eyes. "What are you going to do?" I asked, my throaty voice nearly unrecognizable.

After tracing his tongue over his bottom lip, he whispered, "I'm about to steal a kiss from you"—*oh God*—"just like how you stole one from me."

Heart nearly bursting free of my chest, my eyes slid closed. "So what are you waiting for? If you want to, then kiss—"

Chase's lips instantly found mine, silencing the words I was about to speak, and his hand, the one resting on my lower back, descended south of the Equator, sliding over my bottom. I froze as he cupped my jean-clad flesh softly, fully expecting my demons to begin their usual song and dance.

Surprisingly, they stayed dormant.

Huh... well, would you look at that.

Relaxing once more, I melted into him, my body gone completely boneless.

Groaning, he nipped my bottom lip, and my breath hitched as my cherry-glossed lips parted.

He took full advantage.

Dipping his tongue into my mouth, he sampled my taste, giving me a hit of his in return while simultaneously working me into a heated frenzy, the likes of which I'd never experienced before.

Skin on fire and needing a whole lot more of him, I looped my arms around his neck, melding my body to his. Hands shaking from excitement, I slid my hands into his hair, silently demanding that he deepen the kiss, giving me more of the very thing my starving body craved.

But he never got the chance.

Like the first time our lips touched, an unwanted interruption sliced right through the euphoric veil blanketing each of us, completely obliterating the moment.

Only this time, it wasn't Anthony who shattered the peace that only Chase had been able to give me.

Instead, it was the incessant ringing of his phone.

A phone which I wanted to shatter.

Annoyance washed over me at the sound of the high-pitched ringtone. I was so close to throwing a full-fledged hissy fit that it wasn't funny. To say I was a bit agitated at the way things were unfolding would have been the understatement of the century.

"Sweetness," he said, once again resting his forehead against mine. "I've gotta get that. It may be—"

"Answer it," I said, interrupting him. "It's okay."

As irritated as I was, I understood his need to take the call. So, unwinding my arms from his neck, I took a step back, unhappily extracting myself from his warm embrace.

Jaw clenched, he pulled the phone out of his pocket, and without checking the Caller ID, he pressed it to his ear. "What?" he snapped, his irritation matching my own. Eyes narrowing before mine, he turned, giving me his muscular back.

"What do you want? I'm goddamned busy," he snarled a second later. "Fine, I'll be there in an hour."

My brows furrowed.

He'd just gotten here.

Now he was leaving?

Ending the call, he shoved the phone back in his pocket. Hands fisted, his shirt-covered back rose as his chest expanded, the unchecked anger that simmered in his veins nearly reaching a boiling point.

Though I had no idea who had just called him, it was obvious he wasn't happy about what they had to say.

Wanting to comfort him, I placed my hand between his shoulder blades and gently massaged the flesh that laid beneath. "You okay?"

I dropped my arm when he spun around, his eyes blazing. Refusing to meet my gaze, he stared past me, his attention focused on something behind me. "I'm fucking fine." I flinched at his harsh tone, one which I'd never heard from him before. "But, I've gotta go."

Alarms began to ring in my head.

Nodding, I took a step back as trepidation settled in my belly. "Okay," I whispered, unsure of what else to say or do. "Are you...?" Swallowing around the lump in my throat, I took a breath. "Are you still going to meet me later or—"

"I don't know," he snapped.

My chin trembled. "I don't understand..."

It was the truth.

For over a week, we'd had plans to spend the night at the fair together. My family, along with some of the ladies that worked at the shelter would be there too. When I'd first brought the idea up to him, he'd seemed excited.

Extremely so.

But now...

Well, I didn't know what to think.

Clearing his throat, he pulled his keys out of his pocket. "I've got some shit to handle, but I'll try to meet you there like we planned." The air surrounding us shifted, and after a second, I realized the coldness that nipped at my skin was coming from him. "I'll call you later and let you know if I can make it."

I blinked back tears. "Okay."

Stepping forward, he leaned down and pressed his lips to my cheek in what felt an awful lot like a consolation kiss. It made my skin burn and my stomach roll. Something was off. Like, really off. I just didn't know what it was or what it meant for us.

"I'll call," he repeated, his voice flat and monotone.

Replying wasn't an option.

Between the grief causing a stranglehold in my chest and the voices in my head screaming, *I told you so*, doing anything other than breathing was impossible, and even that was hard.

Without sparing me another glance, he silently turned and walked away, taking a piece of my tattered heart with him.

———

Wet paper towel in hand, I was standing in front of a clouded restroom mirror, viciously scrubbing away the fresh tear tracks that stained my flushed skin when the bathroom door swung open and three girls—all of which I recognized—stepped inside.

My stomach immediately dropped.

This isn't good...

"Well," Bianca, of all people, said, her pretty face twisting into an ugly sneer. "If it isn't the new girl."

Knowing that nothing good would come of this encounter, I tossed the used towels into the trash beside me and turned, more than ready to make a hasty exit.

But it wasn't that easy.

Though I had nothing to say to someone like Bianca, nor the posse of mean girls that flanked her sides, she had plenty to say to me. "You're not thinking of leaving, are you?" she asked, tilting her head. "Because if so, I'm afraid I'll have to insist that you stay, at least until we have a long overdue chat."

Shaking my head, I moved toward the door. "There's nothing for you and me to say to one another."

Done with the entire situation, I went to pass her, but before I could, she wrapped her bony fingers around my forearm, halting the steps I'd only just begun to take. My eyes flared, then narrowed in response. "Let me go."

Ignoring my demand, she tightened her grip. "You're wrong, Trashley. I have plenty of things to say. First, let's start with the reason that you're spending so much time with *my* boyfriend."

I almost laughed.

The girl was crazy.

That much was obvious.

Chase wasn't her boyfriend.

He didn't even like her, something he never failed to remind me of each time we ran into her at school.

"I know what's going through that pretty little head of yours," she continued, moving her make-up-laden face closer to mine. "And let me just tell you, new girl"—she paused—"you are completely wrong."

Bull-freakin-crap.

Chest heaving, I ripped my arm free of her hold. I didn't give a flying crap how tough Bianca thought she was, I refused to let her intimidate me. She may have succeeded in doing so on the first day of school, but it wouldn't happen again. I'd dealt with being pushed around for far too long, by bullies much more sinister than her.

Enough was enough.

"Save your breath," I whispered, my voice surprisingly steady. "I want no part of whatever trouble it is that you're trying to stir up."

She chuckled humorlessly. "Are you sure? Because if the shoe were on the other foot, I'd want to know if I was secretly the laughing stock of the entire school."

I froze. "What do you mean?"

The malevolent smile she wore grew. "You didn't really think that Chase liked you, did you? I mean, I know you're most likely gullible, not to mention desperate, but come on."

When I didn't reply, she took it as permission to keep talking. "Oh sweet little Trashley. Chase has only been spending time with you because Ryder Jenkins bet him two-hundred bucks that he wouldn't be able to seduce you before graduation rolls around."

It isn't true...

She's only saying it to hurt me.

Even as the words echoed through my head, doubt crept into my mind as the sound of my hammering pulse filled my ears.

Aware that her words were having the desired effect, Bianca continued, not missing a beat. "Why do you think Ryder came into the library that day?"

Silence.

Then, "Since you're likely too dumb to figure it out, let me break it down for you."

This bitch...

"After Chase failed to seal the deal, something that's never happened before, Ryder decided to step in and finish what he couldn't."

My temple pulsed. "You're lying."

"Am I?" she asked, eyes twinkling.

"You *are*." I prayed she was. "And I know you are because a girl like you would never allow her boyfriend to sleep with someone else, bet or no bet."

My words were confident.

But my heart wasn't.

Lifting her hand, she stared blankly at her flawless manicure. "Guys like Chase are never faithful," she stated matter of factly with a shrug. "But I don't care if he plays around since it's me that he always comes back to." Her eyes met mine once more. "*Always.*"

I'd heard enough.

Letting my emotions get the best of me, I took a page straight out of my mother's book and said, "You're so full of shit, Bianca, it's no wonder your eyes are turd-brown."

Her hand twitched, and for a second, I thought she'd smack me. If she did, I fully intended to pop her right back. I wasn't kidding when I said enough was enough.

Feeling as though my head would explode, I looked at the other two girls, who were, of course, blocking my exit. "Move," I growled. "Or I'll move you myself."

They looked at each other, then back at me before stepping to the side.

After taking three big steps, I wrapped my hand around the door handle, but I stopped short of making my exit when Bianca said, "By the way, I'm sorry Chase had to cancel y'all's fair plans. I know how much you were looking forward to it, but even though cash is involved, my man is getting tired of this charade." She giggled. "Don't worry though. I'll make sure to keep his mind off you since he'll be with me *all* night instead."

Her words...

They *hurt*.

Mainly because they were true.

They had to be since the only people who knew about our fair date was my family, Chase, and myself. Not even Grandmama knew, and that was saying something. There was no way for Bitchy Bianca to know what we had planned.

Not unless Chase told her.

That realization hit me like a ton of bricks, knocking the air straight from my pained lungs.

Every word, every action, and every stolen kiss...

It had all been a lie.

The phone call, the one in which he turned cold and left immediately afterward, was probably fake too. At that point, I was busy wondering if Bianca had been the one to call him, giving him the out he needed to bolt.

Anger raged inside me at the thought, but the agony that radiated through my chest as a result of my heart splintering into millions of jagged little pieces was too much to bear.

I was about to lose it.

Completely.

Flat-out refusing to let any of those girls see the tears that were seconds away from spilling down my cheeks in an unending tsunami of grief, I flung open the bathroom door.

Then, doing what I did best, I ran.

———

I'd finally stopped crying.

It had taken me nearly the entire ride home from the mall, but I'd managed to get my emotions partially under control by the time Carissa pulled her decade-old Corolla into my driveway.

And thank God for that because I wasn't in the right state of mind to tell my parents why I was such a mess... yet again.

I jumped in my seat, my senses on high-alert as Carissa shifted the transmission into park and unbuckled her seatbelt. Twisting at the waist, she turned, looking back at me. "Do you want me and Heidi Bug to walk you in and stay a bit?"

I shook my head. "No," I replied, my voice a mere whisper. "I'll be fine. Promise."

"You sure?" she asked, her concern-filled eyes locked on mine. "Because we don't mind at all. Neither of us has anywhere particular to be."

"I'm sure," I said, trying my best to assure her. "The Dadinator and Lucca are home to keep me company. Besides, I'll probably just head upstairs and take a nap. My head is killing me."

Heidi scoffed. "Screw a nap. I say you pop an Excedrin or two, and then we go find that two-timing twatwaffle and run him over. I bet he'd make one hell of a speedbump." Eyes wide, she snapped her fingers. "No, wait. I have a better idea. Since you don't want to tell Anthony and Shelby what happened, I say we call Grandmama. I'm sure she'll be more than happy to shoot him right in his cheating ass."

Carissa's eyes flared. "She totally would."

"He'd deserve it too," Heidi added, nodding. "The dickhead must think he's slicker than owl shit to try and pull something like this. Especially with you. I swear if he were here I'd poke his eyeballs out with my keys."

My heart hurt something awful, yet I still laughed. "Slicker than owl shit?" I asked, leaning my head against the car window next to me. "That's a new one."

Carissa's eyes lit up. "Now I know how to make you laugh. All we have to do is release our inner rednecks and let our Southern tongues do all the work."

Heidi chuckled. "I think I like this game."

Carissa smacked her sister's arm. "I came up with it, so I'm going first. Alright, let me think..." She paused and tapped her finger against her chin, seemingly mulling something over. Then, "I've got one!"

A faint smile played on my lips. "Tell me."

"So that Bianca hussy," she said, sneering. "When she walked out of the bathroom after making you all upset, she had her nose stuck so high up in the air that she would've drowned had a rainstorm come."

"That's no joke," Heidi said around laughter. "And did you see those pants she was wearing? They were so tight I could see her religion!"

I had no earthly idea what that even meant, and though my throat was awfully raw from the sobs that had poured out of me an hour before, neither thing stopped my laughter, because for a moment— even as brief as it was—Heidi and C's antics made the pain go away.

Well, more like dulled it.

Like my heartbeat, it never truly ceased pulsing through my veins.

"As for Chase," Heidi continued, rolling her eyes. "If that girl really is his girlfriend, then he's an idiot. Why, I swear there must be a tree stump in a southern Georgia swamp with a higher IQ."

At that, my laughter died.

"Chase isn't stupid," I whispered, the unrelenting torment that held my soul captive returning. "Even if he has been playing me, I still saw pieces of him that I know were real, and each one of them was as beautiful as he was."

"*Crap*, Dimples," Heidi said, face pale as could be. "I'm so sorry. I didn't mean—"

"I know," I whispered, forcing a half-hearted smile. "I'm not mad at you. I'm just—"

"—hurt," Carissa finished for me.

I nodded. "I am. Badly."

Eyes flashing with anger, Heidi tensed. I had no doubt that there was a lot she wanted to say, but to avoid upsetting me further, she kept her mouth shut.

"Thanks for letting me tag along with you girls to the mall," I said, wrapping my hand around the door handle. "I had a lot of fun. Well, until..." Closing my eyes, I shook my head and popped open the door. "If I don't see you at the fair, I'll call one of you later tonight. Lifting my free hand, I blew them both a kiss. "Love you both."

Without waiting for either of them to reply, I jumped out of the car and slammed the door shut behind me.

Feeling another cry-fest coming on, I bolted up the front porch steps, my purse in tow, and burst through the unlocked stained-glass door.

I was about to hoof it to my room but came to an abrupt stop in the middle of the foyer when something in the living room caught my eye.

I blinked, my brain working overtime to figure out what the flash of white I'd seen was. Having disappeared behind Anthony's oversized recliner, I didn't get a chance to have a second look.

It didn't matter though.

Lucca, bless his heart, came to the rescue. "Issy!" he screamed, popping out from behind the sofa. Pointing to the recliner, he smiled. Big. "Ook, Issy! Issa dog!"

A dog?

The thought had just slid through my head when suddenly a ball of white fur charged me, eating up the distance between us in a matter of seconds. I screamed and fell back onto my butt as it lunged at me, tackling me to the floor.

"Oh my God!" I half laughed, half cried as the dog started to lick my face, starting at my chin and ending at my forehead.

"You said you wanted a dog," Anthony said from somewhere close. Eyes pinched shut to avoid having my poor eyeballs licked out of my skull, I couldn't place where he was. "Now, you have one. The problem is, I think he's crazy." He paused. "Which means he'll fit right in with your mother."

Gently placing my hands on the side of the dog's furry face, I held him steady as I sat up and opened my eyes, getting my first good look at him. When I realized what kind of dog he was—not that it would have mattered—I started crying.

White husky.

Beautiful blue eyes.

"You got me a husky?" I asked Anthony, tears pouring down my cheeks. "Just like I wanted?"

Shoulder leaned against the living room doorway, he nodded. "The day you agreed to be my daughter, I swore that I'd spoil you rotten. This is me doing that."

My broken heart swelled as I wrapped my arms around the panting dog's neck and buried my face in his thick-but-soft fur. "Thanks, D-Dad," I stuttered, the maelstrom of emotions tumbling through me, nearly choking me to death. "From the bottom of my heart, thank y-you."

Anthony cleared his emotion-clogged throat. "Dad?" he asked, his voice raspy. "Is that what you're calling me now?"

Vision blurred, I nodded. "If it's okay with you. I mean, I sorta think it's time."

The smile he beamed my way was so bright, there was no mistaking it through the hazy cloud of tears clouding my vision. "Me too, *Principessa*. In fact, I think—"

Whatever he was about to say was cut short when the heavy front door swung open, and the Crazy Old Biddy stepped inside holding an aluminum foil-covered casserole dish in her hands. "Felix!" she hollered. "Bring my grandcat down here, you old goat! I made him a special tuna—"

Her eyes flared when she caught sight of me, plus the dog in the middle of the floor. "What in the good Lord's name is that?" she asked, clutching her pearls with her free hand.

Dad chuckled. "That's Ziggy Bear," he said. "He's Ashley and Lucca's new dog."

"Dog?" Her voice was one of disbelief. "That ain't no dog. It's a dadgummed polar bear!"

Grandmama continued hollering, but I had no idea what she said, because Ziggy licked my face again, stealing every bit of my attention.

"Hey, buddy," I whispered, looking him in the eyes. "My name is Ashley Jo, and I think you and I are going to become the best of friends."

His reply came in the form of a short howl, followed by another lick across my cheek.

And just like that, one of the most heartbreaking days of my life literally became one of the most beautiful moments I'd ever experienced.

Chapter Sixteen

CHASE

I was losing my damned mind.

Since leaving the mall, I hadn't been able to reach Ashley.

I'd called her at least half a dozen times and sent more texts than I could count, yet each call went straight to voicemail, and my messages remained unread.

It was pissing me off.

Though I wasn't mad at her for obviously ignoring me, I sure as hell *was* mad at myself and the horrible way I'd behaved earlier. I had no right—absolutely no damned right—to act like an asshole toward *her*, the sweetest girl I'd ever met.

The words I used, and the tone I'd taken...

I deserved to have my ass kicked for both.

Suffice to say, I'd messed up.

Badly.

I just hoped I hadn't destroyed things beyond repair. If I had, I'd never forgive myself for breaking her heart, especially when I was pretty damned sure she was in the process of stealing mine right out of my chest.

From the first moment I laid eyes on her, I knew she was different, and even if I still didn't understand how or why our connection happened, I refused to deny its existence, because deep in my gut, I knew that Ashley was meant to be mine.

It was a truth I felt soul-deep.

Blowing out a breath and needing to talk to her more than anything else, I dialed her number one more time.

To my disappointment, it didn't even ring. Just like the times before, it went straight to her automated voicemail greeting.

"Goddammit," I mumbled, waiting for the greeting to end so I could leave a message. "Baby, please turn on your damn—"

Beep.

"Ashley, it's Chase," I said, fighting to keep my voice steady. "Sweetness, listen. I'm sorry for the way I acted earlier. Even though my words and anger weren't aimed at you, I had no right to behave the way I did." That was putting it lightly. "I've told you before that I won't stand by and let someone treat you like shit, and that includes myself."

If I could've kicked my own ass, I would've.

"I messed up, beautiful girl, and I fully expect you to rip me a new one for it. Hell, I deserve nothing less. Just please call me back. I can handle you being angry, and I can handle you crying, even if it does tear me up to see and hear, but I can't deal with not knowing whether you're safe or not."

Lifting my hand, I pinched the bridge of my nose. "I'm not sure what time I'll make it to the fairgrounds, but I'll be there, waiting for you next to the Ferris wheel."

Fist clenched, I was tempted to slam my hand into the dash. Somehow, I found the strength to resist. "I hope you're there too."

If she wasn't, I'd find her.

One damned way or another.

"Miss you, Sweetness."

Out of words to say, I ended the call, my frustration reaching a record-breaking level, and glanced at the illuminated numbers on my dashboard.

Nearly two hours had passed since I'd received a call from my twisted fuck of a father, the last person I'd wanted to hear from.

With a demand to meet him, followed by a well-delivered threat stating that he'd show up at the fire station where Ty worked if I didn't, I had no other choice but to bend to his will and drive to the abandoned parking lot he'd picked.

If he showed up at the station, it would only end one of two ways. The first would involve Ty being hauled to county lockup for assault and battery, while the second would involve Clyde physically attacking my brother, which was always one of his favorite pastimes.

Neither was an option.

The problem was, I wasn't sure what the asshole wanted, though I had a pretty good idea. And that idea? It involved—

Tap, tap, tap.

I snapped my head to the left, my gaze going to the window next to me when someone tapped on the glass three times in rapid succession.

When I saw who was standing there, his psycho eyes hidden behind a pair of Ray-Bans, my temper instantly flared, nearly blowing the top of my head off.

Consumed with thoughts of Ashley, I hadn't even seen him pull up.

It didn't matter though, because he was there all the same.

Mad as hell over the entire situation, I opened my door and slammed it into his side, hitting the service weapon attached to his utility belt with a thud. He stumbled back, a snarl forming on his stubble-covered face.

"Watch it, Clyde," I said, jumping out of my Jeep, the very same one Ty had bought me the day I was offered a conditional scholarship to CSU. "Wouldn't want you to get hurt, now would we?"

Anger brewed in my father's hate-filled eyes.

Too bad I didn't give a shit.

"One day, kid," he fired back, right cheek twitching. "One day, you're going to get exactly what you deserve."

What exactly did he think I deserved? I may have been a hothead who had a tendency to use his fists instead of his words in certain situations, but I wasn't a bad person. I didn't go around causing trouble or purposely hurting people.

Unlike him.

"You want to hit me? Maybe even beat my ass like you used to do my big brother's?" I lifted my hands and beckoned for him to come closer. "Because if so, then come on. I'm not fucking scared of you. Not anymore."

It was the truth.

The evil bastard had terrified me when I was a kid.

But now? The thought was laughable.

He may have been big, but so was I.

At eighteen, I was six feet three and weighed two-thirty. The man standing before me may have been a formidable threat years before, but right then, he was nothing more than an old man who'd spent far too many years surviving on cheap liquor and fast food.

When he made no move to swing at me, I leaned back against my car, appearing relaxed even though I was anything but.

Crossing my arms over my chest, I chuckled. "Start talking, asshole," I said, not the least bit amused. "You called me and demanded I meet you here, so go ahead and tell me exactly what the hell it is that you want."

Eyes narrowed into tiny slits, he plastered on the same sadistic grin he used to wear each time he beat Ty until he no longer possessed the strength to stand.

I fucking *hated* him.

So much.

"What I want," he said, finally speaking. "Is what I'm *owed*."

He had to be kidding me.

One look at his face, and I realized that nah, he wasn't kidding.

"And what is it that you think you're owed, dipshit? Cause the only two things I can think of end up with you in either a casket or a jail cell. Take your pick."

His hand went to his gun, casually resting on it.

Refusing to show any fear, I didn't react.

"What I'm owed," he snapped, "is a shit-load of money."

I'd like to say it was the first time he'd ever asked Ty or me for money, but it wasn't. Not even close. The only difference between this time and the ones that came before, was that he'd called me instead of Ty.

I gritted my back teeth together so hard I was surprised they didn't crack. "Hate to break it to you, old man," I replied, my temper climbing even further. "But I don't have any money. In case you haven't noticed, I don't exactly have a job."

It was the partial truth.

Because of football and then conditioning workouts during the off-season, I'd never had time to get a part-time job like a lot of other kids my age.

Instead, I picked up shifts at my Papaw's private security company when he needed someone to fill in. It wasn't lucrative, nor was it steady, but it was something at least.

Getting to spend extra time with Ty, who worked there when he wasn't on shift at the fire station, was just an added bonus.

But none of that mattered.

I doubted my father was interested in the lousy three-hundred bucks I had in my checking account.

No, if he was asking me for money, then it meant he was desperate. And by desperate, I mean he likely owed a bookie or loan shark a shit ton of cash.

A habitual gambler, he'd never been good with money.

The dumb fuck.

I can't begin to tell you how many times he'd come to Ty, the same kid he'd spent over a decade abusing, expecting him to hand him however much cash he needed.

It was complete bullshit.

"You're going to get me what I need, Chase," he said, pulling me from my thoughts. "Or else you'll regret it."

Threats on top of more threats.

It's how he operated.

Never seemed to get him very far though.

"How much cash you need this time, Clyde?" I asked, more out of curiosity than need. "One, two grand?"

"Five," he answered, no hesitation. "And not a penny less."

Laughter spilled out of me. "You have got to be kidding me," I said, uncrossing my arms. "You want me to get you five grand? And where exactly am I supposed to get that kind of money? Go ahead, tell me, since I'm sure you already have it figured out."

"Ask your brother or your Papaw," he answered, cracking his neck. "I don't give a shit either way as long as you get me what I'm owed."

"You aren't owed shit," I fired back. "I don't know where you get the balls—"

"I fucking raised you!" he screamed, cutting me off. "I raised you, and your worthless goddamned brother after your whore of a mama ran off, abandoning you both!"

Like a wire pulled too taut, I snapped.

Fueled by the rage boiling in my veins, I slammed my clenched fist into his nose without thinking twice.

Bone crunched, and blood poured down his chin as he stumbled back, his sallow eyes filled with the promise of retribution.

"You didn't fucking raise me!" I screamed, my chest vibrating from the force of my words. "My brother did!"

"That no-good, piece of shit didn't raise you!" he screamed in return, cupping his busted nose with his hands. "I did!"

The man was delusional.

Absolutely delusional.

"Yeah?" I asked, swiping my palm across my sweat covered face. "So it was you that cooked my supper, bathed me, and tucked me into bed every night? No, wait, it was you that helped me with homework and taught me how to throw a football, right? Fuck no, it wasn't you! It was Ty, the kid who took over your role the moment I was born!"

Emotion gripped me, nearly overloading every bit of common sense I had. Tempted to pummel his face until the only thing that remained was a broken shell of a human being, I was close to losing it.

The man did *not* deserve to live.

Not after everything he'd done.

"Tell me, *Dad*," I said, the word rolling off my tongue with a foul taste. "Why did you hate my big brother so much? He was just a kid. What the hell could he have ever done—"

"He was born!" he screamed, cutting me off mid-sentence. "He was born, and I hate him for it!"

I was speechless, and for the first time in my life, I looked at the man who'd helped create me with an emotion other than fear and anger.

That emotion? Pity.

"You're pathetic," I said, my voice barely above a whisper. "Pathetic because you can't see what a great man Ty is." I shook my head. "Even if I only turn out to be half as good as him, I'll still be a hundred times better than you."

Never taking my eyes off him—I wouldn't have put it past him to shoot me—I reached behind me and opened the door to my Jeep. "Go find your money somewhere else, because you'll never get a dime from me."

Face red as could be, he smiled, making alarm bells ring in my head. "From what I hear, you've got a great future ahead of you, son," he said, wiping the blood from his face with his hand. "It'll be real nice to see if you make it to the NFL like a few sports journalists are predicting."

Knowing exactly where this conversation was headed, I shot him a go-to-hell look. "Do me a favor, Clyde," I said, climbing back into my car. "Forget I exist." It was my turn to smile. "Better yet, drop the fuck dead."

With nothing left to say, I slammed my door shut, started the engine, and took off.

———

Speeding down the highway, I dialed my brother's number.

Like Ashley, he didn't answer, and instead, his voicemail picked up. "Christ, almighty," I mumbled, turning down the blaring radio. "Everybody is ignoring my ass today."

Needing to say the words rolling around in my head before it exploded, I waited for the familiar beep to sound.

When it did, I let each syllable roll off my tongue without giving any of them a second thought. "Ty, it's me, your favorite pain in the ass. Listen, I know you're probably out on a call since you didn't answer, but I just wanted you to know that I love you, assmunch. I realize I don't say it enough, and that's something I'm going to work on, but I hope you understand how much I appreciate all the shit you've done for me. Without you—"

Pausing, I pulled the phone from my ear and took a breath before beginning to speak once more. "Without you, I wouldn't have made it this far, and even though I don't know what the future holds, I hope I make you proud someday."

Done with the sappy shit, I gripped the phone tight. "By the way, if I don't come home tonight, it's because Grandmama shot and buried me in the backyard since I'm pretty sure I made my girl cry today."

Saying those words...

It made me sick.

"I'm going to hang up in a second, dickhead. But first, I just want to add—be careful on whatever calls you go on tonight, man." Another pause. "Because I sure as hell don't know what I'd do without you. Love you, big brother. Always have. Always will."

I ended the call as a lone tear slid down my cheek.

More than ready to start fixing every mistake I'd made, I stomped on the Jeep's accelerator and held on tight as the engine roared and then rocketed me down the highway toward the Toluca Fairgrounds.

"Please," I mumbled, silently praying to whatever God was listening. "For fuck's sake, please let my girl still be there."

Unfortunately for me, like many that had come before it, my prayer went unanswered.

Chapter Seventeen

ASHLEY

*I*t was half past eleven.

Alone in the dark of the night, I lay on the porch over-hang next to my two-story bedroom window, my eyes fixated on the cloudless, twinkling southern sky.

Exhausted after spending the evening at the fair, my parents plus Lucca were all asleep, and Felix who was working an overnight main-tenance shift at the shelter, had left me in charge of caring for Angel. It was a task that, despite my broken-hearted state, I didn't mind doing one single bit.

Lying at the foot of my bed, curled against a snoring Ziggy, he was sleeping peacefully. The sight made me smile. Not just because they'd bonded the moment they met, but because it seemed as though they were destined to be together.

Like two peas in a pod.

Even though seeing them like that made my heart happy, it also made it hurt too. The pain was straight-up agonizing as images of Chase's smiling face danced in the forefront of my mind, bringing with them a slew of unanswered questions, each more pressing than the last.

Though I hadn't spoken to him since the mall, I had seen him at the fair. The problem was, he didn't see me. Seated atop the Ferris wheel with Clara, I'd been looking down at him as he literally looked everywhere but up.

Once the ride came to a stop, I'd acted like a complete coward and dodged him by scurrying off to talk with Clara's boyfriend, Brantley—who also happened to be Evan's twin brother, as well as my new neighbor—about a part-time job opening at his newly established law firm.

It was a job which I'd secured.

While my parents were proud as could be of me getting hired right off the bat, I was anything but. With the events of the day bearing down on me, I just wanted to crawl into bed and sleep for a week.

Thanks to the toxic-venom Bianca had spewed all over me, combined with the way Chase had acted right before walking away earlier in the day, my head was a mess.

And my heart? It just *hurt*.

As hard as I tried—and trust me, I'd analyzed every word, facial reaction, and past encounter—I couldn't make sense of who was lying and who was telling the truth.

Part of me wanted to believe that Bitchy Bianca was attempting to start trouble, but what would the point of that be? Lies certainly had the potential to tear Chase and me apart before we ever truly got started, but they wouldn't get her the one thing she wanted, which was him.

However, the other part—the anxiety-riddled and damaged one—had trouble believing that everything Chase had said and done since we met was genuine, even if Bianca was spilling half-truths.

The crux of the matter was this—why would a guy like him, want a girl like me, when Bianca was an option?

The truth was, as cruel as she could be, she wasn't screwed up in the ways that I was, and I had no doubt that she could give him things that I couldn't.

Things that all guys craved and needed.

My vision blurred as a wave of fresh tears filled my eyes. I'd once thought that after escaping Dominic, my life would get easier, and for a while, it had.

But now everything was changing.

With my world shifting on its axis once more, I felt myself falling right back into the endless blackness that awaited me.

Only now, I saw no way out.

After witnessing firsthand the peace Chase's mere presence offered my tired soul, he'd quickly become the balm that soothed me. All it took was one look into his eyes, and the storm that raged inside of me would instantly calm, making it easier to breathe.

He'd become my rock-steady.

And without him, I would be lost.

More than ever.

Truth be told, it didn't matter if Bianca had been lying or not. Chase and I simply had no future. Where he was everything beautiful and good, I was corrupted beyond redemption and stained with permanent filth.

No matter how heartbreaking it was to admit, he deserved better than my broken pieces.

And that's all there was to it.

I pushed to my elbows and glanced down at the street below when the low hum of an approaching car's engine reached my ears. Living on a dead-end street meant we never got much traffic, and considering almost every neighboring house was dark, I had no idea who was out and about at this hour.

It was a question I needn't have pondered long.

"What is he doing here?" I whispered, my heart thumping away. Sitting up completely, I watched as Chase, of all people, parked his black Jeep Laredo next to the curb forty yards up the street before killing his lights. "Oh my God, tell me he isn't going to get out."

When he popped open the door a second later and jumped out, I had my answer. But it wasn't until he quickly looked around and then started sprinting directly toward me that I realized exactly what his plans were.

Eyes as big as saucers, I stared, completely dumbfounded, as he cleared the picket fence that lined my front yard in one swift move, followed by my mama's beloved azalea bushes. Crouching low to avoid the motion-sensor lights attached to the front porch, he crept to the far side of the veranda like a ninja and temporarily ducked out of sight.

Completely frozen to the spot where I sat, I waited with bated breath as the flower-covered lattice attached to the side of the house creaked when he began to climb it.

Shoulders tensed, I waited for it to snap right in half since the flimsy piece of wood was meant to support climbing roses, not a full-sized man.

Oh, this is bad...

Really bad.

I exhaled, my heart continuing to jump around in my chest, banging against my ribcage until he pulled himself onto the overhang, less than five feet from where I was, hidden in the shadows.

Terrified that one of my parents might have heard him, I quickly whisper-hissed, "What in the name of sweet baby Jesus are you doing?"

Having not seen me yet, he stumbled back, nearly falling right off the roof.

Twisting to the side, I lunged for him, but luckily he was able to right himself before it was too late.

Finding his balance once more, he smiled, his bright blue eyes gleaming beneath the brim of his ball cap. "Hey, Sweetness," he whispered. "Missed you tonight when you didn't show up at the Ferris wheel."

My eyes narrowed.

He couldn't be serious.

Feeling every bit of anger I'd experienced earlier in the day roar back to life, I climbed to my feet. "Why?" I spat, arms crossed. "Didn't your *girlfriend* keep you company?"

His smile disappeared, but I couldn't tell if it was because he'd been busted or because he was genuinely confused.

154

Unable to stop myself and momentarily not giving a crap if we got busted, I let the vile words that Bianca had aimed my way roll off my tongue, each tasting more poisonous than the last. "What happened, Chase? I thought you and Bianca were supposed to spend *all* night together?"

"Ashley," he started. "Beautiful girl, what—"

Taking a cautious step back, I held my hands up, halting whatever he was about to say. I didn't want to hear it. Not when I couldn't decipher my butt from a hole in the ground, much less a well-rehearsed lie from what was the heart-shattering truth.

"Just *stop*," I snarled. "I don't want to do this with you. Not now and not ever." Pointing toward his Jeep, I thinned my lips. "I'm sorry that you'll lose the bet you made with Ryder, but I think you should leave. Like, right the hell now. Because quite frankly, I don't want to look at you."

His face morphed, but not with anger.

With pain.

"What the fuck are you talking about?" His voice got louder with each word he spoke, and I had no doubt that my dad, who was an extremely light sleeper, would hear him any second.

If that happened, Chase wouldn't have to worry about falling off the roof because my dad would throw him right off, and my mom would probably shoot him on the way down.

Teamwork, y'all...

"Go home, Chase," I said, turning to climb back in my window. "Before you end up with two broken legs and a couple bullet holes courtesy of my parents. Lord knows we certainly wouldn't want to end your football career before it ever truly got off the ground." Bile churned in my belly at what I was about to say next. "Besides, you'll likely need an NFL-sized salary to support Bianca in the future. The girl obviously loves to shop. After all, that's what she was doing at the mall today, right?"

Vision blurry from tears and mad as could be, I knelt down and slid one leg inside my bedroom. "Be careful climbing down," I said.

"Regardless of the situation, I don't want you to fall and get hurt." I glanced at him, meeting his eyes for what would be the last time. "Even if you *did* break what remained of my stupid heart."

Tears clogging my throat, I slipped inside and turned to slam the window shut. But before I could, Chase followed me in, forcing me to stumble back. Standing tall, he towered over me, the expression on his face nothing less than pissed.

Adrenaline surging, I fisted my hands as rancid fear oozed from my pores. "Chase..." The words died on my tongue as the ability to speak at all vanished.

It didn't matter though.

Chase had plenty to say.

"Fuck my legs," he growled, his broad chest swelling from the force of his deep breaths. "And fuck football. "

How could he say that?

Football was his entire future.

I shook my head. "I don't—"

"I know you don't understand," he interrupted, his cheekbones tinged red. "So I'm going to explain it real damned fast."

I blinked, waiting for him to continue.

"I don't know what kind of bullshit Bianca has pulled, but whatever she said is a lie, Ashley. I never made a bet with Ryder, and I sure as hell had no plans to spend the night with that skank."

Of course, he'd say that.

"I know you're probably all twisted up, trying to decide who to believe," he said, reading me perfectly. "But goddammit"—he hooked his thumb and pointed back at himself—"believe me."

I could feel my psyche beginning to splinter, the grip I had on reality rapidly fraying. "Why?" I asked, placing my hands on my hips. "Why should I believe you? Especially after the way you acted this afternoon."

He didn't hesitate before answering. "Because I may be a hot-tempered asshole who doesn't think before he acts at times, but I *never* lie." Closing the space between us, he cupped my face with his strong hands and tilted my head back. I flinched at the sudden move, but my panic didn't spike, much to my surprise. "And because I'm pretty damned sure that I'm falling for you, beautiful girl."

I'm falling for you.

Four little words.

That was all it took for him to steal the oxygen right out of my lungs. "You can't," I wheezed, my voice a ghost of itself. "You just can't."

"I can," he replied softly, his face less than an inch from mine.

"How?"

Wrapping his fingers around my wrist, he gently lifted my hand and placed it over the place where his strumming heart laid. "You feel that?"

I nodded, my pounding heart falling in sync with his. "I feel it," I choked out, my throat tight.

Releasing my wrist, he slid his hand over the back of mine, lacing our fingers together. "I don't believe in love at first sight," he said, hovering his lips over my ear. "But I know soul recognition exists, because the moment I first laid eyes on you, I knew, Ashley."

"You knew what?"

"I knew that you were it for me," he answered, giving me exactly what I needed. "And you will continue to be it until the day I take my final breath."

Legs shaking, I looked into his eyes, my heart and brain going in different directions. I wanted to believe him so badly, but the scars marring my soul burned, an ever-present reminder of the hell I'd endured and the deception I'd so easily fallen victim to before.

The grip my past had on me was unrelenting, preventing me from—

Take the leap, Chiquita. Carmen's voice rang out in my head, loud and clear, as if she were standing right next to me. *Fall, baby. He'll catch you.*

My resistance faded.

Lightheaded as could be and feeling a tad bit faint, I looped my arms around his neck and buried my face in the side of his throat.

"One day," I said, chest heaving. "I think that I could fall for you too. And that scares me. So much."

"Baby..." Bending the slightest bit, Chase wrapped one arm around my back and slipped the other under my knees. Effortlessly lifting me into the air, he turned and started toward my bed.

But then he froze.

I hiccuped, ready to ask him what was wrong, but stopped short of doing so when a low growl rumbled through the room.

"Who the hell is that?" Chase asked, his voice quiet and laced with a hint of fear.

Wrong time to do so or not, I smiled. "That's Ziggy Bear," I replied, my pride-filled eyes locking on my new furbaby. "Dad found him at an out-of-state rescue and adopted him for Lucca and me."

He blinked. "You mind telling him to stand down then? 'Cause right now, he looks like he's two seconds away from making a meal out of me."

He was right.

Teeth bared, Ziggy was crouched down on my bed, his chest protectively covering Angel. With his butt high in the air and his icy blue eyes locked on Chase, he indeed did look ready to pounce.

"Ziggy Bear," I whispered. "It's okay. Now lay down."

He looked at me, then sniffed the air.

Seemingly satisfied with whatever scent he picked up on, he licked his lips and laid back down, nearly squishing poor Angel in the process. Then with a final huff, he rolled over and proceeded to go back to sleep.

Dad was right...

He is crazy.

"Ashley..."

"Yeah?"

"Sweetness, we've gotta talk, but I don't know where to put you. Don't care what you say, that dog looks a helluva lot more like a wolf than a Husky, and I'm man enough to admit that I'm scared he may kill me if I get too close."

Lightness spread through me, washing away the darkness tirelessly working to sweep me under. "Grandmama said he was a polar bear."

Chase's eyes flared. "Could be that too. He's awfully big for a dog."

Fighting to quiet the laughter that spilled from my lips, I fisted the front of his shirt in one of my hands and stared up at him, taking in every inch of his handsome face.

Long as I lived, I'd never tire of looking at him.

Of that, I was sure.

"Hey, Jock," I said, calling him by the nickname I'd stolen from Carissa. "How about you set me down so I can pull on a pair of pants. Then maybe we can sneak back out my window. Because Lord knows if my mom or dad hear us, you're as good as dead."

He quirked a brow. "You're right. We can go sit in the Jeep, that way we can keep an eye out in case your parents wake up." Gently placing my feet back on the floor, he nodded toward my closet. "Make sure you grab a jacket. It's chilly out there."

Nibbling on my lower lip, I eyed the hoodie he wore.

Reading the want written all over my face, he pulled it over his head and handed it over. "Pants, baby," he said as I slipped it over my head, basking in his unique scent. "I may not mind looking at your pretty legs, but I'll be damned if I let anyone else gawk at them. Though I doubt anybody else will be out."

His words warmed me.

Surprisingly enough.

Though they ringed of possessiveness, they didn't alarm me. In fact, they were sort of sweet, and such a stark contrast to the awful things Dominic used to say when referring to me as his property.

The two of them...

They weren't the same.

Not even close.

Finally understanding that, I walked to my closet and promptly pulled on a pair of pants before slipping my feet into my boots.

Then, following the demands my heart made, I didn't give it a second-thought before placing my hand in Chase's.

A second later, we made our escape.
Together.

Chapter Eighteen

CHASE

$\mathscr{I}$ couldn't stop staring at Ashley.

Eyes wet with unshed tears, she clutched my phone tight in her hand. Though she hadn't wanted to, I'd made her scroll through every text and phone call, proving to her that one, I didn't even have Bianca's number and two, we sure as shit never talked.

Then, I explained to her about the phone call from my dad, followed by meeting him on the other side of town. I'd left out most of the details—she didn't need that ugliness in her head—but she still got the gist of what had happened.

My girl was smart like that.

Problem was, everything quickly became too much for her to handle.

Overwhelmed and exhausted, she'd started to shake after declaring that she hoped my father, piece of shit that he was, caught the plague.

As funny as her words had been, seeing her like that, her eyes filled with both hurt and regret, made my blood boil.

I had no idea how I was going to deal with Bianca's trouble-making self once we came face to face again, but I wasn't about to let her walk away unscathed after the shit-storm she'd caused.

Because of her, I'd almost lost the girl who had quickly become my entire universe.

That was unacceptable.

"I'm sorry," my Sweetness whispered, her voice barely audible. "I know I shouldn't have believed anything she said. I just..." Expression riddled with guilt, she turned her head, meeting my gaze. "I don't even understand why you like me."

"Like you?" I replied, chuckling. "Ashley, I'm pretty sure I confessed to falling for you not even thirty minutes ago." Her gaze dipped to the console that rested between us, but I kept talking. "And I'm fairly certain you replied that if I'm lucky, one day you'll fall for me too."

Picking at her chipped black nail-polish, she kept her face down, hiding her pretty features from me. "Want to know a secret?"

"Yeah, Sweetness," I replied without hesitation. "I do."

She looked back up, giving me a glimpse of her gorgeous face. With the moonlight caressing her porcelain skin, she looked hauntingly beautiful. I couldn't get enough of it. "I never knew what love truly felt like until the day I met Carmen and Jade," she whispered, taking me by surprise.

My brows furrowed as I wracked my brain, trying to place those names. I was pretty damned sure I'd never heard her say them before, else I would've remembered since I hung on her every word.

Blowing out a pent-up breath, she continued. "I was fifteen by then. Before them, no one had ever cared."

I didn't understand that shit at all.

How could someone not care about her?

It was impossible not to.

"Tell me about Carmen and Jade, baby," I said, tucking a stray lock of hair behind her ear. "Who were they?"

Averting her gaze, she looked out the windshield once more. Lower lip trembling, she sank back against the leather seat. "They were my best friends," she whispered in reply. "But he took them from me."

Took them?

I didn't fucking get it.

"Who took them?"

Features morphing with agony, she clenched her eyes shut. "Dominic did."

I hated the sound of his name.

Arms wrapped around her middle, she dug her trembling fingers into her sides and bounced her legs up and down, the anxiety that constantly plagued her rushing forward. "Carmen tried to save me from him, and because of that, he made them go away."

Anger skyrocketing over that bit of information, I sunk my teeth into the inside of my cheek in an attempt to keep my rage in check. I didn't know much about this Dominic fucker, but he was lucky that he was locked up in the Georgia State Pen where I couldn't get to him. If he wasn't, I likely would've killed him for all the hurt he'd caused Ashley.

Her torment...

I couldn't stand it.

"So he alienated you from your friends." It wasn't a question, but a statement. "Classic goddamned abuser," I mumbled, the urge to sling-shot my hand into the steering wheel growing with each second that ticked by.

Ashley shook her head and used the sleeve of my hoodie to wipe away her tears. "That's not it at all. He was more than an abuser," she said, pouring salt into the festering wound carved across the front of my heart. "A whole lot more."

Needing to touch her, I reached over and plucked my phone from her hand. After tossing it onto the dash, I slid my palm across hers and twined our fingers together. "You know you can tell me anything, right?" I caressed her knuckles with my thumb, willing her to believe me. "There is nothing you can say that will change the way I feel about you."

"That's where you're wrong," she whispered, her hand shaking. "I have so many secrets. Most of which would make you run screaming in the opposite direction. There is no doubt in my mind that if you knew even a handful of the sins that I carry inside here"—she lightly tapped her chest—"you'd never speak to me again."

Not a chance in hell.

I didn't care what all she'd been through or how scarred she was, in the end, she would always be my Sweetness. Besides, who the hell was I to judge? I had more issues than Playboy.

Wanting to prove to her that she was wrong, I gave her hand a slight squeeze. "Try me. Tell me something, one of your darkest secrets, and watch it not change a thing."

As closed off and guarded as she could be about her past, I didn't expect her to reveal a single secret.

Imagine my surprise when she did.

Turning her face to meet mine once more, she whispered, "I was only nine. Just a little girl."

I swallowed and schooled my expression, fighting like hell to appear calm despite feeling anything but. "What happened when you were nine?"

"That's when I was raped for the first time."

Raped.

First time.

The words echoed through my head, sending me into one helluva tailspin.

Out of everything she could've told me, I never expected that.

With the vein in my temple pulsating with each beat of my heart, I fisted my free hand, squeezing it tight. "Baby..." My voice was distorted and staticky, almost alien sounding. "Who?"

Two words.

That's all I could manage.

"I can't recall his name. I must have blocked it out I guess," she replied, her wounded eyes staring into mine. "Just like I don't remember what he looked like. But you can bet that I remember the way his skin reeked of sour sweat and stale cigarettes." Dropping her head back, she exhaled. "It's always the smell that stays with you. That and the pain."

I shifted in my seat. "How'd it happen?"

A smile, one of anguish and not happiness, curved her lips. "He was my mother's landlord." Jesus Christ. "One month, after blowing her disability check on powder and booze, she didn't have a way to pay him." She paused. "So I became the payment."

Silence reigned between us.

Even though I had a million things I wanted to say, none of them comforting, I kept my mouth shut, afraid that if I let a single syllable slip out, I'd word vomit a verbal tirade of epic proportions.

That wasn't what Ashley needed right now.

No, the only thing she did need was my arms wrapped around her, which was something I intended to give her.

Twisting at the waist, I scooped her up into my arms. Settling sideways on my lap, she leaned against me, burying her face in my neck on her own accord.

Holding her as tight as I could without cracking her ribs, I gently rocked her back and forth, moving as much as the seat would allow. "I'm so fucking sorry," I said, running my fingers through her silky hair. "You didn't deserve that shit. No child does."

"No," she said as her tears wet my skin. "They don't. But as horrible as it was to endure, and as much as it still hurts to this day, I've always been glad it was me in a twisted sort of way."

A helluva lot confused, I jerked my head back, wanting to see her face. "What?"

"I know it probably sounds sick, but it's how I've always dealt with the things that life has thrown at me," she replied, fisting the front of my shirt in her hands. "By knowing that the monsters weren't hurting anyone else as long as they were busy stealing what I didn't freely give, then I could cope because I felt like I was saving others. I know it makes me sound deluded, but I sort of thought I was a superhero, taking the pain so other little girls, ones just like me, wouldn't have to."

At her confession, a piece of me broke.

To this day, it's never healed.

Doubt it ever will.

Unashamed by the tears that filled my eyes, I didn't bother to wipe them away as they fell. Instead, I concentrated on Ashley's pain versus my own and slid my hands into her hair. "You said they. Meaning there was more than one." She trembled harder. "Was the second monster Dominic?"

Gripping my shirt tight, she shook her head.

And just like that, another piece snapped.

Completely shattered.

"Who was it, baby?"

"Ricky," she replied, her wide stare vacant. "He was my mother's boyfriend and he..." Shaking her head, she arched her back, shoulders quaking. "I tried to tell her what he'd done, but she didn't believe me. Instead of taking my side like she should've, she called me a whore and said I was trying to take him from her. Then she kicked me out."

I may not have known the slightest thing about Ashley's mother, other than what she'd just told me anyway, but I hoped I never ran into her.

As I've said before, I'd never hit a woman, not even a low-life bitch like the one who birthed my Sweetness, but I wouldn't think twice before pointing Grandmama or Shelby in her direction.

I'm not even trying to be funny.

Though Shelby hadn't given birth to Ashley, she loved her just as much as she loved Lucca.

As for Grandmama? She'd go straight-up nuclear if she found out what all Ashley had been through at the hands of the one person who was supposed to love and protect her.

Hell, so would Pop, Shelby's father.

Matter-of-fact, her entire family would.

Mine too.

Ty didn't know Ashley, not really, but he'd blow a gasket if he ever caught wind of the horrific details I was being told. And Christ, I didn't want to think about what Heidi would do. She and Carissa both loved Ashley, but Heidi was a whole lot more confrontational.

She wasn't crazy by any means—not like Shelby—but when it came to my girl, she'd come out swinging.

Of that, I had no doubt.

"Tell me." Releasing my shirt, she cupped my cheeks with her frigid palms. "Tell me you don't look at me any differently now."

"Ashley, I—"

"Chase, please," she cried, working herself into hysterics. "I need you to tell me that you still see *me* and not the little girl who was raped because her mother cared more about getting high than she did her own baby."

That's when I lost it.

Placing my hands on her waist, I lifted and turned her the slightest bit, forcing her to straddle my lap.

Taken by surprise, she gasped, her eyes flaring for the briefest moment. Quickly grabbing my shoulders, she clutched me tight while steadying herself.

Then she dropped her gaze.

But I wasn't having it.

Slipping my index finger under her chin, I tilted her head back. "Give me your eyes," I demanded. "Now."

When she did as told, I cupped her cheek with one hand "I'm about to say something, Sweetness, and I want you to listen to every word I speak. Then, I want you to let each of them sink in until you never doubt me again. Got it?"

Wide eyes locked on me, she nodded. "I've got it."

More than ready to make her understand, I quickly continued. "The only thing that I see when I look at you is a girl who's crawled through hell and come out the other side a warrior. And baby, what those men did to you, and what your mama allowed them to do—that's not on you. Those are their sins, and theirs alone, to bear."

"But there's more," she said between gasps for breath. "So much more."

Without realizing what she was doing, she lifted her arm and covered her tattooed wrist with her hand, gently massaging it. It wasn't the first time I'd seen her do it, and though I didn't have the slightest clue about the meaning behind the tat, it was obvious that it meant a helluva lot to her.

"You can tell me anything, Ashley. No matter what time of the day or night, I'll always be here to listen. And *nothing* you say will change the way I feel about you."

Covering her hand with mine, I licked my lower lip. "Having said that, you want to tell me about this?" I asked, gesturing toward her wrist.

She froze, her body stilling.

"If not—"

I snapped my mouth closed when she pulled her hand away, revealing the design which consisted of the letter A plus a small heart.

Elegant and simple, it fit her perfectly.

Sniffling, she took a shaky breath and traced her fingertip along the black ink. "One day I'll tell you," she whispered. "But not today."

I was fine with that.

But little did my girl know, the day she spoke of was quickly approaching, and when it arrived, one of her deepest buried secrets would rise to the surface, bringing with it an endless stream of pain. And when that happened, I would do the only thing I could to help her.

I'd carry her through it.

Chapter Nineteen

ASHLEY

A week had passed since our missed fair date.

While I was still a tad bit upset about letting the events that happened that day steal my happiness, along with what could've been a handful of great memories, a couple of good things had come from it all.

First, Bitchy Bianca was now a thing of the past thanks to Chase putting her in her place in front of nearly the entire school. Not only did he call her out for the lies she told, but he made sure to let everyone know exactly how delusional she was when it came to their supposed relationship.

After the confrontation, she'd run out of the school cafeteria in tears, something that usually would've hurt my heart to see, but she had it coming. The girl was nothing but a bully, and though I knew I likely hadn't been her first victim, I'd prayed I would be her last.

Second, after confessing two of my most shameful secrets to Chase, I felt lighter. Not only because I cleansed them from my soul, but because he hadn't seen me as a victim like I feared.

Instead, he'd seen me as a survivor.

And that meant the world to me.

Part of me wished I could tell him everything else, but that wasn't a possibility. If he learned the things I'd been forced to do while under Dominic's control, I feared he truly would walk away.

It was one thing to be a victim. It was another to be what some would view as a willing participant.

And although I hadn't agreed to the horrible acts *el diablo* made me perform under the threat of death, plenty of people would have placed the blame on me.

She wasn't a child.

She could have walked away.

She could have gotten help.

She could have said no.

While I didn't want to believe that Chase would be one of *those* people, the victim shamers, I couldn't be sure.

I mean, he hadn't seemed like one when I'd confessed about the awful things that happened to me back in Kentucky, but people viewed child rape and prostitution differently, even if the latter was still conducted without the consent of the victim.

It was a hot-button issue, and one I was passionate about.

For obvious reasons.

Which, speaking of consent...

I was moments away from making a decision regarding how I wanted to be touched, a first for me. My body, my choice, for the first time in my life.

Needless to say, I was a ball of frickin' nerves.

Stomach twisted in a thousand knots, I stood next to my closet door and stared at Chase, who was laying on my bed, his fingers laced behind his head. Sculpted biceps on full display, just looking at him made me ache in places I'd never ached before.

"Chase," I mumbled, fidgeting in place. "Is it okay if I try something?"

Pulling his attention from the black and white documentary that played on the small TV sitting atop my dresser, he quirked a brow. "What do you want to try?"

Feeling like I may faint at any moment, I bit my bottom lip, not knowing how he would react to what I intended to do next. But with my parents, Felix, and Lucca all out of the house, I needed to get a move on if I wanted to conquer the first of many demons blocking my way to finding the path to healing.

Be brave, I told myself.

You can handle this.

It's just Chase.

No one else.

"I want to try and touch you."

That got his attention.

Slowly removing his hands from behind his head, he wordlessly crooked a single finger, beckoning me closer.

Nervous as could be, I nodded and headed his way. Reaching the bed, I stopped. "Can you"—I pointed to his hands—"I mean, will you put those back behind your head?"

It was a request he obliged.

Glancing at my door to make sure the lock was engaged—it was—I pulled in a deep breath and summoned every ounce of courage I harbored inside me.

Then, with my heart beating double-time, I pinched the hem of the blue dress that I wore and ripped it over my head, leaving me in nothing but a simple pair of white panties.

Eyes locked with mine, Chase didn't drop his gaze, an action I thought he'd immediately take. "Ashley," he said, jaw clenched. "Tell me I can look at you."

His words, combined with his deep baritone made my toes curl, while the simple fact that he'd asked for my permission before looking went straight to my heart, making it swell.

Fighting the urge to cover my bare breasts with my hands, I replied, "I want you to look at me. Chase, please, I—"

Burning up, my words died on my lips as his sweltering gaze raked across my chest, sending the butterflies that lived in my belly into a frenzy. Swallowing, I stood straighter, a hint of desire working its way through me as his eyes glazed over right before mine. Feeling a little bit lost and a whole lot foolish, I forced a shaky smile.

"I don't know what to do," I whispered, the plan I'd made and meticulously gone over at least a hundred times quickly going to hell in a handbasket. "I had this all worked out in my head and now..."

"Sweetness." I watched with rapt attention as he raised his hands in the air, keeping them in full view as he sat up, his eyes hooded with undeniable desire. "Let me take the lead on this."

Unsure, I took a small step back.

"I won't hurt you," he continued, his smooth voice caressing my silky skin. "I'd die a thousand painful deaths first."

Call me foolish, call me hopelessly naïve, call me whatever, but I believed him.

God help me, I did.

"Chase..."

"I'm right here, beautiful girl," he said, his chest expanding and then deflating. "Not going anywhere, either."

I didn't doubt him.

Not for a single second.

Pushing my bangs from my eyes, I climbed onto the bed, kneeling next to his hip. Unsure what to do with my hands, I rested them on my thighs. "Can you take your shirt off?"

Fisting the cotton material behind his neck, he ripped it off in one smooth move, bearing his upper body to me for the first time.

Hard pecs and defined abs...

It was all I saw.

Feeling heat build in my core, I shifted in place, moving my hips from one side to the other. "Can I touch you?" The words tumbled from my lips effortlessly, surprising me. I'd expected to be scared and filled to the brim with trepidation.

But I wasn't.

The only thing I felt was anxious.

That was normal, right?

Gently wrapping his fingers around my right wrist, Chase placed my hand on the left side of his chest, directly above his galloping heart. Its strong rhythm bled into my palm, helping to calm my ever-present anxiety.

"Ashley, baby, tell me that I can touch you," he said, mirroring the words I'd spoken moments before. "Because unless you say yes, my hands are staying right where they are."

My throat clogged with emotion.

Though he knew a small blip of the ugliness that comprised my past, he'd never understand how much those words meant to *me*, a girl who'd never been given a choice.

Voice completely lost, I couldn't answer.

So, instead, I chose to give him permission in another way, one that made me feel empowered and beautiful, both feelings that were new to me.

Raising up the slightest bit, I swung my right leg over his hips and climbed on top of him, straddling his waist. A gasp—one of shock and a small amount of fear—spilled from my lips when my center bumped the hard-as-steel erection lining his sweats.

"Ignore it," he said, teeth gritted. "Crazy fucker has a mind of its own."

The short burst of laughter that tumbled out of me quickly turned to a low moan when he adjusted his hips, bouncing me the slightest bit in return.

It was such a small move, but one that gave me my first taste of something other than pain.

Out of all the times my body had been forced to accept another, I'd never felt anything close to pleasure. But with just one unintentional twist of his hips, Chase had given me a hint of the ecstasy to come.

An ecstasy that only he could give me.

"Tell me what you need," he said, his voice quiet. "I'll only do what you want."

"Promise?" I asked between shaky breaths.

"I swear it."

Removing my hand from his chest, I straightened. "Kiss me."

Wasting no time, he sat up straight, pressing his chest to mine. I hissed, the small contact burning my skin.

"Want me to stop?"

I shook my head, knowing I needed to work through the pain and agonizing memories that were beginning to stir. "Just don't close your eyes." It was such a silly-sounding request but one that I desperately needed. "It keeps them away."

My voice cracked as the past fought to rush forward.

"Who, Ashley?"

Shaky hands cupping his handsome face, I moved my lips closer to his. "The demons," I replied honestly. "When you look at me it makes them go away."

Arms wrapped around me, he trailed his fingertips down my spine, making my back arch. "Then I'll never look away. Not until we vanquish every last one."

With each word, he chipped away the walls surrounding my heart. Before long, there would be nothing left to protect me from falling irrevocably head over heels in love with him.

Done with the space between us, I touched my lips to his, stealing a kiss. Hungry for more than sweet and simple, I ran my tongue along the seam of his mouth.

I gasped when he nipped my bottom lip in return.

Using the opening I'd handed him, he slipped his tongue inside, sliding it against mine. His taste—a mixture of coffee and chocolate—invaded my mouth, searing its way into my memory forever.

A small moan—the second—escaped me as lust built inside me for the first time, causing the pain I'd felt the moment his chest touched mine to fade into the background.

Eyes locked with mine, he slid his hands up my sides, ghosting his fingertips over my ribs, leaving a trail of chill bumps in his wake.

I melted.

Breaking our connection, I cupped his shoulders, digging my nails into his tanned skin. "I need more." I paused. "Just not... just not all of it."

Making sense of the riddle I'd spoken, he nodded. "I'm going to put you on your back. That okay?"

Though fear climbed in my throat, tightening an invisible band around my larynx, I nodded. "Just don't—"

"I won't look away," he said, finishing what I'd started to say. "Not now, and not ever."

I held on tight as he flipped our positions, pressing my back into the mattress. Hovering over me, he spread my legs wide, slipping his lean hips between them. "This okay?"

No.

No, it wasn't.

But not for the reason that one might think.

Having him above me, his gentle touch caressing my skin was nearly my undoing. I needed more of it, needed more of him. "Touch me," I demanded, running my hands down his arms, memorizing every dip and curve of his muscles. "Anywhere."

It was a scary thing for me to say, but again, this was Chase.

He wouldn't hurt me, and if I said stop, he would *stop*.

He wasn't a monster.

He wasn't a demon.

And he wasn't *el diablo*.

Simply put, he was mine.

And I wanted to keep him.

Forever.

Sitting up, he wasted no time before hooking his fingers into the sides of my panties. Gaze never leaving mine, he gave them a slight tug, slipping them no more than an inch down my smooth thighs. "You sure you want this?"

"Yes."

One simple word.

That was all it took.

Pulling my panties free of my body, he tossed them to the floor next to my bed. A moment of doubt crept in, bringing with it panic and shame, but Chase quickly squashed all three when he looked down at my naked breasts, followed by my glistening flesh.

Gazes locking once again, he palmed the outside of my thighs. "You're exquisite, Ashley," he whispered. "Everywhere."

That's when the first tear fell.

Crooking my finger like he'd done minutes before, I silently demanded he come closer.

Lips parted, he did as I asked and blanketed my body with his.

Hooking my legs around his hips, I twined my arms around his back, anchoring myself to him completely.

Then, I kissed him once more.

Mouths fastened together, his hands slipped beneath me, cupping my bottom. Holding me tight, he broke our kiss, ripping his lips from mine.

I whimpered as he pushed to his elbows, putting inches of space between his. "I need to see you, Sweetness," he said, lowering his hips. "If you need me to stop, then tell me."

I nodded, not knowing what he would do next.

Holding my breath, I waited as he shifted in place.

But that same breath quickly left my body when he lowered his hips, grinding his impossibly large—seriously, it felt huge—sweatpants-covered erection along the seam of my bare center making me jerk, then moan.

"Chase," I cried out, clutching his triceps as he did it again, effortlessly sending bolts of pleasure through my body. "Please"—I lifted my head, looking down at the place where his body touched mine —"don't stop."

A bead of sweat fell from his temple, landing on my cheek. "I'll never fucking stop."

And he didn't.

Keeping his gorgeous eyes on mine, he continued to move, carrying me to a place I'd never been to. One where pain didn't exist, and pleasure consumed you, down to the very essence of your soul.

Feeling close to bursting at the seams, I moaned, tightening my legs like a vice, refusing to let him leave me. Not that he would've. Lost in the moment just as much as I, his pace increased. Muscles bunching beneath my sweaty palms, he groaned. Then, "Goddammit, baby, I can't keep this up."

Knowing exactly what he meant, I arched my back, the pressure building in my core about to explode. "I need..."

The words wouldn't come.

Mainly because I didn't know what I needed.

I wasn't a virgin—not even close—but all of this was still new to me.

Thankfully, my guy knew exactly what to do.

Shifting his hips without losing our connection, he lifted my hips, grinding down on me harder and hitting a place that I desperately needed him to stroke. "I'm not stopping until you—"

My mind blanked, my hearing dulled, and I swear to the heavens above that my soul completely left my body a second later when something deep inside me imploded.

Pleasure so intense I could hardly breathe ripped through me, electrifying every nerve in my body as my core convulsed, clenching and releasing, over and over.

Above me, Chase tensed.

Dropping down, he hovered his chest over mine as he rode me harder than before, stealing every ounce of pleasure from me he could and prolonging the waves of ecstasy that washed over me, pushing every dark thought back to where they belonged, deep into the abyss.

"Fuck, Ashley!" he jerked, his erection twitching as he followed me into oblivion, a place where only he and I existed, our twined souls holding each other tight.

Hearts beating in sync and panting for breath, our lips met once more.

Seconds ticked by.

Minutes passed.

Then, when he finally broke the kiss, he touched his forehead to mine and cupped my face. "Sweetness," he said, still out of breath. "What you just gave me... like you, I'll treasure it forever."

A smile tipped my lips as a single tear slid down my cheek. "Does this mean you're planning on keeping me?"

"Forever, Ashley," he replied, stroking my cheeks with his thumbs. "And not a minute less."

Forever.

It was the sweetest promise he'd ever made.

And one he fought to keep.

Chapter Twenty

CHASE

hank Christ for my gym bag.

The lone thought tumbled through my head as I dug through the black bag I'd retrieved from the back of my Jeep minutes earlier.

With the grey sweats I'd worn to Ashley's house now stained with come—hers and mine—I needed to change.

Else Shelby would kill me the minute she got back from wherever it was that she went after dropping Lucca off with Hendrix and Maddie. And Christ, if Moretti found out, I'd probably end up in lockup with a large man named Tiny.

Not even joking.

What we'd done...

It was the last thing I was expecting after I drove Ashley home from work and followed her upstairs to her room, where we planned to do homework after she changed. But when she stepped out of her closet wearing that loose but short dress, my mind went into free fall.

As for when she asked me to touch her...

Well, there's no damned way I could've said no.

Don't get me wrong, I was in no rush to have sex with her—I knew she wasn't ready—but I still wanted to show her that I could be gentle and make her feel good without hurting her just as the pieces of shit who came before me had.

'Cause let's be real here.

I would literally put a bullet in my own head before I took something that she wasn't ready to give. That just wasn't how I operated. Deep down, I think Ashley knew that too.

But I still needed to prove it.

As my big brother always said...

Actions are what counts.

Words don't mean shit.

"Brought you this," Ashley said, pulling me from my thoughts. Twirling a cold bottle of water in the air, she walked into the room, looking more beautiful than I'd ever seen her.

Eyes alight with happiness and cheeks tinged pink thanks to the orgasm I'd given her, she was breathtaking.

"Thanks, Sweetness," I said, taking the bottle from her hand.

Laying it on her bed, I pulled a fresh pair of pants, along with briefs—because, fuck boxers—from my bag.

Ashley looked from the clothes in my hand to the front of my soiled sweats. Eyes flaring, she ducked her head, a hint of a smile playing on her lips. "Uh," she said, looking toward her door. "I'll give you some privacy."

Was she kidding me?

She'd already felt my cock through my pants, I didn't care if she saw it. Especially since I didn't have anything to be ashamed of. Not trying to sound conceited or vain—I've never been either—but I had a body most women drooled over, and my cock sure as hell wasn't small.

"Baby, stay. I don't have—"

She jumped in place when the front door opened, then slammed shut.

Oh fuck.

"Oh my God," she squeaked, shaking her hands in front of her. "She's back early." Eyes wide, she looked at my pants one last time. "Hurry up and change!" Pointing toward the door, she added, "I'm going downstairs to intercept her. That's the only way you're making it out of this alive."

Without another word, she took off.

Knowing she was right, I quickly zipped my bag and tossed it in her closet, hiding it in case Shelby did come upstairs.

Then, I moved my ass and changed clothes faster than the speed of light. But being the idiot that I am, I haphazardly tossed my dirty clothes in the same direction as my bag, not bothering to shove them in it.

However, I did have the good sense—yeah right—to straighten Ashley's bed, which she normally kept in tip-top shape just like the rest of her room.

I'd only gotten glimpses into her past before Anthony and Shelby took her in, but it was obvious that she cherished and cared for every little thing they'd given her. She even kept a blind duster next to her window.

Who the hell dusted their blinds regularly?

Definitely not Ty and me.

Then again, we didn't even own a blind duster.

Shaking my head, I pulled on my discarded shirt, covering the scratch marks running the length of my back and turned, heading out of the room. I'd only made it five steps down the hall when a giant ball of white fluff suddenly appeared, his icy blue eyes boring into my own. Beside him stood a long-haired cat, his mesmerizing tail flicking from one side to the other.

One looked ready to eat me while the other looked like it just wanted a nap. Hell, I didn't blame the cat. If I was him, I'd sleep all day too.

Stock-still, I lifted my right hand. "Alright, fur butt one and two," I said, pointing from Ziggy to Angel. "I'm not robbing the place, I'm not hurting your family, and I don't have enough fat on me to be tasty, so there's no reason for you to eat me." I quirked a brow. "Got it?"

Angel answered by yawning.

But Ziggy, that damned dog, he huffed.

It was obvious he didn't like me, though I had no idea why. Well, actually, I did. "Listen to me you overgrown marshmallow. She was *mine* first." The dickhead growled in response, but I wasn't backing down. Pointing at myself, I repeated, "Mine. Not yours. And if you think—"

I snapped my mouth shut when the front door banged once again. Whether it was from being yanked open or slammed shut, I didn't know. Then, I heard people, definitely more than just Shelby and Ashley, moving around.

Christ, had Shelby called Grandmama to come help kill me?

I sure as hell hoped not.

I could handle one of them at a time—maybe—but not both at once.

Shit...

Slowly moving past Cujo and his sidekick, I inched toward the stairs, straining to hear what was happening on the bottom floor.

Voices, ones I couldn't decipher, floated through the air, but I couldn't understand a word being said.

But then I picked up something that made the hair on the back of my neck stand on end.

Ashley crying.

No, Ashley sobbing.

Followed by, "She's beautiful."

No longer caring if Shelby or anyone else was waiting downstairs to murder me in cold blood, I moved. Taking the steps three at a time, I reached the bottom in no time. Racing through the foyer, I came to a sliding stop at the entrance to the living room where everyone— Ashley, Clara, Evan, Grandmama, Shelby, and a woman I didn't recognize—all gathered, along with one other person.

And that person? It was a baby.

An itty bitty one.

Hidden from everyone but Evan's view, I had no idea what was going on, but one look at my girl's face and the brokenness gleaming in her eyes as she gazed at the little bundle Shelby held securely in her arms, and I knew that she was moments away from falling apart.

Within hours, that's exactly what she did.

———

My chest was cracking wide open.

Sitting in the middle of the sofa, I stared at Ashley, who sat across from me in a wooden rocking chair, holding the baby from before in her arms. Gently rocking back and forth, she ran a knuckle down the side of the little girl's face.

A little girl who'd just become her new foster sister.

And if Anthony and Shelby had their say, Gracie, that was the baby's name, would *permanently* become her sister.

Abandoned via the Georgia Safe Haven law mere days before, she had instantly become a ward of the state, and according to the social worker whom I'd seen earlier, she'd be available for adoption immediately.

As her new foster family, the Moretti's got first dibs.

That was great and all—hell, more than great—but something was going on with Ashley, and it wasn't sitting right with me. Honestly, I was surprised Anthony and Shelby hadn't picked up on the shift in her demeanor.

Couldn't really blame them though.

With everything happening, it was easy to miss stuff. But I never missed anything, not when it came to my girl. Every pain-laced word, every fresh tear, every forced smile...

I noticed it all.

"Sweetness," I whispered, not wanting to wake the baby. "Talk to me."

Swallowing, she glanced around the room, finding it empty of everyone but me. Wanting to give her time to bond with Gracie, Anthony, Shelby, and Lucca had all reluctantly gone upstairs for a bit, giving her the space they knew she needed.

"She's beautiful, isn't she?" she asked, sniffling.

Leaning forward, I nodded. "Yeah, she is. Prettiest baby I've seen in a while." Knowing it was better to just ask the question that burned the tip of my tongue instead of beating around the bush, I tapped my knuckles on the coffee table in front of me and blew out a breath.

"Beautiful girl, I need you to tell me what's wrong." Her brow furrowed, but she said nothing. "If I don't know what's broken, I can't fix it."

My words were her tipping point.

Shaking her head, she clutched Gracie tight as she started to cry. The pain on her face, combined with the agony that I witnessed flooding her eyes was enough to make my chest tighten so hard I could barely breathe.

"You can't fix it," she cried, fighting to stay quiet. "Nobody can."

Bullshit.

I'd crawl through hell if I needed to in order to stop her heart from breaking. I couldn't stand to see her hurt. Given the option, I would've taken every ounce of trauma, torment, and whatever else from her and suffer through it myself if it meant she was free of it all.

And that's no lie.

"I *can* fix it," I fired back, my tone harsher than I intended. "I just need you—"

I ceased speaking when she turned her wrist the slightest bit and glanced down at her ink, her tear-laden eyes filling with an emotion akin to grief. "You don't understand."

She was right, I didn't. "Then make me. All you have to do is talk to me. I know it's your default, but you have to stop bottling shit up. If you don't, it's going to tear you to pieces."

Her eyes met mine when she looked up. "I'm already in pieces," she said, shaking her head. "And I'll never be whole again. Not without her."

Her...

I had no idea who her was.

But I was about to find out.

Heart pounding, I tensed my shoulders, preparing for the verbal chest punch I knew was coming. "Who was she?" My question was met with silence, so I pushed harder. "Whoever she was, Ashley, she deserves to have her name spoken."

I was spouting pure horseshit.

I didn't know if the person she was referring to was worth

mentioning or not. The only thing I did know was that she obviously mattered to Ashley, and therefore she mattered to me.

"Sweetness, talk—"

"Her name was *Addie*," she said, her face twisting as she sunk down into the chair, holding onto Gracie with everything she had. "And she was the most beautiful baby in the world."

Blood running cold, I stood. "Who was Addie?"

It was a question I wasn't prepared to hear the answer to.

Not in the least.

She started to stand, but then crumpled, sliding to the floor in front of the rocking chair. I rushed to her, terrified she'd drop the baby, but she didn't. A bomb could have gone off, and she wouldn't have let Gracie go.

Dropping to my knees beside her, I scooped her and Gracie up into my arms. Standing, I carried them back to the couch where I held onto both girls—one big, one tiny—with all my might.

Resting my chin on the crown of Ashley's head, I repeated the same question from moments before. "Who was Addie?"

Knowing her answer would rock me, I braced myself for the impact her words would have.

Then, between sobs, my girl gave me the answer I sought. "Addie was my baby," she said, quiet as could be. "And I loved her with my whole heart."

My Sweetness was a mother.

She had a baby.

A little girl.

"Where is she?"

Silent sob after silent sob jerked her body. "Because of him, she's gone now too," she whispered, every ounce of pain she felt bleeding into her voice. "Forever."

At that, my heart shattered.

———

"Please don't tell..."

Ashley's whispered words were like a dart to my heart as we stood in her dark backyard, staring through the French doors that led to the kitchen where the rest of her family sat, each of them taking turns holding baby Gracie.

"Chase, please," she begged, nearing the edge of a second breakdown. "No one can know."

I didn't understand that.

At all.

"Why? Ashley, if you're worried about someone judging you, you don't have to—"

Slamming her eyes shut, she started to rub her tattoo. "It's not about people judging me," she said, her tone holding a bite. "It's about not slicing open scarred wounds when doing so won't do anything but hurt me worse than I already am. Addie was my baby"—hooking her thumb, she pointed at her chest—"*mine.*"

Pausing, she took a breath.

"You may think you know what I went through at the hands of Dominic, but you don't have a clue." Shaking her head, she crossed her arms and took a step back. "No one does, and it needs to stay that way."

She was right.

I didn't know what she'd suffered through.

But I intended to find out.

Knowing that she wouldn't straight up tell me any of the stuff he'd done—well, no more than I'd already figured out—I asked, "What did he go to prison for?"

Gathering her long hair atop her head, she secured it in a messy bun, giving me a clear view of her beautiful face. "A lot of things. Possession of a firearm by a felon, drug trafficking, assault, attempted kidnapping."

My spine snapped straight. "Attempted kidnapping?"

What. In. The. Absolute. Fuck!

My girl nodded. "Here's a fun story for you in case you haven't already heard it." I had a feeling this story wouldn't be fun at all. "After I managed to get away from him, I ran to the shelter for help.

It's how I met my mama."

A small smile graced her lips, easing some of my tension. "But Dominic found me and tried to take me back by force. Luckily for me, the Mominator saved me"—her smile grew—"again."

Well, hell...

"And my dad got the honor of arresting Dominic. You know, after he slammed his face into the concrete a time or two."

That earned a laugh from me.

But any amusement I felt quickly died when Ashley's face dropped once more, her unending torment returning full force. "My dad keeps tabs on him. He knows about every infraction he receives, is notified each time he changes cells, and even shows up at any court appearances he has, whether they have anything to do with me or not."

That wasn't surprising.

Most men were overprotective of their daughters, but Anthony took it to a whole new level. Didn't blame him though. If I ever had a little girl, especially one as sweet and perfect as Ashley, I'd move Heaven and Earth to keep her safe.

"You sure he doesn't know about Addie?"

She flinched, her heartbreak visible. "It's not possible. There's no record of me giving birth to her because I never went to a hospital."

Her tears returned, cascading unchecked down her face. Unable to stand it, I wrapped my arms around her and pulled her into my chest, hugging her tightly. "Keep talking, beautiful girl. I'm listening."

She nodded against me, grasping my shirt in her hands. "She was beautiful, Chase. Tiny but with a head full of dark hair."

Entire body trembling, I knew she wouldn't be able to keep this up much longer. Seconds away from falling apart once again, she was barely hanging on.

"I only got to nurse her once," she said, giving me most of her weight. I took it, holding her up when she couldn't do it herself. Like I always promised I would. "I didn't know what I was doing, but I tried so hard because even if it only lasted for a second, I wanted to be a good mama to her."

"You were," I assured her. "I know you were."

Feeling her begin to fall, I reached down and scooped her up into my arms like I'd done many times before and held her against my chest. Unfocused eyes looking at the sky, her head lulled back as she stared off into the distance, her strength wholly depleted.

"But none of that matters because now she's gone, and the only thing I have to remember her by are a handful of memories and a cheap tattoo."

"Ashley," I said, my voice unsteady. "Sweetness, what happened to her? I know you said she's gone, but—"

"Please don't make me say it," she interrupted, doing her best to turn in my arms. "Not today."

I couldn't force her to say a thing.

Especially not when she was this hurt.

And goddammit, she was *hurt*.

Pressing her face against me, she clutched my shirt once more, her white-knuckled grip nearly tearing the fabric. "Don't let go, Chase," she begged, trying to get as close as possible. "If you do, I'm afraid I may break."

That wasn't an option.

So, I did as she asked.

And for over two years, I didn't let go.

Through the constant nightmares, soul-shattering panic attacks, and heart-wrenching tears, I held her, I loved her, and I kept her secret.

But it didn't matter.

Because in the end, her demons still won.

Part Three

FROM HERE WE FALL

"Sometimes the darkness lives inside you, and sometimes it wins."

— Alexandra Bracken

Chapter Twenty-One

ASHLEY

Two Years Later

He'll be here soon...

I stood next to the brightly lit Ferris wheel amid the Toluca County Fairgrounds. Anxious as could be, I fidgeted in place, the yellow sundress I wore twirling around my thighs with each of my movements as I waited for Chase to show.

Twenty-two lonely days had passed since I last saw him, and I was ready to burst right out of my skin. Busy with conditioning camp at Charleston Southern, he hadn't been able to make the hour and a half commute home like he normally did every weekend.

I'd wanted to drive up and see him, if only for a second, but we both agreed it was an idea guaranteed to backfire. Hearts and souls entwined, there was no doubt in either of our minds that once our gazes locked, he'd blow off every responsibility he had at CSU in favor of spending time with me.

That wasn't an option.

With less than a year to go until he officially announced that he was foregoing his senior year in favor of entering the NFL draft, stepping out of line now would be both detrimental and foolish.

He'd worked so hard.

I couldn't let him throw it all away.

Even if waiting to see him did suck.

Like, majorly.

But luckily for me, I'd been able to keep busy. Between taking classes at the community college, working full-time at Morgan Law Firm—the same job I was offered two years before in almost the exact same spot—and volunteering at the shelter on weekends, I had plenty on my plate.

Plus, I had my family.

I had my friends.

And I had my crazy dog.

Each of them made the wait for Chase's return that much more tolerable. Between my nutty overprotective parents, my hyper little brother, and my sweet as pie little sister, there was never a dull moment around the Moretti house.

And don't even get me started on Felix and Angel.

Completely blind, Angel knew his way around the house just fine, but even if he hadn't, it wouldn't have mattered. Felix, bless his heart, carried him everywhere. He and Gracie—whose adoption was finalized over a year before—took Angel and Ziggy on walks every night.

Ziggy pranced around on a leash.

But Angel? He rode in a babydoll stroller.

It was frickin' adorable.

And let's not forget Grandmama.

Crazy as ever, she always kept things interesting.

Between zipping around town in the pink Cadillac convertible Brantley had bought her as a thank you gift for setting him up with Clara, and meddling in everyone's business, she was always on the go. The woman may have been in her eighties, but she had more energy than I did at twenty.

It was complete insanity.

But it was Grandmama so what—

My thoughts were suddenly lost when the hair on the back of my neck stood on end and an eerie awareness washed over me, one which I only felt when my guy was near.

Yes, *my* guy.

Though we still weren't officially boyfriend and girlfriend—I had issues, y'all—we still belonged to each other without question. We had since the very beginning, but it had taken me almost two years to reach the point where I found the courage to start breaking down every wall I'd constructed.

It was a work in progress, much like the Sistine Chapel. It was a labor-intensive, slow, methodical process. Nothing about it had been easy. But I was hoping for a beautiful outcome.

As hard as I fought, my demons pulled me in one direction, while Chase pulled me in the other, trapping me in a constant game of tug-of-war. But thanks to the family who chose to love me, the boy-turned-man who had stuck with me through it all, and the friends whom I couldn't get rid of even if I tried to beat em' off with a stick, my heart was healing.

Slowly but surely.

Though the darkness still came for me most nights in the form of nightmares, and the soul-crippling panic still found a way to bloom in my chest when the memories became too much, I was managing it better.

Keeping my promise to Carmen had helped too.

Since escaping Dominic, I'd graduated high school, I'd fallen for a boy my own age, and I'd even started working toward my degree.

Just like she wanted.

And although I didn't know where she was or if Heaven even truly existed, I prayed that I'd made her and Jade proud. Because I certainly was proud of them. No matter what society thought, I saw my girls for who they truly were.

Beautiful and smart with hearts of gold.

But I still missed them.

Fiercely.

Not a single day went by where I didn't think of them, and not an evening passed in which I didn't sit at my bedroom window and talk their ears off. And sometimes, in the quietest part of the night, I could've sworn I heard them whisper something back.

Which didn't surprise me one bit.

My guardian angels in life, it was apparent they'd continued to watch over me in death.

"Miss Ashley!" I turned my head to the left, spotting Ethel Baucom, one of Grandmama's bingo buddies right away. Smiling from ear-to-ear, she pointed toward the fair entrance from where she stood next to the funnel cake stand. "I spy with my little eye something that belongs to you." If possible, her smile grew. "Girl, you better go get him before someone else tries to snatch him up."

"Thanks, Mrs. Ethel!"

Mirroring her smile, I followed the trajectory of her finger.

A heartbeat later, I saw him.

Chase...

Dressed in the same style grey sweats he always wore, a navy fitted t-shirt, and his favorite ball cap, he looked similar to what he did two years before when he saved me from face planting into the cafeteria floor.

Only now, he was more beautiful.

If that was even possible.

Eyes already locked on me, he came to a standstill forty feet away. "Yo, Sweetness!" he hollered, drawing more than one set of eyes. Arms stretched out to the side, he quirked a lone brow. "Do I get a hug or what?"

Unable to contain myself, I took off, completely uncaring that so many were watching the scene before them play out. Flip flops slapping against the gravel-covered ground with each step that I took, I pumped my arms wildly, running as hard as I could without tripping over myself.

Within arm's reach, I launched myself forward, slamming my body into his. He caught me, then stumbled back, my hundred and ten-pound weight knocking him off balance. For someone who was used to being tackled by guys nearly three times my size on a regular basis, I thought it was hilarious.

"Jesus, beautiful girl," he said, wrapping his strong arms tightly around me tight. "When I go back to camp next month, I'm telling Coach to put you on the team since I know damned well you hit harder than most defensive ends."

I'd heard that before.

And after spending two years at Chase's side, I finally understood what he meant.

Well, sort of.

"I only tackle you." Wanting to be closer to him, I looped my arms around his neck and pulled him down to me, his chest nearly touching mine. "And you know it."

"I do know it," he replied, smirking. "Now, are you going to kiss me, Ashley Jo? Or do I need to steal what I want?"

Pulse skyrocketing, I raked my tongue over my bottom lip. "You can't steal what I give you freely," I whispered, lightly trailing my acrylic-tipped nails over the back of his neck. "Just like you can't steal what's always been yours."

His gorgeous blue eyes stared into mine, irises twinkling. "Yeah?" he asked, sliding a single hand into my hair. "And what exactly has always been mine?"

There was no hesitation on my part. "Me."

A surprised squeak slipped past my lips when he tugged on my dark locks the slightest bit, forcing me to bend back over the arm he had wrapped around my lower back. Then, with my face tilted toward the gorgeous night sky, he dusted his full lips over my gloss-covered ones in a teasing caress that seemingly came as natural as breathing.

"I've missed the hell outta you." Emotion clogged my throat, making speaking an impossible task. "And I'm about to show you exactly how much."

It was the last thing he said before taking my mouth in another kiss, this one both heated and passionate, stealing my breath and stirring my soul as a vortex of emotions whirled around us, blanketing us both in warmth and security.

I want to stay just like this.
Forever.

Lost in the moment and completely mesmerized by the way it felt to be wrapped up in his strong arms, one of the few places I felt utterly safe, I didn't take notice of the person who'd walked up next to us, holding a hot pink teddy bear in one hand and a smoked turkey leg that was nearly bigger than her in the other.

But I sure heard her when she huffed out a breath and said, "Lord have mercy, you two. Don't you know this is a dadgummed family event? Y'all can't be neckin' like that in front of God and everybody. That's what dark parking lots are for, ya big dummies! Besides, the boy is just home from football camp. It ain't like he just got back from blasted war!"

Frustrated as could be, Chase pulled his lips from mine and growled. "Swear to Christ, every time I kiss you, it attracts some type of crazy."

I smiled, the corners of my eyes crinkling. "Sure does. And it seems this time we captured us a Crazy Old Biddy," I whispered, knowing full-well that Grandmama would overhear me. "I hear they're soon to be on the endangered species list."

"You little hussy!" Grandmama barked, her tone teasing. "I'm gonna put your butt on the endangered species list right next to me if you keep talking that sorta way. Don't you know I can't croak for at least the next fifty years? I've got grandbabies to protect and towns-people to terrorize!"

People to terrorize?

I didn't doubt that one bit.

Chase slipped his hand free of my hair as I stood, straightening my dress. "Are we on the list of people you plan to terrorize?" Spinning me in place, he pulled me into him, my back meeting his front. "'Cause if not, we've got stuff to do."

"Yeah? What'cha got to do?"

Waiting for his response, she took a bite of her turkey leg, smearing her fuchsia-colored lipstick in the process. Grease and turkey juice dripped down her chin, making her look a hot mess, but she didn't seem to care. The only thing she was focused on right then was Chase and me.

A blind man could've seen the curiosity burning in her eyes, and Heaven knows I could only imagine the thoughts running wild through her head. For the past year, she'd been waiting on us to announce that we were officially dating, and with each day that passed, she was just getting more and more impatient.

Truth be told, so was I.

The problem was, though their voices were quieter, my demons still stirred, and I simply couldn't stomach the thought of them causing Chase more pain than they already had.

Over the years, I'd fought to distance him from the darkest parts of me. But after holding me through dozens of panic attacks and witnessing the PTSD-driven bouts of depression I slipped into from time to time, he'd seen it all; the good, the bad, and the hideous included.

But I was still scared to take that final step.

Terrified really.

The fact that I still harbored a thousand secrets didn't help matters any. Chase may have known about my sweet Addie, but she was the only pure thing that ever came from me. If he found out about the life I'd been forced to live while under Dominic's thumb, he'd walk.

After all, whores weren't meant to be loved.

It was a fact the voices in my head never let me forget.

With a gentle caress of his knuckle down my cheek, Chase captured my attention, pulling me from my murky thoughts. I leaned into the touch, my eyes fluttering closed. "When we planned to meet here earlier, you promised me a ride on the Ferris wheel, Jock," I whispered, the butterflies in my belly coming to life. "You've never broken a promise before. Don't start now."

Sliding his finger under my chin, he tilted my face back. "Look at me." His voice was hoarse, proving I wasn't the only one overcome with a myriad of emotions. Doing as he said, I opened my heavy-lidded eyes and peered up at him. "I will never break any promise I make you." Tracing his thumb along my jaw, he dipped his face closer to mine. Noses nearly touching, he exhaled. His minty breath wafted over my face sending my heart into overdrive. "Not ever."

"I—"

Whack!

My words faltered when Chase jerked, and garlic-scented poultry juice splashed across the side of my face. Eyes nearly popping out of my head, I swung my gaze to Grandmama and the turkey leg she held up in the air as if she were wielding Thor's mighty hammer.

"Did you just fucking hit me with a piece of meat?" Chase all but hollered.

Confused, I swung my gaze to him.

Then, I almost choked.

Grease, combined with a few tiny pieces of eviscerated meat clung to his reddened cheek, marring his tanned skin and acting as irrefutable proof that the Crazy Old Biddy had indeed popped him with an over-sized piece of Southern-fried fair food.

Oh. My. God.

Seriously, oh my God!

"Grandmama," I said, my tone admonishing. "What in the world are you doing?"

She quirked a brow, challenge sparking to life in her eyes. "I'm tryin' to knock some dadgummed sense into one of you's!" she hollered, one hand going to her hip. "Why, if you two don't yank your heads outta your butts, I'm gonna pull out my flyswatter and go to town on 'em!"

Yank our heads out of our butts?

Good gravy.

She had lost her mind!

"It's bad enough that I'm having to work overtime to get your brother"—she pointed at Chase before swinging her finger to me —"and your best friend to see what's right in front of their dag-blasted faces. Now I've gotta spend my precious bingo time workin' my magic on you two knuckleheads too. I swear," she continued, wavering the turkey around in the air, "it's more work than herdin' cats!"

I narrowed my eyes. "What do Ty and Heidi have to do with Chase and me?"

Puffing out her chest, she pinched her lips into a thin line. "'Cause all four of you are blinder than bats drunk on liquor!" Stepping closer, she dropped her arm, along with the fried weapon she'd used to pummel Chase with and looked at me. "When a man turns you stupider-than-a-stump with just one kiss, then you hang on to him, Ashley Jo." Her brows climbed her forehead. "Especially when his lips meeting yours makes your dadgummed toes curl so hard your feet almost snap right in half."

I blinked, unsure of how to respond.

"Now," she said, taking a bite of turkey. "If y'all don't mind, they are about to have a pull-up competition thingamabob over yonder at the t-shirt stand. I'm first in line."

Wearing a disgusted look, Chase swiped the grease and meat from his face. "Grandmama, you can't do a pull-up. Your damned arms will break slap off."

"Boy, you better thank the good Lord above for football," she said, exhaling frustratedly. "'Cause you don't know whether to check your ass or scratch your watch half the time. Course I ain't gonna do no pull-ups, but you can bet your sweet behind that I'm gonna be watching from the front row."

Of course, she was.

Pull-ups meant muscles, and muscles were Grandmama's drug of choice.

Well, that and moonshine.

Shooting me one last look—one which I couldn't read worth a flip —she turned and headed in the opposite direction, waving her turkey leg at anyone who got in her way. Before she was out of earshot, I heard her yell, "Outta my way, people! I've got pictures to take and tushes to pinch!"

"One day," Chase said, watching her go. "She's going to end up in jail on charges that your daddy won't be able to get her out of."

I shrugged because yep, it would probably happen. "Good thing Brantley is a defense attorney then," I replied. "He already spends half his time getting her out of traffic tickets even though that isn't his area of expertise. I mean, just last week she got cited for parking in front of a fire hydrant while some guys from Station 41 put out a shed fire." I nearly rolled my eyes at what I was about to say next. "You know she was just gawking at them, but she swore before God and everybody that she was just making sure her tax dollars were being put to good use."

Chase chuckled.

Then, without giving me any warning, he snaked his arm around my lower back and pulled me into him. Our fronts collided, almost knocking the air from my lungs. "We've spent enough time on the Crazy Old Biddy," he said. "It's time for you and me to have some fun."

The smile that tipped my lips nearly split my face in half. "Yeah? And what did you have in mind?"

I shuddered when his tongue raked across his bottom lip, leaving a trail of moisture behind. "For starters, I'm buying you a funnel cake. Then, I'm going to win you a teddy bear three times the size of the one Grandmama had."

My heart swelled with each word.

"And finally, I'm going to take you on every ride here." Resting his forehead against mine, he tucked a stray lock of hair behind my ear. "Because tonight, we're going to do everything you missed out on as a kid."

My chin wobbled. "I'd like that," I whispered, tears filling my eyes. "I'd like it a whole lot."

He brushed his lips against my forehead before standing tall once more. "Let's go then." Taking a step back, he bent at the waist, lightly shoved his shoulder into my belly and lifted me into the air. Arm clamped over the back of my thighs and the skirt of my dress, he started to move.

"Chase, put me down!" I yelled as both amusement and mortification worked its way through me.

"Not gonna happen," he replied, tightening his hold.

"Fine!" I said, faux exasperation dripping from my voice. "But if you're going to embarrass me in front of half the county, then the least you can do is buy me a caramel apple to go with my funnel cake."

"Anything you want, beautiful girl. All you have to do is say the words, and it's yours."

Every word he said was the truth.

Because that night, he spoiled me rotten.

And I loved every bit of it.

Chapter Twenty-Two

CHASE

*a*nthony Moretti looked ready to kill me.

It was a normal occurrence for us.

Standing in the open door, his arms crossed over his chest, he glared at me just like he'd done the first time I'd shown up on his porch two years earlier.

The only difference between then and now is that one, I wasn't carrying Ashley's purse in my hand, and two, Lucca was now glaring at me instead of looking at me in confusion like he'd done back then.

Like father, like son.

Christ.

"You've got exactly three seconds to explain to me why I shouldn't have my wife come out here and shoot you where you stand," he said, looking from my bare chest to Ashley, who I held in my arms, her face buried against me. Eyes closed, she was half asleep. "If she's drunk—"

"She's not drunk," I cut in, interrupting him. "And neither am I. She got sick on the Tilt-a-Whirl after eating nachos."

I cringed thinking back to the moment I realized shit was about to go bad. Face tinted green, Ashley had grabbed her stomach with one hand and covered her mouth with the other. Locked in tight, there was nothing either of us could do except let nature takes its course.

And fuck me, there had been vomit.

Vomit every-damned-where.

On me. On her.

On the people in the car behind us.

I'd almost puked at the sight.

"I got her cleaned up as best I could, but she needs to shower." Catching a whiff of the smell coming off me, I shuddered. "And so do I. I'll use the garden hose, I don't give a damn, but she needs to be washed off before she breaks out. You know her skin is sensitive, and who knows what was in those nachos."

The murderous look on Moretti's face softened at my words. Stepping to the side, he pulled Lucca out of the way and nodded toward the stairs. "Take her up to the bathroom across from her bedroom. I'll have Shelby meet you up there after she gets done putting Gracie to bed."

Disappointed that I wouldn't get to see Gracie, I instinctively pulled Ashley closer, holding her a little tighter. I wasn't ready to let her go. Not yet. The three hours we'd spent at the fair weren't enough.

Not even close.

When I didn't react, Moretti shot me an expectant look. Gritting my back teeth together, I headed inside and up the stairs. Knowing that my time with her was ticking away with each step that I took, I moved as slow as I could, drawing it out.

Once upstairs, I carried her into the bathroom like Anthony said. The moment I stepped through the door, her signature peach scent invaded my nose. Between the bottles of body wash, body spray, and lotion situated around the small room, the sour smell clinging to my skin vanished.

Thank fuck for that.

"Baby," I whispered, jostling her the slightest bit. "You've gotta wake up. You need a bath, and your mama is on the way to help you."

She cracked one eyelid half open. "I'm twenty, Jock. I don't need my mama to help me bathe."

I smiled at her smartass comment. Back when we first met, she didn't have a whole lot of fight in her, but now my girl was full of sass at times.

Shelby was to blame for that.

No doubt.

"Yeah, but you got awfully sick, and I don't feel right leaving you. What if you pass out? You could fall and hit your head, and then I'd lose my absolute—"

"You're staying," she said, opening both eyes wide. "If anybody is going to see me naked, it's not going to be my mother. I love the woman, Lord knows I do, but just no."

I raised a lone brow. "You'd rather me see you naked?"

The look she shot me was one of disbelief. "You're kidding me, right?" she asked, sliding her hand up my chest. "Chase, you've seen me naked before. Don't get why now would be any different."

She was right.

I'd seen her naked more than once.

And I had every soft curve memorized.

In fact, the only thing I didn't have committed to memory was how it felt to be inside her. Mainly because I'd never experienced it. Since the first time we messed around in her bedroom, we'd had plenty of repeats, but we'd never gone any further.

My girl was... delicate.

Which I respected.

It didn't matter how long it took for her to work past her issues, I'd wait. Determined to make her future brighter than her past, I wouldn't take something she wasn't willing to give. Just as I wouldn't push her into a relationship until she was one-hundred percent ready.

I wasn't a monster.

"Baby," I said, chuckling. "Difference between then and now is your parents are home. Do I need to remind you of what'll happen if your mama walks up here and sees me undressing you? To hell with Moretti and his service-issued weapon. It's Shelby and her .45 that scares me."

Little Miss Sassitude rolled her eyes. "She won't shoot you. Not when the babies are home." She smiled. Soft and sweet. "She might feed you to Ziggy though."

Death by giant marshmallow.

That would be an embarrassing way to go.

Especially since the little shit was just waiting for the chance to eat me. I couldn't even walk through the house without him glaring at me disapprovingly. The dog was more temperamental than Shelby!

Doing as she said—well, more like demanded—I put her feet on the floor and helped her stand straight. Hands on her hips, I held her steady as she found her balance. "My stomach doesn't feel right," she mumbled. "Not at all."

Pinching the hem of her dress, she eyed the door. "Lock that, please."

Knowing I was likely signing my own death warrant by doing so, I nodded and twisted the lock, engaging it. Ashley shifted, and when I looked from the door to her again, my mouth ran dry.

She'd ripped her dress off, baring her braless chest.

The perfect handful, her breasts were perky with upturned, rose-colored nipples. I wasn't a tit man by any means—legs were my kryptonite—but hers were perfect.

Averting my gaze, I moved past her and reached into the shower, turning on the water. I adjusted the knobs, playing with them until the water was warm but not too hot—perfect for her sensitive skin.

When I turned back to face her, she was sliding the lacy white bikini-style panties she wore down her smooth, toned legs. Refusing to gawk—even if I wanted to—I sat on the closed toilet in front of where she stood and dropped my gaze to the tiled floor.

Don't make her uncomfortable.

Her body isn't yours to take.

It belongs to her.

"Chase." My whispered name falling from her bow-shaped lips sent chills racing down my spine, something that didn't often happen to me. "Want to know a secret?"

Still focused on the ground, I nodded. "Yeah, Sweetness, I do."

Tracing her nail across my jaw, she moved closer. Then, sliding a finger under my jaw, she lifted my face. "Look here." My eyes instantly landed on the small scar directly beneath her belly button.

"This," she said, caressing her thumb over the top of it. "Is from my sweet Addie."

That was when it hit me.

It wasn't a scar.

But a single stretch mark.

"I don't know why I didn't get others," she whispered, continuing the slow strokes. "But I think having just this one makes me love it even more." A single tear fell from her eye before splattering onto the floor. "And I love it because it reminds me that she was real." Another tear. "And that if only for a moment, she was mine."

That crushing pain, the same one I felt deep in my chest each time she talked about Addie returned, stealing the goddamned breath from my lungs. All this time later and she still hadn't told me what happened to her baby, but I had a feeling—a bad one—that she really was gone.

For good.

Knowing some of the vile shit Dominic had done to Ashley, it wouldn't have surprised me if he'd hurt an innocent child, especially since my girl had said time and time again that her baby was gone because of him.

If I ever found out he killed Addie...

Hell, I didn't know what I'd do.

But it was a truth I wasn't sure I'd ever learn. With her determined not to tell anyone about that particular secret, I doubted I'd ever get to the bottom of what really transpired. And it's not like I could press her for more information than she was willing to give.

Over Addie, Ashley would shatter.

She'd come so far in the past couple of years, but being forced to confront those demons would be her downfall, and as selfish as it sounds, I wasn't going to risk losing the girl who unknowingly held my heart in the palm of her hand.

Not for any reason.

"She will *always* be yours," I whispered, staring at the inch-long mark. "It doesn't matter what happened, Sweetness. No one can take that away from you." I looked up, meeting her watery gaze. "Can I touch you?"

A small nod.

That was the answer she gave me.

Resting my hands on her hips, I leaned forward, stopping when only an inch separated her belly—one which had produced life—from my face. Then, with my eyes locked on hers, I kissed the small mark, allowing my lips to linger above the place where her little girl had once lain, the sound of her mama's heartbeat filling the space where she grew.

"I'm sorry, Ashley," I whispered, a lump forming in my throat. "So damned sorry."

More tears fell.

But not just hers.

Slowly standing, I wrapped my arms around her and pulled her into me, hugging her tightly. Face buried against my chest, she hugged me in return, her small body trembling against mine as steam filled the small room, blanketing us in wet heat.

"Want to know another secret?" Her voice was quiet as could be, barely audible over the running shower.

Chin resting atop her head, I closed my eyes. "Yeah, baby, I do."

Fingers digging into my lower back, she sunk further into me.

Then, after pulling in a deep breath, she whispered five little words, all of which were the sweetest I'd ever heard.

Those words? *She should have been yours.*

I opened my mouth to reply—because hell yes, Addie should've been mine—but I didn't get the chance to speak before someone banged against the locked bathroom door, rattling the hinges.

Boom!

"Open this damned door right this second, or else I'm gonna boot it the hell down!"

Fucking Shelby...

"Well," I said, squeezing her one last time as I smiled ear-to-ear. "Seems the executioner has arrived. Let's just hope she makes it quick."

Ashley leaned back and tipped her face to meet mine. "Thank you."

"For what?"

"For always being here for me."

Sliding my hands into her hair, I lightly touched the tip of my nose to hers. "I will always be here for you, Sweetness. Until the day I take my final breath."

Chapter Twenty-Three

CHASE

I woke to the sound of ringing.

Still half asleep and assuming it was Ashley calling, I snatched my cell off the nightstand and pressed it to my ear without glancing at the Caller ID. "Morning, baby," I said, rolling to my back. "You feeling any—"

"It's about time you answered."

I froze at the sound of the familiar voice.

Blinking to clear the sleep from my eyes, I jerked upright, my grip on the phone tightening. "What *the fuck* are you calling me for?"

A humorless chuckle sounded through the speaker, followed by, "Can't a father call his son?"

Father?

Not even close.

"We've been over this, *Clyde*," I spat, my blood pressure skyrocketing. "You are not my damned father. Never have been. Never will be."

His heavy breaths bounced between us, and I had no doubt he was close to putting his fist through whatever wall he was closest to. "You listen to me, you ungrateful little bastard," he growled, making his disdain for me obvious. "You and I need to meet, and it needs to happen soon, else there will be consequences."

He had to be shitting me.

Dropping my head back, I fisted my free hand. "Let me go ahead and cut you off at the pass, old man. I don't have any money, which I'm sure is what you want, so save your bullshit, yeah?"

Silence.

Then, "Saw that article in the paper."

He'd lost me.

"I don't have a clue what you're rambling—"

"The one that said you were gonna skip your senior year and enter the draft," he interrupted, making my blood boil. "Newspaper even said you were expected to go in the first round."

Madder than hell, my eye twitched. "Yeah, and what's that got to do with you?"

Another humorless chuckle. "Like I told you some time ago, I intend to get what's owed to me, one way or another."

Some time ago? I hadn't seen or spoken to the sperm donor who'd helped create me in over two years. Matter of fact, the last time we'd been in contact was the night Ashley thought I ditched her for that snake, Bianca.

He'd harassed Ty since then.

But he hadn't come directly to me.

Mainly cause my brother ran interference.

Which needed to stop.

Now.

"Listen, shithead," I said, needing to reiterate the point I'd made the night I slammed my hand into his nose, likely breaking it. "I'm going to say this one last time. I don't give a damn what you threaten me with, you will never get a dime from me, whether I make it to the NFL or not."

I didn't care if I landed a trillion-dollar payday, I would set fire to every last penny I received before he got his scumbag fingers on a single cent.

That was a fact.

"I *will* get what I'm owed, son," he replied, his voice filled with a mixture of hate and confidence. "One way or another."

The man was delusional.

Not only did he think he could threaten me into giving him money —why the hell would I do that?—but he actually thought there was a snowball's chance in hell of making me bend to his will, whatever it may be at the time.

He'd lost it.

Completely.

"Open your eyes, Clyde, because I'm not sure any of this is sinking in," I said, through teeth clenched. "I'm not a scared kid anymore, and I will not be pushed around by a degenerate gambler with a badge who spends most of his time so drunk he wouldn't be able to find his ass if he put his hands in his back pockets."

Grandmama would love that line.

"Not kidding, you twisted fuck. Don't call me ever again," I continued, heat climbing the length of my neck. "Or better yet, just drop dead."

I ended the call after saying my typical good-bye to him and tossed the phone across the room. It bounced off the wall and landed in a pile of dirty clothes on the floor. Thankfully it didn't shatter, but at that moment, I wouldn't have given a shit if it had.

Madder than I had been in a long time, I was close to letting the anger that simmered beneath my flesh get the best of me. Like many times before, my hand twitched with the urge to hit something. But I wasn't going to do it. I refused.

I will not be like him.

I am better than that.

Needing to get up, to move, to do something in order to calm down, I jumped off the bed and slipped on a pair of basketball shorts. Then, I headed into the living room where I nearly ran straight into Ty, who was coming up the hall, his face covered in smoke and soot.

Even though I was twenty, his presence still calmed me the same way it did when I was six and continuously pissing the bed out of fear every night. It was something that continued to happen until I was eight, and Ty moved out, taking me with him.

Clyde hadn't given a fuck that I was gone.

Never even came and looked for me.

Why would he?

He didn't give two shits about me.

Even when he tried to shake me down now, he didn't pretend to care. He just flat-out demanded what he wanted and expected it to be handed to him for whatever reason.

Said a lot about his mental state.

The psycho was losing his grip on reality.

And right or wrong, I hoped he'd break completely before long.

The world would've been a lot better off if he no longer existed in it, sucking up precious oxygen and polluting the air with his toxic bullshit.

Quirking a brow, I looked at Ty, who was carrying a duffle bag over his shoulder. "Rough night?"

He nodded, dropping the bag to the floor. "You could say that. Had a three-alarm fire over in Garrison."

Garrison?

That was like twenty minutes from his station.

"How bad was it?"

Ripping off his smoke-laden shirt, he tossed it past me, toward his room. "It was at one of the old cotton mills. Cap thinks the fire started in one of the processing rooms, and it went up from there. Ended up catching two neighboring buildings on fire. There's nothing left of any of them now."

"Anybody get hurt?"

He shook his head. "Nah, but Cole's dumbass about died trying to save a mama cat and her litter of kittens," he said, referring to Hendrix, Ashley's uncle. "He got them out, but an incinerated beam fell just as him, Kyle, and I made it to the exit. Missed him by an inch."

Well, shit...

"The cats alright?" I'll admit, my brother may have been a fireman, but I didn't know much about fires or smoke inhalation except that they were both bad. "'Cause if they died, he better not tell Ashley. She'll cry for a month."

That was no joke.

My girl had a hard time coping with some people, but not animals. They were the balm that soothed her. Hell, I was certain she loved Ziggy more than people most days.

Not that I blamed her.

The giant marshmallow may have been a disgruntled dick at times, but he was one of the best dogs I'd ever encountered.

And damned if he didn't love my girl.

He wasn't a trained therapy dog by any means, but he'd still learned to quell her panic when an anxiety attack was coming on.

The first time I saw him do it, I couldn't believe it.

"All the critters are fine," Ty replied, wiping his eyes. "Cap dropped them off at the emergency vet as soon as the scene was under control. Last I heard they were stable. Just had a little smoke inhalation."

"Good." Relief washed through me. "You going to shower and sleep now? Or you got something else to do?"

He rubbed his palms down his face, then looked over at me, his blue eyes—ones identical to my own—staring into mine. "I gotta eat first. You want to grab breakfast? Ruby's will be packed, but we can go down to the Coffee Hut on Main."

Unable to help it, I smirked.

I knew exactly why he wanted to hit up the Coffee Hut. "Bug is down at the Hut, isn't she?" His eyes narrowed, and I chuckled in response. "Still can't believe you haven't put a ring on her finger."

Though he may put me in a headlock for it, I couldn't resist teasing his brooding ass. The fact was, my big brother had been in love with Heidi, Ashley's best friend for a while now.

But she'd blown him off at every turn.

Things were starting to change now though, and I had no doubt they'd be married before anyone could blink. Call it a feeling, call it a premonition, whatever, but despite their hang-ups, those two were meant to be together.

Just like Ashley and me.

One day we'll get there.

Baby steps.

"Yeah, she probably is there," he said, a knowing smile on his face. "And if she is, it means Ashley is too."

That was all I needed to hear.

"I'll get dressed."

It was his turn to smirk. "Thought so, dipshit." Shaking his head, he unbuckled his belt and ripped it free of the loops holding it in place before tossing it on the floor at his feet. "I gotta shower first, so give me twenty minutes, and I'll be ready."

I nodded, indecision stirring inside me.

Still irritated as fuck, I wanted to tell Ty about the phone call I'd gotten moments before because I needed to vent to somebody who understood before I blew a gasket. Problem was, if I told him, he'd be the one who lost his shit.

And I couldn't let that happen.

Ty had already received more than one phone call from Clyde over the same bullshit I'd just handled, and he'd dealt with the deluded fuck each time. The man needed a break from fighting my battles.

I'd handle this one myself.

Reading me like a book, he lifted his chin in the air. "There something you want to tell me? 'Cause you look all sorts of twisted up."

I wasn't a liar—not in the least bit—but that day, I looked my big brother in the eyes and lied my ass off. "Nah," I said, forcing a smile. "Just ready to see my girl."

He jerked his chin down once, not buying my bullshit for a second. "If you say so." He nodded back toward my room. "Go get dressed. I'm going to hop in the shower."

Doing as he said—like always—I turned and headed back to my room without saying another word.

"Chase!" he hollered, making me look back at him over my shoulder. "Heard Shelby almost killed you last night."

My eyes narrowed. "How did you—"

"She called Cap at the station," he said, referring to Shelby's dad.

Most called him Pop, but the guys down at the station all called him Cap because that's what he was; their captain. "Told him she may need help hiding a body."

Great.

Just fucking great.

Everybody knew Pop was nuts when it came to Ashley. The man loved his entire family, but Ashley was special. She'd been remarkably close to him since day one, and I had no doubt he'd tear me to shreds without thinking twice if the need called for it.

He was temperamental like that.

"How did you get out of there without her murdering you?"

That was a simple answer and one which made me smile big as hell. "My Sweetness," I replied. "Shelby spoils her, and even if she wanted to shoot me, she wouldn't hurt Ashley like that."

And thank Christ for that.

Because for a minute, I could've sworn I was a dead man. Especially after Ashley jumped in the shower and I opened the bathroom door, only to be greeted by a murderous looking Shelby.

I was lucky she didn't rip my eyes out.

Ty shook his head. Yet again. "One day, Chase," he said, toeing off his boots. "That woman is going to beat you black and blue."

Most likely.

"Yeah, but—" My cell phone suddenly rang, echoing through the apartment. Irritation prickled my skin once more.

Better not be Clyde again.

Jaw ticking, I pointed toward my room. "I'm going to get that. Shower, assmunch. We've got places to be."

Ty flipped me off in reply but said nothing.

After returning the gesture, I headed back into my room.

Grabbing the phone from the dirty pile of clothes where it had landed—*I really need to wash that shit*—I picked it up, and unlike last time, I looked at the screen.

A smile spread across my face.

Lifting the phone to my ear, I answered quickly. "Hey, beautiful girl," I said, leaning a shoulder against the wall. "Missed the hell out of you."

"Missed you too." Like magic, her sweet voice soothed me, calming the anger that still held me in its clutches, its hold unrelenting. "Heidi and I are headed over to the Coffee Hut. Want to meet us there?"

My smile grew. "I'll be there in about thirty minutes."

"Good," she replied, blowing out a small breath. "I'll see you there then. Bye, Jock."

"Bye, Sweetness."

She ended the call, and I tossed the phone on the bed.

Then, with excitement stirring in my chest, I got dressed.

Chapter Twenty-Four

ASHLEY

*I*t was outreach night at the shelter.

Everyone, including all the ladies' families, were gathered in the storage room, preparing care packages for the people who lived on the streets surrounding the shelter.

In less than an hour, we would split up into teams and deliver them on foot. The entire thing had been my idea—go me!—and I was excited to see it put into action.

Knowing full-well what it was like living on the streets, I wanted to do anything I could to ease people's pain. It didn't matter if the people we encountered were prostitutes, drug addicts, or whatever else, they needed someone to care.

And that someone would be me.

Like I told the ladies when I pitched the idea to them, no one deserved to go hungry just as no one deserved to go without basic hygiene products such as tampons, deodorant, and toothpaste. All were included in each package, along with snacks and other small items such as condoms, an item that sex workers desperately needed access to.

"Ashley Jo!"

I snapped my head up from the package I was preparing and looked across the room, instantly finding a beaming Hope. "You might want to head upstairs," she said. "You've got company at the back door."

Excited raced through me.

But my mama, who stood beside me, didn't share my amusement. Growling, she shook her head. "That damned boy. I can't run him off no matter what I do. Threaten to cut his nuts off, and yet he just keeps coming back. It's like he has a danged death wish or something."

She was only joking.

Well, sort of.

Shaking my head, I hollered back at Hope, "Thanks, Itty Bitty!"

Sealing the package I held tightly in my hand, I gently bumped my shoulder into my mama's. "I'm going to let Chase and Ty in. You want to come?"

Eyebrows nearly reaching her hairline, she looked at me with an amused expression. "Depends. Are you going to let me toss him down the stairs on the way back?"

That was a hard pass from me.

"Nope," I replied, smiling. "Since I'd like to keep him, I'd rather you not break his neck in a forced fall."

Her eyes bulged. "*Keep* him?"

Anxiety stirred in my chest at her expression.

Crap, crap, crap!

Why did I open my mouth?

Blowing out a pent-up breath, I slipped the package into a plastic bag. "I like him," I replied, my voice a mere whisper. "And I have since the beginning. Don't really see that changing anytime in the future."

She blinked, an emotion I couldn't read brewing in her eyes. "Ashley Jo, I'm about to ask you a question, and I want—"

"—nothing less than the truth," I finished for her, having heard the same line a hundred times before. "That's what you were going to say, right?"

Jerking her chin down, she nodded. Then, "Are you in love with Chase?"

It was a question that stole my breath.

Not because I didn't know the answer—I surely did—but because admitting it to myself, much less aloud, was hard.

Like, really hard.

"I care about him," I replied, fidgeting in place. "A whole lot. But I'm—"

"—scared." It was her turn to finish my sentence.

I nodded. "He still doesn't know," I told her truthfully. "Not about what I was. I mean, he knows Dominic abused me, and he knows he hurt me... in *those* ways"—I paused—"but he doesn't know the rest." My vision blurred thanks to the tears rapidly filling my eyes. "If he did, he'd walk."

Fully expecting my mama to agree with me, I was nearly knocked right off my feet when she shook her head and cupped my cheeks with her soft, warm hands. "I'm fixing to say something, and I want you to listen to each word carefully."

Oh Lord.

I could only imagine what was coming.

"Ashley Jo Moretti, you are one of the most beautiful people I've ever met. You're strong, you're sweet, and you're smart as a whip." Her eyes glossed over as tears filled them. "You're also my daughter which makes you extra special." Chin wobbling, she smiled. "But what you are *not,* is what those men did to you, sugar."

She was wrong.

I was every bit what they did to me.

At least what they'd made me become.

Tainted.

Broken.

Used goods.

"And I will not stand by and watch you potentially throw away one of the best things that has ever happened to you because you're scared." I opened my mouth to speak, but she kept talking, not giving me the chance. Big surprise there, right? "Dominic," she snarled, "and those other men have taken enough from you already. Don't allow them to take another damned thing. Do you understand me?"

I froze, unable to reply.

Even if what she said was true—and that was a big if—I still had so many secrets, most of which I could never reveal.

Heart twisting, at that moment, I wanted nothing more than to tell her about Carmen and Jade, and then Ellington. But above all, I wanted to tell her about Addie.

Doing so was impossible.

Dominic would never be brought to justice over Carmen and Jade's deaths—it just wouldn't happen—and if I told her about Ellington, it would open a can of worms that I'd never be able to close.

And Addie...

My sweet baby girl.

If Shelby knew my biggest secret, the one that weighed heavily on both my heart and soul, she might never forgive me.

And if I lost her...

Well, I wouldn't make it.

Using a technique the woman who birthed me had taught me—may she rot in the shit-hole where she currently resided—I swooped and swerved, steering the conversation in a different direction. "I thought you didn't like Chase?" I forced a laugh, but there was no humor behind it. "Is he growing on you?"

Dropping her hands from my face, she crossed her arms. "That little turdnugget may be growing on me just a bit." It was about time! "But don't tell him that. It'll go straight to his danged head, and his melon is already big enough."

That earned a genuine laugh from me.

"I won't tell him"—I held my pinky up in the air—"pinky promise."

Smiling, she hooked her finger around mine. "Now go get the pain in the ass before he chews through the shelter door."

I nodded, and unable to stop myself, I wrapped my arms around her, hugging her as hard as I could. "Thank you," I whispered.

"For what?" she replied, hugging me back.

"For not killing him."

She snorted. "Trust me, sugar, it was touch and go there for a bit. Your daddy already had a place picked out to hide the body and all.

Even bought a special shovel for the occasion." Burying her face in my hair, she rocked me from side to side as I smiled against her. "Just take it slow, okay? Just because I gave you my blessing doesn't mean it's time to hit the gas like a NASCAR driver and rush into things."

"I won't. I swear it."

Releasing me, she took a step back and nodded toward the door. "Go before I change my mind and decide to run the jock over with Hendrix's truck."

She didn't need to tell me twice.

Blowing her a kiss, I turned and took off.

———

I opened the back door to find Ty and Chase standing on the concrete ramp that led to the gravel-covered lot.

Butterflies in full-flight, I smiled at my guy.

"Hey, Sweetness," he said, holding out his arms. "Do I get a hug or what?"

It was the same question he always asked, and one I answered by throwing myself into his waiting arms.

This time was no different.

Biting back a squeal, I slammed my body into his without hesitation.

Wrapping my arms around his torso, I buried my face against his chest and took a deep breath, pulling his scent deep into my lungs.

Then, feeling eyes on us, I glanced over at Chase's big brother. He was such a handsome guy which wasn't surprising considering he and Chase looked almost identical. The only difference between the two was their haircuts and age difference.

While Chase was only twenty, Ty was around thirty.

"Hey, Ty," I said, smiling. "Heidi is inside waiting for you."

And waiting she was.

I swear the poor girl was about to come out of her skin.

I wasn't sure how Ty had gotten through to Heidi, but she'd gone from pushing him away at every turn, to wanting to spend every waking moment with him.

It was such a drastic change, but one that made me ecstatic, because Ty made her happy.

I couldn't ask for more than that.

His spine snapped straight. "Where?"

Biting back a giggle, I leaned further into Chase, who was silently holding me, watching my exchange with his brother. "She was in the storeroom downstairs last I saw."

He nodded and pointed from me to Chase. "You two coming?"

Chase tightened the arm he had twined around my lower back. "Give us a few minutes, then we'll be right behind you."

Grabbing the door handle, Ty shook his head. "Stay out of view of the cameras. If Evan sees y'all all hugged up, he'll radio Shelby. We all know what will happen then."

I flinched, because yeah, we did.

She'd either threaten to shove her cowgirl boot up his behind, or she'd chase him around the parking lot with Grandmama's borrowed flyswatter.

Despite giving me her blessing just minutes before, she tended to get dramatic like that.

"She'll get over it," Chase replied, his tone a tad hard. "Ashley's twenty, not twelve."

That was true.

But I wasn't exactly a normal girl either.

With a past darker than coal, my parents went overboard trying to protect and keep me safe.

Chase understood that though.

If he didn't, he would've dipped long ago.

"Don't say I didn't warn you," Ty replied, pointing at me. "When her mama whoops your ass, don't yell at me for help."

Chase smirked. "Don't tell me you're scared of Shelby Moretti, big brother."

"I sure as shit am," Ty fired back, making me giggle. "And if you had a lick of common sense, you would be too. You don't ever mess with a Mama Bear, especially one whose husband is a homicide detective that knows how to get rid of a body without getting caught."

With that, he walked inside.

"That always makes me laugh," I said, looking up at my guy.

Grabbing a lock of my hair, he wrapped the dark strand around his finger. "What does?"

"Seeing such big strong men act like they are terrified of my mama. I mean, she's an entire five foot three."

"Beautiful girl, Shelby may be small, but you tend to forget about some of the things she's done in the past."

I did tend to forget.

Not ever about what she'd done to save me from Dominic, but many people didn't know what she'd done to save Lucca from his biological father.

The moment he threatened Lucca's life, she'd ended him.

As in, she'd killed him.

Without a second thought.

It's what I should've done too.

If only I'd been stronger...

I'd still have my girl.

Throat clogging with suffocating regret, I swallowed, fighting to hold back the tears that I knew were likely to fall. "Hey," I said, forcing a shaky smile. "Do you mind if we go for a walk? I could really use some fresh air before we go back inside."

Knowing that something was bothering me, but not wanting to set off my anxiety by asking, Chase took one of my hands in his and lifted it to his mouth, where he pressed a soft kiss to my knuckles. "Anything you want."

Despite the hurt swelling in my chest, I melted. "Thank you."

Lacing our fingers together, he extended an arm, gesturing for me to lead the way down the ramp. "Ladies first."

I rolled my eyes. "How chivalrous of you."

"Yeah, well, you know me," he said, "always acting all proper and shit."

"Oh, good heavens." I took a step and tugged his arm, wanting him to follow me. "You're so full of it, I'm surprised your eyes aren't brown, Chase Jacobs."

Pulling his hand from mine, he clutched his invisible pearls, a faux look of hurt plastered on his perfect face. "How dare you," he said, stumbling back. "Your words, Sweetness, they wound me."

Feeling the darkness weighing me down momentarily abate, I glanced over my shoulder toward the back lot of the shelter. "Wanna know what else will hurt?"

He lifted his chin in the air. "Tell me."

"Getting outrun by a girl."

His eyes narrowed. "You think you can outrun me?"

I shrugged. "I don't think anything. I know I can."

"Oh yeah? Then how about you put your money where your mouth is. You run, and if I catch you, I get something I want."

I tilted my head to the side, excitement nipping my nerves. "And what is it that you want?"

"I'll settle for a kiss. But not one of those quick ones. I want a deep one. One that lasts."

Heat bloomed in my cheeks.

"Okay," I replied, agreeing to his terms. "But if I make it to the back gate without you catching me, then you have to wear a shirt the day you go back to camp that says, 'my girlfriend beat me at tag.'"

Chase's eyes twinkled. "Girlfriend, huh?"

I shrugged, refusing to say more.

"Alright, I'll wear the shirt. If I lose. Not that I'm going to."

"We'll see." I took a small step back, fully prepared to bolt. "Ready?"

He nodded. "Whenever you are."

I pulled in a breath.

Then, without giving him any warning, I turned and ran for it.

But even as fast as I was—which was faster than most girls—I never stood a chance. At the end of the ramp, Chase's arms wrapped around me from behind. A squeal slipped past my lips as he lifted me off the ground and pulled me into him, my back against his front.

Moving around the rear of the building, he dropped my feet to the ground and then spun me around before pushing me up against the brick.

Arms caging me in, his chest rose and fell as he dipped his face to within an inch of mine. Noses nearly touching, he stared into my eyes, his gaze hungry. "Got you, Sweetness," he said. "Now it's time to pay up."

Skin overheating, I slipped my hands under his shirt and rested my palms against his granite abs. "First, you need to know a secret."

"Yeah?" He dropped one hand and placed it on my hip, giving it a slight squeeze. "Then tell me what it is."

Lightly digging my nails into his skin, I lifted my right leg and hooked it around his hip, pulling him closer.

He groaned in response but made no move to further touch me.

He'll never take what I don't give.

He's not like them.

Lightheaded as could be, my heavy-lidded eyes slid half shut. "I never intended to win," I admitted. "Because I wanted you to catch me."

His lips dipped closer. "That's good, baby. Because I had no plans to ever let you get away."

Emotion rising once more, my heart swelled. "You can't let me go, Chase." I slid my hands around to his lower back, anchoring myself to him. "Even if I run, please don't ever let me get too far."

"I won't," he whispered. "I swear it." Swiping away the single tear that had rolled down my cheek, he dropped his forehead to mine. "I love you, Ashley Moretti." The unexpected confession stole my breath. "And I'll never stop."

Not giving me a chance to respond, he slammed his lips down on mine and did exactly as he wanted.

He kissed me long.

He kissed me deeply.

And he kissed me hard.

Chapter Twenty-Five

ASHLEY

y hands wouldn't stop shaking.

Standing in the shelter's main office, I stared at the young girl seated across the room, her tear-streaked face bruised and puffy.

Less than thirty minutes before, my outreach group, which consisted of Ty, Heidi, Chase, and me, had found her on the street, terrified and close to freaking out.

She'd been on the run.

From her father, of all people.

A drunk who made her sit in the car while he pounded down drink after drink at the local Watering Hole, he'd beaten the crap out of her after she tried to get out of his vehicle and leave.

Ty, in turn, had beat the crap out of *him* once the worthless monster came looking for his daughter, only to find us with her.

Chase had told me numerous times that his dad had beat Ty more times than he could count, but up until that moment, I'd never witnessed Ty be anything but kind.

But when the girl's daddy showed up...

He went ballistic.

Not that I blamed him.

If he hadn't done it, I would've tried.

Though I was well aware that violence wasn't the answer, I still wanted to throw that man a butt whooping like he'd never experienced before. He'd hit his daughter, his beautiful fourteen-year-old little girl.

They didn't make them any lower than that.

Knowing that I needed to comfort the girl—Mackenzie, her name was—I slowly crossed the room, making sure to keep my hands visible at all times and sat down in the seat directly across from her.

"Hey, Mackenzie," I whispered, wrapping my arms around my belly. "I don't know if you remember, but my name is Ashley. I work here along with the other ladies that you met a few minutes ago."

She sniffled but said nothing.

"I know you probably don't want to talk right now, and that's totally okay, but I just want you to know that you're safe now. I understand how terrifying this whole ordeal is, trust me, but just know that no one else will hurt you."

And they wouldn't.

Every single person who worked at the shelter would willingly throw themselves in between Mackenzie and her father if he showed up, trying to cause trouble.

Not that I expected that to happen.

Because I didn't.

With the way Ty pummeled his face and body, I doubt he could even walk.

But as I said before, he deserved it.

When Mackenzie didn't speak, I continued. "Is there anything I can get you? A drink perhaps? Maybe something to eat?"

Silence.

"Okay," I whispered, a small smile on my face. "I'm going to leave you alone so you can catch your breath. But I'll be right outside the door in case you need anything, alright?"

More silence.

Then, when I started to stand, she whispered, "Please stay."

It was a request I was happy to oblige.

Sitting back down, I crossed one leg over the other and leaned back in the chair, waiting to see if she'd speak again.

I didn't have to wait long.

"Is my aunt coming now?"

I nodded. "Yeah, honey, she is. Maddie already got in contact with her, and she's on the way. May take her a bit to get here, but she's coming."

She blew out a relieved breath, which, in turn, lessened my anxiety.

"I like my Aunt," she said. "She's nice to me." That made me smile. "And she doesn't..."

I tilted my head to the side. "She doesn't what?"

One tear after another streamed down her cheeks.

Reaching over, I grabbed the box of tissues from Maddie's desk and offered them to her. "Here, sweet girl. Take a few of these."

Taking the whole box from my hand, she grabbed a handful of tissues and wiped her face, then blew her nose. "My Aunt Patty," she started. "Doesn't hit me." Shaking her head, she bounced her legs, unable to sit still. "Not like him."

"Mackenzie—"

I snapped my mouth shut when her heartbroken gaze met mine. "Why does he hate me so much?" The hurt in her voice nearly broke me. "I always try to be good. I listen to what he says most of the time, do my homework and don't act up. I don't understand..."

Her voice trailed off as the sobs started.

Needing to comfort her, I stood up and moved to the empty chair next to her. Holding out my hand, I asked, "Can I hold your hand?"

She nodded, then put her hand in mine.

Lacing our fingers together, I caressed the back of her knuckles with my thumb. Feeling my throat tighten, I swallowed, fighting to make it loosen. "I've been where you are," I whispered, needing to erase the pain that brewed in her pretty eyes. "I spent my entire childhood wondering how my mama, the woman who'd given me life, could hate me so fiercely."

"You did?"

"I did."

"Was your mama mean?"

I bit back a humorless chuckle. "My mama was lost. Much like I expect your daddy is."

Her brows furrowed. "What's that mean?"

"It means that their hearts are full of hurt, and instead of working on getting better, they take that same hurt out on others. It isn't right, and it isn't okay, but sometimes the world can be ugly."

Feeling as though I would burst into tears at any moment, I pulled in a deep breath and worked to center myself.

Keep it together.

Show her how to be brave.

"But the world can be a beautiful one too," I continued, holding her hand tight. "Like tonight. What happened to you, sweet girl, will never be okay. But it happened, and you survived. Now, you'll get your second chance. And that second chance? It's going to be a lot better than what you leave behind."

"Did you get a second chance?"

I didn't miss the twinge of hope in her voice.

Lower lip trembling, I nodded. "Yeah, I did. And it started here, at this very shelter."

"Really?" she asked, eyes widening to the size of saucers. "How?"

I shifted in my seat, some of the heaviness weighing me down suddenly lifting. "Do you remember the blonde woman that came in here a few minutes ago? She was wearing a pair of denim shorts, a white button-up shirt, and knee-high cowgirl boots?"

Mackenzie nodded. "I liked her boots."

I laughed. "Well," I said, smiling. "That woman's name is Shelby, and she saved me from all the bad stuff that I was running from when I wasn't much older than you."

"Really?" she asked once more.

"Really. She even adopted me, so now I get to keep her forever."

My heart climbed into my throat as I watched the pain that filled Mackenzie's eyes vanish before mine. "You see, my life was really ugly there for a while, but then it got better and a whole lot more beautiful."

"Do you think mine will get better?"

"One second."

Releasing her hand, I stood and rounded Maddie's desk. Opening the top drawer, I pulled out a business card. Along the backside of it, I wrote my phone number, followed by my mama's.

Moving back to her side, I kneeled next to her, bringing us eye-to-eye. "I want you to do something for me, okay?" Pointing at the phone numbers, I continued. "When you leave here, if your life doesn't get better, you call me, and I promise I will fight with everything I have to fix it."

Taking the card from my hand, she stared down at the numbers, a look of disbelief in her eyes. "Ashley," she whispered, clutching it tightly. "Even if it does get better, can I still call you? Because I like you, and I don't have many friends."

I choked back more tears.

"You can call me, or you can text me. It doesn't matter which." Pinching a stray lock of hair between my fingers, I tucked it back behind my ear. "Whenever you need to talk, even if it's about simple, everyday stuff, then I'm your girl. Morning, noon, or night, I'll always answer."

She looked up, meeting my gaze. "Can I hug you?"

It was one of the sweetest questions I'd ever been asked. "Yes, you can hug—"

A squeal, followed by a burst of laughter escaped my lips when Mackenzie jumped into me, knocking me back onto my butt. "Thank you," she said, hugging me tightly. "Thank you a whole lot."

Squeezing her tight, I rocked her from side to side just as my mama had done me hours earlier. "You're welcome, sweet girl." Burying my face in her dirty blonde hair, I breathed her in, memorizing her scent while praying that I'd see her again one day. "I just want you to do one more thing for me."

She didn't move, nor did she speak. Instead, she just continued to lean on me, hugging me with every bit of strength she had.

"In the future, when you get the chance, I want you to tell someone who's struggling that it will all get better. All we have to do is hold on and keep fighting until it does."

She nodded against me. "I promise I'll tell someone else what you told me. That life can be ugly, but that one day it'll get a whole lot more beautiful."

It was a promise that warmed my heart.

And one that Mackenzie kept.

Chapter Twenty-Six

CHASE

*a*shley was sitting on the edge of my bed.

On *my* bed.

It was a first.

She'd been in my apartment plenty of times before, but I'd always made sure to steer clear of my room when we hung out because I didn't want her to feel pressured into doing something she wasn't ready to.

But now, she was here.

In my room.

Wearing my t-shirt.

Fuck. Me.

"Are you sure you don't mind if I stay in here with you tonight?" she asked, biting into her bottom lip. "Because I don't mind camping out on the sofa—"

"You are *not* sleeping on the goddamned couch," I snapped, interrupting her. "I'll sleep on the floor first."

She dropped her gaze to her lap and picked at a piece of lint on my shirt. "I don't want you to sleep on the floor," she whispered before looking up again. "I want you to sleep with me"—she paused—"in your bed."

I couldn't stop the wonky smile that tipped one corner of my mouth. "Yeah?"

She nodded, her pretty brown eyes void of any hesitation. "Yeah."

Unsure of what to do, I crossed my arms and looked around, searching for divine intervention. As much as I'd fantasized about falling asleep with Ashley tucked safely in my arms, I was a helluva lot unprepared.

Did I strip down first?

Did I just jump in?

"Chase." My girl's voice held a hint of humor. "What are you doing?"

Realizing it was better just to tell her the truth, I held my hands up and chuckled. "Sweetness, I have no idea what I'm doing here. This extends beyond my areas of expertise."

Smiling, she stood from the bed and crossed the room, coming to a stop in front of me. "Before we do anything else, we need to talk."

I did not like the way that sounded.

Not a damned bit.

Sliding my hand into her hair, I pushed the silky strands free of her face. "What do you want to talk about, beautiful girl?"

She fidgeted, her anxiety stirring. "You and me."

I'm not even going to lie. At that point, I was close to freaking out. "What about you and me?"

I don't know what I was expecting her to say exactly, but it sure as hell wasn't the words that came out of her mouth next.

Those words? *I want this to be real.*

My brows furrowed. "What do you mean? This is real. Me and you—"

She silenced me by pressing a single finger to my lips. "What I mean," she started, "is that I want us to be official."

Her words hit me straight in the chest, and for a brief moment, I just stared at her, hoping like hell that I'd hadn't become so desperate that I was hearing shit now. "You want to be my girlfriend?"

The damned lip biting was back. "Yes. That's why I made that joke about the t-shirt back at the shelter."

"Are you sure about this?" I asked, sliding my hands down to cradle the sides of her neck. "Because if you aren't ready, then I'll wait."

Lower lip trembling, she looked toward the window, her gaze locked on the star-filled sky. "Do you want me, Chase?" She turned her head back my way; our eyes met. "Like, truly want me?"

"More than my next goddamned breath."

Hands on my stomach, she caressed my skin, along with the muscles that laid beneath. "Then I'm yours."

Two years.

That's how long I'd waited.

And now it had paid off...

Because Ashley Moretti was finally *mine*.

Pulling herself out of my hold, my girl took a step back. Eyes on my face, she slowly raised my shirt up before pulling it over her head and dropping it to the ground by her feet, leaving her in a small pair of panties.

Baby pink.

Sheer.

"If we're going to do this," she said. "Then, I need your help."

Determined to keep my eyes on her face, I clenched my hands, blinking repeatedly. "What do you need me to do?"

Lifting her hand, she ran a fingertip down my chest, then my stomach. Reaching the top of my pants, she hooked her finger in the waistband and pulled me forward.

"What I need," she whispered, her voice throaty sounding, "is for you to conquer a few of my demons." Conquer her demons? I'd spent the last few years fighting to do just that. "And to do that, I need you to make love to me."

My mind blanked.

My heart dropped.

And my cock? That fucker grew.

Exponentially.

"But I need you to go slow," she continued. "And you can't—"

"I won't look away," I interrupted, already knowing what she was going to say. "Swear to God, I won't look away."

Satisfied with my answer, my girl turned and moved back to the bed. Climbing atop it, she laid back and bent her knees at the waist.

Fists clenched, her face was pulled tight, her breathing labored, making it evident that she was scared.

No, more like terrified.

"Nah," I said, shaking my head. "We're not doing it like this."

Her brows furrowed as confusion set in. But I gave her no time to ask questions before moving forward and scooping her up into my arms.

Holding her slight weight tight, I turned and deposited her on top of my dresser, bringing us almost face-to-face.

Wedging my hips between her spread thighs, I circled her wrist with my fingers and placed her shaking hands on my chest, directly above my heart. "Feel that?"

Uncertainty filled her eyes as she nodded.

"That beats for you, Sweetness. It has since the moment we met, and it will—"

"—until you take your final breath," she finished for me.

"Good girl," I replied, my lips tipping. "At least you listen to me sometimes."

That got a smile out of her. "Well, I can't listen all the time. What would be the fun in doing that?"

I chuckled. "Sounds like something your mama would say."

Knowing I was right, she shrugged.

"But I need you to listen to me now. Every single word." With her eyes holding mine steady, I continued. "I know you're scared, and I get why, but I need you to understand that I will *not* do anything that you don't want me to. It doesn't matter how heated shit gets. If you get uncomfortable, scared, or want it to end, you tell me, and I will *stop*. Immediately."

"Why?" Gaze dipping to the ground, she shook her head. "I don't understand why you're so good to me."

Hearing her say those words...

They broke my heart.

"The reason is simple," I replied, trailing my fingertips up the outside of her bare thighs. "Because I love you, Sweetness."

Her head jerked up.

It wasn't the first time I'd said those words to her, but there was something about this time that was different. It was almost like she was finally hearing them instead of just letting them go in one ear and out the other.

"I've loved you since I was eighteen-years-old, and I will love you until the very end. Bottom line."

Resting her hands atop my moving ones, she pulled in a breath and met my eyes once more. "Want to know a secret?"

I smiled. "Always."

"I love you too."

Four words.

That was all it took for my heart to stop.

"And I have for a long time. I just..."

Cupping her face, I took her mouth with mine, silencing the words she was about to speak. Words that I knew would tear her up to say.

When our lips finally parted, and she exhaled, I kissed away each tear that rolled down her cheeks.

A reminder of how hurt she still was, I hated to see her cry.

Damned well *hated* it.

"Say it again, Ashley." I'm not the least bit ashamed to admit that I wanted to hear those words—the ones I'd waited so long to hear—fall from her lips once more.

I needed them.

Just like I needed her.

"I love you, Chase Jacobs," she whispered, her shoulders shaking. "Now, make love to me."

Heart in my throat, I nodded. "Wrap your arms around me, baby." When she did as I asked, I lifted her from the dresser and moved her to the bed, where I laid her flat on her back. On my knees, I leaned back, fisted my shirt behind my neck, and ripped it over my head. "We're going to take this slow."

"Promise?" She needed me to reassure her.

I gladly did. "I fucking swear it."

Grasping her hips, I dropped my mouth to hers, nipping her bottom lip between my teeth. Her hands flew to my shoulders, her fingers digging into my flesh in return.

Breaking our connection, I jumped off the bed long enough to push my sweats and briefs down in one jerky—not to mention uncoordinated—move.

Swear to Christ, I almost toppled over and face planted on the floor as every ounce of swagger I possessed went flying right out the damned window.

My antics made Ashley laugh.

Wasn't really the vibe I was going for, but I'd take it.

At least until her gaze dropped to my cock.

Eyes bulging, she shook her head. "I think I changed my mind," she said, pinching her lips together. "I know I've seen it before, but now it just seems bigger." She paused and pointed at it. "I don't know how that... *thing* will fit.

If the situation hadn't been what it was, I would've laughed.

But my girl looked genuinely scared.

Shit was *not* funny right now.

I looked down, my gaze landing on my angry-looking dick. "We'll make it work."

Climbing back on the bed, I kneeled between her sexy-as-hell legs and hooked my fingers in the sides of her panties. "Ready?"

She nodded. "Ready."

In one quick pull, I yanked them off and tossed them behind me. Then, feeling as though I was about to come out of my damn skin, I slid my hands up the insides of her thighs and slowly spread her legs, revealing her slick flesh to me.

My mouth began to water.

"Every time I think you can't get any more beautiful, you do." Trailing my fingers over her pelvic bone and up her belly, I traced invisible lines on her creamy skin, drawing patterns that only my eyes could see.

Hands stopping beneath her breasts, I met her stare. "Can I touch you?"

Lips parted, she nodded as her chest rose and then fell, her pants for air coming quicker each second.

Never taking my eyes from hers, I leaned over her and pulled one nipple into my mouth. Back arching, her head dropped to the pillow as her hands found my hair.

Tugging on the locks, she pulled me closer, refusing to let me come up for air.

Not that I was complaining.

Releasing her flesh with a pop, I trailed my lips down her belly, stopping only to nuzzle her lone stretch mark with my face.

Ashley's breath hitched at the move, and I knew—I damned well knew—that if she lifted her head again, I'd see tears in her pretty brown eyes.

"Sweetness, look at me."

She pulled in a breath and pushed to her elbows, surprising me.

And yeah, there were tears.

"Watch me, beautiful girl," I whispered as I crawled down her body and positioned my broad shoulders between her legs. "Watch what I do to you." Trepidation danced over her features, and I did my best to alleviate the anxiety I knew was thrumming through her system. "I have you, Ashley. Always, baby."

"I know you do," she replied. "Because you promised."

That I did.

More than ready to wash away every ounce of fear and pain she'd felt at the hands of another, I licked her sweet pussy from bottom to top in one swipe.

Her entire body tightened as she cried out, her hands finding my short blond locks a second time. "Chase," she whimpered, her hips searching for the pleasure I'd only given her a hint of. "Please..."

"You keep saying my name," I replied as I hooked her legs over my shoulders. "Remember who it is that's touching you."

Another scream came as I dove back in, licking, sucking, and nipping her tender flesh, memorizing her reaction to every move as I learned every little thing that drove her wild.

Eating her pussy with everything I had, I slipped one finger inside of her and groaned when her wet heat clamped down, pulling me deep. *Fuck. Me.*

"Goddamn, Ashley," I mumbled against her. "Just. Goddamn."

Slipping a second finger deep inside her tightness, I sat up and leaned over her, blanketing her body with mine. Attacking her lips with mine, I delved my tongue deep, fucking her mouth the same way I was about to fuck her pussy.

Feeling her insides clench and quiver against my fingers, I pulled them free, stopping the orgasm that was about to wash over her.

Panting and on the edge of looking a tad bit homicidal, my girl glared at me, her eyes narrowed into tiny slits. "Why in the name of sweet baby Jesus did you stop?"

Remaining silent, I leaned to the side and pulled a condom out of my nightstand drawer. After tearing the foil open with my teeth, I sheathed my throbbing length. "When you come for the first time in my bed, it'll be with me deep inside of you."

Her eyes flared.

Cock in hand, I sat back on my calves and pulled her toward me, positioning her ass on the top of my thighs. "You ready for this?" I asked as my thumb found her clit. She jerked as I rubbed the nub, once again priming her for the explosion I was about to give her. "Cause if not, we can stop."

"Chase," she said, moaning. "Don't stop."

"I won't."

Dropping her bottom back to the mattress, I hovered over her once more and hooked her legs around my hips. Positioning the head of my dick against her entrance, I lowered myself to my elbows, bringing us chest to chest.

Our eyes locked.

"You ready?"

Her bottom lip trembled, and I could see the panic beginning to brew.

Flat out refusing to let it steal her away from me, I slid my hands into her hair, twining the strands around my fingers. "It's me, Sweetness," I said, feeling my heart twist. "And from this moment on, it'll only be me."

Giving me a shaky nod, she blew out a breath. "Don't look away."

I swallowed, a myriad of emotions swelling in the base of my throat. "Never."

Winding her arms around my back, she dug her nails into my shoulder blades, clutching me tight. "I'm ready. Take me."

With one slow thrust of my hips, that's precisely what I did.

Sinking into her, I finally claimed her as my own...

It was Heaven.

Nothing less.

"Chase!" she screamed, arching into me.

Resting my forehead against hers, I inhaled as she exhaled and pulled her essence deep inside me. "I finally found it," I whispered, my eyes glazing over with tears. "After all this time, I finally found it."

Ashley's tears started to fall as I began to slowly move. "What," she started. "What did you f-find?" She stuttered and then moaned as I twisted my hips, dragging the head of my cock along her G-spot.

Chest so tight I felt like I would burst, I pressed my forehead to hers. "My home, Ashley Jo." Another thrust; a second twist. "In you, I found my home."

Each word was the truth.

Before Ashley, I'd been lost.

And now, with her heart belonging to mine, I was found.

Chapter Twenty-Seven

ASHLEY

*M*orning came far too soon.

Seated at the small kitchen table in Chase's apartment, I watched as he dug through the pantry for something to eat while my oatmeal—which Ty had cooked for me—cooled.

Blinking to clear the sleep-induced fog blurring my eyes, I lifted my arms in the air and stretched. "Where's Heidi Bug at? She's usually up before everyone."

After leaving the shelter the evening before, Heidi had spent the night with Ty—a first for her—while I stayed with Chase. Because she was staying at the apartment as well, my mama hadn't thrown a full-fledged hissy fit when informed that I wouldn't be coming home at midnight like I originally planned.

Well, she'd thrown a fit.

But thanks to Heidi's smoothing-over skills, she hadn't shown up at the apartment door, gun in hand, ready to drag me back home.

My dad either.

Then again, he probably didn't even know I'd stayed with Chase yet. Thanks to being stuck on overnight shifts for the past few weeks, he didn't make it home until mid-morning most days, which meant I had a bit of time before he quite possibly showed up, pissed off as all get out.

"She's in the shower," Ty answered from the stove where he was plating scrambled eggs. "Should be out any minute."

Stirring my oatmeal, I silently nodded.

"This is complete horseshit."

I snapped my head up, my eyes finding Chase at the sound of his voice.

Wearing a pair of black sweats, no shirt, and sporting a headful of mussed hair, he looked more gorgeous than normal.

And that was saying something.

Chase was easily the hottest man I'd ever laid eyes on, but he wore the whole fresh-out-of-bed look like no other.

It was yet another thing I loved about him.

Love...

Never in my life did I think I'd be in a position where I loved a man, especially after everything I'd been through, but I can honestly say that at that point, I was head over heels in love with Chase Jacobs.

And I'd had sex with him.

More than once.

Though I'd experienced it, part of me still couldn't believe it was a reality. After the hell I'd been through, I'd spent the last two years convinced that being intimate with him was a feat I wouldn't be able to achieve.

I was wrong.

Big time.

A combination of patient and loving, Chase had given me exactly what I needed without taking something that I hadn't offered. Reading my reactions without error, he'd pressed forward when I wanted more and pulled back when I'd reached my limit and needed to regain my bearings.

He'd promised to go slow.

And he'd sworn to never look away.

As always, he'd kept his word.

And it was because of him—the man I'd fallen irrevocably in love with—that I'd been able to conquer a handful of my demons and take back a part of me that was stolen long ago, all the while learning to enjoy the pleasure he could give me.

"What's the matter now?" Ty asked, carrying the eggs to the table where I sat.

My guy didn't reply as he sat the bowl down onto the countertop and shoved his hand into a box of cereal, fishing around the contents. What he was looking for exactly, I didn't have a clue.

"These assholes forgot my stickers." Scowling, he pointed at the front of the package. "It says right here that they're included with my purchase. They cheated me."

Lord have mercy...

Here we go.

"You're kidding me, right?" Ty asked, his hand on the back of the chair across from me. "Seriously, tell me you're joking."

"I'm not kidding you, and hell no, I'm not joking," Chase replied, face twisting in annoyance. "The stickers were the entire reason I bought this nasty, sawdust tasting crap instead of my regular Lucky Charms. I was gonna give them to Gracie."

My heart warmed at my little sister's name. Though she was a tiny terror who was convinced she ruled the house—gee, I wonder where she got that from—she was one of the best things to ever come into my life.

Full of sass and smiles, I loved her so much.

So did Chase.

"Guess you'll just have to find another way to bribe her into liking you," Ty mumbled, taking a seat.

Pushing my hair back from my face, I rested my elbows on the table. "He doesn't need to bribe her. Gracie already loves him," I said. "Lucca, though"—I smiled—"that's a different story."

Chase scowled harder, his eyes narrowing. "It's because he knows your dad hates me."

I rolled my eyes and blocked him out as he went on a tirade, each word he spoke a tad harsher than the rest.

"My dad doesn't hate you, nor does he despise you," I said, once he was finished. "He just doesn't trust you."

And that was a fact.

"He has no reason not to trust me."

That wasn't exactly true. "You have a penis," I whisper-hissed. "That's reason enough."

At least it was in my dad's eyes.

Ty chuckled. "Your girl makes a solid point, bro. If I were Anthony, I wouldn't trust you either."

Chase looked ready to come out of his skin. Eyes narrowed, he fired back, "Thanks a lot, big brother. You're supposed to be on my side. Ya know, teammates and shit."

"I'm just saying," Ty replied, with a shrug. "When I have a little girl, you can bet your ass I'm not letting any man with a fire hose dangling between his legs come within fifteen feet of her before she's thirty, maybe even forty."

I'd burst into faux laughter to hide the fact that my heart was cracking at Ty's words. Obviously, he was looking forward to having a little girl, and yet I'd had one, but I didn't have her.

And it was all because of Dominic.

Don't cry, don't cry, don't cry!

"Can't you have a son?" Chase's words cut through the heart-wrenching fog surrounding me. "I mean, damn, Ty, I can't handle a girl. What if she wants to play dress up? Or have tea parties?"

A mess of emotions, I was going to blow a gasket. Speaking before I could put myself in check, I shot a glare Chase's way. "If she does, then you'll put on a pretty pink dress and sit down for a cup of imaginary tea." His mouth gaped, but I wasn't done with him yet. "Let me tell you a little secret, Jock."

I forced a smile.

"When it comes to little girls, you swallow down every ounce of pride you have, and you do what makes them happy. Since you and my father can't seem to have one civil conversation, how about you ask Hendrix? He'll tell you."

Angry and on a roll, I didn't let up.

"Want to know how many times I've seen that man have a tea party with Melody and Maci?" I tapped my fingers atop the table. "He even lets them paint his fingernails and put bows in his hair. He and Pop both do."

It's what any good father would do, and what I would've done as a mama if I'd been given a chance.

El diablo ruined that for me.

"Hey, Ashley," Ty said, giving me something to focus on other than the geyser of anger and hurt that spewed inside me. "Next time you see Cap getting his nails painted, send me a picture."

A genuine smile crossed my face. "That I can do."

"I'm not letting anybody paint my fingernails," Chase mumbled, starting back up where he'd left off. "My toenails maybe, but—"

Boom, boom, boom!

I flinched when someone slammed their heavy fist against the apartment door three times in rapid succession, then paused before doing it once again.

Boom, boom, boom!

Jumping up so quickly my chair skittered backward, I hollered, "I'll get it! I'm sure it's my dad... or my mom." I bit my bottom lip. "Oh God, please let it be my mom."

Knowing full-well what would happen if it were my dad and Chase answered, I ran out of the kitchen and through the living room.

Reaching the door, I disengaged the deadbolt and yanked it open without bothering to check the peephole.

It was a huge mistake.

Because right there, standing directly in front of me, was a man that I'd seen many times before. And that man? He was Dominic's main fixer, a corrupt cop with an unquenchable thirst for underage girls.

Jade in particular.

The things he'd done to her, the pain he'd made her feel...

Every bit of it came rushing back, making my stomach churn as bile climbed the length of my esophagus. I can't tell you how many nights Carmen and I had taken turns cleaning her up and then holding her close as she cried herself to sleep after spending a mere hour in his sadistic presence.

I hated him.

So damned much.

Hovering between rage and gut-wrenching agony, I briefly wondered why he was at Ty and Chase's door. But with one look, the question floating around my head was answered.

His hair, eyes, and bone structure...

They were identical to both his sons.

Oh God...

With the realization that my boyfriend's father was not only the man who'd terrorized the girl I'd once considered to be my sister, but that he'd also been the one to later dispose of her and Carmen's bodies on Dominic's orders, I stumbled back a single step.

"This isn't happening," I whispered, tears blurring my vision. "It's not."

The fixer, whose real name I didn't even know, smiled. "Well, I'll be damned," he mumbled, running a shaky hand down the side of his stubble-covered jaw. "It's D-boy's *Tesoro.*"

Moving into the doorway, he leaned against the frame and raked his bloodshot gaze over me, stopping at my chest. "I know someone who would be real interested in seeing you again."

Without having to think, I knew exactly who he was referring to.

Ellington.

Panic rising, I slapped my hand against my mouth and fought to bite back the scream climbing high into my throat.

Sucking on his teeth, he rubbed his finger along the dark bag beneath his right eye. "Reckon I should arrange that little meeting. Would make for a nice payday for me." He paused. Then, "But maybe I'll try you out for myself first. You're not my type, but—"

The man snapped his mouth shut and smiled deviously when Ty's booming voice rang out. "You son of a bitch," he snarled. "You made one hell of a mistake in coming here."

Ty swooped around me, putting himself in between his father and me as Chase yelled, "Get the hell away from her!" Grabbing my wrist, he pulled me into him, wrapping one arm around me. "Did he touch you?"

"N-no," I stammered.

The smile on the fixer's face grew as he watched Chase hold me tight while running a hand all over my body, searching for any injuries.

My world crumbled at the sight.

He knows what I really am.

Now he's going to tell.

And I'll lose Chase.

Forever.

Chest tightening, my hearing dulled as Ty and the fixer continued to speak, throwing one verbal barb after another at each other.

But though I was spinning out of control, I still heard the fixer when he said, "Chase, stop hiding in your brother's shadow and come on over here, son. You and I need to have a little chat about our future."

My insides splintered.

I didn't know what type of future the monster was referring to, but I knew without a doubt that there would no longer be one for Chase and me.

"How about you bring your pretty little girlfriend over here too?" he continued, sending me spiraling more than I already was. "I'd love to get to know her better."

My legs began to give way as Ty shoved his forearm into the jerk's throat and pushed him out into the hall, slamming the door closed behind him.

I started to fall, but Chase caught me just in time, taking my weight. Scooping me up, he cradled me like a baby against his chest just as Heidi bolted down the hall toward us, her terrified eyes the size of saucers.

Her mouth moved, but I couldn't make out a single thing she said.

After shooting me one last glance, she bolted out the door and straight into the hall, disappearing from sight just as the apartment walls began to close in on me.

Feeling myself detach, I looked up at Chase for what I thought may be one of the last times. "Chase." My words were strained, barely audible. "Please..."

Rushing back to his room, he laid me on his bed and climbed in next to me, holding me close. Cupping the side of my cheek with his hand, he said, "Ashley, baby, you're fine, just concentrate on the sound of my voice. It's just a panic attack."

Hearing his voice hurt, because I knew I wouldn't hear it much longer.

How long until he walks away?

"Sweetness, you're safe." He hugged me tighter, holding me just as he had through dozens of panic attacks in the past. "Just breathe for me, beautiful girl."

Tears fell from my eyes, but the pain in my chest began to dissipate, vanishing into thin air.

Numbness took its place.

"Goddammit, baby. Fucking fight to stay with me. Just breathe!"

I had no fight left in me.

As for breathing...

Once he left me, I'd suffocate.

"Ashley"—a tear fell from his eyes and landed on my cheek, mixing with my own—"I have you. I always will have you." He paused. "And I will never let go."

He was wrong.

He would let me go.

Because in the end, I gave him no other choice.

Chapter Twenty-Eight

ASHLEY

*E*verything was falling apart.

That truth was crystal clear as I sat on the floor next to my bed, my back pressed against the box spring, clutching Ellington's phone in my hand; the same one I'd stolen from him seconds after thrusting Carmen's knife deep into his thigh.

A move that I wished had killed him.

Unfortunately, I wasn't that lucky.

Though I didn't stick around to see what happened next, I'd scoured the local newspapers from the safety of the shelter the week that followed, searching for any news of what had come of the incident.

I'd found plenty.

Hailed District Attorney stabbed in botched carjacking, the headlines had said. *Suspect, an unidentified black male, remains at large.*

Just as I'd predicted, he hadn't gone to the police with the truth. He wasn't that stupid. Sick and psychotic? Yes. Dumb? No.

As cowardly as I could be, he knew that if he'd pointed the finger my way, I would've turned the phone, along with every sick piece of evidence it held over to an authority that was out of Ellington's corrupt reach.

But none of that mattered now.

No matter what steps I'd taken to ensure he never came after me, and despite how hard I'd fought to escape the demons from my past, everything was coming back around to destroy all the precious things I'd gained.

And it was all thanks to a man who'd spent his life hurting others in the vilest of ways possible. If Clyde Jacobs, a man whose name I'd only just learned, had never shown up at Ty and Chase's door, I could've continued to cope.

If only I'd been left alone, I knew I would've kept getting better, and most importantly, my secrets, the very ones that meant my end, would have stayed buried in the blackness which resided deep inside me.

Exactly where they belonged.

It was a moot point now because Dominic's most used fixer not only knew where I was, but he was fully aware of how much I meant to his youngest son; the very one he was trying to sink his claws into in order to secure a payday in the near future.

It would only be a matter of time before Ellington was aware of my location as well. That's if he didn't how already.

Which, I had a feeling he did.

Knowing him and with my luck, he'd probably had somebody watching my every move for the past two years. Honestly, part of me was surprised that he hadn't tried to retrieve the phone already.

Doing so would've been a risky move, one that had the potential to backfire if not executed just right. Also, my dad was a cop. That had likely been my only saving grace.

But as I said before, it didn't matter any longer. Because soon, whether I was ready or not, my sins would be revealed, and with them, my darkest secrets would be thrust into the light.

Hiding was no longer an option.

Not as long as Clyde Jacobs was still breathing.

Which brought me to the reason I sat all alone in my room, his phone clutched tightly in my shaking hand. If the truth was going to come out, which it soon would, then I couldn't be around when it did.

My heart was already broken.

My stained soul beyond salvation.

As horrible of a person as it made me, I refused to sit back and wait for the moment my family and friends, the very people who'd chosen to love me even when I couldn't love myself, found out every one of my ugly truths.

Truths that would warp how they saw me once they learned of the horrible things I'd done and allowed to happen.

Forever.

So, right or wrong, I was going to do what I did best and run, because leaving was my only choice even when I realized that in doing so, I would break everyone's hearts.

But what other choice did I have?

When my parents found out about Addie—a story that Clyde knew all too well—they would see me for exactly what I was.

A coward.

As for Chase, the moment he found out that Dominic hadn't been the abusive boyfriend as I'd allowed him to believe, but rather a sadistic pimp who sold me to any and everyone who offered him a couple hundred dollars for the chance to do anything they wanted to me instead, he'd walk away.

Well, *almost* anything they wanted.

There were two exceptions.

One, their lips were never allowed to touch mine, a rule that Ellington broke without fear of the consequences. It was an action that led to me being grazed by a bullet and to Carmen and Jade being murdered right in front of me.

He killed them because of me.

Every bit of it is my fault.

Two, a condom always had to be used; no exceptions. It was a rule that was followed without fail by everyone except the man who'd made it. The same man who, within months of finding me standing in front of the bus station, my life in tatters, had gotten me pregnant with his baby.

A baby he wouldn't allow me to keep.

When it's born, he'd said. *I'll handle it.*

And by handling it, he meant that he'd toss my child—*mine!*—into the swamps out on Highway 9 the moment she took her first breath. It was a threat he'd meant, and one I never allowed him to follow through with.

In the end, it didn't matter.

She was still gone, and a piece of me would be missing forever. Because without her, the beautiful little girl that I'd given life to, my soul would never be whole again.

Just as my life would forever be empty without Chase. For two years, he'd been my entire world, my rock, and the main person who held me together each time I felt myself beginning to fall apart.

And soon, he would be gone.

But it wasn't just knowing that I was about to lose him that tore me to shreds. It was the fact that I knew—I frickin' knew—that once he learned each of my ugly truths, that he'd never look at me the same again.

No longer would I be his Sweetness.

Instead, I'd be the whore who'd been passed around to dozens, if not hundreds of men, numbers that most couldn't fathom.

Already teetering on the edge of losing what remained of my mind, there was no way I'd be able to handle seeing the love he had for me vanish the moment he found out that the girl he once thought was beautiful, was instead hideous.

Both inside and out.

"Ashley..."

Startled by the sound of my father's deep voice, I jumped in place and swung my teary-eyed gaze to the door where he stood, his shoulder leaning against the frame.

"Can I come in?"

Quickly slipping the phone beneath my thigh to hide it from his eyes, I nodded. "Sure."

He moved into the room and sat down next to me, his back pressed against the bed just as mine was. Blowing out a breath, he reached over and took my hand in his, twining our fingers together.

His warmth seeped into me, causing my tears to fall faster. I would miss my entire family so much, but my dad was special. Always had been. Without him...

I didn't even want to think about it.

"*Principessa*, I need you to tell me about Sergeant Jacobs," he said, squeezing my hand tight.

I closed my eyes, replaying the scene from hours before through my head.

After waking up in Chase's bed after his dad's visit, my entire body trembling from the panic that remained, adrenaline still coursing through my veins, my father had been sitting there, waiting for me.

Arriving minutes after Clyde, he'd witnessed the confrontation between Ty and his father outside in the hall and after telling the eldest Jacobs to kick rocks, he'd stormed inside the apartment only to find me completely checked out thanks to the panic attack coming face-to-face with Dominic's main fixer had caused.

And that's when he knew.

Clyde Jacobs and I had a connection.

One which, knowing my father, he wouldn't rest until he figured out.

Needing to be closer to him, I leaned my head against his shoulder as the blackness began to stir, pulling the oxygen right out of my lungs.

"Tell me, sweetheart," he said. "How do you know him?"

As much as I wanted to tell him every ugly detail, I couldn't force the words to come.

"Alright," he said after a few minutes of my silence. "How about this—I'm going to ask you a question, and if the answer is yes, then all you have to do is squeeze my hand."

That I could do.

At least I thought so.

Nodding against him, I scooted closer, pressing my side against his. Even at twenty, I needed him to make me feel safe, especially from the demons that stirred inside me, their cruel taunts repeating on an unending loop in my head.

"Breathe for me, Ashley," he whispered, his thumb stroking the back of my hand.

Doing as he said, I took a breath.

Then, "*Principessa*, squeeze my hand if you know Clyde from the time you spent with Dominic."

Squeeze.

"Alright," he said in reply. "Did he work for Dominic?"

Squeeze.

"Good girl." He turned his head and pressed a kiss to the top of mine. "Now, did you ever see him commit a crime?"

I hesitated for the briefest moment.

But then I did as he'd asked.

I squeezed his hand once more.

His body stiffened. "Did he ever touch you?"

I didn't squeeze his hand.

He blew out a breath in response.

"Thank fucking Christ," he mumbled, his arm trembling against mine. "Now—"

"It wasn't me he touched," I said, cutting him off.

Blackness rising, my head felt as if it would explode as my secrets rose to the surface, and what little good remained in me demanded that I tell my father, the man I trusted with my whole heart, what happened, no matter what the consequences may be.

They mattered, the voice in my head said.

And their final truths need to be told.

Completely breaking, I ripped my hand from his and covered my ears as I rocked back and forth, my shoulder blades hitting my bed over and over.

"Ashley, sweetheart, what—"

"He killed them!" I screamed as my mind bent, nearly fracturing. "He killed them, and it's all my fault!"

Footsteps sounded, and I smelled my mother's distinct perfume as she ran into the room, her eyes wide. "What the hell happened?" she shrieked, concern and fear both bleeding into her voice.

Scooping me up into his arms just like Chase had done hours

before, my father held me against him as he stood and sat down on the bed, taking me with him. "Tell me, Ashley." His stern voice cut through the hysteria, reaching the sane part of me—as small as it was —that remained. "Who did Clyde kill?"

Clutching his dress shirt in my hands, I shook my head, my hair falling into my eyes. "Not Clyde," I said, my throat tight. "*Dominic.*"

My father's eyes hardened before mine. "Tell me who."

A sob broke free from my chest as I latched onto the tiny amount of courage I possessed and whispered, "Carmen and Jade." I took a shuddering breath. "Their names were Carmen Santiago and Jade Allen." Another breath. "And they were beautiful."

Pulling his eyes from mine, he looked at my mother. "Sunshine, get me my phone."

A combination of heartbreak and straight up-rage etched on her face, she nodded once.

Then, she raced out of the room.

————

The glass of water shook in my hand as I sat in the middle of the sofa, my head bowed.

"It's all my fault," I cried, insides twisting. "Every bit of it."

"How?" my dad, who stood in front of me, his trembling hands resting on his hips. "How is what Dominic did to those girls any of your fault?"

My head snapped up, my tear-filled eyes finding his furious ones. "Because they were trying to help me!" I shrieked, my shrill voice rising with each word. "They were trying to help me, and Dominic killed them for it!"

My mama, who looked more enraged that I'd ever seen her, glared at my dad. "Tell me you can do something," she said, hands fisted. "Because if not, I'm sure as shit going to!"

"What did he do with them, *Principessa*?" Dad asked, his tone hard but steady. "Where are their bodies?"

I clenched my eyes shut as the memories from that night battered me, one after the other. "*Clyde*," I spat, chest aching, "disposed of their bodies within minutes of Dominic murdering them. But it wasn't until *el diablo* tried to kidnap me from the shelter that I learned the bastard had dumped them in the swamp."

Room spinning, I pulled in a breath.

I will not let the blackness take me.

Not until they know.

I will not fail.

Not this time.

"Which swamp?"

Setting the glass on the coffee table in front of me, I bent forward and laced my fingers behind my head, rocking back and forth. "I don't know."

After a few moments, when he said nothing more, I lifted my head and glanced from my mama to him, reading the myriad of emotions flitting across their faces.

But it was my dad's that made my entire body still.

Lips thinned in a straight line, all it took was one scrutinizing look at his face to see that I'd been one-hundred percent correct when thinking that Dominic, and by extension Clyde, would never be brought to justice over what happened to my girls.

And it was because of his sullen expression, combined with that realization, that any control I still possessed snapped right in half.

Both heartbroken and pissed, I jumped up, the injustice of the entire situation nipping at my raw nerves, sending me into a manic-fueled tailspin. "Dominic and Clyde both deserve to rot for what they did to Carmen and Jade!"

My mama opened her mouth to say something, but I kept yelling, my lungs burning from the exertion, without giving her a chance to get a word in edgewise. "They may have been nothing more than street whores, but they mattered!"

"*Principessa*—"

"No!" I screamed, holding up both my hands. "You don't get to call me a princess because that is *not* what I am. Like my two best friends who died on a dirt-laden floor of a miserable trap house, I am *nothing!*"

"You are not nothing!" My mama screamed, losing the control she was struggling to maintain on her infamous temper. "You are my daughter and—"

"They were someone's daughter too!" I fired back, not giving a crap how disrespectful I was being by yelling at her. "Jade's parents died in a car crash when she was thirteen. They were good people, both teachers, but they were alone in this world, and she had nowhere to go. So she was sent into foster care." My entire body vibrated with rage. "And that's where she was raped for the first, second, and third times."

It made me sick to think about.

"Months after the first attack, she ran away to escape it all, but in the end, she fell into Dominic's waiting arms, and suddenly the hell she lived back in foster care was nothing compared to what he and Clyde put her through."

"What did Clyde do to her?"

My knees shook at my father's question.

Don't falter.

Hold steady.

Speak your truth.

One of them at least.

"He raped her!" I screamed, my hysterical voice echoing throughout the house, which was thankfully empty of anyone else. Across the street at Grandmama's, Lucca, and Gracie hadn't been home since my dad carried me through the front door after leaving Ty and Chase's apartment. "And that was *after* he beat the crap out of her!"

My mama's eyes slid closed as ghosts from her own past rushed forward, bringing with them one painful memory after another. "What about Carmen?" she asked, wrapping a single arm around her belly.

Sob after sob jolted me.

"Carmen was a Colombian beauty queen," I said, pride filling me. "But she ended up with Dominic after her cartel-connected boyfriend auctioned her off." My stomach rolled, the urge to vomit increasing.

"She couldn't cope, so she started shooting up, which Dominic let her do because it made her more pliable."

I hated him.

Hated. Him!

"In the end, she was a shell of the woman she'd once been, and more than ready to die, she sacrificed herself to save Jade and me."

Dad, who was one of the most controlled men I'd ever encountered, looked close to shoving his fist into a wall, something Chase would have done if he'd been there.

A hot scalpel sliced across my heart, cutting me deep as his handsome face flashed through my mind.

Don't think about him now.

Just don't.

"How did Jade die?"

I blew out a shaky breath at my dad's question. "Dominic accused her of stealing from him and shot her. I tried... I tried to save her, but he hit m-me"—my voice broke—"and I couldn't get u-up."

Unable to stop herself, my mama rushed forward and wrapped her arms around me, pulling me into her. I willingly went, accepting every bit of comfort she offered, even though I didn't deserve an ounce of it.

"Tony," she whispered, resting her chin atop my head as I buried my face in her neck and gave myself over to the agony ripping through me. "Tell me you can do something."

With nothing good to say, he didn't answer right away.

Like Chase, he wasn't a liar, and since his hands were tied—something I was sure of—he wouldn't plant false hope in either of our heads.

"Legally? No," he finally said, relaying a truth that I'd always known. "If Jacobs disposed of the girls' bodies in the swamp, then there won't be anything left. And without any evidence, we won't be able to secure an arrest warrant, much less a conviction."

My mama hugged me tighter. "You have Ashley."

A humorless chuckle spilled from my chapped lips. "No grand jury will listen to me," I said, the pain in my chest spreading through my entire body. "Not after they find out what I was."

And definitely not with Ellington as the DA.

"Tony, do something!" she yelled at my father, her body vibrating with rage against mine. "I don't care how illegal or dirty it is, you do something because those bastards hurt those girls"—she paused as tears of her own began to fall—" and they hurt *my* daughter!"

As straight-laced as they come, I didn't expect my dad to agree to her emotion-fueled demand, so when he dipped his chin once in agreement, my legs almost collapsed.

Pulling his phone from his back pocket, he headed out of the room. "Where are you going?"

Dad stopped walking at mama's question.

Jaw ticking, he glanced at us over his shoulder. "First, I'm going to have a conversation with Ty down at the station, and depending on what he says, I'm planning on placing a call."

mama raised her chin in the air. "Who's that call gonna be to?"

His cheek twitched, something that only happened when he was extremely pissed. "Someone a lot goddamned scarier than Dominic West and Clyde Jacobs could ever hope to be." Another twitch. "Arianna Ivanova."

I had no idea who that was, but one day in the future, I would find out.

And when that day came, I would see first-hand that my dad had been right. Arianna Ivanova truly was more terrifying than *el diablo* could ever think to be.

And a whole lot deadlier too.

Chapter Twenty-Nine

CHASE

I was about to snap.

After only having seen Ashley a handful of times in the past few weeks, I was more than ready to rip the apartment to pieces. I had no idea what was going on because she'd completely shut down on me. Ever since my fuckface of a father had shown up at the door, she'd pulled away, building wall after wall to keep me out.

It was bullshit.

Don't get me wrong, I didn't blame my beautiful girl because obviously something had triggered her sudden change in behavior, but hard as I tried, I couldn't put my finger on what had done it.

Yeah, she'd come face to face with my dad, bastard that he is, but I wasn't sure if that's what had caused her to backslide or not. I mean, yeah, she knew what an abusive piece of shit he'd been to Ty, but he had never hurt her.

If he had, he'd be dead.

As a fucking doornail.

Either way, it wasn't okay, and I blamed Clyde completely. The only regret I had was not getting the chance to beat his ass once Ty was through with him.

If Ashley hadn't flown straight into a panic attack, one which left her mentally checked out, I would have done it too, the consequences be damned.

I just wish I knew what he said to her.

But I doubted it was something I'd ever get to the bottom of.

"That piece of shit," I hissed from where I sat in the middle of the sofa, my fisted hands resting on my thighs. "Swear to Christ, if I ever see—"

"Who are you talking to?" Heidi, who stood in the hallway, holding a cup of coffee, asked. "I know I'm deaf and all, but even I could hear all that huffin' and puffin' you've been doing from the other end of the hall."

One corner of my mouth tipped in a smile. "I keep forgetting you live here now, Bug," I replied, honestly. "Sorry."

She waved a dismissive hand in my direction. "No reason to be sorry. It's a big adjustment for everybody. Plus, you didn't disturb me. Well, maybe you did a little. But only because I was trying to figure out what you're all pissy about."

I chuckled. "You should know."

Tilting her head to the side, she looked at me with a questioning expression. "What do you mean?"

I leaned forward, the urge to slam my fist down onto the coffee table increasing with each second. "Ashley's your best friend," I replied. "You going to tell me you don't know something is going on with my girl? You two are normally joined at the hip. She must've said something."

Sadness filled her eyes, making my chest ache.

Closing the space between us, she took a seat next to me and placed her cup on the end table. "She hasn't said anything to me." Her chin wobbled the slightest bit. "She'll usually answer when I call, but she doesn't..." A tear fell from her eye as her voice momentarily trailed off. "I feel like she's going backward, and I don't know how to help her. The more I try to pull her back in, the harder she pushes me away. She's just..." Leaning back on the sofa, she crossed one leg over the other and wrapped her arms around her middle. "It's like something inside of her broke, and I can't stand it."

I couldn't stand it either.

But I didn't know how to fix it.

I'd called, I'd texted, and I'd even shown up at her house multiple times only to have Shelby turn me away because Ashley was sleeping, something she seemed to be doing an awful lot of lately.

Which, speaking of sleep...

I'd never seen Shelby look so rough. Moretti either for that matter. Last time I saw them together, both had bags under their eyes, and Shelby looked pale as hell. It seemed like she'd lost a little bit of weight too, and I know that shit wasn't on purpose. A woman who prided herself on being curvy, there was no chance she was dieting.

I might've been slow when it came to certain things, but it was apparent both she and Moretti were struggling. I knew exactly why too.

Ashley.

My stomach twisted at the thought. My girl was hurting, and there wasn't a damned thing I could do as long as she continued to isolate herself.

"Has Shelby said anything to you?"

Heidi shook her head. "Not really. Just said she's going through a rough patch, but she and Tony are trying to pull her out of it. Pop and Grandmama too." Thinning her lips, she drummed her fingers atop her thigh. "This all started when your dad showed up. Do you think seeing him would trigger something?"

My jaw clenched. "Her ex was abusive, Heidi, and she has PTSD because of it. I'm sure coming face to face with someone just like him could've done some major damage. The only problem is, I don't know how we can make things better. She's struggled before, but never for this long, and never this hard."

Saying those words pissed me right off.

My fucking father.

He'd done this.

"Her ex," Heidi mumbled, an emotion I couldn't read flashing in her eyes. "You talking about Dominic?"

I nodded. "You know something I don't?" Judging by the way her eyes flared the slightest bit at my question, I couldn't help but wonder if she did. "My girl have more than one abusive ex?"

Turning her head, she ripped her gaze from mine. "No."

My eyes narrowed.

Something was off.

"You sure about that?"

Heidi swallowed and shook her head. Picking her mug of coffee back up, she took a sip. "I'm sure."

I opened my mouth to start interrogating her because it was obvious that she was holding back, but stopped short of doing so when my phone rang.

Please let it be her...

Heart pounding so hard I thought it may explode, I ripped my phone from my pocket and pressed it to my ear. "Hello?"

"Chase..."

I blew out a pent-up breath. "Ashley, baby—"

"Can you come get me?" she asked, her voice unsure and timid.

She didn't even need to ask. "Of course I'll come get you. You at home? If so, I can be there in ten minutes." It was a twenty-minute drive from my apartment to her house, but I'd break every damned manmade traffic law in order to reach her as fast as possible. "Sweetness, answer me."

"I'm at home." She sniffled, and my heart cracked. "I'm so sorry, Chase," she whispered, the pain she was fighting like hell to hold back bleeding into her tone. "I know I'm hurting you by staying away, but I don't mean to. I just... I'm a whole lot of broken right now."

A lump formed in my throat.

I couldn't breathe.

Could. Not. Fucking. Breathe.

"You're not broken. Bent, yeah, but not broken," I croaked out, my voice foreign-sounding. "Never broken."

Another sniffle. Then, "Can you bring Heidi with you? I miss her so much."

My eyes met Heidi's. "Of course I'll bring Bug. She needs to get out of the house anyway. She's starting to look paler than normal and

—" I grunted when Heidi punched me in the arm. "Ow, goddammit. You punch hard as hell for a girl."

Ashley giggled through the phone, and I smiled. "You laughing at Heidi kicking my ass, Sweetness?" Before she got the chance to reply, I looked back over at Bug. "Hit me again. This time harder. Don't give a shit how much it hurts, my girl thought it was funny."

Heidi did not disappoint.

One quick jab straight to the chest, and I sucked in a harsh breath. "You didn't have to hit me in the tit!"

Ashley's giggle turned into a full-blown laugh.

Heidi though? She flipped me off.

The little shit.

Her and Ty are perfect for one another.

Shaking my head, I stood and moved away from Heidi. She may have been short, but she wasn't weak. "We're leaving now." I was antsy and ready to hold her in my arms. Immensely so. "I'll be there in ten. Love you, beautiful girl. Always."

I held my breath, waiting.

Come on, baby.

Say it back.

"I love you too," she replied. "Always."

At her words, my anxiety vanished.

My pain abated.

And my heart? It soared.

Without wasting another second, I ended the call.

Then, together, Heidi and I bounced.

Chapter Thirty

ASHLEY

I was selfish.

Utterly and completely selfish.

I had absolutely no business calling Chase and asking him to come and pick me up, especially when I knew that things between us were crumbling and before long, everything we'd worked to build would be nothing but dust.

But I couldn't stay away.

I'd tried, God knows I had, but I'd failed.

More than once.

The invisible rope that tied his heart to mine was too strong, and when it grew taut in a silent demand that I find the man who I knew was my soulmate, everything in me would ache with a ferocity that I'd never experienced until he and I were face to face once more.

I hated it.

But I loved it too.

And yet, it was killing me.

Killing. Me.

With the threat of my past being exposed looming over my head like an ax prepared to strike, I'd made plans to walk away before he learned the truth.

As worried as I had been about him leaving me once he found out who—or rather what—I truly was, I couldn't wait for that to happen. Losing him was going to destroy any good that remained in me, but letting him be the one to pull away wasn't an option.

Bad as it sounds, I would've rather he hated me for breaking his heart, than look at me with disgust when he learned of the life I'd been forced into at fifteen. Because let's face it, even if he understood that I had no choice but to do the things I'd done, he still wouldn't want me, and thinking that he possibly could was not only foolish but dangerous.

I just wasn't good enough.

I never had been.

And I never would be.

Chase was going into the NFL for heaven sakes, and as talented as he was, I had no doubt he'd become a star. A man like him, in a position like that, deserved a whole lot better than a damaged former teen prostitute with more problems than she could count.

I'd been stupid to think I could keep my past from him.

Like Grandmama always said, secrets can only stay hidden for so long.

Obviously, she was right.

As for Heidi, she deserved better too. Beautiful, sweet, and possessing a heart of gold, she needed a best friend who was her match. Not me, a girl who'd been broken since she was a child.

You see, Chase and Heidi, they were good...

But me? I was poison.

And everyone who got to close suffered.

Carmen.

Jade.

Addie.

My sweet baby Addie...

Turns out, loving me was lethal. It was a truth my family was coming to understand, and one which I refused to let Chase and Heidi learn.

No matter how much it hurt, I had to walk away, had to let them go before it was too late.

But first, I needed one more day to pretend that everything was going to be okay and that my family, my heart, and my entire world weren't close to imploding.

And it was because of that need that I found myself in the backseat of Heidi's car, straddling Chase's lap, his cock wedged deep inside me as I rode him with abandon, his strong hands cupping my bare breasts.

Parked at the end of the nearly empty drugstore parking lot, hidden from any passerby's eyes, we made love as Heidi waited inside for a prescription to be filled, something that would take half an hour according to the pharmacist.

Head dropped back, I cupped his shoulders as I rolled my hips, taking every inch he had to give. Wanting to memorize the feel of him twitching inside me, rapidly reaching the point of no return, I closed my eyes and concentrated, cataloging every beautiful moment that I moved atop him as he grunted and cursed beneath me, his firm-yet-gentle hands caressing every curve I possessed.

"Ashley..." The sound of his voice sent chills racing down my spine. "Baby, look at me."

I didn't want to look.

Because if I did, my heart would break.

I just knew it.

But as always, when it came to Chase, I couldn't resist. So I did as he asked and lifted my head, meeting his gaze. His hands came to my cheeks, cupping them softly as I slid my arms around his neck and buried my fingers in his short locks, tugging on the blond strands.

"I love you," he said, touching his sweaty forehead to mine. "So goddamn much."

I blinked to keep the tears that were filling my eyes from falling. "I love you too," I replied, unable to stop the truth from slipping past my lips. "With every broken piece of me. Don't"—I moaned as he hit a spot deep inside me, one which only he'd ever touched—"ever forget that."

Our lips met.

I savored his taste, along with the feel of his mouth on mine as he dropped his hands to my hips and lifted me before pulling me back down on his length. The thrust was hard, and I cried out as my body screamed for more.

"Chase!"

Biceps bunching, he continued to drive into me while yanking me down, forcing me to feel every bit of the pleasure that he was capable of giving me. "I'm going to come, baby," he said, his eyes on mine. "You've gotta get off."

Driven by desire, I shook my head.

My orgasm was within reach, and as messed up as it may sound, I wanted him to come inside me. I wanted to feel it, to feel *him* this one time because after the moment was over, it would never return.

This is the end.

"Come in me. I—" My words were replaced with a scream when my orgasm burst free, obliterating my ability to speak, to think, to do anything but feel.

So that's what I did.

Pleasure, heartbreak, bliss, agony.

I felt it. All of it.

Repeatedly.

Body trembling, I dug my fingers into Chase's shoulders as his cock jerked deep inside me, and he yelled—yes, yelled—as his own orgasm hit him, pulling wave after wave of pleasure from his body as his come lashed my insides, coating my walls in warmth.

"I love you," he groaned, repeating his words from seconds before as his fingertips gripped my hips. "Forever."

I dipped my head, hiding my face from his view as the first tear fell.

Deep in my heart, I knew that loving me was going to destroy him.

Unfortunately, I was right.

———

I was frozen in fear.

Panicked, I sat next to Chase in the backseat of Heidi's car and watched as a uniformed police officer approached the driver's side of the vehicle, the lights from his squad car reflecting in the rear and side-view mirrors.

No one else seemed overly concerned, but even before I got a good look at the man walking up to Heidi's window, his hand resting on his gun, I knew things were about to go bad.

Though I may not have been the smartest person in the world, I had more street smarts than most, and one thing I'd learned long ago was to always listen to my gut.

And right then, my gut was screaming at me to run.

The problem was, I couldn't do that.

I may have been prepared to walk away and break Chase and Heidi's hearts in the process, but I wouldn't leave them to the monster who lurked close by, his intentions anything but good.

"Chase," I whispered just as the officer tapped on Heidi's window, his scarred knuckles visible through the tinted glass. "That's..."

Heidi rolled down the window, unaware of who stood on the other side.

But Chase knew.

Unlatching his seatbelt, he leaned forward, his jaw clenched tight.

"Chase," Heidi said quietly, finally catching on to what was happening. "Whatever he says, don't get out of the car."

"Fuck that," he growled, leaning closer to her. "Let me handle this, Heidi. He's here for me."

No, he wasn't.

He was there for both of us.

"No," she replied, shaking her head.

"Heidi—"

I screamed as my best friend's door was pulled open, and Clyde Jacobs' hand suddenly circled her small bicep. "Come here, bitch. It's time you and I had a chat."

In a flash, he yanked her from the car and onto the scorching Georgia asphalt that made up the desolate stretch of Highway 9, where we sat parked on the shoulder of the road.

"Heidi!"

Mind-numbing fear climbed high into my throat, completely immobilizing me as Chase jumped out of the car.

Knowing that I needed to move, that I needed to save her—like I should've saved Carmen and Jade—I closed my eyes and drew in a breath.

Get out of the car!

If you don't, she'll die!

They both will!

Behind the vehicle, shouting ensued as I fought with my body to move, something which was proving impossible as I remained stock-still, wholly frozen to the spot.

Get up!

Just as I latched onto the courage to move, I heard Clyde chuckle. Then, "Looks like I grabbed the wrong girl."

Before I could react, my door was ripped open, and I was forced out of the car. In mere seconds, Clyde had my back pressed to his front and a single arm wrapped around my chest, anchoring me in place.

Ten feet away, Heidi climbed to her feet from where she'd been on the ground, her hands and knees covered in torn skin and blood. My heart twisted at the sight.

Lifting the service-issued gun he held—one which I hadn't seen until that moment—Clyde pointed it at Heidi's chest.

Just like Dominic had done Jade.

Oh God no!

"Don't you fucking move!"

Thankfully, Heidi didn't flinch.

But Chase did.

When he charged forward, his face twisted with rage, Clyde moved his arm, aiming the gun at him.

"Chase!" I screamed, my legs almost giving way as a whole new level of fear washed through me.

At my shout, he froze mid-stride. "Go ahead, Dad," he snarled. "Fucking shoot me! Then you'll never see a damned dime."

No, no, no!

I cried out as Clyde squeezed me tighter, his grip nearly crushing me.

"Ashley," Heidi whispered. "Look at me, Dimples." Our gazes locked. "It's going to be alright," she said. "I promise."

It was a lie.

Nothing would be alright.

Not ever again.

"Heidi... please..."

She nodded, her eyes filling with tears. "It's going to be okay," she assured me once more. "I'm right here, and I'm not leaving. I will *never* leave you."

Each word broke me a little more.

She might never leave me.

But I was leaving her.

I had no other choice.

What was happening right then, at that very moment, only solidified that decision in my head further.

Clyde laughed. Hard. The sound was cruel and malicious; two things I expected. "This is rich," he said. "The disabled bitch is comforting the town whore. I've seen a lot of shit in my day, but this truly takes the cake." His words lashed me, chipping away at what remained of my soul. "Out of all the girls," he continued. "You had to choose this one. Hell, I can't say I blame you. She's a pretty little thing. I bet *Detective Moretti*," he spat, making his disdain for my father known, "just loves tucking her in at night."

I began to spiral.

Falling into the abyss.

Around me, the world faded.

Chase's voice rang out, but I just couldn't understand a word he was saying as my sight blurred, my eyelids becoming heavy. But even as far as I'd already slipped, I felt the moment Clyde nuzzled the side of my face with his own and breathed my scent in.

My belly revolted.

I was going to puke.

"Let this serve as a warning, Chase, one which I suggest you fucking heed," he said before running the barrel of the gun down the side of my face.

Unable to move, much less scream, I merely stood there, my mind close to checking out as my body slipped into a catatonic state "You will let me have a taste of what's been coming to me since the day you were born. Or else I'll have to find a different way to earn a little cash." Grinding his erection into my back, he made the meaning of his threat perfectly clear.

He's going to sell me...

Just like el diablo did.

With no warning, Clyde unwrapped his arms from my chest, grabbed a handful of my hair, and shoved me forward. I stumbled, nearly falling, but Heidi caught me before I hit the asphalt.

Pulling me into her warm embrace, she held me tight and ran her hands through my hair, trying her best to comfort me as Clyde and Chase kept talking, their raised voices echoing through the afternoon air.

"I've got you," she whispered, running her hand up and down my back. "And I swear I won't let anyone hurt you ever again."

It was a promise she intended to keep.

But one she should've never made.

Chapter Thirty-One

ASHLEY

"*E*verything is going to be okay, Sissy."

I looked up from where I sat on my bedroom floor, Ziggy draped across my lap, at the sound of Lucca's voice.

Clutching Ellington's phone in my hand, I blew out a shaky breath as my gaze landed on my brother, followed by my sweet Gracie.

Seeing them standing there, their beautiful faces stricken with confusion nearly killed me. They had no idea why I was crying, nor did they understand why our shared mother was downstairs throwing an absolute hissy fit as she called every bar in town trying to hunt Clyde down.

More pissed than I'd ever seen him, Dad, along with half of Toluca PD were on the hunt, searching for him as well. I wasn't sure what would happen once they found him, but I hoped and prayed that he'd either end up in jail or dead in a ditch somewhere.

If my father found him, the first would happen.

But if Grandmama or my mama got their hands on him—something which was a real possibility since the Crazy Old Biddy was out and about looking for him too—it would be the latter.

The moment he'd pointed a gun at Heidi and made such sick

threats toward me, he'd sealed his fate, and no one in my family would stop until the situation was handled.

Not that it really mattered.

Come morning, I'd be long gone.

I'd cost my family enough pain.

I couldn't bear to hurt them anymore.

Though I knew me leaving would tear them apart, I also knew that they'd one day heal and forget I ever existed. But if I stayed, it would just be one problem after another for them, forever.

I couldn't handle that.

Just like Chase didn't deserve a scarred whore for a girlfriend, my family didn't deserve a broken daughter that did nothing but cause them problems.

End of story.

Forcing a shaky smile onto my tear-streaked face, I dropped the phone between my legs and extended my arms, beckoning both Lucca and Gracie to come closer. "Come here my little monsters."

Without missing a beat, they both ran to me and dove into my arms, slamming my back against the bed, which was directly behind me. Ziggy, lucky little turd that he was, moved out of the way just in time and ran out of the room, avoiding a collision.

Me though?

Both kids knocked the air right out of me.

Wheezing, I fought to pull in a much-needed breath. "You little frickin' turkeys," I said, lungs screaming. "You almost killed me."

Gracie plopped onto my lap and turned, burying her face against my chest. Body moving on autopilot, I wrapped an arm around her back and buried my face in her golden-blonde hair before kissing the crown of her head. "Love you," I whispered, feeling my heart begin to twist, then shred. "So damned much."

"You said a bad word!" Lucca practically hollered, his dark brown eyes—ones which were identical to Pop and Hendrix's—twinkling before mine. "Mama is gonna kick your butt."

Gracie huffed. "You no tell," she said, her toddler-sized voice high pitched but full of seriousness. Lifting a hand, she wagged a single finger from side to side. "No, no, tell on my Ashy."

The forced smile I wore turned genuine.

But then it fell.

Completely vanishing.

And it did so because I realized these were the last few moments I'd ever spend with either of them.

The realization hurt.

A whole lot.

Lucca huffed in return, clearly offended. "I won't tell."

Gracie's eyes narrowed. "Good."

Running my fingers through Lucca's curly black hair, I swallowed, the pain in my chest increasing with each second that ticked by. "You know that I love you, don't you, little man?"

Lucca nodded. "I love you too."

His words hit me straight in the gut.

"But you can't cry no more," he continued, thinning his lips. "I don't like it, and it makes mama upset."

It did make our mama upset.

Which was another reason for me to go.

All I did was hurt her, the woman who'd saved me. It wasn't right, and it surely wasn't fair.

It needed to end.

"You won't see me cry anymore," I said, fighting back the sob that was building in my throat. "Promise."

He nodded. "Okay."

Focusing my attention on Gracie, I slipped my finger under her chin and tilted her head back, forcing her sapphire-colored eyes to meet mine. "I love you, Goldie. With every broken piece of me."

She stared up at me, confusion dancing on her freckle-covered face. "Uv you, Ashy. Ever and ever and ever."

I felt like I was suffocating. "Forever and ever and ever."

Wiping away the tears that continued to stream down my cheeks without fail, I focused back on Lucca. "I need you to do something for me."

He quirked an expectant brow.

I almost smiled.

Almost.

"I may be gone for a little while"—I pulled in a quick breath—"so I need you to take care of Ziggy for me, okay?"

He crossed his arms over his little chest. "Where are you going?"

It was an answer I couldn't give him. "Just promise me."

"Okay," he agreed, his eyes filled with confusion, just as Gracie's had been moments before. "I will."

"Alright, Goldie," I said, squeezing Gracie tight. "I need you to do something too."

"Yeah!" she squealed, obviously excited.

Brushing her bangs out of her face, I said, "I need you to keep an eye on Angel for me while I'm gone. Make sure Uncle Fe-fe doesn't overfeed him."

"O-tay," Gracie agreed, bobbing her head enthusiastically. "Me take care da cat." She paused. "And Un-ka Fe-fe."

Hands trembling, and knowing I needed to get them out of the room before I broke down completely once more, I kissed Gracie for what I thought would be the last time. "Love you so, so much, Gracie," I whispered, my voice breaking. "Don't ever forget that okay?"

She cupped my cheeks, just as Chase always did. "I uv you, Ashy."

Another crack formed across my heart.

"I don't like this," Lucca said, capturing my attention. "My stomach hurts."

Reaching over, I ran a knuckle down the side of his cheek. "Love you too, ya little turd. Everything will be okay. Promise."

It was a lie.

Nothing would be okay.

"Gracie! Lucca! Go brush your teeth, it's past your bedtime!" Both kids jumped up at the sound of our mother's shouts from downstairs. "I mean it, don't make me come up there!"

Standing, Lucca grabbed Gracie's hand, helping her climb to her little feet. His assessing eyes roamed over my face, taking in every inch of my expression. "Will you be here in the morning?"

I nodded. "I'll be here..."

It was the truth.

Come morning, I'd still be around.

But by afternoon I'd be gone.

That was the plan at least.

"Now, y'all had better get a move on before the Mominator comes up here and rips us all a new one."

Gracie giggled because she knew that even though Mama yelled at times, she'd never rip anything. She'd throw herself down the stairs first. "Remember what I said, you two. I love you both." I pressed my palm to the place where my broken heart laid. "With every broken piece."

Raising her free hand in the air, Gracie blew me a kiss. "Uv you."

Lucca rolled his eyes. "Girls."

"Hey!" Gracie hollered, ripping her hand away from his. "Hush!"

At that, more shouts came from downstairs. "I don't hear water running! You two have exactly three seconds. One, two—"

"Bye, Ashley!" Grabbing Gracie's hand once more, Lucca took off, dragging her with him.

Despite the heart-wrenching agony exploded through every inch of my body, I smiled as I watched them go. But the moment they disappeared through the door, everything started to collapse around me.

My chest, my stomach, my head.

They all hurt.

So bad.

But knowing I still had two phone calls to make, I picked up Ellington's phone and slipped it between my mattress and box spring, the same place I always kept it and stood. Then, grabbing my own cell off my nightstand, I plopped down on my bed.

Hands shaking, I stared down at the screen, watching as the illuminated numbers changed with the time. "This is the right thing to do," I whispered, clutching it tightly. "It always has been."

Swallowing down my grief, I quickly scrolled through my contacts and dialed the first number. Lifting it to my ear, I waited for the person on the other end to answer.

It took exactly four rings.

"Hello?"

I dropped my head forward, the pain becoming nearly unbearable. "Heidi..." I paused, my grief choking me. "Are you okay?"

"I'm okay," she replied. "Are you?"

Deciding it was better to tell her the truth than a lie, I shook my head. "No... because I have to let him go."

"What?" she asked, sounding panicked. "What do you mean you have to let Chase go?"

I'd only said *him*...

Yet she'd known.

"One day he's going to find out," I whispered, my biggest fear rising to the surface. "And when he does, I can't be here."

"Ashley—"

"I'm going to break his heart," I continued, interrupting her. "And he's going to hate me because abandoning him is the one thing I swore I'd never do. But I'd rather him hate me for walking away, than look at me with disgust when he finally realizes exactly who, and what, I am." Heidi said nothing, so I kept talking. "I'm not what he thinks I am. I'm not... *good*."

"You have gotta be shitting me," she fussed, sounding just like my mama. "Ashley Moretti, you are one of the best damned people I've ever met. You may not realize it, though I don't know how that's even possible, but you are—"

"—a whore," I interjected, harshly.

"You are *not* a whore."

"Yes, I am. You know it, I know it, and most everyone in the entire town knows it. It's only a matter of time before Chase finds out. After today, I'm sure he'll start digging—*if he isn't already*—and when he does, he's going to find enough dirt to bury every feeling he's ever had for me."

"No... I won't let you throw away one of the best things that has ever happened to you because of fear that someone else instilled in your head. Especially when that someone is a child-abusing scumbag who I'd like to stab in the eye with an icepick!"

She pulled in a breath.

"You are not what was done to you as a child, nor are you what was done to you as a teenager. Those things that happened to you, as horrible as they were, do not define you, and what those people forced you to do isn't your fault either. You were a victim, Ashley. And now you're a survivor."

She didn't understand!

Her words were beautiful.

But my reality wasn't.

"I can't do this," I said, feeling myself begin to break as panic crested and crashed inside me. "I can't keep pretending to be something I'm not, and I can't live in a place where people hang my darkest secrets over my head, like a guillotine poised to strike."

Losing every ounce of control I still possessed, which admittedly wasn't much, I picked up a glass off my nightstand and slung it across the room, watching as it shattered into dozens of little pieces. "I'm not what he needs," I said, between sobs that were now breaking loose, one after the other. "And I'm not what you need either."

"You are *not* leaving me! Ashley," she cried, her voice cracking. "You can't go. Please just let me come get you. I'm on the way to the station, but I can turn around. Are you still at home? Please talk to me..."

Legs buckling, I collapsed, my knees hitting the ground. Covering my mouth with my hand to muffle my screams, I wailed into my palm as every ounce of pain and anguish that I felt poured out of me in an endless stream.

"Ashley, I'm begging you, say something."

I dropped my hand, fisting it on the carpet beneath me. "I'm so sorry," I whispered, a combination of snot and saliva sliding down my face.

"Dimples, you can't—"

Heidi's voice disappeared as a horn sounded through the phone, followed by a blood-curdling scream, one which I knew belonged to her.

"Heidi!" I yelled, my heart leaping high into my throat.

Her only answer came in the form of more screams. In the background, the sound of squealing tires and a second horn followed.

Then, impact.

"Heidi!"

More screaming; more impacts.

Boom!

Boom!

Boom!

Boom!

Boom!

"Bug, please!" I continued to bellow, my screams mixing with the sounds of metal groaning and glass exploding.

One final crash, and an eerie silence echoed through the speaker.

Mouth gaping, I dropped my phone to the floor and jumped to my feet. Staring down at the screen as if it were a snake about to strike, I slowly crept past it and to my bedroom door. Then, snapping out the fog that surrounded me, I took off down the hall.

"Mama!" I wailed. "Help me!"

She came flying up the stairs just as I reached them. "Ashley, honey, what—"

Grabbing her by the arms, I began to shake her. "Heidi's hurt!" I cried, my face mere inches from hers. Waving my hand toward my bedroom, where my phone remained. "Help her, please!"

Wide-eyed, she wrapped her hand around my jaw, holding my face tight. "Where?" she asked, her voice calm and steady, whereas mine was the exact opposite. "Ashley, answer me! Where?"

My chest rose and fell as I fought to get the words out.

Talk!

Don't let her die like Carmen and Jade!

"S-she," I stuttered, the boa constrictor wrapped around my throat, tightening its hold. "On the way to the s-station. She w-wrecked. I c-can't—"

She released my hand and turned before bolting down the stairs. "I'm getting help! Stay here!" Reaching the first floor, she bolted toward the kitchen, disappearing from my view.

Alone in the silence, I broke.

Collapsing once more, I hit the floor, hard, and bent forward, pressing my forehead to the carpet. Hands clenched, I slammed them against the floor as I began to scream, as loud and as long as I could.

Over and over.

"Oh God," I hollered, the pain shattering me like the glass I threw at my bedroom wall. "What did I do?" A complete mess, I sat up, clasped my hands, lacing my fingers together, and looked up. "Please," I begged the heavens above. "Don't take her from me. Not this time," I cried, rocking back and forth. "If you need someone"—extending my arms, I slowly climbed to my feet—"then take me. Please... just take me."

It was a cry that went unheard.

Just like all of the ones which came before it.

Chapter Thirty-Two

ASHLEY

*I*t was a Friday morning.

Consumed with grief, anguish, and the inability to fix anything I'd broken, I sat next to Heidi's hospital bed, holding her hand. With Ty sleeping in a chair opposite me, the room was silent except for the steady beep of the machine that monitored every beat of her fragile heart.

With only my demons to keep me company, concentrating on the steady cadence that pulsed through the surrounding air kept me grounded because it was proof that she was still alive.

And fighting.

Eight harrowing days had passed since her accident, and not once had she woken up. Riddled with trauma, including a fractured skull, serious spinal injury and extensive cerebral edema, the doctors weren't sure she'd ever open her eyes again.

It was an outcome that I feared.

And one that would be all my fault.

Just like everything else.

Taking her limp hand in mine, I laced our fingers together, careful not to touch the IV port protruding from her bruised skin. "Bug," I said, looking at my best friend and the girl I loved like a sister.

"You've been sleeping long enough, sweet girl. I need you to wake up now."

Silence met my ears as I glanced at Ty.

Like everyone else, he was a mess.

Barely holding it together, he didn't eat, hardly slept, and I was reasonably certain he hadn't left the hospital once in the past week. If it hadn't been for Maddie and my mama forcing him to shower and change clothes, I doubt he would've even done that.

Not that I blamed him.

The man loved Heidi with his entire heart, and not knowing whether she would ever come back to us was killing him, one excruciating second at a time.

Again, every bit of it was my fault.

Well, not all of it.

The person—a man whose blood alcohol level was over three times the legal limit, that had crossed the yellow line, hitting Heidi head-on—was responsible too.

I hated him like no other.

Leaving nothing but torment and scars—both emotionally and physically—in his wake, he'd been nothing short of evil. A man who'd spent his entire life terrorizing others, feasting on their pain, and reveling in the misery he caused, he was a monster.

And his name was Clyde Jacobs.

May he rot in the fiery pits of hell.

Pronounced dead at the scene of the accident, he no longer served as a threat to Ty, to Chase, nor to me, but in one final act of wickedness, he may have succeeded in stealing one of the most beautiful souls I'd ever encountered from all of us.

It wasn't fair.

Not at all.

Like Carmen and Jade, Heidi had never done anything to anyone. She didn't deserve the crap situation she'd been handed, one which I'd helped personally deliver to her.

If I hadn't called her, and if I hadn't told her that I was leaving, maybe she would have been paying better attention, and maybe—just maybe—she wouldn't be lying in the hospital right then, her body both broken and battered.

Because of my weakness and inability to cope with the life I'd been handed, one of the people I loved with every beat of my scarred heart was fighting for her life, a life which hung in the balance, perilously close to slipping away.

It was killing me.

Though my hands had been sullied with blood ever since I watched Carmen and Jade be murdered before my eyes, the stain continued to grow, tarnishing my tainted soul even further.

Part of me doubted it would ever stop.

Not unless I made it.

Which was something I'd fight to do.

"Heidi, please," I whispered, my hand shaking against hers. "Open your eyes for me." When no response came, not even the slightest bit of an eye flutter, the pain in my chest grew, branching out and spreading like wildfire.

Growing more desperate, I squeezed her hand the slightest bit. "I promise I'm not going to leave anymore"—throat tightening, I swallowed—"and I swear I'm going to do my best to get better."

Still nothing.

"But I need your help because I can't do this without you." A single tear slipped down my cheek as I trailed my fingers up her inner arm. "Especially not when I'm still going to lose *him*." I pulled in a shuddering breath. "I told you I'm not going to run anymore," I continued. "And I'm not. But even with Clyde dead, I can't change who I am, nor what I was." My eyes slid closed on their own accord as a hint of the agony to come stirred in my belly. "It's time for me to let him go"—another breath—"even if I don't want to."

Continued silence.

Straddling the precipice of losing my mind, I knew I needed to go. Me breaking down in that room, with my best friend busy fighting for her life, wasn't the right thing to do. Even someone as screwed up as me realized that.

Standing, I gave Bug's hand one last squeeze before leaning over her bed and pressing my lips to her pale cheek. "I love you, Heidi. With every broken piece of me," I whispered as my heart completely shattered. "I'll be back tomorrow, first thing, and I expect to see your pretty blues the moment I walk through the door. If not, I may just shove my foot up your behind." A shaky smile crossed my face, but it didn't last long before vanishing completely. "Please wake up." The tears falling down my face and clogging my throat began to grow, their numbers increasing ten-fold. "It's selfish, I know that but I've lost enough already—*with more to come*—and I can't lose my best friend too."

I kissed her one last time.

Then, with my heart in pieces, I left.

———

My soul is dying...

The heart-wrenching thought echoed through my head as I sat on the living room floor, my shaking arms wrapped around my torso. Rays of sunshine kissed my skin through the large bay window to my right, but it did little to heat my frame. The coldness that possessed me, oozing from the marrow of my bones, was too strong.

I'd never be warm again.

Tears, ones which never seemed to stop, filled my tired eyes before spilling onto my trembling thighs. A cruel reminder of the most recent nightmare I found myself stuck in, I hated the sight of them.

The only thing I hated more was myself.

"Ashley," Chase said, from behind me where he sat on the sofa, his concern-filled gaze boring holes into my back. "Beautiful girl, talk to me."

Eyes sliding closed, I dug my fingers into my sides, flinching at the familiar bite of pain. Knowing that the time had come for me to destroy every last tie binding him to me, I took an anguished breath.

Then, with my stomach in knots, I whispered the five words I'd rehearsed a million times, understanding full-well what would happen once they were spoken.

Those words? *I can't do this anymore.*

In an instant, the surrounding air shifted, becoming colder with each tick of the grandfather clock that stood tall in front of me, its refinished face seeming to mock me as time moved on while the world around me stood still.

I'm going to destroy him.

He's going to hate me.

I'll never get over him.

He'll move on.

"Yeah," Chase said, his voice deep as could be. "You're gonna need to explain that one, Sweetness. What can't you do?"

Digging my fingers in deeper, I tilted my head to the side, one tear after another falling. "This. Us," I whispered, unrestrained hurt swirling in my empty stomach. "I can't do either any longer."

A black cloud formed at my words.

Sorrow rained down, drenching me in pain.

Chase's sneakers squeaked against the hardwood as he jumped to his feet. Rounding me, he stood before me; pure beauty mixed with undeniable panic. "What do you mean you can't do *us* anymore?"

Life, being the cruel bitch that she was, began to slowly wrench my chest wide open, eviscerating my tired heart one tiny slice at a time. "You and me..." My voice trailed off as ice slithered into my veins, chilling my aching flesh further. "We don't belong together."

His eyes hardened. "What the hell do you mean we don't belong together?"

Bending my knees, I folded in on myself, pulling my legs into my chest. "I'm not a good person, Chase. I never have been," I replied, each word shredding me a little more. "And it's time you see that."

"What kind of bullshit are you spouting off?" he hollered, crossing his arms over his muscular chest. "Ashley, I fucking love you! I know you've got problems, but it doesn't matter how much you struggle. As I've told you time and time again, I will love you through every bit of it!"

No, he wouldn't.

Not when he found out that his Sweetness wasn't so sweet.

I'm nothing but a whore.

Tainted. Broken. Worthless.

Jackhammering heart nearly imploding, I climbed to my feet, standing on my wobbly legs as grief hit me in waves. Both grueling and heartbreaking it was *killing me.* "If you love me," I said, forcing my voice to remain steady. "Then let me go."

His head jerked back as if I'd slapped him. "I will *never* let you go!"

He didn't have a choice.

Because I wasn't giving him one.

Standing my ground, I threw back my own string of harsh words, hoping they'd nick his heart enough to leave.

Though I knew that I was doing the right thing by pushing him away, my resolve wouldn't last. My love for him—as toxic as it may have been—was too strong.

"You don't have a choice!" It was one of the few times I'd raised my voice at him, and judging by the hurt that filled his eyes, my harsh voice and cruel words hit their mark. Still, I wasn't done. Not yet. "You have always said that it was my choice! My choice if you touched me and my choice if I loved you. And this, us being together," I said, pointing from him to myself, "is my choice too."

Body quaking, he glared at me, betrayal dancing in his eyes. "So, what, you're just going to choose to stop loving me now?"

That would never happen.

And as much as I didn't want to admit the truth to him, I couldn't hold myself back. "I will *never* stop loving you!" One of the fraying strings holding my heart in place snapped. "Not ever! But, Chase, I can't do this. Not anymore." Stumbling back, I slid my hands into my hair, fisting the locks tight. "My entire being is splintering at the seams, and I'm so frickin' consumed with secrets, regrets, and guilt that I can't even breathe!"

"Ashley, I'll help—"

No, no, no!

"The only way you can help me is by walking away!"

"Fuck that," he barked, hands going to his hips. "Two years ago, I swore that I would never stop holding on, and I meant it! If you think for one second that I'm going to let your demons—"

"You have no choice!" I yelled, my shrill scream echoing through the empty house.

Both hurt and furious, he fisted his hands, and even though I knew he'd never harm me, I flinched, my eyes slamming shut.

It was a reaction he didn't miss.

"It's because of him, isn't it?" He didn't give me a chance to reply before continuing to shout, his every emotion bubbling up and out of him. "It's because of that piece of shit that you want me to walk away! What, you think I'm going to turn out like him? Ashley, I am not abusive, I never will be, and I will fucking die before I hurt you. You have got to goddamned trust—"

"You don't know anything about what Dominic did to me!" I screamed, interrupting him. "And you will never know because I won't tell you! Not when every truth I've buried would erase every bit of love you've ever had for me!"

It was more than I wanted to say.

But the words wouldn't stop.

"*Nothing* you say will ever change the way I feel about you." He was wrong. So damned wrong. "How many times do I have to say that?"

"You may think that now, Chase, but you don't know my secrets and you—"

Face twisting, every ounce of softness he'd portrayed minutes before vanished. "Because you won't tell me!" he snarled. "I may not know whatever shit it is that you've got buried in your head, but, baby, one thing I do know without a doubt is this. Those hidden truths you've locked away are toxic, and they are exactly what is poisoning you, along with everything we have!"

Toxic.

Poison.

He'd hit the nail on the head, driving a railroad spike straight through my chest with just two words. "You're right," I whispered, my frantic shouts turning to a mere whisper. "I am poison, and everyone that gets too close dies." With my world shifting on its axis, I staggered backward, leaving pieces of my shattered heart in my wake. "It's best you see that now instead of when it's too late."

"That's not what I..."

Brows furrowed, he reached for me.

But I evaded his grasp, stumbling back once more. My back met the living room wall with a soft thud, rattling the pictures affixed to its surface.

"It doesn't matter what you meant. The truth is the truth, just like my past is my past. I can't change either. The only thing I can change is what I allow to happen from now on. And I can't...."

My dark locks stuck to my sweat-slicked skin, and I shook my head, the words not wanting to come. "I *can't* be with you. Not when a million things are waiting to rip us apart, and not when I know that you're too good for me."

Agony-fueled tears, ones mirroring my own, began to fall from Chase's eyes. Cascading down his high cheekbones and angular jaw, they dripped to the floor, each one in sync with the drops of blood that seeped from my maimed heart. "My father, the monster who helped create me, is dead, and shit is supposed to be easier now that he's in hell where he belongs."

He paused, his jaw clenching. "But right this second, I feel like I'm right there beside him, kneeling at the devil's goddamn feet, because what you're doing, what you're *forcing* me to do, hurts worse than an eternity of damnation ever could."

Another of my fraying strings broke.

"I can't force you to want me," he said, his tears falling faster. "But I am begging you to keep me because I love you, Ashley Jo Moretti. I love you with every piece of me."

"I love you too, but—"

"So then that's it then," he interrupted. "After all this time and after everything we've been through, your demons are still going to win."

It wasn't a question.

It was a statement.

And one which was true.

"It's the only way."

Eyes never leaving mine, he shook his head. "No, Sweetness, it's not. But it's the way you chose, and because of that, I don't have any choice but to walk away. Not after I swore to you that I'd never take something from you that you weren't willing to give. And if you aren't willing to give me your whole heart, as broken as it may be, then I can't keep you either."

The final string snapped.

And I broke like never before.

Full out sobs jerked my body as Chase closed the space between us and gently pressed his lips to my forehead. "You will always be my girl," he whispered, his tears falling onto my cheeks and mixing with my own. "And I will love you until the day I take my final breath."

Without another word, he walked away.

Legs collapsing, I fell to the floor, the pain streaking through me becoming unbearable. And it was there, in the center of my parents' home, that my soul, along with every bit of light that remained in me, flickered out.

Part Four

FROM ASHES LOVE RISES

"True love will always be enough."

— Shelby Moretti

Chapter Thirty-Three

CHASE

Eighteen Months Later

$\mathcal{M}$y footsteps echoed throughout the concrete tunnel that led from the stadium to the secure parking lot where my SUV sat, parked near the entrance.

Like always, I was the last one to leave, and with nothing but the sound of my steady pace to keep me company, my mind wandered to the same place it always did.

To *her*.

529 days had passed since I did as she asked and let her go, the sounds of her heart-wrenching wails following me as I walked away and crossed the street where I climbed into my Jeep.

A crying, fucked up mess, I'd just stuck my fisted hand into the dash, busting my knuckles wide open when I'd caught sight of Grand-mama standing next to her Cadillac, purse in hand.

Eyes fixated on Ashley's house, the tormented look on her face mirrored my own as she wept, the oversized pink sun hat she wore atop her head shaking as her body quaked with each of her sobs.

If a sliver of my heart remained intact, it would've broken at the sight. But the moment Ashley told me I had no choice but to walk away from everything we'd fought to have, the entire thing shriveled up and died, leaving nothing behind but ash.

Since then, I hadn't seen her.

As much as it gutted me not to hear the sound of her quiet voice or smell the sweet scent of her peach perfume, I knew it was for the best. Messed up as it may seem, I didn't know if I could be close and not pull her into my arms.

It was one helluva problem to have considering that in less than forty-eight hours, my brother was getting married to the one and only girl he'd ever loved.

Heidi.

A miracle in every sense of the word, not only had Bug survived the accident which should've killed her, but she was thriving. Though she'd never walk again thanks to the spinal injury she'd suffered, she was doing good.

Real damned good.

I only wished I could bring Clyde back from the depths of hell where he no doubt now resided, just so I could kill him all over again with my bare hands. The piece of shit had abused my brother, ruined my childhood, terrified my girl, and almost killed Heidi.

I truly hoped the devil was shoving a pineapple right up his sorry ass on the daily, sans lube. Christ knows he deserved nothing less. Not after all the torment he'd caused, the pain he'd doled out, and the permanent scars he'd inflicted.

But none of that mattered anymore.

Because he was gone.

Dead.

Burning in hell.

And we didn't speak his name anymore.

Not ever.

Reaching the end of the tunnel, I crossed the dark parking lot and jumped into my Jeep, the same one I'd had since my senior year of high school. It was a curse because I couldn't even sit inside it without seeing her.

Window rolled down, dark hair blowing in the wind. Bare feet and painted toes propped up on the dash. The sound of her cries as she confessed to being raped as a child.

Every memory, both good and bad, haunted me each time I sat behind the driver's seat. I'd considered—more than once—selling it and buying something new, but I could never bring myself to do it.

I'd already lost Ashley.

I couldn't lose the memories too.

Without them, I'd die.

And that's not me being overly dramatic. Empty on the inside, I already felt like I was slipping away. If what little I did still have of her disappeared, it would be my undoing.

Of that, I had no doubt.

Starting the engine, I drove out of the parking lot, made a right on Stadium Drive, and followed the path that would lead me to the interstate. Once on the highway, I sped to my apartment, more than ready to climb into bed and forget the hours that had passed.

Sleep never brought me peace—ever—but each time I laid in bed at night and closed my eyes, I could pretend.

No longer faced with reality, I imagined I was back in high school, tucked away in the corners of the library with Ashley sitting across from me, a pile of books between us.

I also fantasized about being back in the apartment that I'd once shared with Ty, tucked in my bed, with my girl wrapped up in my arms.

But mostly, I let my mind take me back to the night we stood in her bathroom, her nude body pressed against me as she whispered the confession that had come to mean more to me than anything else ever had.

She should have been yours.

One sentence.

Five words.

They had hit me straight in the chest.

Because yeah, Addie should've been mine.

Just like her mama always would be.

Making it home, I parked in the garage reserved for tenants who lived in the same downtown building as me, jumped out, and made my way toward the entrance.

At the front door, I was greeted by Leo, the smiling security guard who patrolled the property each night. "Good game tonight, Jacobs," he said. "Heard you rushed for over a hundred yards. That's what's up man."

I lifted my chin in the air but said nothing in return. I never did. Not anymore. The only time I ever spoke was during team meetings and on the field. I didn't want any friends. Hell, I didn't even want acquaintances.

All I wanted was my Sweetness.

And that would never change.

Not until the day I die.

After riding the elevator to my top floor apartment, I moved down the hall until I reached my door. My open laptop rang with a FaceTime call notification as I slipped inside.

Knowing that it was my brother, I tossed my wallet and keys onto the small table by the door and headed into my kitchen. Seated at the six-person dining table, I answered the call.

I smiled when my brother's face appeared on the screen, followed by a giggling Lily Ann, who was Heidi's toddler niece and Carissa's only daughter. "Ace!" she hollered, waving frantically. "Saw you pay!"

The kid never failed to warm my cold, dead heart.

"Yeah? Did you see me get the crap knocked out of me by that linebacker who broke through the line and about broke me in the process too?"

She nodded and clapped her hands once. "You went boom!"

That got a chuckle out of me. "Yeah, sweet girl, I sure did."

Ty quirked a brow. "Should've been paying attention. Then you could've dropped back and made a run for it. Could've easily picked up the first down that way."

He was full of shit.

The pocket collapsed before I could blink. Wasn't going to argue with him though. If there was one thing I'd learned about my brother, it was that the idiot always had to have the final say. Which was funny considering he was marrying Heidi, 'cause he sure as hell never got the final say with her.

Karma sure was a bitch.

"Sure," I replied, biting back the *fuck you* I wanted to sling his way. "I'll try to keep an eye out next time, big bro."

He smirked, not missing the pissiness lining my tone. "What time are you coming into town tomorrow? The trip from Atlanta takes you what... two hours? Rehearsal supper is at six, but you know Grandmama is going all out. She's got a big ol' family breakfast and lunch planned. Between her and the rest of the Crazy Chick Club," he said, referring to all the women who worked at the shelter that Ashley volunteered at, "I'm about to go flippin' nuts."

I had no doubt all the ladies were driving him batty. Over the last couple of years, each one of them had moved onto the same street as Ashley and Grandmama, buying up all the adjoining properties. Hell, Ty even built Heidi a house at the end of the cul-de-sac directly next to Carissa and her husband, Kyle's house.

It was a gorgeous place.

Though it wasn't big and it wasn't fancy—something Heidi would've despised—it was really nice with its simple brick exterior, open floor plan, and huge, fenced-in backyard.

It was the perfect place to raise a family.

Not that I knew anything about that.

"Ty, bro," I said, getting back to the conversation at hand. "I probably won't get there until right before the rehearsal supper."

His jaw clenched as irritation brewed in his stormy blue eyes.

Kissing Lily Ann on the head, he lifted her off his lap and stood her on the floor next to him. "Tink, how about you go play with Ryker for a bit?" He pointed to Evan and Hope's oldest son. "He's over there with Colby and Wyatt."

"Otay!" she replied, throwing her arms up in the air. "I uv Ry Ry!"

Without another word, she took off running, disappearing out of my view.

Ty turned, his pissed-off gaze meeting mine through the screen. "Stop being a little bitch," he snapped, getting straight to the point. "Heidi and I both want you here early. So unless you're planning on having my future-wife run your sorry ass over with her wheelchair while Grandmama simultaneously beats your butt with her flyswatter, then I suggest you get your ass here."

I pulled in a breath, my pulse skyrocketing. "It's not that easy," I bit out, my back teeth clenched. "Not when—"

"You're going to see her, Chase," he said, interrupting me. "She's Heidi's maid of honor, and whether you like it or not, you're going to have to deal."

"It's not that—"

"I know it's gonna hurt," he replied, cutting in once more. "And you know I wouldn't ever ask you to do something that would tear you up inside, but this is my wedding."

He was right about that.

Despite my feelings and the emotional kick to the balls I knew was coming, I had to show up, I had to hold it together, and I had to be there for my family.

It's what they would do for me.

Hell, it's what they *had* done.

Even from her hospital and physical rehabilitation center beds, Heidi had fought to keep me together after Ashley, and I split. Her body may have been broken, but her mind was strong, and like my brother, she'd helped ground me when I came close to falling apart.

She'd done the same for Ashley.

They never gave me all the details about what was going on with my girl, but they kept me in the loop with the big stuff.

For instance, a year after I walked away, she earned her two-year degree in Early Childhood Education and had become a preschool teacher, something she'd always wanted to do.

She still volunteered at the shelter in her free time, and I doubt she'd ever stop, but five days a week she taught at the Tiny Tots Academy in downtown Toluca, the same school Lily Ann attended.

According to Heidi, she was happy there.

It was all I'd ever wanted for her.

To be happy.

If only I could've made her that way...

"I'll be there as early as I can," I replied, swallowing down the mixture of trepidation and excitement that climbed into my throat, blocking my airway. "I swear it."

He nodded. "That's all I can ask for."

"Do you want me to come straight—"

"Ashley Jo!"

I snapped my mouth shut when Melody, Hendrix and Maddie's oldest daughter ran through the room, her arms opened wide, heading for the front door. Gut twisting, I clenched my fists tight as I waited for my girl to come into view.

It had been eighteen months.

Eighteen damned months.

And she was there, just out of sight.

"Ty," I said, shoulders trembling when I didn't see or hear her. "Turn your phone."

"Chase—"

"Turn your goddamned phone!"

A second later, he turned it.

And there she was.

My Sweetness.

My beautiful girl.

My entire world.

"Christ," I whispered, taking her in from head to toe. She looked the exact same, except now her hair fell to the top of her shoulders instead of cascading down her back. I loved it, but not near as much as I loved the hoodie she wore.

A hoodie that belonged to *me*.

The first night I ever snuck her out of her house, I'd given it to her to wear. She'd never given it back. And now I knew why.

She wanted to keep it.

Just like she'd wanted to keep me.

The realization ricocheted through my head, slammed into my

skull, and sent my heart into overdrive. Ashley had wanted me, hell, she'd fucking loved me. But I'd walked away, leaving her to the demons that never ceased in tormenting her because I was a heart-broken fool who thought I was doing what was best for her.

I'd been wrong.

Point blank, I. Had. Fucked. Up.

Majorly.

But I was about to fix it.

Come hell or high water.

Growing up, love was something I never thought I'd care to fight for. But then I fell in love with a broken-hearted girl who possessed a beautiful soul. And now, years later, after I'd already loved and lost her, I was suddenly ready for war.

"What's going on in your head?" Ty asked, wide-eyed. Having raised me since I was a baby, he could read me like a book; therefore, he knew shit was brewing. "Talk to me, Chase."

"I'm coming home," I said firmly. "And I'm taking back what's mine."

He arched a brow. "And what's that?"

"Ashley."

With nothing left to say, I slammed my laptop shut, ending the call. Then, sick and tired of being without the woman who was the other half of my soul, I headed for the door.

Chapter Thirty-Four

ASHLEY

*I*t was a Sunday night, at half past nine.

For the past couple of hours, myself and the rest of the ladies who worked at the shelter—minus Carissa who was sick, and Charlotte and Wendy since they were on shift—had been going over wedding plans, ensuring that Ty and Heidi's big day went off without a hitch.

We'd just finished everything up when Grandmama suddenly hollered, "You ran over my dadgummed toe with that spiffy new motorized wheelchair you got," from the kitchen where she'd been fussing with Heidi over floral arrangements. "And you did it on purpose, ya little hussy!"

And here we go...

"You smacked me with the flyswatter because I told you that I don't want baby's breath in my arrangements!" Heidi hollered right back, pointing a newly manicured nail in the Crazy Old Biddy's direction. "And if you whack me with it again, I will run you down like a dog."

Maddie and Clara, who were sitting on either side of me, both looked ready to choke from laughter, while my mama, who sat in the

301

rocking chair across the room, holding a sleeping Gracie on her lap, did her part to egg stuff on. "Run over her other foot, Bug!"

Hands on her hips, Grandmama spun around. "You listen here, Blondie," she said, eyes narrowed. "I will tear your rear-end up. I don't give a good dadgummed who—"

Hope, bless her heart, chose that moment to burst through the front door, her blue-black hair in disarray. "Somebody better have wine," she said, completely out of breath. "Because after what I just went through, I need a bottle"—she paused—"actually, make that three."

Clara's laughter died.

Jumping up as if she thought something was wrong, she looked ready to rip somebody's head off if need be, which wasn't surprising. Clara and Hope had been best friends since they met, but after marrying twin brothers—Evan and Brantley—they were now sister-in-law's.

"What happened?" Clara asked.

Hope clutched her chest and exhaled. "Your nephews, that's what!" I fought back laughter. "I only went home for twenty minutes, but I swear they are going to be the death of me. All three of them. They've learned how to coordinate their special brands of crazy. I never stood a chance at trying to get them in bed." When my mama laughed, Hope swung her gaze her way. "Keep laughing, Shelby Ray, and I'll send them to your house for the week."

Mama shrugged. "Send 'em. I've got duct tape."

Oh for heaven's sake!

Maddie blew out a breath. "I feel your pain, Itty Bitty. I only have one boy, but Maddox is Hendrix's son, so that counts for something, right?"

Hope blinked. "Uh, yeah. I mean, we're talking about Hendrix here. You'll be lucky if Maddox doesn't steal a car by the time he turns twelve."

I should not have laughed.

I really shouldn't have.

But I couldn't help it.

Mainly because what Hope said was true.

My Uncle Hendrix was...

Well, he was a troublemaker.

Maddie shrugged. "Then again, it's not him being his father's carbon copy that I worry about. It's having her"—she pointed at the crazy old woman standing less than ten feet away, her ruby red lips pursed—"as his live-in Grandmama that scares me."

Two weeks earlier, Hendrix, Maddie and their three kids—Melody, Maci and Maddox—had moved into Grandmama's house instead of buying one of their own. It's what Grandmama had wanted since she was getting older and could use the help around the house.

Plus, her house was big, yet empty now that Maddie's father, Keith, had moved out to live with his now-fiancée, Charlotte.

She was lonely too.

Whether she'd admit it or not.

"Now, listen here," Grandmama started. "I ain't done a dadgummed thing." She stuck her nose up in the air and closed her eyes. "I'm an angel."

"Shit," Clara said, dragging out the last syllable. Hearing her, a woman who rarely cursed, say such a thing shocked me. Yet I still found it hilarious. "Grandmama," she continued. "I think it's time for you to see a doctor because clearly, you have lost your—"

She snapped her mouth shut when Heidi's front door swung open, and Brantley stuck his head inside. Gaze instantly finding his wife, he smiled. "Firecracker, you coming home tonight? Or you planning on staying over here?"

Clara blinked before running her heated gaze over Brantley's broad chest and arms. "I'm coming home." Turning, she grabbed her purse off the end table where it sat next to mine. "Bye, y'all. I'll see you at breakfast in the morning."

"Bye, Clara," I said before turning my attention to my former boss and one of the nicest men I'd ever encountered. "Night, B!"

Brantley winked my way. "Night, Shorty."

Once they were out the door, Hendrix, of all danged people stepped inside, his eyes searching the room for Maddie. When he found her, he smiled, just as Brantley had. "I'm not asking if you're staying here,

Pretty Girl," he said, making his way toward his wife. "I'm just taking you home, to my bed, where you belong."

Maddie yelped in surprise when he bent down upon reaching her and tossed her over his shoulder in one fell swoop. "Bye, ladies!"

A chorus of goodbyes followed as Hendrix grabbed a lock of my Mama's hair, giving it a quick tug. "Later, brat. I'll see you tomorrow."

She responded by flipping him off.

Hope scrunched her nose as Hendrix and Maddie disappeared out the door. "He's such a caveman."

I snorted. "And Evan's not?"

"No, he's a brute. There's a difference."

"Well," Grandmama said, suddenly looking tired as could be. "Guess it's time I hobble my old derriere home. Tomorrow is gonna be a long day and sweet baby Jesus knows I ain't no spring chicken no more."

One corner of Heidi's mouth tipped. "Well, since you're doing all the work for my wedding, I suppose I could give you a ride." Tapping her lap, she continued. "Come on, Crazy Old Biddy. Climb on."

Grandmama blinked.

Then, she moved.

Climbing on Heidi's lap, she gripped the metal frame tight. "Let's boogie!"

Heidi pulled back on the electronic lever that controlled the chair, and like a rocket, they both took off. Out the door and down the wheel-chair ramp they went, Grandmama's cackling laughter floating through the night air.

Mama, who was the only other adult left after Hope followed Heidi out, stood, taking Gracie with her. "Sugar, I'm gonna get your little sister home, and then I'll be back to help you pick up the mess the ladies made. Just give me ten minutes."

Standing, I waved a dismissive hand in her direction. "I've got it. Won't take long at all."

Lips thinned into a straight line, she stared at my face, her eyes searching my expression for something. "You holding up okay?" she asked, readjusting Gracie in her arms.

I nodded as a lump formed in my throat. Knowing exactly where this conversation was headed, my heart sped up. "I'm going to be fine," I whispered, the urge to fidget in place overwhelming me. "I'm not the same person I was eighteen months ago. I'm stronger now." At least, I tried to be. Some days it was hit or miss. But keeping myself distant from everyone had helped.

Present but silent had become my motto.

"I know you and Dad are worried about me falling apart the moment I see *him*, but you don't need to be."

I couldn't even bring myself to say his name.

"I've been going to therapy, plus the new medication Dr. Wilson put me on helps. I'm going to be fine." I didn't know who I was trying to convince more—her or me. "And if I start to spiral, I know to reach out and get help."

"You have been doing better," she said, nodding. "But, sugar, I also know you still love him."

I did still love him.

No doubt I always would.

"That boy was your best friend," she continued, her throat clogged with emotion. "And even though you've come a long way, I still see that same emptiness in your eyes that I saw eighteen months ago when y'all broke up."

Leave it to my mama to shoot straight from the hip. I mean Jesus! "I think a part of me will always be empty without him," I replied, honestly. "And you're right, I do still love him. But sometimes love isn't enough. Even when we want it to be."

"You're wrong, baby," she replied, her eyes glazing. "True love will *always* be enough."

My brows furrowed. "What are you—"

I ceased speaking when headlights flashed through the open front door.

"That's your daddy pulling into our driveway," she said, staring outside, an expression I couldn't read plastered on her face. "Let me get your sister home before he throws a full-fledged hissy fit, and then I'll hoof it back over in a few." Dipping her chin, she shot me a look that I knew meant business. "This conversation isn't over, Ashley Jo. Before the sun rises tomorrow, you and I are gonna talk this out."

Knowing there was no way for me to get out of whatever craziness was running through her head, I nodded. "Okay."

Flicking her hair back over her shoulder, she turned and walked out, leaving me alone in the house. "And people say I'm crazy," I mumbled, shaking my head as I headed toward the kitchen where most of the mess existed.

Once there, I grabbed an empty trash bag and moved around the room, picking up paper plates, random sheets of paper, and soiled napkins before tossing them away. Then, I dropped the bag and snatched up the three empty bottles of wine littering the island. "Good heavens," I whispered to the empty room. "My ladies are turning into a bunch of winos."

I spun around, intent on throwing each one into the recycling bin.

But I didn't make it that far.

Because when I turned, I came face to face with a man whom I hadn't seen in eighteen months, and one who, after all this time, still held my beating heart in the palm of his hand.

He looked exactly the same, only now he was bigger, his muscles more pronounced.

Knocked completely off-kilter, I dropped my hands, letting one of the bottles fall to the tile floor where it shattered on impact, sending bits of broken glass flying around the room. But, being that I was utterly dazed and all, I didn't react.

Instead, I just stood there...

My eyes locked on his.

Head spinning, my heart climbed high into my throat as my belly began to flip, awakening those stupid butterflies that resided there. Glossed lips parted, I inhaled, waiting to see if he'd say something.

Thankfully, I didn't have to wait long.

"Nice shirt, Sweetness."

Sweetness...

My heart both melted and broke.

"Chase," I whispered, chills bumps breaking out along every inch of my skin as my eyes drank him in from head to toe. *I've missed him so much.* "Why are... I mean, what are you doing here? I didn't think you were coming until tomorrow."

"Seems I left something behind when I blew out of Toluca all those months ago." Raking his tongue over his bottom lip, he slipped his hands into the pocket of his sweatpants, ones which hung low on his lean hips. "And I'm here to get it back."

My chest rose and fell as the surrounding air thickened, making it nearly impossible to breathe. "Yeah?" I asked, forcing myself to remain still and not swoon like a frickin' fool. "And what is that?"

He didn't hesitate. "You."

His answer rocked me.

To my core.

And before I could blink, he moved.

Coming to a standstill in front of me, his sneaker-covered toes touching my booted ones, he cupped my face. "Five hundred and twenty-nine days," he whispered, touching his forehead to mine in a move that was both familiar and comforting. "That's how long I've been without you."

My lungs seized.

"This shit ends now, Ashley."

It was the last thing he said before slamming his lips down on mine.

Chapter Thirty-Five

CHASE

*M*y girl was running from me.

Yet again.

Some shit never changed.

Chasing her out of Heidi's house, I took off down the concrete drive and up the sidewalk, making sure to keep her in view but not get too close. I'd already crossed the line by kissing her without permission, but dammit, the moment she looked up at me with those twinkling brown eyes of hers, I lost control.

It wasn't okay.

And it wasn't acceptable.

An apology was in order, but first, I had to catch her without spooking her more than I likely already had. "Ashley!"

Expecting her to run faster, I stumbled, nearly tripping in place when she came to a sudden stop and whirled on me, her face a mask of both anger and confusion. Hands going to her jean-covered hips, she glared my way.

If the situation hadn't been so messed up, I would've smiled, because damn she was gorgeous.

Holding my hands up in a placating gesture, I stopped when ten feet separated us, giving her plenty of room to breathe. "Sweetness, listen, I'm—"

"Don't you call me that," she said sharply, her tongue acting as a verbal whip. "You had no right. Absolutely *no* right!"

She was correct.

I had no right.

Take nothing she doesn't offer.

Her body, her choice.

"I'm sorry," I replied, genuinely. "I realize I crossed a line, and it's something I swear I won't do again." That was the damned truth. If I was going to fix everything I'd allowed to remain broken for a year and a half, then I couldn't do something so stupid—not to mention selfish—again. "It was a mistake I don't intend to repeat."

Visibly relaxing, she crossed her arms and shifted her weight between her feet. The small move made me smile because it meant I still affected her. I just hoped like hell it was in a good way.

If she was scared of me...

Hell, I didn't want to think about it.

"Okay," she replied, dipping her chin.

Turning back around, she started to walk off, but I wasn't having that. "Ashley, wait." Her shoulders tensed as I approached her from behind, the sound of my heavy breaths and pounding pulse filling my ears. "Baby, turn around."

Dropping her head back, she stared up at the starry night sky. "Why are you doing this?"

For a moment, I froze, unsure of what the hell to say. Part of me knew that if I told her the truth, she'd likely bolt. But the other part, the one that was a whole lot louder, was sick of the hidden truths that stretched between us.

The bullshit needed to end.

Right then.

So I did what my gut screamed at me to.

"Because I'm still in love with you," I replied, cutting straight to the chase. "Eighteen months may have passed, but my feelings for you haven't changed. Not one fucking bit."

Righting her head, she pulled in a shaky breath and rocked back on her heels, making her dark locks sway. "You're not supposed to love me anymore," she whispered, pain filling her voice. "You're supposed to hate me."

"Why would I ever hate you?"

My voice was one of disbelief.

Wrapping her arms around her belly, she slowly turned, bringing us face to face. Tear-filled gaze locked with mine, she tilted her head to the side, a ghost of a smile playing on her bee-stung lips. "Because I broke your heart." A single tear fell. "I broke your heart to save your soul, and you should hate me for that."

My hands twitched with the need to touch her, but I didn't dare. Instead, I slid my hands into my pockets, concealing the way they twitched from her eyes. "You did break my heart, but it wasn't your fault."

It was a fact.

My girl had issues.

Major ones.

But they weren't her fault.

She'd been neglected, beaten, *raped.*

Plus had her baby taken from her.

If I'd lived through the things she had—at least the things I knew of—I would've been a helluva lot more bent than her. And there was so much shit I didn't know about. But I was sure as hell going to find out every detail.

No matter how long it took.

"Nothing that has ever happened to you is your fault." She opened her mouth to speak, but I didn't give her the chance. "And before you say I don't know anything, you're right, I don't. But it doesn't matter, because when you found Shelby, you were just a scared seventeen-year-old girl running for her life. Whatever happened before that day doesn't matter."

"You're wrong," she said, just as I knew she would. "Chase, my secrets—"

"Will hold absolutely zero fucking power over you the minute you let them free," I interrupted, determined to get through to her. It was something I'd failed to do before, but I would *not* fail again. "It doesn't matter how bad they are, how twisted they may seem, or how much they tear you up inside, they will not change my feelings for you."

It was a line I'd said a thousand times.

But one I only needed to click once.

Come on, baby...

Talk to me!

Sniffling, she looked away, her eyes going to the ground by her feet. Digging the toe of her right boot into the concrete, she looked close to falling apart. "What do you want from me, Chase?" She lifted her head; our eyes locked. "Because I don't have a whole lot left to give."

"The same thing I've always wanted." I paused and drew in a breath. "You. Bent pieces and all."

"Bent..."

I nodded at her non-existent question. "Bent. Not broken. *Never* broken."

Something flashed in her eyes, but hard as I tried, I couldn't decipher its meaning. "Talk to me," I said, no more like begged. "Ashley, please."

"Want to know a secret, Jock?"

My chest burned, searing closed one of my many gaping wounds at the sound of the nickname. "Always, beautiful girl."

"My feelings haven't changed for you either," she whispered, the smile she wore shaky. "Doubt they ever will."

Having said all she needed to say, she turned and started to walk away once again. But like before, I wasn't having that. "Wait." She stopped mid-stride and turned her head, uncertainty written on her features. "You once asked me to never let you get too far, even if you ran." It was a request I'd never forgotten. "I swore I wouldn't. And I won't. Not from this day forward. I messed up by leaving you adrift for this long, but I'm done." Absolutely and *completely* done. "I'll give you the space you need, but I'm not walking away again. Not ever."

Close to bawling, my girl nibbled her bottom lip, trying her best to hold it together. "You're crazy, Chase Jacobs," she murmured. "Like, a whole lot of crazy."

I wasn't crazy. Dumber than a box of rocks for letting this shit go on? Yeah. But crazy? Nah. "I'm just a man trying to give the woman he's always loved exactly what she deserves."

She blinked slowly. "What do I deserve?"

My answer was simple. "The world."

Pounding the truth into her head every day until it finally took root was something I intended to do. Because the heart of the matter was this—Ashley deserved everything I could give her, including a future that was a helluva lot brighter than the darkness I was determined to free her from.

And that was the damned bottom line.

Chapter Thirty-Six

ASHLEY

*T*he moment I stepped through the front door, I found Heidi, Clara and my mama waiting for me in the living room, all three of their watchful gazes locked on me as if they were afraid I'd bolt at any second.

I understood Heidi and Mama being there, but not Clara since she'd gone home with Brantley just minutes before.

What the hell is going on?

"Come here, sugar," Mama said, pulling me out of the questions running through my head.

Knowing better than to disobey her, I moved into the living room, my pace no faster than a snail's.

"What is this?" I asked, looking from one woman to the next. "An intervention?"

My attempt at humor fell flat.

"That's exactly what this is," Heidi replied, choosing to take a no-nonsense approach to whatever was going on. Arms crossed over her chest, she leaned against the back of her wheelchair, brow quirked. "It's been a long time coming."

Uh-oh.

I chuckled nervously. "What kind of intervention?"

Mama, who looked two-seconds away from losing what remained of her mind, stood from the couch where she sat next to Clara. "The kind where one or all of us is gonna cuss and throw one damned fit after another until you finally hear the words we've been saying for the past year and a half."

Clara nodded and pointed at Mama. "What she said."

"I don't—"

"You," Heidi said as she steered her wheelchair in my direction, "are going to quit being so hard on yourself and you're damned sure going to quit distancing yourself from me, something that you've done since the night of my accident."

"Heidi—" I started.

"Don't you Heidi me," she interjected, her blue eyes piercing my face. "I know you blame yourself for what happened, and I have tried and tried to be patient, but I am all outta tries, Dimples." Her chin wobbled the slightest bit, causing guilt to build in my chest. "You are my maid of honor, my best friend, and the little sister I never had."

The little sister I never had...

Hadn't I said the same thing about Jade?

Heavens, I missed her. Carmen too.

"And I am done with you keeping me at arm's length," she continued, her expression pinched. "Because as we all know, I am far too needy for that mess."

"Isn't that the truth?"

"Zip it, Red," Heidi barked at Clara as she bit back a smile. "Now, back to what I was saying." She paused. "My wedding is tomorrow, and as my beautiful maid of honor, you owe me a favor. And this right here is me calling it in."

My anxiety climbed, but I kept it under control, refusing to surrender myself to its unrelenting grip. "What kind of favor?"

Tears filled Heidi's eyes, and I knew that the words she'd speak next would rock me to my core, much like Chase's had moments before.

Once again, I was right.

"The kind where you forgive yourself," she said, her voice firm but filled with emotion. "You've carried guilt, along with a lot of other stuff that wasn't yours to carry for far too long." When she started to cry, her tears tripping over themselves as they flowed down her face, I nearly lost it. "And it's time for you to let it go." Placing a hand over her heart, she patted her chest. "As your best friend, I'm asking you to do it for me."

"Heidi—"

"If not for me, then do it for Lucca and Gracie, because they need you," she continued, not giving herself a chance to take a single breath. "Or do it for your parents. Maybe even do it for the big, extended family that all of us have created out of choice, not obligation." Shoulders shaking, she pulled in a breath. "Better yet, do it for Chase, because without you, he will *never* be whole again."

"Bug—"

"And if you can't do it for any of us, then dammit, I want you to do it for *yourself*, Ashley Jo, because simply put, you deserve a lot more than what you've been getting."

Her words were fierce.

Her expression stern.

But my soul? It was exhausted.

I was so tired of fighting with the demons that continued to torment me, day in and day out. I just wanted it all to end. But I didn't know how to stop it. I couldn't just flip a switch and turn everything off.

I was messed up, I knew that.

Though I'd gotten better, it had come at a cost.

And that cost was numbness.

It scared me to death.

Looking from one woman to the next, each who had been through her version of hell, I whispered the truth that stirred in my belly, making me feel sick. "I don't know *how*," I cried, dropping the mask of indifference I'd grown accustomed to wearing. "I've lived with my demons for so long, ever since I was a little girl, and I..."

Words failing me, my voice trailed off.

"You'll know how when the time is right," Clara said, offering me a sweet smile. "Trust me. It took me a bit, but when that moment came, I found the strength I needed to conquer every monster."

"You did?"

She nodded. "I did, sweet girl. And I have no doubt that you will too."

"Yes, you will, sugar," Mama said, grabbing my attention. "And if for some reason you don't, then I'm sure as shit going to do it for you. I will find a way. 'Cause quite frankly, I am sick and tired of seeing my oldest baby so full of hurt." Wiping away the tears that leaked from the corners of her cornflower-blue eyes, she smiled. "And if anyone dares repeat a lick of what I'm about to say, then I will deny it until the day I die."

Heidi chuckled.

"You," she said, pointing a finger at me. "Belong with Chase Jacobs. End of story. And if you let that boy slip away because your head isn't in sync with your heart, then Ashley Jo, you are making the mistake of a lifetime."

Annoyance flared in my chest. It wasn't directed at her but at myself. "If you're so sure about all this, then why didn't you tell me this eighteen months ago?"

"You weren't ready eighteen months ago," Heidi answered for her. "But now you're stronger. Still lost, but stronger."

"They're right," Clara added, nodding. "It's time."

Mama nodded, mirroring Clara. "Damned straight."

Feeling their determination hit me square in the chest, I sucked in a deep breath. "So, what do I do?" I asked, running my shaking fingers through my hair. "I mean, how do I do this?"

"You do what every woman in this family has done before you when faced with darkness," she said, her entire body vibrating. Fisting her hand, she lifted it, knuckles facing me. "You stand up, and you frickin' fight."

"She's right," Clara said. "Standing up to the voices in your head isn't going to be easy—in fact, it's gonna hurt—but when your demons hit, Ashley Jo, you hit back twice as hard."

"Exactly," Heidi added, nodding. "And when you get knocked down, you climb your butt right back up because that is what *we* do. So, listen to me when I say that you are not going to stay down," she continued. "Not anymore."

My stupid chin trembled. "What if I can't get back up? I'm not—"

"Then we will dadgummed pick you up."

I snapped my head to the left at the sound of Grandmama's tear-filled voice. Standing in the open doorway, her eyes wet with emotion, she stared at me, her lips thinned. "Grandmama..."

"You are *my* grandbaby, Ashley Jo Moretti," she said, chest puffed out. "And that means something, whether your little behind realizes it or not." Closing the space between us, she cupped my face with her aged, shaking hands. "A year and a half ago, I found you laying on the living room floor, crying so hard you couldn't breathe." Her hands shook harder as her tears began to fall. "Something inside my old ticker broke that day, and it ain't beat right since. Now you gonna fix that for me? Or am I gonna have to keep walking around more wonky than usual?"

My mind spun at her question.

Could I fix it?

Could I fight?

Was I strong enough?

When push comes to shove, you fight, Chiquita. Carmen's words, the ones she'd spoken the night she died while trying to save Jade and I echoed through my head. *You always fight.*

She'd wanted me to fight, but I'd failed her instead. It was a mistake I'd be damned if I repeated.

So, at that moment, with the taste of Chase's stolen kiss still lingering on my lips, I made a decision.

And that decision? It was to go toe-to-toe with the blackness that stirred inside me, holding my soul captive.

My battle wouldn't be an easy one.

But that was okay.
Because I wouldn't surrender.
Not ever again.

Chapter Thirty-Seven

ASHLEY

I couldn't stop crying.

Standing in the center of Grandmama's backyard where Ty and Heidi's reception was in full swing, I was a ball full of emotions.

Between watching my best friend marry her soulmate in a beautiful yet simple ceremony, and the pregnancy announcement—hers—that followed, I was a certified hot mess.

Being escorted down the aisle by Chase didn't help things either. Not when the mere touch of his strong hand against mine sent me into a tailspin from which I could barely—and I do mean *barely*—ground myself.

The man was wreaking all sorts of havoc on my system. Not ready to deal with the emotions that his presence conjured up, I'd been dipping and dodging his every move since I stepped foot in Grandmama's house first thing that morning.

The problem was, he was *everywhere*.

And because he was everywhere, I wasn't the least bit surprised to see him headed my way from the other side of the yard, a look of determination etched on his handsome face.

Eyes never leaving mine, he navigated through the ocean of bodies that separated him from me, increasing his pace with each step until he was right there, smack dab in front of me.

"Sweetness..."

My eyes slid closed as his deep voice washed over me, awakening parts of me that had been dormant since I forced him to walk away all those months ago. No longer did numbness inhabit every square inch of my insides.

Pain mixed with regret did.

"What do you want, Jock?"

Standing less than a foot away, he leaned closer and chuckled, his chest nearly touching mine. The smell of his spicy cologne met my nostrils, and I swear my knees weakened. It simply wasn't fair for a man to be so pretty while smelling so good.

There was no defense against that.

"You know what I want," he said, his lips far too close to mine for comfort. "But just in case you need a reminder—it's you, beautiful girl."

Lungs burning, I bit my bottom lip.

Don't cry.

Just breathe.

My tear-filled gaze fluttered open, our eyes locked. "We've been over this, Chase," I said, my voice shaking the slightest bit. "There's a reason we broke up. I'm not—"

"Ashley Jo Moretti, swear to Christ, if you say that you aren't good enough for me, I am going to lose my absolute shit right here and now, in the middle of my brother's goddamned wedding reception."

That couldn't happen.

Frustrated and feeling all sorts of twisted up—*that's putting it mildly*—I blew out a pent-up breath. The night before, I'd made myself a promise that I was going to fight and conquer every demon that possessed my soul, but I couldn't do that *and* handle Chase.

One at a time was enough.

"Why are you doing this to me?" I asked, belly beginning to hurt. "You know I can't..."

My words vanished when he cupped my jaw, his thumb caressing my flushed skin. "Tell me what's wrong," he demanded, his voice soft yet firm. "And don't bullshit me either. I could see the pain dancing in your eyes all the way from the other side of the yard. Now, I want to know what's causing it so I can fix it."

The urge to hide from him, to curl into myself, to do anything but speak my truth was so strong it nearly crushed me, rendering me to a pile of broken bones and useless flesh. "You can't fix it," I replied, the grief that welled in my chest squeezing my heart. "Nobody can."

"Fucking try me."

Swaying on my feet, I latched onto his wrist, holding him tight.

"Ashley," he said, his voice morphing into one of concern and slight panic. "Baby, talk to me." Wrapping an arm around my lower back, he pulled me close, and for a moment, just a tiny blip of time, I leaned into him, letting him take my weight as I took every ounce of comfort he offered.

Chin resting atop my head, his finger traced patterns up and down my spine in slow, comforting strokes. "I have you," he whispered, swaying me from side to side the slightest bit. "You're fine, beautiful girl. Just breathe for me."

Burying my face in his shirt-covered chest, I did as he said and took a breath, pulling his scent, one that would be burned into my memory until the day I die, deep inside, where it melded with my soul, comforting the very thing that hurt the most.

"I promised myself that I would fight," I said so only he could hear. "But I don't know how I'm supposed to do that when every buried secret and hidden truth is eating me alive, destroying me more than my inner demons ever could."

Unwinding his arm from my back, he cupped my cheeks and tilted my head back, forcing my face to meet his. I hiccuped, my tears barely being held at bay. "Let them out, Ashley," he said, his Adam's apple bobbing up and down. "You release them and remove their power to hurt you another second."

My fears, the ones I'd had since the moment I realized I was beginning to fall for the man standing before me, his comforting touch delivering my heart the strength it needed to keep beating, rose, nearly suffocating me.

Shaking my head so hard that my hair began to fall from the loose up-do Clara had spent forever perfecting, I inhaled, the agony increasing tenfold. "You'll leave," I said. "You'll leave, and I can't handle that. Not less than a day after you showed back up here and reminded me what it feels like to have my pounding heart fall back in sync with yours."

"How many times do I have to say it?" he asked, his voice cracking. "Ashley, I fucking love you, and that includes every part of you. Even the bad shit that you think will make me turn my back."

He can't love me.

Not when I'm nothing more than a whore.

Stumbling back, I ripped myself from his hold. My soul screamed in gut-wrenching agony at the loss of his heat against mine, but I couldn't stand to be close anymore. Not when I knew that the toxic waste about to spew from my mouth would turn the love filling his eyes into nothing but disgust.

Above us, the storm clouds that had been gathering for the past hour lit up the sky with streaks of lightning as thunder boomed all around us.

Its ominous sound created the perfect setting for the nightmare that I was about to conjure up with a few lashes of my sinful tongue.

Done with the shackles binding me in place, I decided it was time to let every shameful secret out. Because even if I lost everything, my soul would finally be free.

I was officially *done.*

"You think you love me, Chase?" I asked, blackness swirling around me. "Well, you're wrong. And I know you're wrong because whores like me are meant to be used and battered, and then discarded like the trash we are. Not loved." The world beneath my feet crumbled. "*Never* loved."

"Ashley, what the hell are—"

"You thought Dominic was my boyfriend?" I asked, just as the sky opened up and heavy rain began to fall, pelting us with each of its frigid drops. "You were wrong again. I may have been his dirty little obsession, but truthfully, I was nothing more than my sadistic pimp's highest-paid whore."

Silence.

Then, "What *the fuck* did you say to me?" Eyes narrowed, he cocked his head to the side, the tendons in his neck cording as he glared at me in revulsion, the love he had dissipating with every second that ticked by.

"I told y-you," I stammered as everyone around us ran for cover from the thunderstorm that roared above us, when little did they know, an even bigger storm swirled around Chase and I, its mighty force more than prepared to rip each of us apart until nothing but broken pieces remained. "I told you that once you knew the truth about my dirty past, you'd stop l-loving m-me."

My knees knocked together as humiliation froze my insides, turning everything beneath my flesh into a tundra, completely void of anything resembling life.

I felt like I was dying.

Right there, on the spot.

Needing to get away before what remained of my psyche shattered, I turned to the side and bolted, heading straight for the gate that separated the backyard from the front. Both my parents screamed my name as I burst through it at top speed, not slowing the least bit when I hit the concrete drive.

The echo of footsteps sounded from behind me, but I didn't stop to think about who they could belong to, nor whether they were striking the ground faster than mine. My only focus was on escape, just as it had been the day I stabbed Ellington in his thigh and made a run for it.

Ellington...

Thinking his name sent a fresh new wave of torment crashing through me as I high-tailed it across the street, up the front porch steps and through the front door of my house.

Soaked from head to toe, my boots skidded against the hardwood foyer floor, and I careened into the bottom of the stairs, slamming my shins into the bottom step.

Ignoring the throbbing pain the collision created, I rocketed up the stairs, down the hall, and into my room where I dove for the side of my bed, ignoring the burn that covered my knees as my carpet tore into my flesh, leaving tiny patches of cream-colored fiber embedded in my ripped skin.

"Telling one truth isn't enough," I said as I jammed my hand beneath my mattress and ripped out the phone I kept hidden there. Clutching it tightly, I held it against my chest as I jumped to my feet, my heart beating so hard I expected it to fail at any moment. "It just isn't enough!"

Following the path I'd taken seconds before, I ran back out the house and headed back across the street, to the place where I'd find my father, the person I needed to see more than anyone else.

I never made it that far.

Stumbling to a stop in the center of the street, I stared through bloodshot eyes as Chase stood in the middle of the raging thunderstorm, his wedding clothes soaked through and his face streaked with what I knew were tears.

"Ashley!"

My mother, followed by nearly my entire family ran for me, but I ignored the whole bunch of them. Eyes focused on the man I loved like no other, I didn't breathe, much less move as I waited for him to speak.

Lightning flashed above us as thunder cracked nearby, shaking the ground beneath my feet.

"Ashley!" Again my mother screamed from the sidewalk where my father had a tight hold on her, refusing to let her come to me. "Let me go, Tony!"

"She needs this, Sunshine," he replied, his words holding a meaning I didn't quite understand. "She has to do this. It's the only way."

Focus on Chase...

"Tell me, Chase," I hollered, the tears that blurred my vision nearly blinding me. "Tell me that you don't love me anymore. Tell me so I can let g-go!"

Expression unreadable, he stared at me with unfocused eyes. Then,

"I will never not love you," he replied, his words like a sledgehammer to the belly. "Why would I ever stop loving the girl who has owned me —heart, body, mind, and soul—from the second I saved her from face planting into our high school cafeteria floor?"

"But I'm... I'm a—"

"You are *mine!*" he screamed, his face turning red. "What you were forced to do by one of the real-life monsters who took pleasure in tormenting you doesn't matter to me. The only thing I care about"—he pointed at his chest—"is what's in here."

I didn't believe him.

Part of me wanted to.

But the other part...

It had been hurt too many times.

"And baby, whether it's scarred or not, you have one of the most beautiful hearts I've ever seen. Bottom damned line."

"Chase—"

I bawled like a fool, my mouth slamming shut so hard my teeth rattled as he dropped to his knees in the middle of the road amid a deadly thunderstorm and extended his arms. "You want me down on my knees begging? You want me to plead? Well, here I am, Sweetness. On bended knee."

He paused, his shoulders shaking as he cried, his heart breaking before mine. "I'm begging you, Ashley. Just let me love you, baby. Let me love you the way you were always meant to be loved. With every piece of me, and with every breath, from now until forever."

The phone slipped free from my hand, clattering to the pavement as I cupped my hands to my mouth, my warm breath fanning against my shaking palms. Like many times before, I had a choice to make. I could either push Chase away for the final time and destroy us both in the process, or I could do as he asked.

I could let him love me.

For once, it wasn't a hard choice.

Dropping my arms, I steadied myself, my legs nearly giving way. "I want you to love me," I cried, my insides a tangled maelstrom of emotion. "And I want you to keep me forever."

Jumping to his feet, Chase charged me.

In less than ten steps, he twined his arms around my back and lifted me into the air. Hands on his shoulders, I continued to cry as my forehead rested on his, my tears raining down onto his face. "I love you, Ashley Moretti," he said, his voice cracking with each word. "And as I've said many times before, I will love you until I take my final breath."

"I love you too, Chase Jacobs," I whispered, wiping the tears from his face. "With every broken piece."

Chapter Thirty-Eight

CHASE

*U*nchecked rage warred inside me.

I'd known my girl had been hurt and had assumed the sort of pain she'd suffered had been due to domestic violence and sexual assault, but what she'd told me... I couldn't even think about it without feeling as though the top of my head was going to blow right off.

Dominic had been a pimp...

She'd been a prostitute.

With those two truths, bile climbed into my throat. Not because of what she'd been, but because I knew beyond a shadow of a doubt that she hadn't been a willing participant. But even if she had, it wouldn't change the way I felt about her.

People made mistakes.

All the damned time.

I may have been a hot-headed prick, but I wasn't a judgmental ass clown. Hell, I had plenty of faults of my own.

Everyone did.

In the end, none of that crap mattered. The only thing that did was that we learned from our screw-ups and became better people somewhere down the road.

As for my girl, her heart was golden.

And her soul? It was beautiful.

To hell with her past.

The only thing I cared about was *her*.

Which, speaking of...

She wouldn't stop shaking.

Eyes closed, she sat next to me at her parents' dining room table, her trembling hands tucked firmly between her knees.

Arm gently touching mine, she fought to pull in one breath after another as both Moretti and Shelby sat opposite us, their pain-filled eyes never leaving her gorgeous face.

"I can't do this anymore," she whispered, visibly swallowing. "The secrets have to come out. If they don't, my demons will win, and that..." Voice trailing off, she turned her head to the side. "That just isn't an option. Not after all this time."

Across the table, Shelby appeared ready to fall apart. It wasn't a normal sight to see. Strong as hell and a badass in every sense of the word, not much rocked her. When it came to her kids though, she was vulnerable.

Just like I would be.

Eyes fluttering open, my girl turned her attention to her Mama. "You once told me not to let the men who'd hurt me take more from me than they already had." Another pause. "This is me finally listening."

"We're here, sugar," Shelby said, shoulders shaking as Moretti wrapped an arm around her and pulled her into his side. "We'll always be here. No matter what."

I held my breath, waiting for Ashley to throw out her normal line of, *not once you find out my secrets.* Surprisingly the words didn't come.

Instead, she nodded, her pretty eyes filled with moisture. "I know you're always going to be here." She turned her head, finding me. "I understand that now."

Thank Christ!

Relief unfurled inside me.

"Which is why I'm finally ready to speak my truths," she continued. "It's time to silence the demons destroying my soul by taking their power, and not feeding into the madness. Just like Chase told me to."

Resting my hand on her thigh, I gave her flesh a slight squeeze. "You've got this," I told her. "Just let it all out."

A shaky smile played on her lips as she nodded and laid one of her hands atop mine. "I've got this," she said, repeating the line I'd just told her. "I've always had it."

That she had.

Pulling in a deep, cleansing breath, she looked forward once more, facing her parents head-on. "Both of you know parts of my story, but I'm about to tell you everything. I just... please just let me get it out, and then you guys can ask any questions."

Moretti nodded.

Shelby too.

"My first memory is of a man touching me where no little girl should ever be touched," she said, her fingers digging into mine. "I don't know how old I was, but I hadn't started kindergarten. So, three or four, maybe?"

I fisted my free hand but held steady, refusing to let the fury boiling inside me out.

"After that, it never stopped. I'd get months of peace depending on which man Wanda was dating at the time, but the bad guy always had a way of finding me. I don't know if it's because she just didn't care or if they targeted her because she had me. Either way, what happened, what she *allowed* to happen, isn't okay. It wasn't then, and it's not now."

She was right about that.

I'd never met Wanda, her birth mother before, but if I ever came face to face with her, I would gladly sit back and watch as Shelby Moretti stomped her ass from here to kingdom come.

"When I was nine"—knowing the story to come, I froze —"Wanda offered me up as payment when she couldn't afford the rent." Moretti's eyes flared, but like me, he stayed silent. "After he..." My girl paused, clamping her eyes shut. "After he *hurt me*, I couldn't walk too well, so Wanda called the school and told them I had the flu. I didn't go back for over a week, and no one ever found out."

Shelby shifted in her seat.

She looked a second away from having an aneurysm. I felt her pain. Quite damned literally. Though I'd heard the story Ashley had just told before, it still hurt.

A helluva lot.

My girl...

She'd been through hell.

"Then," Ashley continued, holding strong. "The day I turned fifteen, Wanda brought this guy named Ricky, home." Teeth gnawing on her bottom lip, she shook her head. "He was the worst. I tried to avoid him as best as I could, but within a week of moving in with us, he started sneaking in my bedroom at night."

I didn't know Ricky.

Had obviously never met him.

But I hoped he was dead and sharing a cell in the deepest pit of hell right next to Clyde.

"I would prop a chair against the door to keep him out, but one night I was so tired"—another pause, another deep breath—"and I forgot. I woke up with him on top of me."

Chest heaving, Moretti dropped his head back, his infuriated eyes fixated on the ceiling.

"The next morning, I told Wanda. I didn't expect her to do much, but part of me still wanted her to do something because she was my mother, and I was... well, I was her daughter, and she should've loved me enough to protect me."

That was when the first tear fell.

Not when speaking about the rapes, but when talking about how the woman who birthed her didn't love her.

It. *Killed.* Me.

Pulling my hand from beneath hers, I scooted closer and curled my arm around her shoulder, hugging her close. She leaned into me, her soft body melting into my hard one.

"You've got this, Sweetness," I whispered. "Keep going, beautiful girl."

A quick nod. Then, "Instead of doing something to help me, she accused me of trying to steal Ricky from her and kicked me out with nothing more than the clothes on my back." I had a lot of shit I wanted to say at that moment, but once again, I refrained. "But I found a way back inside."

I hadn't heard this part.

"I waited until she and Ricky were doped up real good later that night and snuck back in through my bedroom window. Once inside, I stole every last dollar they had. It wasn't a whole lot, but it was enough for me to buy some food and a bus ticket." She smiled. "That's how I made it to Georgia. When I walked into the terminal in Miner's Cove, I told them I wanted on the next bus out. Toluca was it."

For that, I was thankful.

I couldn't stomach the idea of her having landed somewhere else.

Without her, I'd be lost.

Fact.

"When I got off the bus, I didn't have anywhere to go, so I ended up sleeping behind the station." Shame filled her eyes as she dipped her head. "Dominic found me within two weeks."

"Ashley Jo," Shelby said, unable to remain quiet a second longer. "We know what Dominic forced you to do, sugar. You don't need to—"

"Every truth," she whispered in reply, cutting her Mama off. "I need to speak them all."

Understanding flashed in Shelby's eyes. "Okay, baby," she said. "You speak every last one."

"When he found me, the first thing he told me was that I was beautiful. Then he bought me some food and gave me his jacket. After sitting with me for a bit, he offered to take me home with him. Said I could sleep in his spare room, the one his baby sister stayed in when she came to visit." Shame washed over her features, gutting me. "I went without hesitation, but I found out real quick that he was nothing but a liar. He didn't have a sister, and the only room he intended for me to sleep in was his."

By then, she'd been trapped.

"A week later, he took me on my first call. When I refused to do what he and the client demanded, he took me back to the trap house where he, I, and the rest of his girls lived. The first thing he did when we stepped inside was pull Jade aside." More tears. "He made me watch as he..."

"Just breathe, Sweetness," I said, pressing my nose to the crown of her head. "We have you."

Digging her nails into my wrist, she nodded and then continued. "He made me watch as he raped her. Over and over. She cried for it to stop, begged for me to help her, but I couldn't..." Her shaking grew more intense. "After that, I tried not to anger him again."

My heart was ripping in half.

Tearing right down the middle.

And that feeling, the one that I could've sworn would be the death of me, only intensified when my girl fisted her hand because I knew—I fucking knew—exactly what was coming.

"But I failed when I got pregnant." Shelby's entire body stilled as Moretti blew out an audible breath. "Dominic was so pissed. He couldn't take me in for an abortion because people would ask too many questions, so he beat me. Repeatedly. But I never miscarried. How that happened, I still don't know. But months later, on the filthy bathroom floor of that same trap house, I gave birth."

Shelby slammed her hands over her mouth, silencing the scream I knew was seconds away from escaping. But Ashley, my brave girl, didn't hesitate as she continued to speak, banishing one demon at a time. "She was beautiful. Most beautiful baby I'd ever seen."

My face found her hair again.

I breathed her in, my heart in tatters.

"As much as I wanted to, I couldn't keep her. Dominic had sworn to kill her the moment she was born, and I knew if I didn't get her out of that house before he returned from the drug run he'd left on, she was dead. Me too, because I wouldn't let him take her from me without a fight."

Of that, I had no doubt.

My girl faltered when it came to some things, but there was no doubt in my mind that she would've fought to the death to protect her baby...

To protect *Addie*.

"So I did the only thing I could. I bundled her up in one of his shirts, nursed her for the first and last time, and then left."

A tear slid down Moretti's cheek.

"Ashley, baby," Shelby cried, barely hanging on to her sanity. "Where did you go?"

My girl sat straight, her tear-filled eyes meeting her mother's. "Carmen and Jade went with me to surrender her. I walked her into Toluca Memorial Hospital and handed her over to an ER nurse." The first sob hit. "Just like Gracie's birth mom d-did."

Shelby jumped up, her chair skittering backward, but Ashley still didn't stop.

"I'd had Jade write a letter to social services asking them to keep the name I'd given her, but I don't know if they did. I don't know where she is or if she ever got adopted. All I know is that she will *always* be my Addie."

"What did you tell, Dominic, *Principessa*?" Moretti asked, his face marred with tear tracks.

Just like mine.

"Carmen told him that she died," she replied, finally breaking down. "She told him that she died and so she buried her in a vacant lot over on Maple Street. He never questioned her, never checked. The only thing he cared about was that my baby, my beautiful little girl, was gone."

With that, Shelby broke.

Rounding the table, she pulled Ashley up from the seat where she sat, buried in my side, and wrapped her arms around her. Sob after sob jerked her body as she held onto her oldest daughter and cried every bit of pain she felt out.

"Please don't hate me," Ashley said, her tears still falling. "I wanted to keep her, but he'd have killed her... or sold her, and I couldn't—"

"Hate you?" Shelby asked jerking back so she could look my Sweetness in the face. "What you did was the most selfless thing a mother could ever do, Ashley Jo Moretti. And don't you ever forget it."

Ashley swayed, her legs nearly buckling.

Jumping up, I wrapped my arms around her from behind as Moretti did the same to Shelby and Ashley both. "Anything else you need to say, *Principessa*?" he asked, holding two of his girls tight. "If you've got anything left, say it. Let's finish this."

"The p-phone," she stuttered, breaking apart. "It's my last s-secret."

Moretti furrowed his brow as she glanced over at the older iPhone that sat in the center of the table, its screen black. Slowly reaching over, he picked it up and powered it on.

Ashley cried harder at the sight and buried her face in Shelby's neck, hiding from whatever it was that Moretti was about to find. "*Principessa*, what is—"

His words died as his eyes flared.

Left in the dark, I had no idea what he was looking at as his thumb moved across the screen, over and over, but the enraged expression he wore, one which served as a warning of the hell about to be unleashed, was unmistakable.

"Moretti," I said, face twisting. "What the fuck—"

Face red as hell, he stepped back and pulled a bawling Ashley from Shelby and I's arms. Then, he dragged her close, hugging her so tight I doubted she could even breathe. "My beautiful, brave *Principessa*," he said. "I'm going to fix this. Don't care what I have to do, I'm going to handle it."

She nodded against him. "Promise?"

Dropping his arms, he cupped her cheeks, forcing her to look at him. "I swear on my life that you will get justice this time. One way or another."

His eyes met Shelby's as he pressed a kiss to my girl's forehead. "I'll be back," he said, sliding the phone into the front pocket of his dress shirt. "Don't wait up."

He looked at me. "Take care of our girl, yeah?"

Our girl.

Hearing him say that did funny shit to my heart.

I nodded. "I have her. Always."

Without giving me another glance, he headed into the living room where he retrieved his service gun and badge. Attaching both to his belt, he pulled on a jacket and moved toward the front door.

Confused, Shelby hollered out, "Tony! Where are you going?"

Turning his head, he peered at us over his shoulder. "To burn the corrupt town of Toluca, Georgia to the goddamned ground," he replied, his voice colder than I had ever heard it before. "Starting from the fucking top."

Before Shelby could form a reply, he opened the door and slipped outside, disappearing from sight, and leaving us to sweep up the broken pieces that remained after each of Ashley's bombshell confessions.

So that's what we did.

We picked up every jagged piece.

Then, we glued them back together.

Chapter Thirty-Nine

ASHLEY

I went home with Chase that night.

Though free of the weight my buried secrets had placed on my soul, I still hurt. Whether the agony came from reliving the torment that each painful memory brought forth or the fact that I'd spent so much time plagued with unnecessary fear, I didn't know.

The only thing I could be sure of was that I wanted to fall asleep in his arms, enveloped in his secure embrace.

We'd lost so many moments.

I didn't want to lose one more.

And it was because of that, that I found myself sitting next to him on the end of his bed, one of my legs crossed over the other. "You're awfully quiet," I whispered, taking one of his hands in mine. "Anything you want to talk about?"

He ran his strong hand over his clean-shaven jaw. "I was just thinking about your two friends."

A pin pricked my heart at the mention of Carmen and Jade. I hadn't told him about them back at my parents' house because it was a story they'd already heard. So I waited and then told him every morbid detail during the hour-long road trip back to Atlanta, where he lived.

I'd also told him the truth about his father, one which about killed me to reveal. Not because I gave a crap about Clyde—I didn't—but because I knew it would upset Chase.

And boy did it upset him.

The moment he found out that his father had not only raped Jade—repeatedly—but also disposed of her and Carmen's bodies after Dominic murdered them, I thought he would stick his fist through the windshield.

Needless to say, he was *pissed*.

Extremely so.

"If Clyde were still alive, I'd kill him myself. As for Dominic," he spat. "I should pay another inmate to murder that sorry fuck. I'm sure someone would be more than happy to shank him."

It was a ledge I talked him down from.

I mean, as much comfort as Dominic's death would bring me, I figured spending the next two decades behind bars was just as good.

After all, I doubted he'd ever walk out a free man.

As I said before, my dad kept tabs on him, including every infraction he'd received. And those infractions? They were vast. I doubted it would be long before he killed someone and was sentenced to life. Or that somebody killed him.

Which would be just fine with me.

"I know you said there won't be anything left of their bodies"—I cringed, his words a gut-punch—"but what if we still had some type of memorial put in place for them? I don't know, Sweetness. I just think they need to be remembered. By more people than just us."

My chin trembled at his words.

"They would have loved that."

"Yeah?" he asked, smiling.

I nodded. "Yeah." Dropping my gaze from his face, I picked at the hem of the dress I'd changed into before leaving home. "Both of my girls would've loved you." I knew they both would have. Carmen probably would've threatened to cut his balls off if he hurt me though. "Jade, especially."

His smile grew. "How about you? Do you love me?"

I closed one eye and lifted two fingers. "Just a little bit."

A surprised squeal escaped my lips when he quickly twisted at the waist, placed his hands on my hips, and lifted me onto his lap, forcing me to straddle him. "Just a little bit, huh? Guess I need to work on changing that."

When his lips trailed down the sensitive juncture of my neck and shoulder, I moaned and dropped my head back. "What—"

"What I'm doing," he interrupted, hearing my words before I spoke them. "Is you." He ghosted a hand up my back before sinking it into my hair, where he fisted my locks, tugging them tight. "Can I touch you?" His teeth nipped my neck as I gasped in shock. The move was rougher than any he'd made before. "Remember, it's always about what you want, beautiful girl. So tell me, if I can have you or not. Because if not, I need to stop—"

My hands went to his shoulders, where I dug my acrylics into the slab of muscle that laid beneath. "Don't stop." Readjusting, I pressed my center down on his hard cock, loving the way his rigid length felt against my aching flesh.

Any fear that I'd once felt at being touched by him was long gone, nothing but a distant memory. "Take what's always been yours," I continued, goading him. "Chase, please—"

In one swift move, I was flat on my back and a hairbreadth later, he fisted the front of my dress in his left hand and jerked up, ripping the airy fabric from my body. A tearing sound filled the room, followed by the jingle of his belt as he yanked it free of his pants.

"You make me fucking crazy," he said, pulling off his shirt, followed by my panties and bra. "So goddamned crazy."

Laying down atop me, nothing but the pressed fabric of his slacks and briefs separating us, he took my mouth with his. Possessing it completely, he swirled his tongue around mine and groaned, the taste of me seemingly driving him wild.

Fingers sinking into my hair, I twined my legs around his hips as he shifted them, grinding his erection against my folds. "Jock," I said, ripping my mouth from his. "Please, I can't..." Head spinning, I searched for the words, my ability to speak nearly vanishing. "I *ache*."

My words were his undoing.

"To hell with this shit," he mumbled, sitting back on his calves. "I'll take my time and do this right later, but right now, I just want to fuck you."

Right or wrong, his dirty mouth turned me on, something I never would have expected.

But this was Chase.

My Chase.

Everything with him was different.

After popping open the button of his slacks, he tugged the zipper down, freeing his erection from behind his briefs. Harder than I'd ever seen it, the head was purple, the crown glistening with drops of pre-come. Teeth sunk into my bottom lip, I touched my finger to the slickness and brought it to my mouth, relishing the taste of him on my tongue.

Neck tendons corded, he lifted my legs, resting my smooth calves on his shoulders. "You're trying to kill me," he mumbled, fisting his rigid length in his hand.

Gripping it tightly, he pumped his palm up and down it as his free hand went to my pussy. His thumb found my clit as he sank two fingers deep inside my sheath.

My back arched at the feel of his touch.

His name fell from my parched lips.

"That's right," he said, sliding his digits in and out of me as his thumb circled my sensitive nub, sending bolts of pleasure careening through my lower belly. "You say my name. *Mine.*"

"Chase," I moaned, doing precisely as he said. "I want you inside of me." I rolled my hips, forcing his fingers impossibly deep. "I need—"

My words dissipated as he pulled free of my body and lined his throbbing cock up with my entrance. "Sweetness," he said, chest heaving from the force of his pants. "I don't have a condom. I never bought any after you. There was no point."

I burned hotter at his confession.

Chase being with another girl had never even crossed my mind.

Why would it? Even at my worst, I was all he ever wanted, even if I couldn't see that truth.

"No condom," I replied, rolling my hips once more. "I have an IUD. We're good."

It was one I'd had put in the minute Shelby took me for a checkup after she'd adopted me. At the time, I had no plans to have sex, but I refused to take a chance on getting pregnant if something else—something bad—happened again.

Chase looked at me funny, an expression I couldn't read appearing. "Want to know a secret, Sweetness?"

Knowing that whatever he was about to say was important to him, I nodded. "Tell me."

"After you ended stuff between us, I prayed you were pregnant from that one time we didn't wrap up in the back of Heidi's car. It's selfish as hell, but I thought if we had a kid, you wouldn't push me away." He smirked. "See, beautiful girl? You're not the only crazy one in this relationship."

I playfully smacked his arm. "I am *not* crazy. That title goes to Grandmama."

He cringed. "Baby, I am less than a second away from sinking my cock into your tight pussy. Now isn't the time to be bringing up the Crazy Old Biddy."

"I—" My reply morphed into a shocked moan as Chase slammed home, giving me every inch of him in one hard thrust. "Oh God!"

Blanketing my body with his, he held my nape with one hand and cupped my bottom with the other. "Put your hands on the headboard," he barked, the tendons in his neck cording again. "And keep them there, else I'm going to fuck you through the wall."

The moment my palms touched the wooden headboard, he withdrew and slammed into me once more. Panting for breath, he erased what remained of the space between us, pressing his broad chest to my soft one.

Pinning me to the bed, he supported himself with his elbows as his hard pecs scraped across my nipples, making my back bow with each thrust of his hips.

"More, I groaned, turning my head to the side. "Please, Chase, I want *more*."

It was a demand he obliged.

My heels dug into his butt as he drove into me, stabbing me with his cock over and over again. Gasps, followed by grunts and pants, fell from my lips as the slapping of his skin against mine echoed through the room.

Tugging on my hair, he held me tight as his fingers dug into my skin, the pace of his frantic thrusts increasing with each twist of his adept hips.

Sweat dripped from his brow as the hand gripping my behind lifted me the slightest bit. I screamed as he hit a deeper spot, the small change in angle giving him better access to parts of me he'd never reached.

"So"—thrust—"good!" he yelled.

Screaming his name in return, I scraped my nails down his back, marking his tanned skin for the whole world to see. I didn't give two craps that his entire team would likely see the claw marks the next time he changed in the locker room.

I *wanted* them to see each one.

Because he. Was. *Mine.*

"Ashley, goddammit," he cursed, jaw clenched tight. "Baby, I'm not gonna last..."

Knowing exactly what I needed, I pulled his hand from my hair and slipped it between us, silently telling him what I wanted.

"Fuck yes," he said, drilling into me so hard his balls bounced off my ass with each full thrust.

Fingers finding my clit once more, he rolled my nub between them, giving me exactly what my body craved.

Orgasm building, I cupped his face with my shaking hands. Our eyes locked. "Don't look away," I demanded, my core tightening around his swollen cock. "Not ever."

Foreheads touching, he stared down at me, our exhaled breaths mingling before we both pulled them back into our lungs. "I will never"—thrust—"look away."

My heart swelled as the orgasm that had been building since he forced me onto his lap finally broke free, shattering me in the process.

Scream after scream, moan after moan, and more curse words than I'd ever uttered in my life flew from my lips as wave after wave of pleasure consumed me, numbing my body of any other sensation.

Above me, Chase's thrusts became more and more erratic until he suddenly yelled out, his body stiffening above mine as he came inside me, pouring himself into me. "Fuck, Ashley," he said, panting for breath. "I'm pretty damned sure I just saw Heaven."

Pressing my lips to his, I kissed him, as his heart pounded against my chest, his pulse entirely in sync with mine. "You are my Heaven," I whispered against his mouth, fully aware of how silly yet truthful my words sounded.

Chase groaned as he pulled out of me and rolled onto the mattress beside me. I turned, facing him, and he lifted me onto his chest, holding me tight. "You're mine too," he replied, nuzzling his face into my hair. "Forever, Sweetness."

Eyelids fluttering close, I snuggled into him, nearly crawling beneath his skin. "Forever, Jock."

It was the last thing I said, because within a matter of minutes, I was fast asleep.

-

-

Chapter Forty

ASHLEY

I was going to be sick.

Seated in the lobby of Toluca PD, I stared at the door to my left, not so patiently waiting for my dad to walk out. A little over an hour had passed since he'd called me at work and told me to get my butt down to the station. Since he didn't elaborate as to why, I was ready to come out of my skin with worry.

And my poor stomach...

The stupid thing wouldn't stop churning.

If I hadn't been alone it wouldn't have been so bad. But with Mama at work and Chase back in Atlanta at practice, I didn't have anyone. Sure, I could've called one of the other ladies to come sit with me, but either they were at work or gone with their families.

I'd been tempted to call Grandmama or even Pop, but they were busy too. I swear some days it seemed like my entire family was going in a hundred different directions.

It drove me batty.

"*Principessa...*"

I jerked my head up at the sound of my father's voice. Moving through the now opened door, he wordlessly gestured for me to get up and come with him.

So that's what I did.

Standing, I followed him back through the door and down the long hallway that led to his office. Once we were inside, he shut the door behind him and nodded toward an empty chair next to his desk.

"Sit, Ashley."

I chewed on my bottom lip. "I'd rather stand. Especially when I have a bad feeling that whatever reason you brought me down here isn't a good one."

Blowing out a breath, he slid his hands into the pockets of his slacks. "Your mama will shoot me where I stand if this goes badly," he mumbled, before closing his eyes for a moment. "And if she doesn't kill me off entirely, your Grandmama damned sure will."

I had no idea what he was talking about.

"Dad," I said, brows furrowed. "It's no secret that I'm easily confused at times, but do you mind telling me what's going on?"

Pulling his hands free of his pockets, he crossed his arms and turned to face me fully, his eyes locking with mine. "Jeffrey Ellington was arrested last night."

All the air left my lungs in one quick whoosh. "For what?" I asked, feeling a tad bit faint.

"Sexual Exploitation of a Minor and Possession of Child Pornography, among other things."

"Is it...I mean, is it because of the—"

"It's because of the phone," he cut in, knowing exactly what I was about to ask.

I hated thinking about that danged phone.

It was bad enough that my dad saw the horrendous things that were on it, including me being violated in the most twisted of ways.

But after having to explain to both my mama and Chase the type of videos and pictures that it contained after Dad stormed out, hell-bent on burning down the town, I never wanted to speak of it again.

Not ever.

Feeling beads of sweat form along my spine, I stepped back and leaned against the wall behind me. "Holy crap," I murmured. "I know I gave you the evidence, but I never... Well, I guess I just thought nothing would come of it. I understand it's not your fault, but after you said there would be no justice for Carmen and Jade, I figured there wouldn't be any for me either."

"You were wrong, *Principessa*."

It would appear so.

"What happens now?"

"The judge denied his request for bail this morning, deeming him not only a flight risk but a hazard to the general public, children especially."

Disbelief built inside me.

This can't be real.

It's too good to be true.

"But he's the DA. Can't he just pull some strings and get out of it?" I was hopeful he couldn't, but he had plenty of money plus friends in high places. If anyone could get out of legal trouble, it was him.

"He's not going to be the DA for much longer, and he has more enemies than friends." Well, that wasn't real surprising when I thought about it. "Trust me, more people want to see him behind bars than free."

Mixed feelings swirled inside me.

Part of me was happy as could be that Ellington may get sent to prison or at the very least, knocked off the pedestal he'd perched his predatory-self on long ago. But the other part of me—the jaded one— didn't believe he'd ever see the inside of a prison cell.

Powerful men like him never did.

"Do I need to do anything? Like, fill out a report or something? Is that why you asked me to come down?"

He shook his head. "No, baby, it's not."

My brows furrowed. "Then why?"

"Before I reveal my intentions, you should know that Dominic is in a holding cell downstairs."

Once again, all the air left my lungs, and panic stirred despite the fact that I tried to push it down, back into the depths from which it sprang. "What is...?"

Losing the ability to speak, I pressed my back flat against the wall as my heart pounded against my ribcage.

"He has to make an appearance down at the Toluca Courthouse this afternoon thanks to a new charge they uncovered recently. Bureau of Prisons transported him in from Atlanta early this morning. He was supposed to be logged in at county, but they are at max capacity, so we're taking their overflow until they free up some space."

Oh God.

"Dad, I don't understand. What am I—"

"This is your shot."

Tears filled my eyes though I didn't have the slightest clue as to why. "My shot to what?"

"To sever the last remaining tie."

One sentence.

That was all it took for understanding to dawn upon me. "You want me to confront them?"

Closing the space between us, he gently pinched my chin between his index finger and thumb. "What I want," he said, "is for you to take back every ounce of power they stole from you."

The moment I began to wonder exactly how in the world I'd do such a thing, Mama's words from the night she, Clara and Heidi staged an intervention echoed through my head.

You do what every woman in this family has done before you when faced with darkness, she'd said. *You stand up, and you frickin' fight.*

My back snapped straight.

That was the night I made a decision to go toe to toe with the darkness that lived inside of me. So far, I'd done that. But if I truly wanted to be free, I needed to go head to head with the two men who'd hurt me the worst.

Like Dad said, this was my chance.

And I wanted my damned power back.

Channeling every ounce of strength from the kickass women in my life, I stood tall. Adjusting my purse on my shoulder, I stared at my dad. "Where are they?" I asked, my voice steady. "Because I have a thing or two to say to each of them."

A victorious smile crossed his face.

Turning, he opened the door and stepped to the side, making room for me to exit.

Once I crossed the threshold, he took my hand in his and led me down the hall. At the end, we descended a set of stairs into what used to be the station's basement but now served as overflow cells for the county jail.

My heart pounded the entire way.

But my steps did not falter.

Reaching the bottom, Dad came to a stop and turned, facing me head-on. "You ready for this?"

I didn't hesitate. "Yes."

He nodded, his eyes gleaming with pride. "Ashley Jo, listen to me. There are ten cells on the other side of this door. One is occupied by Ellington and a second by Dominic. Both are secured, and they won't be able to harm nor touch you. Understand?"

It was my turn to nod. "I do."

"Alright, *Principessa*, last chance. You sure you're ready?"

Again, there was no hesitation. "Open the door."

A second later, that's what he did.

After pushing it open, he stepped to the side. "I'll be right here," he said. "If you need me, I can reach you in five seconds flat."

"I'm gonna be just fine."

Like my heart, my words were confident.

It was a first for me.

Exhaling, he nodded toward the row of cells I could see from where I stood. "Go reclaim everything they took, *Principessa*," he said. "And then tell them to go straight to hell where they belong."

I said nothing as I stepped through the threshold and into the hall running between two rows of holding cells. Unlike upstairs, the entire area was dimly lit and had a creepy vibe to it.

It kinda freaked me out.

Still, I wouldn't let that stop me.

I held my breath as I moved toward the end of the cells, but just as I was about to exhale, I caught sight of both monsters.

Secured in cells right next to each other, both sat on their beds, their unfocused eyes staring at the place where I stood, momentarily concealed by shadows.

"Come on, man," Dominic said, clearly thinking I was someone else. "Lunch was over an hour ago. Where the fuck is my tray, *pendejo*?"

My insides twisted at the sound of his devilish voice.

I hated him.

So damned much!

"Come on, white-bread," he taunted, still thinking I was one of the men from upstairs. "Move your ass."

At his words, something inside me broke.

A mixture of pissed off and hurt, I stepped out of the shadows and into his direct line of sight. "*El diablo*," I whispered, my eyes locking with his hate-filled gaze. "It's been a while."

In the blink of an eye, rage began to roll off of him in waves as he jumped up, his slipper covered feet hitting the concrete cell floor with a slap. "*Tesoro*," he sneered, wrapping his hands around the bars of his cell. "Come over here, baby. This little reunion has been a long fuckin' time comin'."

I passed on that.

There was no doubt in my mind that if I got within reaching distance, he'd ripped my head off without thinking twice.

He was that *pissed*.

"I'll never get near you again, Dominic," I said, refusing to cower in his presence. "The only reason I'm here is because I have a few things I'd like to say."

He smiled, his white teeth gleaming thanks to the fluorescent light beaming down on him from above. "Yeah? And what's that?"

"Almost seven years have passed since I fell into your sadistic clutches." He chuckled, but I ignored him and kept speaking. My words had been a long time coming. "From the moment we met, until I managed to escape you, you terrorized me to within an inch of my sanity."

I took a breath.

"You beat me, you raped me, you allowed others to rape me for profit, and you took things from me that I can never get back, including my child and my two best friends."

My heart climbed into my throat.

But I didn't stop.

"I will never forget the things you did to me, but I will no longer allow them to hold me back. I may have once thought of you as a monster, but that's no longer true. Now, you're nothing more than a caged animal."

"You stupid little—" he started.

"From now on, I will be at every court appearance and every parole meeting you have," I continued, cutting him off. "I will do everything in my power to make sure that you never walk the streets a free man again, where you'll have the chance to hurt another person."

Keep going...

Speak your truths.

"You may be the devil, Dominic West, but as of this moment, you no longer hold any power over me." Stepping closer, but not too close, I looked him straight in the eyes and said, "You tried to break me, but you failed."

"You stupid fuckin' *puta*, I own—"

"You don't own a damned thing!" I hollered, letting my emotions get the best of me. A twisted smile spread across my face. "You've been replaced, *el diablo*." His eyes flared, the anger brewing in them clear as day. "Far as I'm concerned you don't exist anymore."

I meant every word.

"But there's something I need you to know, and it's really important so listen up."

White-knuckled grip squeezing the bars tighter than before, he exhaled so harshly his nostrils flared. "Yeah? And what's that?"

Squaring my shoulders, I stood as tall as my five feet two inches frame would allow and glared at him with hard eyes. Then, "I'm no longer your *Tesoro*, Dominic. Now, I'm just me."

"Bitch, you aint'—"

"*My* name," I screamed, "is Ashley Jo Moretti, and whether you like it or not, *el diablo*, I am *done* being your fucking victim!"

Chest heaving, I turned my attention to Ellington, whose face was paler than normal as Dominic continued to cuss and sling one threat after another my way. Ignoring him, I stared at the well-dressed man before me, his beady brown eyes filled with pure terror.

"How does it make you feel, *Jeffrey*, to know that a mountain girl from the hollers of Appalachia is the one responsible for putting you here?" I smiled once more. "Have fun in prison, Mr. Fancy DA. I'm sure there are plenty of prisoners who will just *love* making your acquaintance."

Having nothing left to say, I walked away.

With each step that I took, another of the mental chains that held me captive snapped, completely breaking in half. And with them no longer anchoring me to my demons, I became the very thing I'd always wanted.

Free.

Chapter Forty-One

ASHLEY

*I*t was my birthday.

To celebrate my special day, my entire family had gathered in Grandmama's backyard for a cookout. The smell of charcoal, along with the sounds of laughter filled the air, and although I was happy as could be, a part of me ached with emptiness.

It was a feeling that had intensified over the past few weeks and one which I doubted I'd ever be rid of when such a huge chunk of my heart walked around free of my body day in and day out.

I missed my Addie.

So much.

Though I'd held her for less than an hour, I'd carried her for nine months. The feel of her moving inside me, followed by the smell of her newborn skin was something I'd never forget.

Often times, my mind drifted to both when I thought of her and one question after another—all of them impossible to answer—echoed through my mind.

Was she ever adopted?

Does she love her family?

Is she happy?

Is she safe?

I prayed that the answer to each question was yes. Giving her up had been hard enough, but if I ever found out that I'd taken her from one bad situation and thrust her into another, I wouldn't be able to handle that.

Seriously, my heart would break.

Beyond repair.

"Sweetness..."

I jerked my head up when the sound of Chase's voice washed over me, pulling me from my tumultuous thoughts.

Plopping down next to me atop the picnic table where I'd sat for the past thirty minutes watching the kids play tag, he took my hand in his and leaned over, pressing a soft kiss to my temple.

"What are you thinking about so hard?" he asked, his voice low so only I could hear him. "You look seconds away from bursting into tears. And that can't happen. Not on your birthday. So just tell me whose ass I need to kick, and I'll handle it."

Of course, he would.

"I'm not going to cry," I replied. "I was just thinking about Addie." He made a humming sound but said nothing in reply. "I know I forfeited my right to be her mama when I gave her up, but I still think about her all the time. I just hope she's okay, and that wherever she is, she's happy and safe."

Both were things I'd never felt as a child.

"I'm sure she's fine, baby," he whispered. Wrapping his arm around my side, he pulled me into him, comforting me as best he could.

Head going to his shoulder, I closed my eyes and took a deep breath. "I'm sure you're right. But not knowing—"

"Chase!" My eyes fluttered back open when my father, who was standing near the gate that led from the backyard to the front, hollered my guy's name. "The gift you got my *Principessa* just arrived."

His eyes flicked to me.

A small smile graced his lips.

My interest was officially piqued.

"What did you get me?" I asked, sitting straight. "Cause if it had to be delivered, it better be a pony." I smirked at him. "With a pink tail and an even pinker saddle."

He chuckled, jumping off the table. "Only you would ask for a pony with a pink tail."

Pushing my dark hair free of my face, I scrunched my nose. "Grandmama was the one who gave me the idea."

"Of *course* she was." With a roll of his eyes, he circled my upper arms with his strong hands, massaging my bare skin with his thumbs. "Stay here for me, baby."

My eyes narrowed.

"You're up to something," I whispered, head tilted to the side. "I can feel it."

It was his turn to smirk. "That I am." Lips meeting my cheek, he pressed a sweet kiss to my flesh. Then, "Remember when I told you that you deserved the world?"

I nodded. "I do."

"Well, beautiful girl"—he traced a fingertip down the side of my face—"this is me giving it to you." The meaning of his words were lost on me. "I love you, Ashley Jo. Always."

He didn't give me a chance to reply before turning and walking toward my father, my curious eyes following him the entire way.

"Ashley, sugar." Turning my head to the right, my eyes instantly found my mama. Voice filled with anxiety, which wasn't normal for her, she nervously shifted her weight between her feet, much like I did when on the verge of freaking out. "I need you to stay calm."

Stay calm?

"What in the world is going on?" I asked, brows furrowed. "You, Chase, and Dad are all acting battier than me, and that's saying something." Seriously, it was. "He didn't really buy me a pony, did he? Because if so—"

I snapped my mouth shut and looked back toward the gate when it creaked back open, the high-pitched noise acting as a beacon for my confused self.

When I saw Chase step through it, a small pink backpack hanging from his shoulder that same confusion increased.

Exponentially.

"What is he—"

In the blink of an eye, time stopped as my ability to speak vanished. The world beneath my feet shifted, and I swear to the heavens above that my heart ceased beating.

Gut-punched...

That's what I felt.

Hands flying to my mouth, I slipped off the table, stumbling to my feet. Leaning forward the slightest bit, a sob jolted my body as I stared at the little girl walking beside Chase, her hand tucked safely in his.

A little girl who, in the space of a stuttered heartbeat, I knew was mine.

Dropping my hands, I let the tears that had rapidly filled my eyes fall as I fought to remain upright. Legs nearly buckling, I almost hit the ground, but Mama reacted quickly and curled an arm around my waist, taking some of my weight.

"Breathe, Ashley Jo," she said, tears of her own falling. "Just breathe, baby."

Mouth gaping, I fought to find the words, but they simply wouldn't come, because right there, standing less than forty feet away was my baby...

Mine.

"Mama," I cried, heart nearly bursting out of my chest. "She's—"

"—here," she finished for me, knowing exactly what I was about to say. "And her name is still Addie. Children's Services honored your wish since you did the right thing by surrendering her in a safe environment."

"How?" The simple word miraculously rolled off my tongue, the single syllable strained and nearly incoherent.

"Chase hired a private investigator to find her," she answered, her body quaking against mine. "When we found out she was still in foster care and had never been adopted, we contacted Patty, your and Gracie's ex-social worker. After I explained the situation to her with the help of your Aunt Maddie and Hope, she jumped at the chance to assist us in bringing her home to you, where she belongs."

Oh God...

"Turns out, it wasn't all that hard. Thanks to your daddy and me keeping our foster license current, she was able to transition her into our care"—she paused—"starting today. It was perfect timing too since Children's Services was about to move her anyway. The foster family she's been with the last few years are retiring. Patty said they're good people but getting up there in age."

"W-what," I stuttered. "N-now?"

"Now," Mama replied. "You go meet your daughter. She's been looking forward to meeting you for the past two weeks."

Two weeks?

Reading the confusion on my face, she continued. "Chase has been visiting her. Said that since he's going to be her daddy and all, he thought it should be him that helped transition her into our care, and eventually yours, instead of Tony and me."

Daddy?

My mind was spinning.

Hard as I tried, I couldn't think.

But although I could barely formulate a reply, one question formed on the tip of my tongue. "Does she k-know?" I asked, chest filled with so many emotions I couldn't decipher one from the next.

"She's six, sugar. The only thing Chase and Patty told her was that you loved her very much and couldn't wait to see her. We'll handle the rest as it comes. One baby step at a time."

Wiping away the tears that spilled down my cheeks before splattering onto my chest, I took a deep breath. "Can I... can I go see—"

"Go, hug your baby, Ashley Jo," she cried, unwinding her arm from my back. "It's been a long time coming."

Though I was terrified, I couldn't wait another second.

Running on the need to hold my child—*mine*—in my arms for the first time since I gave her up to protect her, I moved my feet, one step after another.

Halfway to her, I stopped.

And I stopped because she suddenly turned her head in my direction. Stomach twisted in a thousand complex knots, I sucked in a breath and then swallowed a sob as her pretty brown eyes locked with mine.

Tugging on Chase's hand, she briefly glanced up at him. Her lips moved, but I was too far away to hear what she was saying. But then—then!—she looked my way once more and pointed a single finger straight at me.

That was the moment my heart stopped.

Swear to God, it *stopped.*

Then, it nearly burst when she parted her little lips and shouted the words I would have sold my soul to hear.

Those words? *There's my Mama!*

I didn't know if it was the right thing to do or not, but with a million raw emotions and driven by the need to pull my child into my arms, the place she should've always been, I took off, running straight for her.

"Addie!"

To my surprise, she ripped her hand free of Chase's and ran full-bore toward me, her long dark chocolate hair gleaming in the afternoon light. "Mama!"

Seconds later, I came to a stop and dropped to my knees, arms spread wide. Her chest collided with mine, and I wound my arms around her tiny body, holding her tight. "Mama," she said, burying her face—one which was nearly identical to my own—in my neck. "You're here."

Cupping the back of her head, I rocked her back and forth, tears pouring. "I'm right here, baby," I whispered, my body shaking. "And I'll always be here." I paused, fighting to keep from falling apart. "From this day forward."

Even with her slight weight in my arms, and her steady heartbeat bleeding into my chest, I couldn't believe that she was there with me.

Addie...

My Addie.

Leaning back, my sweet girl placed her little hands on my tear-streaked face and looked me straight in the eyes. Head tilted to the side, she gnawed on her bottom lip, the same as I always did when faced with uncertainty. "Promise?"

"I promise," I cried, dropping my forehead to touch hers. "On my life, I *promise*."

It was a vow I would keep.

Always.

———

"Happy birthday, Sweetness..."

Laying on my bed, a sleeping Addie curled snuggly into my side, I looked over at Chase, who lay behind her, his strong arm draped protectively over both of us.

Eyes locked, I remained silent.

The words simply wouldn't come.

There were so many things I wanted to say to him, but no matter how much I wrestled with my frazzled brain, my tongue wouldn't work.

But that was okay.

Because Chase understood.

Smiling, he traced his fingertips up and down my side, drawing invisible patterns against my skin. "Baby, I know you're overwhelmed, so I just want you to lie there and listen to everything I have to say."

I softly nodded.

"For the past few weeks, I've been making plans." That much was obvious. "Big ones. And every single one revolves around you"—he nodded at Addie—"and her." Scooting an inch closer to my girl, he continued. "First things first, I'm buying the vacant lot next to Ty's. It's the last one on the street, and Grandmama won't sell it to anyone but us."

Wait.

Grandmama owned that lot?

Well, color me surprised.

"Then I'm building you a house. Whatever kind you want. I don't care as long as you and Addie live in it with me."

Tears returning, my vision blurred.

"Brantley has already volunteered to represent us in family court so we can get your parental rights to Addie re-established. He's assured me it won't be a problem. We're young, but we'll have a nice home, money, and no criminal convictions. Not to mention, you're her mother. It may take a year to finalize everything, but until then, she'll remain right here with each of us."

My chin wobbled. "Then what?"

"Then," he said, smiling from ear-to-ear. "You're going to marry me."

Eyes flaring, I froze.

"Want to know a secret, Sweetness?"

Tears falling, I nodded.

"The moment Grandmama showed me your picture and asked me to keep an eye on you, I knew you were special. But when your terrified eyes first met mine the following day, that's when I knew..."

Circling his wrist with my fingers, I squeezed him tight. "What did you know?"

He swallowed, his eyes awash with moisture. "That you weren't just some girl I was going to keep an eye on, so her crazy ass Grandmama wouldn't shoot me."

"Yeah? Then what did you think I'd be?"

Pulling his wrist free of my hand, he ran a knuckle down the side of my face. "I didn't *think* anything. I *knew* that you were the mate to my soul and the other half to my heart."

Turning my face into his hand, I started to cry. "Thank you, Jock," I whispered, trying desperately to keep myself under control. "Thank you for saving me," I continued as every broken piece of my heart began to stitch itself back together. "And thank you for loving me when I couldn't even love myself. But mostly, thank you for *her*."

A lone tear—this one belonging to Chase—fell. "This is just the beginning," he whispered, his voice strangled. "Tomorrow is the first day of our forever."

As always, he was right.

Chapter Forty-Two

CHASE

One Year Later

*O*ne play.

With seven seconds left on the game clock, that's all we had time for. And since we were twenty yards out of field goal range, it was up to me to pull a miracle out of my ass and find a way to score.

It wasn't an easy task.

Not when my receivers hadn't been able to catch a damned thing all night and the only reliable running back I had exited the game at halftime with what the team doc suspected was a torn ACL.

Riddled with injuries, my team was falling apart.

And during the goddamned Super Bowl no less.

Seriously, *fuck. My. Life.*

Needing to move my ass, I stood at the line of scrimmage and bent down, sliding my hands under my center as sweat dripped from my brow.

Heart pumping, I stared at the opposing team, trying to read if they would blitz or fall back and play it safe.

They're blitzing.

I gritted my back teeth together at the realization.

"Come on, Jacobs!" One of the dumb fucks standing on the defensive line yelled. "Don't be a pussy!"

I wasn't a pussy.

Not by any stretch of the imagination.

But the last thing I wanted was to lose with my entire family sitting in the stands directly behind the end zone I was facing. Especially not with what I had planned for after the game.

We've gotta win...

Determined to do just that, I glanced toward the end of the field and locked eyes with my girls. Wearing matching jerseys with my name scrawled across the back, both were standing, their hands clasped together, watching me.

Feeling my eyes on her, Addie—*my sweet little Addie*—lifted her hand high in the air and waved while screaming something I couldn't hear over the roar of the crowd.

Standing directly beside her was Ashley, my ball cap, the one I'd been wearing the day we met, perched atop her head. Behind her sat my brother and next to him was Heidi, who held my niece, Brielle, in her arms.

The rest of my family—Crazy Old Biddy, who was wearing a beer hat, included—filled the next two rows, their faces a mixture of excitement and nerves.

But it wasn't them that I was focused on.

It was my girls.

Both of them.

One corner of my mouth tipped in a smile as a plan hatched in my head. More than ready to execute it, I called out, "Set, Green 80, Green 80, Hut-Hut!"

The ball landed in my hands on the second hut.

Dropping back, I cocked my arm, ready to pass as my line formed a shield around me, blocking the headhunters that were coming for me, more than ready to plant my ass into the ground.

In a flash, the pocket collapsed.

Surrounded by opposing jerseys, I lunged to my right, barely evading a sliding hit from one player, followed by a near tackle from another.

Eyes on the route I needed to take, I tucked the ball against my side, and made a run for it, using my speed to swoop, swerve and stutter-step my way out of danger.

Breaking free of any last threats, my gaze found Ashley and Addie again. Both were screaming, jumping, and cheering their asses off.

For *me*.

Seeing that...

It renewed my determination to reach the end zone. And to do that, I ran straight for *them*, the two girls—one big and one small—who were my entire world.

With only twenty yards left until the end zone, I could finally see Addie's lips well enough to read the words she was screaming.

Those words? *Daddy, run!*

Daddy.

That was all it took for my heart to swell. Like Ashley, I loved Addie so damned much I could hardly stand it. She may not have looked anything like me, and my blood may not have run through her veins, but Addie Jo was *my* daughter, just as her mama would soon be *my* wife.

Bottom damned line.

Boom!

The sound echoed around the stadium as I crossed the goal line without so much as being touched, securing the touchdown my team needed to win.

But I didn't even care about that.

Not really.

Instead, my focus was on climbing the wall beyond the end zone.

So that's what I did.

After ripping off my helmet, I clutched the ball tight and scaled the padded wall, quickly reaching my family. Fans screamed my name, and a few tried to reach me, but my brother, Hendrix, Evan, Brantley, Moretti, Kyle, Felix, Keith and Pop all did a good job of keeping them back. Grandmama waving around her goddamned flyswatter like she was brandishing a sword didn't hurt either.

I was reasonably sure that come morning, her crazy ass would be plastered all over the internet, but I didn't care. The only thing that mattered right then was doing what I'd planned to do for the past month.

"Hey, Peanut," I said, lifting Addie into the air. Hugging her tight against me, I buried my face in her hair, breathing in her strawberry-scented shampoo. "Did you see me score?"

"Yes!" she screamed, pulling back the slightest bit. "You won, Daddy!"

My heart hammered against my chest. "I did, baby." Tucking the ball, the one which I'd just scored the winning touchdown with under her arm, I smiled. "This is for you."

"Thank you! Mama look, Daddy gave me a ball!"

Long as I lived, I'd never tire of hearing her beautiful voice.

Swallowing around the emotions threatening to steal the air right out of my lungs, I glanced over at my brother, purposely avoiding Ashley's gaze. If she got one good look at my eyes, she'd figure out what I was up to real quick.

"You got it?" I asked him, chin in the air.

He nodded and slipped me the small velvet box, somehow managing to keep it out of her view. Then, clutching it tightly in my hand, I set Addie back on her feet.

"Jock," Ashley whispered, her voice barely audible over the roar of the crowd. "What are you doing?"

I didn't answer her.

Instead, I dropped to my knees.

Not one. But two.

Ashley's mouth fell open as Addie squealed in excitement. "Look, Mama!" she screamed, repeating her words from moments before. "Daddy is gonna marry you like in the movies!"

"Oh God," Ashley said, her hands flying to her mouth, eyes glazing over.

"There are only two places in this world that I exist," I said, taking her hand in mine. "And that's wherever you are, and wherever Addie is."

My Peanut giggled, warming my heart.

"I have loved you since I was eighteen years old, and I have loved her since the moment I learned her name. And just so we're crystal clear—there is not a damned thing in this world that I want more than to spend forever with both of you."

I paused and slipped the chocolate-diamond ring—one I'd chosen because it was unique and beautiful just like her—free of the velvet box it was housed in. Then, I held it up for her to see. "Do me a favor, Ashley Moretti." Another pause. "Marry me so that I can keep both of you forever. Please?"

There was no hesitation on her part.

Shoulders trembling, she nodded.

"Is that a yes?" I asked, hopeful.

"It's a yes," she said, eyes sparkling. "When it comes to you, Chase Jacobs, it will *always* be a yes."

Always.

It was the sweetest word I'd ever heard.

Epilogue

Six Months Later

*I*t was a Saturday afternoon.

Tired as could be from spending the week moving into the house that Chase had built for himself, Addie, and me, I'd spent the last two hours napping on the sofa downstairs. When I'd passed out, my mini-me had been cuddled up beside me, her soft puffs of breath dancing across my side.

Now though, she was gone.

So was Ziggy, who'd been asleep on the floor next to us.

Normally, that wouldn't have alarmed me since she loved playing in her new bedroom, but the moment that the familiar scent of finger-nail polish hit my nostrils, I grew concerned real freakin' fast.

Oh, this is gonna be bad...

With images of my sweet girl slathering the entire room in the brightly colored polish Mama had bought her a week before, I jumped off the couch and bounded up the stairs.

Completely panicked, I raced down the hall that led to her room, and upon reaching it, I didn't stop to knock before pushing it open and bursting inside.

"Addie, baby—"

My mouth instantly snapped shut when I caught sight of the scene before me.

"Hey, Mama," Addie said, giggling. "Daddy and me are playing."

I blinked as a smile spread across my face. "I can see that." Moving my eyes to Chase, I tilted my head to the side. "Love the lipstick, Jock. The candy apple red looks great against your skin tone."

Biting back a peal of laughter, I skimmed my gaze over him, taking in his appearance from head to toe. "Love the tutu too. It adds a dose of sass to the whole stud ballerina look you've got going on."

I expected him to scowl in my direction.

But he didn't.

Instead, he smiled like a loon and held up his hands. "Like my polish? Peanut said the hot pink looks great on me." He shrugged and put his hands back on the table that separated him from her. "Grand-mama is gonna be jealous as Fudgesicles."

Fudgesicles.

Heaven help me.

"You know," I said, leaning against the doorframe. "I seem to recall a time when you said that you would never let someone paint your nails." I quirked a brow. "It was around the same time you were fussing about stickers missing from your cereal box."

Picking up a bottle of blue polish, he shook it before twisting off the cap. "I *lied*." I could see that. "You want this one?" he asked Addie, his eyes twinkling.

My little girl nodded. "Yep!" Slamming her hand down on the table, she narrowed her eyes and chewed her bottom lip as she watched her daddy paint her little nails. "Hey, Mama, guess what?" she asked me, continuing to watch his every move.

"What is it, baby?"

"Daddy painted Ziggy's nails too!"

As if on cue, Ziggy sprang off the bed where he'd been lounging, apparently more than eager to show off his new pedicure. I couldn't contain my laughter when I caught sight of his purple toes.

White husky.

Purple toenails.

Again, heaven *help me*.

"Well, who is going to paint my—"

"*Principessa!*"

I held up a finger, cutting my girl off. "I'll be right back, baby."

She smiled, and my heart skipped a beat. Just like it always did. "K."

I looked at my Jock, finding his beautiful blues on me. "Behave while I'm gone."

He smirked. "Not making any promises."

Of course not.

After blowing each of them a kiss, I headed back downstairs and found the Dadinator waiting for me in front of the open front door, his hair in disarray, and his tie tugged loose from his neck.

I knew right away that something wasn't right.

"Dad," I said, descending the steps two at a time. "What happened?"

He glanced up at the ceiling before placing his hands on his lean hips and facing me once more. "Ashley Jo, we've gotta talk."

I didn't like how that sounded. "About what?"

"About Ellington," he replied, making my stomach roll.

Why him again?

I swear no matter what I did, I couldn't escape him!

Dad nodded toward the kitchen. "Come on, let's go have a seat."

I shook my head, panic welling in my chest. "No. Tell me now."

He blew out a ragged breath. "Two weeks ago, *Ellington*," he spat, "agreed to testify against Dominic and a dozen other known criminals for a reduced sentence."

That didn't surprise me.

Not in the least bit.

"What's he testifying about?" I asked, pushing my hair back from my face. "Does it have anything to do with me?"

"No," he said, his grey eyes boring into me. "But, it does have something to do with Carmen and Jade."

My spine snapped straight. "What about them? Ellington wasn't there the night Dominic killed them, so there's no way he knows about the murders. I mean, he was, but he left before..." My voice trailed off as my throat tightened.

I didn't want to think about that night.

Not now, and not ever.

"He knows where Clyde dumped their bodies," he retorted, his jaw clenched tight. "Apparently, Jacobs didn't know how to keep his mouth shut after he got a few drinks in him."

"Did you find them?" I asked, my stomach dropping to the floor. "Because if you did, then I need to bury them. They deserve to have—"

"I found them," he interrupted, his cheeks tinged red. "Took a while, but I found both of them."

Months had passed since I last felt my heart crack down the center. But at that moment, I felt it shatter for what must've been the millionth time. I wanted nothing more than to give both my girls a proper funeral before laying them to rest, but I didn't know if I could do it.

Seeing them die had been enough.

I wasn't sure I could bury them too.

With tears streaming down my cheeks, I blew out a breath. "How do I claim their bodies? I know there can't be much left but—"

I froze, completely rooted to the spot when a flash of white caught my eye from the front yard. Brows furrowed, I narrowed my gaze, focusing my vision on the small sedan that sat parked in front of the house, its engine still idling.

"Who is that?" I asked my dad.

I felt rather than saw, his hand clamp down on my shoulder. "*Principessa*, I told you—"

My hearing dulled as I watched a woman climb out of the driver's side of the car, her long, tawny hair blowing in the slight breeze that stirred. It was hair that I would've known anywhere.

"Dad," I cried, turning to face the woman fully. "Tell me..."

He spoke, but with the sound of my pounding pulse filling my ears, I couldn't make out a single word he said.

I was too busy focusing on *her*...

The woman I'd watched die.

Feeling my legs shake, I bent over, my breath quickly leaving my body. "It can't be," I said, clutching my chest as denial set in. "There's no way."

My dad wrapped his arm around my bicep, stopping the tumble I was about to take. "It's her, sweetheart."

Ripping my arm from his hold, I stumbled through the door, tears streaming down my face. Gasping for breath, I fought to remain standing. Then, reaching the porch steps, I did the only thing I could.

I screamed.

"Carmen!"

That was all it took for her to move. "*Chiquita!*" she yelled right back, running as hard as she could toward me, the white summer dress she wore twirling around her legs.

Finding my inner strength, I latched onto it with everything I had and raced toward her.

Meeting her in the middle of the yard, I slammed my body into hers, knocking us both to the ground. "Carmen!" I cried out, my heart both healing and breaking once more as I wrapped my arms around her, holding her tight. "You're here... you're not dead."

The words I spoke...

They sounded ridiculous.

Running her hands all over my body as if to check for injuries, Carmen buried her face in my hair. "I'm not dead, *Chiquita*," she said, her tears wetting the top of my head.

I didn't understand.

Not at all.

And I didn't get a chance to ask a single question before a second voice, another which I recognized immediately, screamed out my name. "Ash!" The slamming of a car door followed, and I pulled myself free of Carmen's hold and jumped up.

This can't be happening...

Heart climbing high into my throat, I nearly crumpled when I saw Jade and her beautiful, freckle-covered face headed straight for me, taking the same route Carmen had taken seconds before.

"Oh, my God... Ashley!"

I was knocked down a second time when she tackled me to the ground. My back met the grass with a thud, but I didn't care because right there, with her body half blanketing mine was Jade.

My sweet, sweet Jade.

And next to us was Carmen.

Neither was dead.

Both were breathing.

I had no clue what was going on or how any of the things I was witnessing were possible, but it didn't even matter, because right there, at that moment, the last two pieces of my once broken heart snapped back into place, completely mending my remaining tattered pieces.

And I became whole.

————

"How?"

The one-worded question rolled off my tongue as I sat in the middle of my living room sofa, my hands shaking profusely as I stared at Carmen, her eyes shining bright. "I watched you die. I watched you *both* die."

"You watched us *almost* die, *Chiquita*," Carmen replied, crossing one of her legs over the other. "But as you can see, neither of us actually croaked."

She winked, and my head grew fuzzy.

For a moment, I could've sworn I was going crazy.

Did I get into Grandmama's moonshine or something?

I shook my head as I clutched an emotional Jade's hand. She hadn't stopped crying since she slammed into me in the front yard. Not that I blamed her. Heaven knows I hadn't quit either.

"Then tell me," I said, looking from one woman to the next. "Tell me how."

"I woke u-up," Jade said, between sobs. "I woke up when Clyde pulled me out of the t-trunk. And I stayed awake as he threw me into the water."

She sucked in a breath, fighting for calm.

Needing to comfort her, I wrapped my arm around her, holding her close, just as I'd done many times before. "It's okay. Just breathe for me."

Doing as I said, she took a second breath.

Then, "He was d-drunk." Not surprising. "And didn't realize I was still alive. Carmen either."

Drunk or not, I couldn't blame Clyde there.

Even I hadn't known they were still alive, and I'd held Carmen in my arms.

Dad, who was sitting on the loveseat next to Carmen, spoke up next. "How did you get out?"

Jade shrugged and swiped away her tears with the back of her hands. "I don't know. I just... did."

"Dominic shot you in the chest," I said, my disbelief evident.

"No, he didn't," she replied, shaking her head. "He got me in the shoulder. Wanna see?"

My eyes bulged as Carmen laughed. "Even from two feet away, that *pendejo* couldn't hit what he was aiming for."

"But what about you?" I asked Carmen. "I saw Dominic stab you." My heart twisted at the memory. "Over and over."

She nodded. "I know you did, *Chiquita*. Seeing you fight against him to save me... that hurt worse than my blade did as he jabbed it into my belly half a dozen times."

Her confession made my stomach hurt.

I'd tried to save her...

So hard.

"But how did you—"

"—survive?" she finished for me.

"Yeah," I replied, needing to know every detail. I'd spent so much time mourning their deaths when I should've been celebrating their survival.

It was just another thing Dominic had stolen from me.

The bastard.

"Well, I almost didn't survive," she said, uncrossing her legs and leaning forward. "If Jade hadn't found the strength to pull me out when she did, and then crawl to the road and stop someone in order to get help, I wouldn't have made it to morning. Between the hemorrhaging and the infection that had already begun to set in, I was dying. Quickly."

"You're okay now, though?"

Again, she nodded. "I'm missing half a spleen, a foot of intestine, and I'm down to one kidney, but I'm here." She smiled. "And I'm clean. Have been since that night."

Unable to contain myself, I squealed like a child, which made her and Jade both laugh.

"Now, *Chiquita*," she said, flicking her gorgeous hair back over her shoulder. "Tell us about you. I hear you've got a man now." She waggled her eyebrows. "Heard he's in the NFL too."

Heat crept up my neck and into my face. "His name is Chase." My smile fell thinking about what I'd need to say next. "But there's something you should know. Chase is Clyde's—"

"They know, *Principessa*," Dad said. "I made sure they knew before I brought them here."

"He did," Jade said, nodding against me. "And it's okay, babydoll. I promise I won't hold who his father is against him."

Relief washed through me.

"I only have one question," Carmen said, a look of trouble spreading across her radiant face. "Does Chase have a brother?"

Jade laughed as I rolled my eyes. "He does, but he's married, so you can't have him."

Carmen blew out a breath. "Such is my luck, *Chiquita*."

A light bulb flashed in my head. "You know what though? I can always hook you up with Pop. He's single as can be."

I thought it was a great idea.

Especially since Pop was a catch.

Built and handsome as could be, I truly didn't understand how he was single.

Mama said it was because he'd loved a woman a few years back, but before he could claim her as his own, she'd run from him, breaking his heart in the process.

He hadn't heard from her since.

It killed me to think about.

"No worries," she replied. "I'm just going to concentrate on work and getting Jade's *culo* through nursing school."

Eyes wide, I swung my gaze to Jade. "You're in nursing school?"

Smiling shyly, she tucked a strand of hair behind her ear. "Started last year. After what we all went through, I wanted to help people. Becoming a nurse is me doing that."

I squealed, clapping my hands together. "I'm so proud of you!"

"I'm proud of you too, Ashley Jo," she fired back. "I mean, look at you! You escaped *el diablo*, stabbed Ellington—*guess Dad told her about that*—finished school and found love. Like, I am seriously so danged proud of you!"

"Sweetness! Can we come down now? Your dad said I had to stay up here until you said I could come down." He paused. "I feel like a damned teenager whose been grounded and restricted to his room."

"Christ," Dad groaned, shaking his head.

Standing from the sofa, I blew out a breath. "I think it's time for y'all to meet someone."

"Yes," Carmen said, smacking the loveseat. "Bring the man down so I can interrogate him a bit."

Lord.

"As fun as that sounds," I said, shooting her a warning look that only made her grin grow. "There is someone else I want you to meet first."

Both ladies looked at me curiously as I hollered out, "Peanut, come down here, baby!"

Footsteps echoed through the house as my sweet girl bounded down the stairs, the plastic high heels Chase had gotten her clicking against the hardwood. I held my breath as I waited for her to turn the corner into the living room and appear.

Thankfully, I didn't have to wait long.

"Mama!" Addie hollered as she sprinted toward me. "Daddy said he's hungry and that—"

She came to a sliding stop when she caught sight of Carmen and Jade.

Carmen, though, she nearly hit her knees when she got her first look at my girl. Hands flying to the base of her throat, she gasped, her shoulders beginning to tremble. "*Chiquita*, is—"

"It's her," I finished for her, much like she'd done to me earlier. "It's my Addie girl."

"Oh God," Jade cried, standing. "She's beautiful."

Yes, she was.

No doubt.

Tilting her head to the side, Addie looked at Carmen, her assessing gaze on her face. "Hi!" she suddenly yelled, her infectious happiness radiating through the room. "I'm Addie!"

Carmen glanced at me, then back to Addie. "Hi Addie, I'm Carmen."

Addie beamed before looking at Jade. "Hi!"

"Hi, baby," Jade whispered, her entire body trembling. "You look just like your pretty mama."

Giggling, my girl ran to me and wrapped her arms around one of my thighs. "Mama, I like your friends. They're beautiful just like you."

"They are," Chase added, suddenly appearing in the threshold of the room. "All three are gorgeous."

Upon seeing him, Jade snapped her mouth shut and blinked.

But Carmen? She whistled. "Well damn, *Chiquita*. I may be a bit jealous. If I could find a man as—"

"Knock knock," a familiar voice called out. "Where's my girls—"

I felt like I'd been hit in the chest the moment Pop, of all danged people, rounded the corner opposite Chase and saw Carmen for the first time.

Coming to an immediate stop, his jaw slackened as his eyes filled with an emotion I could read like a book.

That emotion? Heartbreak.

It made my chest ache.

Seriously.

As for Carmen, she looked like she'd been kicked in the belly. "James," she said, tears filling her eyes. "It's been a while."

At that, everything clicked.

The woman Pop had been in love with, the same one who'd disappeared years back, it was Carmen. He'd been in love with her, the woman who'd fought to save my life, and who in return had almost lost hers.

I was stunned.

To say the least.

"Sweetness," Chase said, picking up on the tension filling the room. "Why don't we head into the kitchen? Give Pop and your friend some time."

Nodding, I grabbed Jade's hand with one of my own. Then, placing my hand on Addie's back, I started to guide us out of the room as Dad followed. "We'll be in the kitchen if y'all need anything."

Drowning in each other, neither Pop or Carmen said anything as we left the room, leaving them alone.

Once in the kitchen, I released Jade's hand as Chase scooped Addie up in one arm—much to her delight—and pulled me into him with the other.

"I think I just saw love," he said, smiling.

I nibbled my bottom lip. "I saw it too."

But I also saw something more.

And that something more? It was hurt.

A whole lot of it.

Pressing a kiss to my forehead, Chase whispered, "I love you, Sweetness."

My worry lessened at his words.

"And you," he said, tickling Addie's belly. "May just be my favorite person in the whole damned world."

My heart melted, and my soul sighed.

I love him.

So much.

Addie laughed until I thought she'd burst as Chase continued to tickle her while focusing his attention on Jade. "I'm gonna go out on a limb here and guess that you're Jade."

She nodded, and regret flashed in his eyes.

He was thinking about Clyde.

"One step at a time," Dad whispered, reading the situation correctly. "That's how we're going to do this. Just one step at a time."

Jade nodded. "I can do that."

"Me too," Chase agreed.

Feeling better about the situation before me, I wrapped my arms around Chase's torso and rested my head on his rock-hard chest. "Say it again."

Knowing exactly what I wanted, he rested his chin atop my head and whispered, "I love you, Sweetness. Until my final breath."

I closed my eyes. "I love you too, Jock. Until my final breath."

The sound of raised voices grabbed my attention. My eyes popped open, and I looked back toward the living room. "Think they stand a chance?"

Chase grunted.

Jade remained silent.

But my dad? He looked at Chase and me. Then, he whispered, "True love will always find a way."

He was right.

Because of true love, Chase and I had found our happily ever after, and maybe, just maybe—Pop and Carmen would too.

The End

Also by J.E. Parker

Redeeming Love Series

Every Moment with You

Every Breath You Take

Every Promise You Made

Every Tear You Cry

Every Wrong You Right

Every Kiss You Steal

Every Sin We Erase

Newsletter Sign Up

Want to be notified about new releases, cover reveals, and ARC opportunities? If so, sign up for my newsletter now.

https://www.jeparkerbooks.com/newsletter-sign-up

Find J.E. Online

Facebook: JEParkerRomance

Facebook group: JE's Romance Junkies

JEParkerBooks.com

Instagram: AuthorJEParker

Bookbub: AuthorJEParker

Twitter: AuthorJEParker

About the Author

J.E. Parker is an American romance author who was born and raised in the great state of North Carolina. A southern belle at heart, she's addicted to sweet tea, Cheerwine, and peach cobbler.

Not only is J.E. married to the man of her dreams (albeit a total pain in the rear), she's also the mother of a herd of sweet (sometimes), and angelic (only when they're sleeping) children. Despite their occasional demonic behavior and bottomless stomachs, J.E. loves her little tribe more than words could ever express.

On the weekends, you can find her sitting on the couch, cheering on (or cursing) her favorite football team, stuffing her face with junk food, and guzzling a bottle of cheap red wine.

When she's not busy making sure her husband doesn't burn the house down or acting as a referee for her fighting children, J.E. enjoys reading, writing (obviously), and listening to a wide variety of music.

Acknowledgments

Ziggy Bear

I miss you, ya giant ball of fluff.
Thank you for loving me, sweet boy.
And thank you for loving my babies.
My heart will never be whole again,
but I'm thankful for every second we had.

Angel Youngren

I never met you, but she loved you,
and therefore I do by default.
Take care of my Marshmallow for me.
Lord knows, he likes to find trouble.
Rest easy, sweet boy.

Christina Youngren

This book hurt.
We both cried, we both cursed,
but somehow we survived.
Words will never be enough.
You've walked me through anxiety attacks,
family emergencies, and moments where I just wanted to give up.
Thank you, Cupcake.
For everything.

Sara Miller

Book number 7!
How the hell that happened, I don't know.
But here's to thirty more!

Tempi Lark

You understand my special brand of crazy, and you don't judge me
for it.
You have no idea what that means to me. From the bottom of my
whacky heart, thank you!

John

I was a mess when you married me.
And I'm still a mess today.
Thank you for saving me all those years ago.
Without you, I'd be lost. No doubt.
Love you, Big Guy.

Until my final breath.

Grandmama

Life hurts without you.
But seeing how much everyone falls in love with you as they read my
books lessens the pain.
I miss you, Crazy Old Biddy.
A whole lot.
I hope you're proud of me.
Because I'm certainly proud of you.

The Parker Squad

You five drive me batshit crazy.
But I wouldn't trade you for the world.
Everyday, I'm thankful to be your Mama.
Love you guys.
With every piece of me.

JE's Romance Junkies

Y'all will never understand how much you mean to me. Thank you for
sticking with me through everything! Without y'all, I never would've
made it this far.

Made in the USA
Columbia, SC
05 December 2021